Miss Peculiar's Haunting Tales, Volume II

By

Susan Buffum

Please contact the author at sebuffum415@gmail.com for permission.

Copyright by Susan Buffum, July 2015

First Edition

July 2015

This is entirely a work of fiction. All characters, names, incidents, organizations and dialogues in this publication are either the products of the author's imagination or used fictitiously and not meant to represent anyone currently living, or deceased.

<u>Dedication</u>

To Kelly for whom I write everything first and foremost.

To the late Alfred Hitchcock who inspired me.

To All my friends who love and support me.

To my family who love and support me, too.

To my husband John.

Susan Buffum

Table of Contents

Susan Buffum

THE MAGIC OF CROSS AND CROWE

"I need a girl!" Simon Crowe announces to wild cheers and cries of "Pick me!" from the SRO audience. Behind him, black-clad stage hands wheel in the props needed for the next trick—a four-foot wide by six-foot high board with the outline of a body chalked on it, a table with twenty-five glinting, sharp, throwing knives. "But not just any girl. I need a brave girl!" He is unbuttoning his black cut-away coat, removing it, handing it off to one of the stage hands. His blood red cravat comes off next. He tosses it from the stage, winks at the twenty-something blonde who catches it. She holds it up like a prize. "I need a girl who can look danger straight in the eye and not bat an eyelash!" He unbuttons his white shirt, first the cuffs, then the collar. He tugs the tails out of the waistband of his pants and finishes unbuttoning it as he paces the front of the stage, his dark eyes searching for the ideal girl. "I need a girl who wants a thrill in her life." Shrugging off the snowy white shirt, letting it fall to the floor, he is now pacing the stage in a snug black t-shirt and black skinny pants that emphasize his tall, sinewy frame. He is a preternaturally handsome young man with raven-black, longish hair that he wears pulled back into a short ponytail, very dark eyes. The females in the audience are literally screaming, begging him to choose them, reaching for him. "I need one girl in particular," he finally says. "A redhead with the initials P and R. I believe she's sitting in section eleven, row H, seat seventeen. Will that young lady please join me on stage right now." He walks to the steps at stage right where he waits for the girl from section eleven, row H, seat seventeen to get over her initial shock, then climb over twenty knees and make her way up the aisle. She hesitates at the foot of the stairs. He looks down at her, holding his hand out to her. "Don't be afraid. I don't bite. I just throw sharp knives at pretty girls." The audience laughs. "Come up here, Miss Rumford."

She climbs the stairs, allowing him to take her hand and lead her to the center of the stage. "How do you know my name?" she asks him.

He cocks his head to one side, looks from her to the audience. "She wants to know how I know her name." He turns to her. "Have we ever met before? Answer honestly."

"No."

"Are you sure? You've never gotten drunk and kissed someone, a stranger maybe, in a dark corner of a club?"

"I don't go out much," she replies, shaking her head. There are some chuckles from the audience. "No."

"Yet, here you are in Vegas, a city full of clubs, here in this auditorium sitting in that particular seat. How do you explain that?"

"Um…I don't know. I just bought a ticket at the door. I didn't plan on coming here tonight."

"No? You didn't come here tonight specifically to be my assistant for this trick?" She shakes her head. "Maybe I have the wrong girl." He turns to the audience. "Is there another girl named Pepper Rumford in the audience?"

"How in the world do you know my name?" she cries, staring at him in disbelief. She is from a small town in north-western Connecticut. This is her first trip to Las Vegas. She hadn't even planned on coming to this magic show but she'd gotten bored watching her parents gamble. She'd used the credit card they had given her to buy the ticket less than an hour ago. It had been the last seat available—section eleven, row H, seat seventeen. The ticket seller had told her that she was lucky to get the seat, otherwise she'd be standing at the back of the room for the whole show.

"A rather big birdie told me," he says, holding out his arm. A large, black raven soars down from high up in the catwalks above their heads, landing on his forearm. Pepper takes a step back, startled by the bird's sudden appearance. "Ravens are rather intelligence birds," he says. "And, like their relatives, the crows, they are attracted to shiny objects. Are you missing something, Pepper? Something shiny?"

She takes inventory of what she is wearing and discovers that she's missing an earring! "I lost an earring," she says. It's a diamond stud, one of the pair her grandmother had given her for her high school graduation. Disappointment is evident on her face.

"Jack?" he asks the raven. "Do you have something that belongs to Miss Rumford?" He cocks a dark brow at the raven that caws raucously. Crowe holds his other hand out, palm up, wiggles his fingers. "Cough it up, buddy. We don't steal from people," he says firmly. The raven caws again, then dips its head into Crowe's palm. When it sits upright, a shiny diamond stud lies in the center of Crowe's upturned palm. "Thank you, Jack! Off with you, now!" The raven launches itself back up toward the catwalks. The audience is applauding the trick. Crowe polishes the earring on his shirt then asks if he can put it back where it belongs. Pepper nods, completely at a loss as to how he has her earring since the only time he has touched her was to take her hand when she came up the stairs. His hands have been nowhere near her face or her head in general. She turns her head and tilts it a bit. He tucks her red curls behind her ear, quickly puts the stud back into her ear lobe. "And now the trick—Find a Girl and Make the Relationship Stick! I found the girl, now let's see if I can convince her to stay with me!"

He leads Pepper to the board. "Are you going to throw knives at me?" she asks nervously.

"Yes," he replies matter-of-factly. "You're a little bit shorter than I thought you'd be. But that's all right." He motions for a stage hand to bring a small wooden platform about four inches high from the wings. The stage hand positions it in front of the chalked outline on the board. Crowe helps Pepper mount the platform, then bends her limbs, positioning her so that she matches the outline on the board. "This is a new trick for me," he announces. "I haven't had a chance to practice it as much as I should have, but, the act was beginning to feel stale, so I figured, why not?" She is staring at him, wide-eyed now and he smiles widely. "Luckily, Pepper has curly hair," he says, indicating the outline. The head appears to have wavy hair. "You're a perfect match. Now," he says, "all you have to do is just hold very still." He walks toward the table near the front of the stage, picks up one of the knives and brings it right to the edge of the stage. "You," he says, pointing to a young man with a shaved head, a face full of studs and rings, tattoos visible on every inch of his exposed skin. "You look like someone who can verify that this is, in fact, a very real, very sharp knife." He offers the knife to the young man who hefts it in his hand, tests the sharpness of the blade against his thumb, and examines the knife, checking to make sure that the blade doesn't retract into the handle. "Are you satisfied that this is a real knife?" Crowe asks.

"Yeah, it's a beauty, man. Very real."

"Every knife on this table is exactly like this one," he says, replacing the knife on the table. He clasps his hands before him. "I ask that all of you refrain from flash photography during this feat. I will be throwing very real, very sharp knives at Miss Rumford in very rapid succession. It is imperative that I remain focused because I wouldn't want to bloody any of my blades." He glances back at Pepper who is staring at him, grim-faced. "Or puncture my pretty assistant, Pepper. Smile, Miss Rumford. This is a magic show, not a funeral!" She musters a smile for him but he can see apprehension in her eyes. "Would you prefer to be blindfolded?" he asks her.

"No," she replies.

"Good, because after the last illusion I performed, I'm fresh out of silk handkerchiefs!" The audience laughs and she gives him a genuine smile. "Okay then! Let's do this!"

With no further fanfare he turns, grabs a knife and hurls it at the board. It thuds into the wood extremely close to the girl's right calf. She flinches. "No! Stay very, very still, Pepper! Look at me!" Her hazel eyes meet his. "You must remain frozen in place," he says, holding her gaze. "Trust me and stay as still as a statue." Her eyes do not leave his. He takes another knife, throws his arm back then lets the knife fly. It slams into the board with a loud *thwack* right alongside her left hip.

In rapid succession, he grabs the knives and hurls them, one after the other, basically outlining the girl with knives. As he is about to release the next to the last knife, a camera flashes brightly in the balcony box to stage left. The knife leaves his hand and there is a collective gasp, then some screams as the audience realizes that the knife has plunged into the girl's palm, pinning her hand to the board. "Pepper!" he says loudly and firmly. "Do not move!" He hurls the last knife. It thuds into the board just at the crown of her head.

He is already walking quickly to the girl, his eyes holding hers. "This is part of the trick," he tells her as he grasps the handle of the knife that has gone through her hand. "It is not really piercing your hand, is it?"

"I don't know," she replies. "No."

He takes an almost imperceptible breath, tugs the knife from her palm in one swift motion, and drops it to the floor where it lands with a solid thump. He grasps her hand that he's folded into a fist with his hand and raises it over her head. "Ladies and gentlemen! Miss Pepper Rumford, my new assistant!" He moves his hand to her wrist. "Open your hand and wave to the audience." She turns her head toward him, tilts her head a bit, searching his face. His dark eyes meet hers. "This is show biz, Pepper," he says quietly. "Wave to the audience, then we'll bow and you're going to leave the stage with me. Open your hand."

She opens her hand and waves as directed. There is no blood, no visible wound. The audience cheers, people jumping out of their seats applauding wildly for they were certain that the camera flash had caused him to miss his mark and stab the girl. He waves his free hand, they bow deeply then he gives her a slight push toward the wings.

As soon as they are no longer visible to the audience, he curses. "That's it!" he shouts angrily. "No cameras allowed! If they want pictures they can take them with their damn cellphones! I want a 'no flash photography allowed' notice in bold print on all future pamphlets and posters! If anyone attempts to enter the auditorium with a camera, that camera is to be confiscated, tagged and returned after the show! I'm sick of this shit!"

"Simon…" says Sebastian Cross, his partner in the show. "Calm down. She's not hurt, is she?"

He glances over at the girl who is standing a few feet away examining the palm and back of her hand, frowning slightly. "I don't know. Not too seriously. She's moving her fingers."

"Go make this right with her," Sebastian says. Then he turns and calls for the three girls who will be assisting him with his next illusion. "I don't know what you were thinking using real knives like that." He shakes his head, white blonde hair falling across his pale-blue eyes.

As Sebastian takes the stage, the girls—Charlotte Cheston, Caroline Wyndham and Cym Snow wait for their cue in the wings.

Simon walks over to Pepper. "Come with me. I'd like to talk to you. We have about twenty minutes while Sebastian does his thing." He takes her arm, steers her through an acre of props and cable, past a cage in which a black panther with golden eyes paces restlessly, to a narrow corridor off which there are a number of doors. He opens the door that has a card with his name on it tacked to it. It's his dressing room. "It's a mess, sorry. Sherry's got a nasty cold. She usually keeps my wardrobe organized." He clears a tall stool, easily lifts her up and sits her on it. "Let me see your hand."

"It's okay," she says. "I think."

He takes her hand and examines it closely, pressing lightly with his thumb, then more firmly. She winces a bit, looks confused by unexpected pain. "It's not bad," he says. "I'm sorry I hurt you."

"I'm not hurt," she replies.

"Yeah, sweetheart, you are, but I cauterized the wound when I pulled the knife out." He's not going to tell her how he managed to do that, doesn't want to have to explain it to her, so he needs to distract her. He lets go of her hand and snaps his fingers. She jumps slightly. "Look." He nods at her hand. She looks at her palm, flips her hand quickly to look at the backside. He can see the shock and horror in her face, steadies her as she wobbles on the stool. "I hypnotized you, and the whole damn audience, too. You're going to be fine, but if you haven't had a tetanus shot recently you need to go to urgent care and get one."

"You put a knife through my hand!" she cries.

"It was an accident. That damn camera flash blinded me! People are so freakin' ignorant these days! So damn selfish, disrespectful and thoughtless! I'm sorry. I'll pay your medical expenses."

"I had a tetanus shot about two years ago after a spider bit me and my leg got infected," she says.

"Then you should be all right." He relaxes, smiles. "You want some wine? A beer?"

"Do you have any water?"

"Sure." He goes to the small refrigerator, gets her a bottle of water, and opens it for her. He hands her the bottle, but as she takes it, the bottle suddenly turns into a bouquet of real flowers. She laughs with delight, her eyes bright as they meet his again. "I really do need an assistant. Are you interested?"

"Um, will you be throwing knives at me on a regular basis?" she asks.

"Yes, every night, among other things."

"I…"

"Pepper Rumford," he says and again her eyes meet his. "I chose you out of all the girls out there in the audience tonight." His words, simply spoken, quickly sink in.

"How in the world did you know my name?" she asks. "How did you know where I was sitting?"

14

"A good magician never reveals his secrets," he replies.

"I didn't even know my parents were coming here tonight. I had no plans to come to this show. It was a spur of the moment decision because I was bored." He nods. "So, really, how did you know?"

"You signed your name on the credit card slip when you bought the ticket. The card is in your mother's name, Phyllis A. Rumford." Her eyes widen. "See, the truth isn't so amazing. People want to believe in magic, want to believe it's real. It's mostly illusion, distraction, manipulation, switches." He shrugs. "I lost my last assistant. She bailed on me the other day. I've been winging it the past couple of nights with Sabrina filling in as needed. We're here six months out of the year, travel four months to other parts of the country to do shows and then crash and re-group for two months in the Berkshires of Massachusetts. We have a compound here and one in the Berkshires, so you'd have room and board. When we travel, the company pays for your lodging and food. We offer health insurance, life insurance, and the use of company owned vehicles so you don't have to worry about owning a car here and there, registering them, and what-not."

"Okay," she says.

"You'll be paid twenty-eight thousand a year to start, which might not sound like much, but you have to remember that you don't have to pay rent, you don't have to buy groceries, unless you want something specific, and you don't have to buy and maintain a car or pay insurance premiums. We take care of all that for the whole company. That's just the starting salary. If you do well and I keep you on, you'll get increases."

"And if I don't do well?" she asks.

He shrugs, gives her a wry smile. "I don't think we have to worry about that, do you? You did great out there tonight. You're a natural."

"I was petrified."

"That'll pass. First night jitters. Plus, I tend to make girls nervous the first time they work with me. I can be a little intense."

"You were funny."

"Was I?" She nods. "So, yes or no, will you stay on and be my assistant?"

She looks at her hand, palm and back. "I don't know. My parents…"

"Bring them to the show tomorrow night. I'll have Sabrina assist me. Let them see what you'll be doing. Then, after the show, I'll treat them, and you, to dinner in Cicero's here at the hotel. Just take them right to the restaurant, tell the maître d' that you're my guests and you'll be seated. Have a cocktail and an appetizer, whatever. I'll join you as soon as I clean up and change my clothes. I'll talk to them, assure them that you'll be well taken care of and happy. Family members get free tickets to all the shows. They can visit you at any time." He pauses then says, "I'm not a psycho."

"No, you're just famous."

"Through no fault of my own." She smiles and some color stains her cheeks. She is a remarkably pretty girl. He feels he's chosen the perfect girl. He had been drawn to her the moment that he'd laid eyes on her earlier in the hotel lobby when she'd arrived with her parents. "Say yes."

"Yes," she says.

He lifts her hand through which he has thrown a sharp knife less than a half hour ago and brings it to his lips, presses his lips to her palm, turns her hand and presses his lips to the back of her hand. "Meet me at eleven o'clock tomorrow morning in conference room D on the third floor here. Just walk in. I'll be there with our business manager, Risley Stroud. We'll get all the paperwork done."

"I live in Connecticut," she says. "I only have two suitcases with me. All my stuff is at home."

"What do you need most from home?" he asks.

"Well, my stuff." She shrugs.

"Specifically?"

"My computer, the rest of my clothes, my music and books, my…"

He abruptly turns his back to her as he walks across the room, opens a closet and removes something, holding it close to his chest. "Your plush tiger that you've slept with since you were three years old? Mr. Stripes, isn't it?" He turns and she gives a cry that is half surprise, half shock. He comes back to the stool and hands the tiger to her. "Rumor has it that he doesn't like to be left behind when you travel."

"How…where….?" She shakes her head, suddenly speechless as she holds the rather worse-for-wear mohair tiger. It is Mr. Stripes! There is no doubt about it in her mind. The tiger is missing one green glass eye and its left ear is half off from her having carried it around by that ear for over a decade. Her mother had always meant to stitch it back on more securely. She's surprised that it hasn't fallen off yet and gotten lost. "How did you get Mr. Stripes? I don't understand this! He was on my bed when we left home!" She looks at him wonderingly. "How on earth did you get him?" she asks.

"Magic," he replies, a dark light dancing in the depths of his eyes.

Sebastian Cross runs a slim, pale hand up through his shaggy, straight, white-blonde hair as he paces the suite Simon Crowe has taken for the next two nights, as he claims that he has business to conduct in town. "Explain to me again exactly how you chose this red-haired girl to be your new partner, or, basically, our seventh sister in the Seven Sisters Illusion?"

"I saw her in the lobby when I was booking the suite and felt drawn to her. She was just way too sweet and innocent to be on her own here in Sin City. I wanted to protect her. I wasn't a-ware at the time that she was attached to two protective parents, but I can handle them. She'll be all signed up with the show by the time I charm them at dinner after tomorrow night's show."

"Answer me this, do you know what the hell you're doing?" Sebastian asks, dropping down into the deep couch cushions with a weary sigh. "You're getting more and more reckless. You threw *real* damn knives at that innocent, trusting, little girl tonight! You shish kabobbed her hand!"

"I had her under my control in a heartbeat. I don't think she even realized what had happened until we were in my dressing room." Simon shrugs. "She's a sweet kid."

"And you're a damned demon. This does not bode well, if you stop and think about it. But stopping and thinking anything through is something you seldom do. You're a spur of the moment, let's raise hell type of guy."

"And you're a damned stick in the mud. If we sat around and waited like you prefer to do our show would be closed down and we'd be on the strip hustling coins, rattling our tin cups for spare change! Trust me on this one, okay? I like her."

"Yeah, well, if memory serves me correctly, you liked your previous assistant, too. And where is she again? Buried six feet under the desert sand, isn't she?"

"I don't know. I didn't ask any questions. I just told Winslow to get rid of her. Maybe he bought her a bus ticket and sent her home." Sebastian rolls his eyes, grimaces. "I didn't kill her."

"Right."

"Was it my fault she just freaked out like that?"

"She saw you in your natural form, Simon! There aren't too many human females who can handle finding themselves in bed with a freakin' scaly demon!"

"My bad. I lost control. I tried to mind wipe her but she was too hysterical."

"So you broke her neck instead."

"I did not!" he cries indignantly. "I just slapped her a little too hard to try to get her to stop screaming like that."

"Pity humans have such fragile cervical vertebrae."

"It wasn't intentional! I forget how powerful I really am after living in human form for so long!" He flops down in a chair with a groan. "I can't keep using Sabrina. She has her own functions in the show. I need an assistant. I saw Pepper and I liked her. I think she'll be great."

"You plan on bedding her, too?"

"No," he replies quickly. "It's obvious I have some control issues when it comes to having female humans in my bed. I'll stick to my own kind. I've finally learned that lesson." He leans his head back, closes his dark eyes. "You don't have to worry about explaining any more disappearances."

"I hope not." Sebastian rises from the couch. "Look, this place makes me antsy. I'm heading home. See you at tomorrow night's show."

Simon rolls his head to the side, opens his eyes to glance at the wall clock. It's after one o'clock in the morning. "Today's show," he corrects his partner.

"Yeah, right. Today. Time flies when you're having as much fun as we are."

"Has it stopped being fun for you?" he asks as he gets up and follows Sebastian to the door. "Really?"

"It's work to create new illusions. I work my ass off, and what do you do? You push the envelope and use real knives and hurl them at a human female who does not have lightning quick reflexes. You could have killed that girl tonight!"

"But I didn't. I nailed each throw."

"Except the next to the last one."

"That was the fault of that asshole in the balcony with the camera! Didn't I say *no* flash photography?"

"Did you break his neck too?"

Simon shrugs. "I would have but he was long gone. Lucky for him."

"Do me a favor and stick to the stuff we painstakingly developed over the years. Leave your devil's trickery and nonsense in the trunk where it belongs."

"I am what I am, Sebastian. After a couple thousand years here I'm pretty goddam bored and restless. These are the best guises that we've ever had. I'm having some fun with it. You need to lighten up a little."

"I am what I am, too, Simon," he responds.

"You're better than I am, but not by all that much."

"Keep reminding me how close I am to being like you. It really cheers me up."

"Go suck on your wing tips and try to get some sleep, unless you're taking a girl home?"

"Charlotte's waiting for me, although she's probably fast asleep."

"Naw, she won't fall asleep until you join her in bed, and then it'll be lights out for her because you're so damn boring."

"I may be boring in bed, but I don't transform into a demon and then break my girlfriend's neck when she won't stop screaming."

Simon scowls. "Goodnight, Sebastian," he says, swinging the door shut.

He turns and finds the girl that he'd picked up in the lounge downstairs leaning against the bedroom door frame. She's naked and gorgeous, but looking at him as if she can't quite believe what she's been hearing while eavesdropping. "What was *that* all about?" she asks. "Did you really kill your last girlfriend?"

Simon ruefully shakes his head. "Sebastian and I have personas in the show. He's the angel, I'm the demon. We fool around all the time, razz one another. The sorry truth of it is my last girlfriend dumped me. She accused me of being too boring because I just practice my craft all day, perform all night." He gives her a dark look. "On stage, not in the bedroom. And that's what killed the relationship."

"Are you going to bore me to death?" she asks as he comes closer.

"I have a boring tool," he says and she laughs.

"Let's put that to some good use then."

"I have an eleven o'clock meeting in the morning."

"You might be a little late for that."

He swings the door shut as he follows her into the bedroom.

Risley Stroud looks up over the tops of his reading glasses as the tall, raven-haired magician enters the conference room where he has been waiting for over a half hour with the pretty girl whose legal name is actually Tessie Rumford, but everyone has called her Pepper all of her life because of her red hair. She seems to relax when Crowe comes and sits down opposite her. "Hey, sorry. Late night. I overslept."

"That must be some pillow you have. It left lipstick on your ear and neck," Stroud replies.

Crowe shrugs. "Much better than finding a lousy mint on the pillow." He turns his dark gaze toward Pepper. "Good to see you again. You managed to get away from your parents. How?"

"They went to a wax museum. I said I'd stay here in the hotel and read. I get creeped out in wax museums. It's a known fact in my family."

"Well, remind me to scratch the wax dummies from the show. Can't have you freaking out on stage when you open a coffin and find a wax body." He gives her a quick grin then turns back to Stroud. "All the paperwork in order to hire this little trouper?"

"She and I have been going over the contract and the addendums while we've been waiting for you." He turns to Pepper. "Are there any further questions?"

"I'll be known as Pepper Rumford?" she asks.

"If that is how you want to be known, that's fine. Have you ever considered a legal name change? It's a simple enough process."

"I might think about it."

"Who are you hiding from?" Simon asks her. "A jealous boyfriend? A stalker? A creditor?"

"I'm not hiding from anyone. Pepper is the name everyone knows me by. If I had to use my legal name, no one would know it's me."

"Do you want people to know it's you?"

22

She shrugs. "I guess it's really not going to matter since my friends don't make a habit of coming to Vegas. They don't have the money for it."

"Then let's just call you Pepper and be done with it? Can we get some signatures on paper here, Ris? I'm starving. I want to grab something to eat after this. Pepper, you want something to eat?"

"I should get back upstairs," she replies.

He studies her for a long moment, then shakes black hair away from his handsome face, reaches up and rubs at the place by his ear where he's been told that he has lipstick stains. "You're still having dinner with me tonight, right?"

"Yes, my parents and I are."

"What'd you tell them about that?" he asks.

"I said that I'd met you at the show when you picked me out of the audience to help you with a trick, and you asked me to dinner for being a good sport about it."

"Did they ask about your hand?"

She looks down at both her hands as they are loosely folded on the table top. She lays them both flat on the table then slowly turns them over. "What about my hand?" she asks, frowning slightly.

He shakes his head. "Never mind. It's not important." He turns to Stroud. "You don't have disappearing ink in those pens, do you?" This makes Pepper smile. He likes the way her eyes light up with mischief at his stupid jokes. She really is a sweet kid. For a moment, he feels a frisson of apprehension, a sense that he should tell her to run and not look back, save herself, but then he feels a fluttery sort of panic in his gut at the thought of losing her when he's only just found her. "Sign the contract, Pepper," he says, picking up a pen

She signs the paperwork. He co-signs as her employer and Stroud signs as witness. Stroud then passes a business check to Simon. He fills it out in Pepper's name in the amount of twenty-five hundred dollars, signs it with a flourish then slides it across the table to her. "Cash it at the bank here and have fun shopping," he says as he rises from his seat. "I'll reserve three of the best seats for tonight's performance if you want to take your parents to the show before dinner, let them see what you'll be doing. Although, I may have a hard time convincing them that I'm not going to corrupt and ruin their daughter if you do bring them."

"I think they said that they want to take naps before dinner because it'll be late and they have a busy day of sightseeing planned today."

"What are your plans for the day?" She shrugs. "Come with me then. We can cash your check and then I'll take you to lunch. I have some things to do this afternoon so you can hit the boutiques, go have a five hundred dollar manicure or whatever."

Risley Stroud stands up. He's placed all the papers in his brown leather briefcase and snapped it shut. "If you'll excuse me, I'll go back to the office and put all this in order and then get Miss Rumford on the payroll. May I suggest that she open a checking account with that check and then call me with the account number so that I can arrange a direct deposit." He removes a business card from his suit coat breast pocket and hands it to the girl. "Don't lose that. Any questions, call me." She nods. "It's been a pleasure to meet you, Miss Rumford. Welcome to Cross and Crowe Productions Limited."

"I always through it should be Crowe and Cross Productions, but that's just my personal opinion," Simon says.

"Sebastian preferred the names be alphabetical," Stroud replies as he heads for the door.

"He's anal like that." Simon comes around the table. "Come with me, Pepper. Let's get your bank account opened."

They go downstairs to the bank in the lobby. The bank manager comes out to personally assist them. He opens the account with the full amount of the check. Simon takes out his wallet and throws in an additional five hundred in cash. "Let's makes it a nice round number," he says. She stares at him incredulously. "That's your pay for assisting me last night onstage," he tells her. He turns to the bank manager and says, "I hired her as my assistant last night. Have you been to the show recently?"

"No, my wife and I haven't been since early last year."

Simon produces a handful of tickets seeming from thin air and tosses them onto the man's desk. "Take her out to dinner and a show tonight. Give the rest of the tickets to your staff here. We've got some new illusions that'll blow your mind this year."

"Thank you, Mr. Crowe. This is very generous of you."

"Are we all set here?" he asks.

"Yes. I'll order some checks for Miss Rumford. Should they be delivered to the company's compound?"

"Yes. She'll be living out there with us."

"You're embarking on a very exciting and interesting career, young lady. Everyone loves a magic show. Cross and Crowe have one of the best shows in the world."

"We're striving to be the best in the universe but it's hard to get good reviews on Jupiter these days." Pepper laughs.

He takes her to the Sinful Cupboard café for lunch where she is absolutely thrilled to discover that they have cream cheese on date nut bread sandwiches with pineapple wedges as a side. Simon lets her order that even though he thinks it sounds appalling. He orders a quarter pound cheeseburger, medium rare and a Coke. She orders English breakfast tea with her dainty sandwiches.

When the waitress goes off to place their order, he just sits across from her, studying her, reveling in her utter cheerfulness. She is an easy going, happy young lady who truly appears to be enjoying his company. "You haven't been drinking, have you?' he asks.

She laughs. "No!"

"Have I been drinking?"

"Probably. You're older than I am and you had a sleepover date last night."

"Are you jealous?" he asks.

"No. That would be like you being jealous of me sleeping with Mr. Stripes. He's just a plaything, too."

"I see. You know all about playthings then?"

"No, not everything."

"But enough?"

"Enough. You see and read lot of stuff on facebook that you sometimes wish you'd never seen. It grows you up fast."

"Stay off of facebook. Stay sweet and innocent for me."

"Too late," she says.

"Damn it all, it's my job to spoil and corrupt you. I hate facebook! It's taken all the pleasure out of my life."

"Don't pout."

He leans back in his seat and studies her even more carefully. Today she has her long, soft, red curls pulled back from her face in a loose plait that hangs down her back. She's wearing a crisp white blouse, an eggplant purple vest, black slacks and black ankle boots. Her vest has silver filigree buttons—three of them. She has the diamond ear studs in, a twisted, double strand silver necklace around her neck. "Why don't you wear gold?" he asks.

"I can't afford gold."

"After lunch, before I go, we're going to the jewelry store and I'm buying you a gold necklace."

"You can't do that!" she cries.

"Why not?"

"I don't know exactly why not, but you can't."

He falls silent and she looks away, nervous now, but still excited to be having lunch with him. He continues to study her, to learn her every nuance. She has a nervous habit of gnawing on the right corner of her lower lip. She has perfect teeth, but he's not sure if her teeth are due to good genes or a brilliant orthodontist and three or four years in braces. Her complexion is porcelain perfection. Her one flaw is a tiny, thin scar on the ridge of her left jaw bone. "You play the violin," he says. Her head comes around, her hazel eyes wide. He looks at her hands. "And the piano."

"How do you know that?"

"The little scar on your jaw is from a string breaking during a vigorous tuning or while playing. Probably a string breaking as you were playing because if you were tuning it you wouldn't have had the instrument so close to your face."

"You're like Sherlock Holmes," she tells him.

He bows his head briefly. "Your mother sent you for dance lessons for about three years but then you balked at going. She relented and sent you for piano lessons instead. From there you became interested in the violin. Your parents were disappointed that you chose an instrument not ordinarily found in a high school marching band. Your mother had played in her high school band and your father met her on the playing field. He played football."

"Is my family history on Google or something? How in the world did you find all this out?"

"I didn't Google you. I'm just deducing this from what I can see."

"You deduced my father played football and my mother was in the marching band just by looking at me? What is there specifically about me that would tell you this?"

"You play the piano and violin. Someone else in your family is musically inclined. I don't feel it is your father therefore it must be your mother. The majority of females do not play in garage bands in high school therefore she must have been in the high school marching band. If she was in the band she either met your father in the band or on the playing field since the band plays at all the big football games. I'm thinking that he's not very musically inclined so he must have been a high school athlete. You're in remarkable physical condition so I would also deduce that he enrolled you in a local gym and you do elliptical and spinning. You move in a very agile manner, very graceful and self-possessed so I'm going to go out on a limb here and say that you were in gymnastics as well and excelled in floor exercise and the uneven bars, but the balance beam was your bane." Her mouth drops open in stunned disbelief. "You fell off the beam and broke your left wrist. I know this because there is still a small bump on that wrist from a slight misalignment of the bones. In cold weather it aches." She nods. "You had a cat named Dusty when you were little."

"I don't believe this!" she cries. "How can you possibly know that just from looking at me?"

"I don't know that from looking at you. I know that because Mr. Stripes whispered it in my ear last night before I returned him to you. He told me all your secrets because you whispered them into his ear when you were growing up. He is the keeper of your deepest secrets and I, being a master at trickery and deception, got him to spill the beans about you."

"You did not! He can't talk!"

"You don't think so? He had quite a lot to say. He told me all about a boy named Caleb who broke your…"

"Stop!" she suddenly cries in a shocked, wounded voice.

"…heart." He regrets not stopping. She has tears in her eyes and a look of betrayal on her face. "Mr. Stripes didn't say anything actually. Don't blame him. He's innocent."

The waitress brings their food and beverages. "Will there be anything else?"

"How about a pistol with five bullets? I want to shoot myself for upsetting my lovely dining companion."

"Only five bullets?"

"Well, I feel very bad but I should have one shot at redeeming myself." The waitress shakes her head as she walks away. Pepper has her head bent. He has unnerved her, hurt her. "I apologize. For what it's worth, that Caleb was an idiot. You're a beautiful, charming young lady and I bet he's kicking himself for treating you like he did."

"He married my best friend Marianne a month after we graduated from high school. They've got two little kids and a third on the way. They're living at her parent's house, in the basement, because he can't hold a job. He's a loser."

"Then you're fortunate that he walked away from the best girl in the world. And I'm very fortunate, too, because by his doing so he set you on the path that has led you here to me. To Vegas. To Cross and Crowe and a career in magic."

"Assisting," she corrects.

"True, but if I didn't have an excellent assistant my illusions would suck because some stuff you just can't do by yourself. Assistants are important assets to a magician. I'm going to work with you and make you one of the best in the business. If you get sick of me you'll be able to go and work for any magician in the world and they'd be grateful to have you. Trust me. You're going to be worth your weight in gold in a very short time." He taps his finger on the edge of her plate. "Now, do some magic of your own and make those disgusting little sandwiches disappear."

"They're not disgusting!"

"Unappealing, then."

"Have you ever even tried a bite of one?"

"No. I never even knew such a thing existed."

"Try a bite because if you've never tried something then you shouldn't say bad things about it since you really don't know, right?"

"Pepper, you're going to wear my brain out with your reasoning everything out." He reaches across the table, picks up one of the little finger sandwiches, takes a bite of it then sets it back down on her plate. He chews the bite, not looking absolutely convinced that it's a tasty delight. He swallows, stabs a chunk of pineapple from the small side bowl and eats that. Finally, he shrugs. "Okay, it wasn't that awful but I don't think I'd actually order it myself." He winks at her. "I just might let you order it and steal a bite now and then." This earns him a flicker of a smile. "Come on, eat up. We have a gold necklace to go in search of next, then you should go back to your room and I should get on with what I have to accomplish today."

She surprises him by getting up, coming around to his side of the table, taking her napkin and dipping it in his water glass. She then pushes his hair back away from his ear and proceeds to scrub the lipstick stains from his ear lobe and neck. "If you're going to go meet another girl for sex you'd better not show up wearing some other girl's lipstick."

"I have a need for diversions," he says.

"That's your business, not mine." She returns to her seat and resumes eating her lunch without another word.

Simon eats his burger but his mind is racing. He's never done this before, pursued a girl that he saw in the lobby like this. He's actually surprised that he's gotten her to agree to be his assistant so easily. She's all signed on. The last hurdle will be convincing her parents that their little girl has not made a huge mistake choosing a Vegas career. He'll probably get a lot of resistance from her father since she's an only child. Daddy won't want his little girl living with a sex fiend magician, especially if Daddy gets even the slightest inkling of how badly the magician wants to bed his little girl. He's going to have to do something he is not very accomplished at—use restraint and caution. Sebastian is the master of those traits. He is not.

"The girl Simon chose from the audience for the knife throwing trick is now his new assistant," Sebastian announces to the six young women he's gathered in the huge family room of the sprawling mansion on the Cross and Crowe compound which sits on an elevated piece of property out in the desert. "Her name is Pepper Rumford. He'll probably be bringing her here as soon as her parents fly back east. I'm fairly certain that they will spend the rest of their vacation trying to persuade their little girl that she's making a grave mistake. I shouldn't say this, but I hope they will be successful in making her see the rashness of her decision, but the truth of the matter is that we need a seventh young lady for the Seven Sisters Illusion and she'll be perfect for that. Therefore…"

"Sebastian, how old is this girl?" Caroline asks.

"I'm not sure. Very early twenties, I'd guess."

"And she has exactly zero experience?" Cym asks.

"None whatsoever." He turns his hands up in a gesture of helplessness. "You know how Simon can be at times. We can only hope that he knows what he's doing this time."

"Does anyone know for sure what happened to Gillian?" Poppy Stowe queries cautiously.

"I'm thinking he put her on a bus with a suitcase of cash and sent her home."

"There's wishful thinking," mutters Piper Sherwood, looking away from the tall, white-blonde haired magician. "I can't picture him doing that."

"Whatever he did, it's over and done with. We can't change the past."

"How does he get away with stuff like that, Sebastian? He'll have the authorities down on our heads one of these days," Charlotte warns.

"Every two hundred-fifty years or so he gets like this. It's a mating thing. He's looking for a mate. He's never reproduced. I think, after all this time, he's getting antsy and anxious about that fact. He hasn't found the ideal mate."

"So he goes out on a limb and picks a little ginger-haired *human* girl he sees in the lobby of the hotel yesterday and manipulates the evening to go his way because he's hot for her?"

"More or less." Sebastian blows out his breath in frustration. "We've all dealt with this phase before. It'll pass."

"Yeah, but what about this poor little girl? Is he going to kill her too?"

"That's why we're here right now. She's a great kid. Very easy going. I'd hate to see something bad happen to her. So, when she gets here, I want the six of you to take her under your wings, so to speak…"

"Or literally," Charlotte adds. He glances at her, gives her a wry look. "Let's be honest with one another," she says.

"Fine," he concedes. "Take her under your wings and keep her safe. I can only do my best to try to keep him in line."

"It's never happened before," Cym points out.

"I can try *harder* to keep him in line."

"You and what army? When a demon gets the lust on him there's not a being in any realm that can contain it."

"Poor Pepper."

Sebastian walks to the bar and pours himself a drink, tosses it back quickly. "Okay ladies, meeting adjourned. What's done is done, and now we all have to deal with it and make the best of it. Welcome her and guide her along the best that you can. If I have to put a restraint on him, I will. He won't like it. He'll be hell to deal with and handle, but if I have to do it, I will, for all our sakes. I won't tolerate a loose cannon. His moorings have been slipping for centuries."

"So, if he mates with her and is successful that would quiet him down, wouldn't it?"

"She's a human being, Piper," he points out.

"So was someone else's famous saintly mother," she retorts.

"Let's not compare apples with rotten apples."

"Is lunch ready yet?" Caroline wonders, rising from her seat. She is also ginger-haired, tall, willowy with light-green eyes. "I'm starving!"

The others all get up and follow her from the room, leaving Sebastian at the bar staring down into his empty glass.

Cicero's looks like a place that Caesar may have taken his wife for dinner if they'd had Vegas-style restaurants back in ancient Rome. There are fluted marble columns, marble railings, grapevines, olive trees, marble statues of the gods and goddesses, marble fountains, an amazing bar. Simon Crowe causes heads to turn when he walks into the foyer of the restaurant. Three women immediately gasp and begin searching for pen and paper on which to obtain his autograph. He pauses to speak to the maître d' who informs him that Miss Rumford and her parents have arrived and have been seated. Simon nods, then turns and looks at the three women who have sort of fenced him in. He quickly signs an autograph for each of them, glances at the husbands who are lined up against the mirrored wall looking bored and somewhat embarrassed by the fuss their wives are making over him. He nods to the men then looks again at each woman in turn. They range in age from early thirties to late fifties. "Ladies, if you return to your husbands and look in their jacket breast pockets you will each find a pair of tickets for tomorrow night's show. Enjoy. Now, please excuse me, I have a dinner engagement and I'm already late with the show running overtime tonight."

The ladies rush to their husbands who all look startled by their wives grabbing for their jacket pockets, but Simon hears their cries of amazement and delight when they find the promised pairs of tickets exactly where he's said they'll be. Simon hears them calling, "Thank you, Simon!" as he makes his way through the crowded restaurant to the reserved table in a quiet corner.

"I apologize for being late. The show ran over by fifteen minutes tonight. Sometimes that happens. It's unpredictable." He smiles at Pepper who looks ravishingly beautiful with her loose red curls pinned up, a few loose coils of hair trailing down the nape of her neck. She's wearing a summery floral print dress—a satiny cream-colored strapless sheath over which there is a delicate watercolor patterned floral print sheer overdress. She has on the gold necklace that he bought for her. For a moment he can't take his eyes off her she is such a vision to him, but then her father stands up, reaches over, his hand extended. "Mr. Rumford," Simon says, grasping his hand firmly. "It's a pleasure to meet you."

"Likewise, Mr. Crowe. You've impressed our daughter. This is my wife, Phyllis. My name is Tom."

He turns and smiles at Phyllis Rumford who is a pretty woman with strawberry-blonde hair. Her husband has dark hair. "I see where Pepper has gotten her radiant beauty from. It's very nice to meet you, Mrs. Rumford." He bows over her hand then lets go of her as he sits down across from Pepper at the table for four. There is a plate of stuffed mushroom caps, an antipasto and a basket of breadsticks on the table that they have been enjoying. Mr. and Mrs. Rumford have cocktails before them, Pepper a ginger ale. "Pepper's told you that I've hired her as my new assistant?" he asks.

Immediately, he feels tension from the direction of her father. His mere presence at the table has already entranced Mrs. Rumford. He has that effect on women, not on men. Men view him as a threat. "Yes, about that...." Mr. Rumford says.

"Before you accuse me of seducing your daughter or leading her astray, I want to assure you that the job I have hired her for is legitimate. She will receive all the training that she needs over the next few months. I am not stealing your daughter, sir. I have offered her a unique and rare opportunity to be a part of one of the greatest magic acts in the world today. There were over nine hundred people in the auditorium that night. Your daughter caught my eye. She is everything I'd hoped she'd be—poised, graceful, possessed of a good sense of humor, brave, trusting and professional. I offered her the job. Since she is unemployed and looking for work, she accepted. I know it happened quickly but this is show business. I cannot be without an assistant because we perform every evening and twice on Saturday and Sunday with matinées in the early afternoon. I needed to find someone fast. I understand you may feel that the offered salary is low but as I explained to her, she will receive free room and board and the use of a company vehicle whenever she needs one. Her insurance premiums are covered by us. She'll have no expenses but her own personal ones. She will receive increases as she progresses in her training and gains experience. You do not have to be worried about her living unchaperoned with me. Sebastian and I maintain our own separate, private quarters on the compound. Pepper will be living in the main house with the other young ladies we employ. She'll have her own suite—a spacious bedroom/sitting room and private bathroom. She's free to decorate her suite however she chooses. She'll live here in Vegas six months out of the year. She will live with us in the Berkshires, which isn't that far from your family home, in November and December. She may go home and visit you for the holidays. She's not a prisoner. It's not a cult. She can come and go during her two months off as she pleases, or she can spend the entire two months with you if that's what she wants to do. The other four months of the year we travel to various venues so she'll have an opportunity to see parts of this country and Europe that she may never otherwise see if she were to take a boring desk job at an accounting firm at minimum wage or whatever. She'll be a part of the Cross and Crowe family. She'll be well taken care of. And I think that she'll be happy with us."

Mr. Rumford sits looking at him, practically glowering at him. "I just wish you'd spoken to me before you whisked her off to sign contracts that we have no idea what they say. She's only twenty-three years old, just out of college with no experience in things like this. Her mother and I have no idea what she's gone and gotten herself into."

"I'll call Risley Stroud and ask him to have copies of the contract and papers Pepper has signed at the front desk for you so that you can look them over. If you have any concerns you may contact Mr. Stroud directly and he can review everything with you. However, at twenty-three, Pepper is legally an adult. At twenty-nine, I am a professional magician and I assure you, I have hired assistants over the past eight years on a number of occasions and have never had a parent raise so much as an eyebrow at my hiring practices."

"What sort of job security is there for her? Why do you go through so many assistants?" Mr. Rumford asks.

Simon glances at Pepper for a moment. She is looking at him, no, watching him, with those lovely hazel eyes, listening to him. She is studying him like he studied her at the café. He returns his gaze to her father. "This is Vegas and my previous assistants have all been single, young females. They met young men, and in one case, an older man, here, fell in love and left to start lives of their own with their boyfriends or new husbands. I am not one to stand in the way of romance and a desire to move on in life. Pepper is not eternally bound to the company. She can pursue her own personal life as she chooses." Here he sees alarm written on her father's face and senses a frisson of anxiety from the direction of her mother. "Let me tell you this which may set your minds at ease. We are a family here and watch out for one another. We are not going to let Pepper be led astray by some rich, please pardon the crudeness of the phrase, bastard, who only wants her as a plaything. Charlotte, Caroline, Cym, Piper, Poppy and Sabrina will be like her big sisters. They'll keep a close eye on her. Pepper will be safe enough here."

"Pepper will fit right in," Mrs. Rumford says. "Charlotte, Caroline, Cym. Piper, Poppy and Pepper. And Sabrina." She smiles.

"Alliterative names, except for Sabrina," Mr. Rumford says.

"You can check with the local police. There has never been a problem involving anyone in our company." He crosses his fingers underneath the table and hopes that they do *not* check with the police.

"We'd like to see where Pepper will be living," Mrs. Rumford says.

Simon turns his head and looks at her. "When are you leaving for home?"

"We leave Sunday morning."

"We have two shows on Saturday, so I suppose you'd better run out there tomorrow morning. Do you have plans for then?" She glances at her husband, shakes her head. "Good. I'll have Adair Radburne meet you here at the hotel. He can take you out to the compound and give you the grand tour. Go with them, Pepper, so you can see where you'll be living. Shelley and Sherry will be there." He turns his head, looks at Mr. Rumford. "Yes, we do like alliterative names, I suppose. I never thought of it that way, but even Sebastian and I have alliterative names. Anyway, Shelly, Sherry and their brother Shawn are our property managers. They manage the compound, order the supplies and so forth. They're responsible for hiring the gardeners, making repairs, keeping the place running smoothly. Pepper can have a look at her suite so she can start getting some ideas on how she wants to decorate it. Shelley and Sherry will work with her on that." He looks at Pepper and smiles. "I'll give you an eight thousand dollar budget to furnish the suite whatever way you want it, and a two thousand dollar budget to decorate it." Her eyes widen at his generosity. "I want you to be comfortable and happy."

"That's extremely generous of you, Mr. Crowe" Mrs. Rumford says.

"That's...outra..." Mr. Rumford begins to say. Simon turns his head and the man seems to remember that this is no ordinary man whom he is having dinner with, but a world famous and, obviously, very wealthy showman. The young man is giving Pepper quite a lot of money to decorate her suite. He wonders if he is as generous with his other employees, or if he has some sort of feelings for his daughter. Pepper has been absolutely radiant since attending the magic show and being chosen by this man to be his assistant on stage. He suspects that she has a crush on the raven-haired, handsome magician and that might be what led her to sign the contract so quickly. "That's very nice of you. But," he hesitates, and then continues, "I'd like to speak to you privately after dinner. Maybe we could go to the bar while the ladies have coffee?"

"Of course," Simon agrees.

The server comes to the table to take their orders. Pepper orders baked fish and vegetables, her mother orders the chicken Alfredo, her father a New York strip steak, baked potato and steamed vegetables. Simon orders a pasta dish with shellfish and calamari. They all order salads. Simon orders two bottles of wine for the table, a burgundy for her father who is eating red meat and for himself because he's not a fan of white wines, and a delicate white wine for the ladies for their fish and chicken. It's not cheap wine by any means and her father clearly appreciates the fact that he's willing to spend money on them.

Simon talks about how he and Sebastian met and merged their separate magic acts into a mega-production unlike anything else ever seen on stage. Pepper asks him about Jack and the panther whose name she learns is Onyx. "Jack, I found in the alley one night. He had a broken wing, possibly from a disagreement with a large bird of prey. I took him home, had him treated, kept him comfortable and fed. We bonded. I started training him before he regained the use of his wing. It was his choice to stay. I took him outside to release him but he decided he wanted to stay, so I worked on acclimatizing him to performing in the auditorium. For the first few weeks he found the catwalks, lighting fixtures and cables more interesting than he found me down on the stage. But gradually, he and I came to an agreement. He does what he's trained to do then I let him have some free choices. He likes the catwalks. However, if anyone spills popcorn, he'll swoop down and indulge himself in that treat." He shrugs. "He finds lost jewelry fairly regularly." Pepper raises her eyes, remembering Jack coughing up her ear stud. She never asked how that had come about. "Onyx was adopted from a big cat rescue shelter in Reno. A collector of big cats had obtained him from a circus that went under. He was under two years old. He had him for a year before he discovered that he had liver cancer, a particularly virulent form of it, and was diagnosed as terminal. He had to scramble to find his cats new homes. Sebastian and I went up and had a look. He adopted the snow leopard and I adopted the black panther. Neve proved to be unsuitable for the show, she's too skittish, but Onyx was a different story altogether. He loves to perform. He'd been around crowds before. He'd performed in the ring. He was used to people, noise, bright lights, and music. He's an amazing animal."

"What did Sebastian do with Neve?" Pepper asks.

"Neve lives with him in his house. She has a suite of rooms designed specifically for her with real trees and rocks she can climb up and lounge on. The rooms are climate controlled. There's a recirculating fresh water stream. She likes to fish. A couple times a month Sebastian will get a half dozen fish and put them in the stream as a treat for her. He takes care of her, but when we're on the road for four months he has a man he trusts who cares of her and keeps her socialized. Jake Miller and I take care of Onyx. I have a lot of respect for my panther but I don't let him loose in my house very often. He has his special quarters attached to my home and I visit him there."

"No risk taking with the big cat?"

"No. He is, first and foremost, a wild animal despite his having been captured as a six-month old and raised around people. He still possesses all the instincts of a predator."

"I don't want Pepper…"

"Pepper will be trained how to work with Onyx. Nothing she will be doing will expose her to any danger from the cat. She will learn all the signs and signals that we've developed, all the commands. She will not work with the cat until I'm confident he's accepted her and is willing to work with her. She'll never be alone with him and he will never be loose near her unless I am also present."

"I don't want her being mauled."

"Neither do I," Simon replies. "We are all very respectful of the cats. Jack, on the other hand, is going to adore her. He's very sociable and curious. He flies around my house."

"That can be messy," Mrs. Rumford says.

"Actually, he's well-trained. He has his perches. There's sand from the desert in trays under the perches. The sand gets changed regularly. He hasn't had an accident in the house since he figured out where he's supposed to go. Ravens are very intelligent."

Their salads are brought. Mr. Rumford talks about his real estate business. Pepper's mother is an agent, selling houses. She was once attacked by a deranged man who posed as a bachelor interested in buying a remote cottage near a river where he could fish in peace. She managed to get away with little more than bruises and a cut on her wrist where he had slashed at her with a fish fileting knife. The man had gotten away as well, but showed up at the office seventeen days later when Pepper happened to be working part time after school. Pepper had been sixteen years old then, had recognized the man from her mother's description of him and his odd behavior. He had demanded to see Phyllis. She had been alone in the office at the time because the receptionist had run across the street for pastries to go with their afternoon coffee and had gotten into a flirtatious conversation with the newly widowed baker. The man had vaulted over the counter and attempted to reach Pepper who had jumped up and run around the far side of the desk. She in turn had vaulted over the counter and fled the store-front office, stumbling out into the street where she had nearly been hit by a police cruiser that was heading back to the police station two blocks away at the end of shift. She'd jumped up onto the hood of the cruiser to avoid being struck and had slid into the windshield, bruising her shoulder and spraining her wrist, but the officer had not been driving very fast and was able to stop without throwing her off the hood. He'd jumped out of the car to berate her for being so reckless but instead pulled her to safety as the crazy man had come running out of the real estate office waving a knife and threatening to slit her throat. The officer had managed to disarm and subdue the man but Pepper had had to help him cuff him. "She is a brave young lady. And as a result of the incidents, I send all of my agents out in pairs and make sure that there are two people in the office at all times. We've had no close calls since." Simon nods

"Tom, you're boring him," Phyllis murmurs.

"I was just confirming his impression that our daughter is a brave girl."

She makes a slight face, turns to Simon and asks, "How did you get into magic?"

"I wasn't any good at anything else I'd ever tried to do." He reaches over, picks up her dinner fork, taps it three times on the table and he's suddenly holding a long stemmed red rose. He hands the rose to her and she smiles, delighted and amazed. He pretends to throw something up into the air, reaches up and her fork is in his hand when he brings his hand back down to the table. He replaces it on her placemat. "I am very good at what I *can* do."

"That was awesome!" Mrs. Rumford cries.

"Do you bend spoons with your mind?" Mr. Rumford asks.

"That is telekinesis and no, I cannot do that." He can but he's not going to reveal all his secrets, not to these people.

"Can you make our hotel bill disappear?" Mr. Rumford asks next as their salad plates are removed and their dinners are placed before them.

"Dad!" Pepper says quietly, shooting him an incredulous look. Her eyes shift to Simon and she is embarrassed to find that he looks offended. "Mr. Crowe is being extremely generous buying us all dinner tonight. He's already done a lot more for me than I ever expected. Don't be greedy!"

"He's stolen my baby from me," Mr. Rumford replies.

"I'm *not* a baby!" Pepper protests, her face flushing a deeper pink.

"My little girl, then."

"Thomas, please! Stop."

"I was hoping Pepper would come to work for the agency."

"Dad, that was so not going to happen and you know it. I don't want to sell houses. That's boring!"

"But you'd be good at it, like your mother is."

"I'll take care of your hotel bill," Simon says.

"Well, that's more like it," Mr. Rumford says, smiling. "Let's have some of that wine you ordered! Fill 'er up!" He holds out his wine glass and Simon fills it to the brim, much to the man's delight.

Pepper wants to melt into the floor she is so humiliated by her father's behavior. She suddenly excuses herself and hurries to the ladies room. Mrs. Rumford gives her husband a quick glare, then excuses herself and goes after her upset daughter. Simon pours wine for himself. "You have a lovely wife and a beautiful daughter. You're a very fortunate man. You own your own business as well. Your lovely daughter has grown up to be a decent, charming, young lady. May I offer a toast to you, sir, for your good fortune in life."

"Thank you, Crowe, that's very nice of you to say so." They salute one another and drink. "Wonderful wine!"

"I'm thinking that I should retire after dinner, so let's skip going to the bar. Let me just come right out and say that I will write you a check for one quarter of a million dollars and leave it for you at the front desk. Would you consider that adequate enough compensation for my having stolen your daughter away from you and the future you had laid out for her?" Mr. Rumford's eyes widen at this out of the blue offer of money in exchange for his only child.

"I didn't mean…" he begins to say, but Simon holds up a hand.

"Yes, I know you didn't. But in Vegas everyone wants to win big. You've been losing at the tables, your wife has been losing at the slot machines. Pepper has been the big winner in the Rumford family with her landing of a plum job that thousands of other young ladies would covet. I am being generous with her because in a few days she'll be left behind while you and your wife return to Connecticut. There will be an adjustment and adaptation period for her. I want her to be comfortable. I want for her to be happy with her decision, her step toward independence from her family. On the other hand, I also want both you and your wife to be happy with her decision, and comfortable with her choice. I feel that by compensating you in this way I will be helping both of you adjust to her being out of the nest. It's really not that large a sum when you think about the current real estate prices. What would a quarter of a million dollars actually get you these days? Perhaps I should give you a half million dollars? Would that be better? What would Pepper's earning potential have been if she had chosen to be a realtor?"

"You're paying her twenty something thousand a year! She would have earned much more selling houses."

"Fine, then. You drive a hard bargain. I will compensate you exactly one million dollars. However, you must understand that you will not get another penny more out of me. I will also inform Mr. Stroud that I want Pepper's starting annual income to be fifty thousand dollars. I will still be paying her room and board and letting her use a company vehicle and paying her insurance premiums. Does that sound satisfactory to you, sir?"

"I didn't mean to imply…"

"Is that satisfactory in your opinion?"

"Yes! It's more than that. Thank you, Crowe."

"Then I will write the check right now and we'll be done with this bit of business." He pulls his personal checkbook from his inside jacket pocket, produces a pen seemingly from thin air and hastily writes out the check, tears it out and hands it to the man who looks at it with a broad smile on his face. Simon sees the glow of greed deep in the man's eyes and grimaces, looks away. He sees Mrs. Rumford and Pepper returning to the table. Pepper has her head bent. "Put the check away now, please. Do not tell your daughter or she will be offended by my basically purchasing her from you." He stands up, holding the chair out for Mrs. Rumford. Pepper seats herself as he does this, so he sits back down, pours wine for the ladies. "Pepper, try this wine. It's delicate and sweet. I think you'll enjoy it." She raises her head and he sees just how miserable she is. "Delicate and sweet, like you," he says, holding the glass across the table to her. She hesitates then reaches out and takes the glass from him. A thrill races through his entire being at the slight brush of her fingertips against his. His hunger for her flares hot as a blue flame but he tamps it down, not without much effort, smiles at her and is rewarded with a slight smile in return.

The remainder of dinner goes fairly smoothly. Pepper, however, never does entirely relax. Their plates are cleared and desserts are ordered, except for Simon who just orders coffee. The coffees come before the desserts are served. He takes his black, drinks about half the cup then apologizes that he has to leave them so soon, but he has had a long day and needs to sleep. He encourages them to stay and enjoy themselves, have anything else they may desire, that he will have the bill charged to his room. "I will let Adair know he's to pick you up in front of the hotel at ten tomorrow morning to take you to the compound for a tour. Sherry or Shelley should be there to show you around. Adair will bring you all back here afterward. Pepper, you have the tickets for to-morrow evening's show?" She nods. "I will see you at the show then. Goodnight."

He wends his way through the restaurant, occasionally being stopped by a female patron who wants her photo taken with him or an autograph, or both. When he is fifteen paces out into the hotel lobby he hears his name called and stops, slowly turns back and sees Pepper coming toward him from the restaurant entrance. She looks almost livid but there is something else in her face as well, hurt. He frowns. That bastard probably couldn't wait to show his wife the check, and now Pepper knows she's been, more or less, sold to the magician by her own father. He waits for her to speak first. A nebula of spectators begins to form around them and he does not like that. He abhors public spectacles. "I can't be-lieve..." she begins to say and he cuts her off.

"Everything you see, no, Miss Rumford, I agree. You shouldn't believe everything you see, because much of what I do is illusion." He takes her by the arm and steers her into the elevator that has just opened and expelled a group of revelers. Quickly, he presses the button for the fifteenth floor and the doors slide shut more rapidly than they would normally do, shutting everyone else out. "What has your pretty feathers so ruffled up?" he asks.

"You paid him *a million dollars* for me? He *sold me to you?*"

"No, I've merely compensated your parents money for their loss of you. You do realize that you are staying here with us, that you won't have an opportunity to go home and see your parents until November? Your father had plans for you." Here she rolls her eyes and makes a face that almost makes him laugh but he holds that response in check. "I was only going to give him a quarter of a million dollars," he says and is surprised when she suddenly slaps his face, surprisingly hard. "Miss Rumford, really!"

"How dare you give him money like that! He's just going to squander it all on stupid stuff! You'd have been better off giving the money to my mother who can at least hold onto money! Now she'll be miserable!"

He is silent for a few moments as he rubs his stinging cheek. She has quite a good arm on her. "I'm afraid I can't undo what I've already done," he says.

"You're a magician!"

"That much is true. I'm a professional trickster but I can't change the check now."

"Then void it, stop payment on it—do something!"

"What if I write another check to your mother in the same amount?"

"Are you kidding me? That's just throwing gasoline on the fire!"

"So what is it that you want me to do, Pepper?" he asks, and is stunned when she bursts into tears as if he has just com-manded her to do so. He doesn't like it when girls cry. He's not good at all at handling feminine tears.

"I don't know!" she cries as the doors on the fifteenth floor slide open. There are several people standing about in the corridor. "I don't know how to fix this mess!"

He takes her arm and steers her toward his private suite, even though he knows there is someone already there waiting for him and this will just make this whole business worse, but he can't stand in the hallway and argue with an hysterical young lady when he's already been recognized and is being stared at. "Come with me." He does not let go of her as he strides quickly down the hall-way. Pepper has to nearly jog to keep up with him. He runs his key card through the reader, throws open the door and hauls her into the living room of his suite where not one, not two, but three naked females are sprawled on the furniture awaiting his arrival. Slightly behind him, Pepper freezes and he feels the tension that makes her nearly rigid as she takes in the scene. And then she is trying to wrench her wrist free of his grasp.

"She doesn't look very willing to join us," observes one of the girls.

"Simon, are you really going to take on four of us tonight? Are you trying to break a record? Or would that be set a personal best record?"

"Oh, he can handle it," says the third girl. "You know how he is."

"Let go of me!" Pepper flares hotly and this time she gives him a hard kick to the back of his right calf.

"Stop it!" he barks angrily. Turning to the three girls, he points to the bedroom. "All three of you, go in the other room and close the door. I'll be with you in a few minutes. I need to take care of this first."

"What's so special about her that we have to wait and she gets you first?"

"She's my new assistant and she is getting nothing more from me at the moment because I have evidently given her more than enough as it is!" He points to the bedroom again. "Move!" They don't look happy about it, but they all go into the bedroom and slam the door shut behind them. He turns back to Pepper. She is half turned away from him, straining to get out the door, back into the hallway. "Hold on for just a minute," he says. "We have something to settle here."

"There's nothing we need to settle," she replies icily. "I'll get the check back from my father. I'll call Mr. Stroud and tell him that everything was a huge misunderstanding, a big mistake. I'll leave the necklace for you at the front desk. I just want to go home. I don't want to stay here. I don't want to be your assistant."

"Stop behaving like a child," he says. "This is not about what you just saw and heard. We're discussing this problem of money that I gave to your father, money you feel he's going to piss away that will make your mother unhappy. That's the issue here." He shakes her arm. "You are young and naïve if you don't think I have a sex life, Pepper. I do and I'll tell you right up front, even though it's none of your business, that it's pretty damn active. You don't need to know everything about me. I don't need to know everything about you. I'm the magician, you're the assistant. Let's keep that straight between us. Now, tell me what you want me to do about the money."

"Nothing. Don't do anything. Just forget about it. It doesn't matter." She tries to tug her arm free again but he's still got a firm grip on her. "Please let go of me."

He has suddenly realized that he does not want to go into the bedroom and have sex with those three showgirls from the exotic dancer bar downstairs. He wants to make love to Pepper and make her his, but he can't do that. And he knows he would only upset her even more if he tried. She's not happy with him. But, he is having a lot of trouble getting his own feelings under control. "If you think of a solution before they fly back to Connecticut let me know what you want me to do." He lets go of her wrist and she rushes to the door. "Pepper, let me give you my cellphone number so you can call me. I probably won't see you again until Monday."

She pauses a moment at the door, then slowly opens it. "No, Simon, you don't understand. You're not ever going to see me again. I'm going home." She slips out into the hallway, pulls the door closed behind her. She does not see what happens in the living room, does not see Simon lose control like he has never lost control of himself before.

All Pepper knows is that, as she reaches the elevator, the fire alarm goes off and people quickly begin exiting their rooms, begin screaming as they rush toward the fire exits. There is definitely smoke on this floor. She is shoved against the wall as there is a general stampede for the stairs. The elevators have shut down. She slides sideways because she can see fire flickering beneath the door of the suite she's just left. Running to the door, she pounds on it with both fists. "Simon! Get out of there! Please! Get out of the room!"

She doesn't know exactly what it is that opens the door and grabs her, hauls her into the burning, smoke-filled room, but it is black, it is very strong and its skin is rough and scaly. It easily picks her up as it races swiftly across the room. She can't scream because she's having difficulty breathing with all the smoke, but as it plunges through the huge glass window she thinks that she's going to die. Her survival instinct kicks in and she writhes around so that she can grab onto the thing that is plummeting toward the ground fifteen stories below. She hears a noise like the sails of a windmill flapping and feels the creatures back muscles bunching and moving. It has wings. She can't see them because she'd squeezed her eyes shut when it had crashed through the window and has not reopened them, basically because the smoke irritated them and they sting. And, she's terrified.

The next thing she knows, her feet are on solid ground. She's sitting on a concrete platform. In the distance she hears sirens and screams. "Are you hurt?" a gruff voice asks. She can't open her eyes. She shakes her head. She's not really sure if she's hurt or not. She's too shocked to take inventory. She feels scaly hands running over her arms and legs, scaly fingers running through her hair, hears bits of glass ticking onto the cement around her. "Not too badly anyway," he growls. "Open your eyes and look at me," it commands roughly, shaking her a bit by the shoulders. Her eyes pop open against her will and she stares up into two red, burning eyes with oval slits for pupils. Before her mind can grasp the fact that she is looking into the eyes of a demon from Hell, her mind suddenly grows still and quiet and the terror dissipates. "Go back to the hotel and find your parents. They'll be worried about you." She hears leathery-like movement. "Even though you won't remember anything of what's just happened, I need to say this. I'm sorry," the thing says. "Now, close your eyes and count to ten before opening them again."

By the time she opens her eyes, she finds that she is alone in an alley, sitting on a loading dock. Scrambling up, she runs to the end of the dock, wobbles unsteadily down the concrete steps then hurries to the entrance to the delivery alley. She discovers that she is across the street from the hotel. There are fire engines and police cruisers, ambulances with blue and red lights rotating, casting eerie patterns all around her. The streets are crowded with hotel guests, casino and restaurant patrons, employees who have evacuated the hotel and spectators. She wends her way through the throng of people, searching for her parents. It seems to take forever, but she finally hears her father shouting at someone that his daughter is missing, is unaccounted for, and that he can't find her.

"Dad!" she cries. Her throat hurts and her voice is raspy. "Dad! Over here!"

She's released from the hospital at nine o'clock the following morning after being treated for mild smoke inhalation and some superficial cuts and a bruised knee. She has no memory of what happened to her after she rushed out of the restaurant, is shocked speechless when her parents tell her that there was a sudden, intense fire in Simon Crowe's private suite and it killed three show girls who had been visiting him. She asks about Crowe and learns that he was trapped in an elevator with seven other guests between the tenth and eleventh floors and was rescued by firefighters. Damage to the hotel was confined mostly to the suite, but the entire south wing of the hotel has been closed by the fire inspector until structural damage can be assessed. The hotel is relocating as many guests as possible to other rooms in the north wing and main building. Since they have rooms on the eighth floor in the north wing they are being allowed to remain there. The casino, bars, restaurants and auditorium are still open. The boutiques in the south wing are temporarily closed due to the power being shut off in that wing.

Pepper's parents tell her that Adair Radburne is still picking them up at ten. He will deliver Pepper and her things to the compound. They will all have a tour of the place where she will be living then she will remain there and Adair will be driving them to the airport as they will be flying home. "Why are you leaving today?" she asks.

"Your father and I have some things to do before Monday morning," Mrs. Rumford replies. "Mr. Crowe has assured us that you'll be fine and we have no reason to think otherwise."

At the hotel, Pepper has to scramble to pack her belongs even though she's only got a weeks' worth of outfits with her. The last thing she grabs is Mr. Stripes off the bed. For several long moments she stands beside the bed holding the mohair plush tiger, fingering its loose ear. She remembers Simon producing it in his dressing room, but she still has no idea how he obtained it. She's just glad that she has it with her as she goes to live in an unfamiliar place. It's a small piece of her childhood, her past that brings her comfort, and today, for whatever reason, she needs that comfort. Something is troubling her but she can't put her finger on it. It does upset her that Simon's suite exploded, but she's glad he was stuck in an elevator and wasn't in it when it happened. That would have been terrible. But the whole thing leaves her uneasy because she's not sure how she inhaled smoke or how she got all the little cuts and scratches. She just cannot find an explanation for that and thinks maybe that's what's making her feel so off balance.

Adair is a man in his early thirties with surfer dude blonde hair and brown eyes. He's tall and athletic looking, tanned and has a wide smile, perfect teeth. He shakes hands with all three of them, loads their bags into the trunk of the black limousine after getting them settled into the air-conditioned interior. Then he slides behind the wheel and pulls away from the curb. Pepper feels a fleeting frisson of anxiety as they merge into traffic and leave the hotel behind, but Adair has the partition between the front seat and rear seats open and he begins telling them all about Vegas, the various hotels and casinos, the shows going on in them and how Cross and Crowe have been a staple of Vegas entertainment for close to a decade.

It takes forty minutes to reach the road to the compound, another ten minutes to get there and five more to climb the rise to where the massive limestone and fieldstone castle-like mansion sits amid manicured desert gardens. There is a Victorian style conservatory full of lush plants between the north wing and a somewhat smaller castle-like structure at the other side of it. Adair tells them the conservatory connects Sebastian Cross's private residence from the main mansion. Simon Crowe's private residence is set back from the mansion and connected by an enclosed walkway. The oval swimming pool lies between the mansion and Crowe's residence. There is a fieldstone bathhouse. Colorful awnings shade part of the patio surrounding the pool. Crowe's house faces the desert. At one side of the structure is a compound where Onyx is kept, featuring indoor and outdoor living areas. There is a carriage house with seven bays with five attached shaded carports at either side.

They will see the main mansion today. He pulls up in front and they go to the door. Adair uses his key to admit them. Once inside he unclips a walkie-talkie from his belt. "Adair to Sherry. Guests have arrived."

"Bring them to the day room. I'll be there shortly with lemonade and iced tea."

"This way."

He leads them toward the back of the mansion, then down a broad hallway to a large, sunny room facing the conservatory. There is an atrium door allowing access to the conservatory in this room, and a row of double glass atrium doors leading out onto the patio surrounding the pool. "Make yourselves comfortable. I'll just go take Pepper's bags up to her temporary room. Sherry will be right along. She'll give you the tour and then I'll drive you to the airport."

"Thank you."

In the rather gothic looking stone house behind the mansion, Sebastian Cross slams open the door of the master bedroom. Simon is in bed, his forearm draped across his eyes. He is unshaven and pale, his black hair a tousled mess on the silvery-colored pillowcase. "Explain to me what the hell happened last night!" Sebastian shouts at him. "And this had better be damned detailed and not just another one of your glossy lies!" He stalks to the window and tears the drapes open, rings rattling. Behind him, Simon groans, clearly in pain. "How the hell did your room explode?

Why were there three naked, dead girls found in your bedroom? And don't you dare tell me that you were innocently trapped in an elevator with seven other people because I don't believe that bull- shit for one second! Start talking!" He turns back and finds Simon in the exact same position as he was when he came into the room. "Well?"

"I lost it," Simon says. "Okay? I screwed something up. I upset Pepper. She started to make a scene so I hauled her up to my suite to try to hash it out with her in private. There were three showgirls waiting for me there. I sent them into the bedroom to wait. Pepper just got even more upset…and she…I think she quit, or told me that she was going to call Stroud and try to quit. She walked out on me and I just…I lost control. You're obviously aware of the results of that loss of control."

"All of goddam Vegas is aware of the results, and probably the entire damn country as well by now. You've blackened our names and reputation good this time, Simon Crowe! And you killed three showgirls besides!"

"That was an accident."

"Just the same, they're dead."

"They'll investigate and discover that the girls were smoking meth in the bedroom. I had flash powder in there and other explosives that we have permits for that we use in our shows that were all legal for me to possess, but the girls evidently got into my stuff while waiting for me and didn't realize the danger. They unwittingly blew the place up. I'll most likely be fined for not having the materials stored properly. The hotel is insured. We're insured."

"What if they throw your ass in jail?"

"I didn't do anything wrong or illegal. I wasn't even in the room."

"But you were. Maybe Pepper is going to remember that."

"No, she won't remember. I took care of that."

"Where is she right now?" Sebastian asks. "Heading home to Connecticut? With her parents at the hotel? In the damn hospital?"

Simon slowly uncovers his eyes. His eyes are red with oval pupils. He rapidly blinks several times and his eyes revert to their human deep, dark brown color with round pupils. He scrubs his scruffy face with both hands. His hands are scratched and he has a few cuts on his arms. "What time is it?" he asks.

"Almost eleven," Sebastian replies.

"Then Pepper is at the mansion with her parents. Sherry's giving them a tour of the place."

"She's here?"

"She's my assistant."

"Are you absolutely sure about that?"

"She doesn't remember quitting, or planning on quitting. She can only remember having dinner with her parents and me last night."

"How did you get her out of the suite?"

"You know how I got her out."

"And no one saw a black, scaly, winged demon jumping through a fifteenth floor window clutching a redhead in its arms?"

"No."

"You weren't caught on any security camera performing this feat?"

Simon hauls himself half upright, leaning on his elbows. "A curious atmospheric condition scrambled the camera reception in that vicinity. There are no recorded images of anything leaping out of the fifteenth floor window with a panicky redhead twisting in its arms and clinging to it for dear life. I may be reckless, but I'm not stupid."

"You're an idiot and a huge liability! Do you know that?"

"I believe you've told me as much any number of times through the years."

"You're going to be the death of both of us!"

He draws himself up further, turns, moves his pillows around then leans back against them. "I don't think I'll ever be fortunate enough to literally die. And neither will you. I'm quite sure you and I are immortal beings. I don't have to cite examples of our extraordinary escapes from cataclysmic disasters in the past, do I?"

"You don't," Sebastian says. "But what you have to do is get this damn demon lust of yours under control!"

"For your information I am not in lust."

"I've seen you like this before. I know what's going on with you. Don't lie to me, Simon."

"All right then! I'm having an issue this time," he admits. "The simple fact of the matter is that I want Pepper Rumford. I want to mate with her. I want her to have my offspring. I want her *now*, not two hundred fifty years from now. The problem is, she's human and I'm not supposed to mate with humans. I know other demons have gotten away with it. They've produced some pretty nasty spawn."

"You leave Pepper alone," Sebastian says.

"Easy for you to say. You can take whomever you choose. It's easy enough for a fallen angel to mate with a human being. It's expected of you. I'm the flip side of the coin. I'm not supposed to touch a human being, never mind bed one. That girl is like a craving in my body. When I'm near her my blood sings in my veins and it's all I can do to keep myself from tearing her clothes off and having my way with her."

"So you stupidly hired her as your assistant. As such, you'll be working closely with her, training her, having close contact with her day after day, and then you'll be performing live on stage with her, touching her, interacting with her on a nightly basis and twice on Saturdays and Sundays! If this is how you manage your problems no wonder you're such a damn screw-up! Really Simon, the better solution would have been to never have chosen the girl in the first place! Am I right?"

Simon blows out his breath in frustration. Sebastian turns from the window and looks back at him, and he sees something he has never seen before. He sees utter misery in the eyes of his longtime partner. He has known this demon for several thousand years. They have lived together, worked together, traveled the world together, performed together, transformed themselves again and again together, but he has never seen this depth of despair in Simon before. "I don't know what to do for you," he says.

"There's nothing you can do for me," Simon replies in a hollow voice. "I have to make Pepper unhappy enough that she'll decide on her own to leave me. I have to talk to Stroud, get him to write a loophole into her contract that he can 'discover' at some future point in time so she can get out of it. I have to let her go. I realize that now."

"Too bad foresight isn't as acute as hindsight, my friend."

Simon looks away. "Just do me a favor, will you? Be her friend. I have to hurt her. She's going to need a friend."

"Simon, she's a beautiful girl. Maybe I'm not the one you should be asking to befriend her. It could go badly."

"Yeah, I know," Simon replies quietly and Sebastian is further stunned to realize that his friend is asking him to take

Pepper as his lover to save her from certain destruction at his own hands. Simon knows he is involved with Charlotte Cheston, so that would mean that he'd have to place his own relationship and happiness in jeopardy to help him. He's not sure he can do that. "Leave me alone now."

"The police have called. They're sending a few people out here to interview you, to get a more detailed description of what was in your suite and all the sordid details of your out of control sex life. As you know, the whole damn world is anxious to get all the dirt on you that they possibly can. We live in a voyeuristic society that literally craves smut. And you, damn you, give the tabloids fodder for their smut mills on a fairly regular basis!" Simon grimaces. "Get up, clean yourself up and, for all our sakes, try to look like a man who is as shocked as everyone else is about what's happened." Sebastian leaves the room, closes the door firmly but he does not slam it.

Simon sits with his head tilted back, eyes closed for several long minutes before finally hurling the covers aside and getting out of bed. Naked, he walks to the window with the intention of drawing the drapes, but as he reaches to pull them closed, he catches sight of people down on the patio. Sherry is leading the Rumfords on a tour of the patio and pool house area. The sun is shining on them all, but it's Pepper's fiery red hair that catches and holds his eye. Her hair is as bright as a bonfire and he feels drawn to her. He groans aloud, in agony. Although his window is closed and there is no way that she can possible have heard him, her head turns and she looks up, her eyes meeting his across the pool. She starts to smile then realizes that he's naked, as he's most likely visible to her from the top of his head to below his navel. Her smile falters for a moment then brightens. She lifts her hand in a quick, almost furtive wave. He finds himself giving her an equally quick salute, then Sherry says something to her and she looks away. He stares at the back of her head for a long moment, grimly watches her reach up and touch the back of her head. He lets the drapes fall closed as he steps back. She is very receptive. It's clear enough to him that she felt the caress of his hand on her hair, only she didn't realize what it was that she was feeling. She probably thought an insect had touched her. And isn't that what he is? A huge, ugly beast of an insect drawn to the bright and beautiful, sweet-nectared flower that she is.

Pepper unpacks her things in the guest room on the third floor because her assigned suite is empty. She has no idea how to furnish or decorate it but Sherry has assured her that she and Shelley will take her furniture and accessory shopping soon. She's given a notebook and a pen and told to write down some colors that she likes and any ideas that she has as to how she wants the suite to look. She's seen how the other girls have decorated their rooms and has been awed by the opulence and beauty of the various suites.

Her parents had enjoyed a quick lunch with her and Sherry. They'd eaten southwest grilled chicken salads, then the Rumfords had said goodbye to their only child and Adair had driven them away from the compound. Pepper had had a bad first hour, riddled with anxiety and doubt, but then Charlotte had come home, followed by the other young ladies, all seasoned assistants of the two magicians. They'd greeted her warmly and begun fussing over, taking her to the attic where there were closets from one end to the other, pulling out clothes and having her try them on. Every kind of costume imaginable is stored in these closets. There are also basic clothes as well—brand new black leggings, black leotards, black t-shirts and gowns, jewel-colored capes. These are the basics that all the assistants have, solid colors that compliment but do not distract the audience from the two magicians as they all work together on stage to perform the illusions that astonish, amaze and delight the people who come expecting a great show and find themselves captive to an amazing experience.

At four o'clock, they all head over to the hotel. Cross and Crowe have not canceled the evening performance. Pepper is expected to assist Simon in the knife throwing act. Her heart speeds up and seems to beat harder when she hears that. She glances at her palm but there is no sign of any injury there. She's also going to quickly be trained to perform in the Seven Sisters Illusion. They are going to rehearse her the minute they get to the theater. They tell her that it's easy enough, to just follow what they do and she'll be fine. Sabrina is going to alter Gillian's costume so that it fits Pepper well enough for tonight.

Pepper is put through the paces of the Seven Sisters Illusion three times before they break for supper, which is served in the dining room off stage left and down a corridor. The Cavalier restaurant in the hotel provides their meals and the food is good. There are twenty-five to thirty people in the dining room eating dinner when Sebastian Cross and Simon Crowe enter. They are in street clothes and both look somber. "Can we have your attention please!" Sebastian shouts. In a few moments, he has their complete attention. "As you know, there was a tragedy in the hotel last night in Simon's private suite. Three young ladies died in a fire that is still under investigation. Simon and I met with the hotel owners and the owners of the Pirate's Cove Club where the girls danced and we've decided that we will proceed with tonight's show as usual. The logistics of reimbursing nine hundred patrons the cost of their tickets is just too staggering to consider. We discussed how tragedies are a part of life in Vegas, and as on the

Broadway, and everywhere else in the known world where performers are found, the show must go on. We will have a moment of silence for the lives lost last night and then we will perform our show to the best of our collective abilities and wow the audience as we always do. Simon is co-operating with the authorities to find the exact cause of the explosion and fire that destroyed his suite and killed those young ladies. We would appreciate it if you did not speak of this tragedy to others. If you have any questions or concerns, please, do not hesitate to approach Simon or me. We will do our best to answer your questions or address your concerns." He looks from face to face. Simon, beside him, seems unusually subdued. "Lastly, we have a new young lady who has joined out troupe tonight. You may have met her briefly the other night when Simon chose her from the audience to assist him with the knife throwing act. Please join us in welcoming Miss Tessie 'Pepper' Rumford to the Cross and Crowe family. She prefers to be called Pepper. With that red hair of hers, I don't think any of you will have any trouble remembering that!" Here, Simon finally raises his eyes and he looks directly at Pepper. She is sitting between Sabrina and Cym. Cym has ginger-colored hair, a pale orangey-red. Pepper's hair is much more vivid in hue. His eye is drawn to it and his hands tingle with the remembrance of the feel of it against his palms and fingers.

"Pepper, I need to see you for a few minutes in my dressing room before the show. When you're finished eating come to me," he says, and then he turns and leaves the dining room.

Sebastian turns his head to watch him go then turns back to the room. "He's still quite upset. Let's give him some time and space to move through this. I'm sure he'll be his old self again once this all settles down."

Pepper is actually nervous when she makes her way to Simon's dressing room. She hesitates then knocks once on the door, hears him tell her to come in. She opens the door and slips into the room she was in just a couple of nights ago. It is surprisingly tidy tonight. He is already partially dressed in his skinny black slacks and white shirt. His black cut-away frock coat is on a hanger behind the door. He is putting on his vest but he can't seem to get the buttons to cooperate. He is obviously getting frustrated with himself.

Pepper crosses the room and says, "Here, let me do that for you."

"You don't…" he begins to say but stops when she looks up and her eyes meet his.

"I do," she says before she looks back down at the jeweled buttons on his vest and quickly works them through the button holes. "There." She steps back. "What do you need to see me about?" she asks.

"The knife throwing act."

"Oh, right."

"I had a talk with Sebastian on the way over here and I've told him that I can't perform that trick tonight. I throw real knives at a real girl and I am having trouble concentrating tonight. Therefore, you will only be performing in the Seven Sisters Illusion this evening. There will be no knife throwing act until I feel I can focus one hundred and twenty-five percent on what I'm doing."

"Oh." She is both relieved and disappointed about this.

"I don't have time to train you for a substitute act as we go on stage in less than an hour, then we perform two shows tomorrow and Sunday. I'm going to have Sabrina assist me tonight and for the matinees and evening shows this weekend. On Monday morning, I'd like to see you in the gymnasium of the mansion and we'll start your training. I think you'll be perfect for the levitation act so I'm putting that back into the show. Gillian was taller and about fifteen or so pounds heavier than you and had trouble with it, so we scratched it from the show. People have always liked it so it's time to bring it back." She nods. "Good luck tonight. I know you'll do well."

"I hope so." She walks to the door, then stops and turns back. "Simon?" He raises his head and looks at her. "My parents wanted me to tell you thank you for everything." He nods and she leaves, closing the door behind her. His dressing room suddenly feels as if all the air has been drawn out of it. The lights seem dimmer. He drops down into a tall canvas chair and stares at the far wall, lost in thought, suffering a misery so profound that it leaves him immobilized.

Sebastian has to track him down and direct him to finish getting dressed. "Do I have to kick your ass to get you to move tonight?" he demands.

"I feel sluggish."

"Maybe you should try sleeping once in a while instead of..."

"Don't go there," Simon warns him.

"Are you going to be able to perform?"

"Here or in bed?"

"Here, where it really matters."

A look of annoyance crosses the dark-haired magician's face. "Yes, of course."

"How did Pepper take the cutting of the knife act?" Sebastian asks as Simon checks his pockets.

"She's somewhat disappointed, but also somewhat relieved."

"What act are you going to train her for first?"

"I've decided to try her with the levitation act. She's very susceptible to hypnosis and suggestion. I can get her in a trance and it'll be a piece of cake to levitate her."

"Just don't drop her."

"Would it kill you to have a little faith in me?"

"Me, have faith in a demon? Yeah, I think that just might kill me after all."

They leave Simon's dressing room and walk to the back stage area where all the props for the show are arranged in the order that they'll be needed. Simon pauses to speak in a low voice to Onyx. The big cat comes and rubs its head against the cage bars, snuffling. Simon strokes its broad nose with three fingers and murmurs to it in an old language. A throaty purr rumbles in the cat's throat and it closes its eyes. "I know how you feel," he whispers before he walks away to join Sebastian as both magicians appear on stage together for the opening act which involves producing everything from silk handkerchiefs to bouquets of flowers, bottles of wine, balloons, playing cards that seem to leap in card showers from their hands, orbs that materialize from their palms, doves, Jack the raven, and a chimpanzee wearing a maroon fez riding a unicycle—all from seemingly thin air. There are random showers of glitter and streamers from clouds that appear high over their heads and drift out over the audience. It is just one trick after another until the stage is littered with objects they have made appear while dressed in their cut away frock coats, slim slacks, vests and white shirts. They then exchange banter at the front of the stage about magic and how long they have been performing together while black clad stagehands sweep up the mess in the dimness behind them and prepare for Sebastian's version of thrusting knives through a young woman, in this case his assistant and lover, Charlotte Cheston. The twist on this trick is that there is a second woman as well, Piper Sherwood, the two women standing back to back, their arms extended outside the cabinet, their wrists bound together. A lower door about a foot high at the base of the cabinet is opened to show their lower extremities from mid shin to foot. Their legs are also bound together. It's an act that always makes the audience hold its collective breath with fear that one or both girls will be run through with one of the long steel swords he uses—a full dozen of them, all examined by members of the audience and determined to be real.

Simon then does a solo act making a deck of cards dance in mid-air to music. Several of the cards stubbornly refuse to perform and he banishes them from the stage. At the end of the trick the deck is back in numerical and suit order but missing the two jokers. He then asks two audience members to join him on stage, usually male, but occasionally he chooses a female who has tight jeans on. He asks these members to check a certain pocket in the clothing they are wearing—and the jokers are produced by the astounded audience members because at no time does he touch them or even get close to them.

The Seven Sisters Illusion follows this act and involves two of the girls and an arrangement of full length mirrors. The girls wear filmy long white gowns with hoods that hide their hair. Their faces are made up identically with pale make-up, dark eye liner, smoky eye shadow and lush ruby-red lips. Pepper has noticed that the girls are all very similar in size. She is the shortest but they have put lifts in her shoes to boost her height. The two girls inter-act with the mirrors, dancing hypnotically to the dreamy music in front of the looking glasses, circling them, coming in view and passing out of view in the mirrors. And at the end, they reach toward the mirror and both pull their mirror images out from the mirror frames twice so that a total of six identical girls are on the stage with a number of mirrors in frames not reflecting the girls. Then, suddenly, a seventh girl appears in one of the mirrors, seemingly trapped within it. The six girls gather around the mirror and act distraught. They spin the mirror around to show there is nothing behind it but the backing. It is only a few inches deep. One of the girls runs off stage and returns with a hammer. The girl in the mirror looks alarmed as the girl outside the frame raises the hammer, opens her mouth in a scream as the hammer strikes and shatters the glass. It appears that the mirror girl falls in pieces onto the floor at the base of the mirror. The mirror is now an empty frame. The six girls gather around the broken pieces on the floor, and then suddenly back away as a seventh girl seemingly materializes from the place where the glass has fallen. In her hands she holds pieces of the broken mirror. It's a beautiful illusion and Pepper does very well for her first time performing it. She is one of the girls drawn from the mirror, the fourth sister.

Backstage, Sebastian gives her a quick hug and an air kiss to avoid getting her make-up on his face. "Well done!" he says before she rushes off to scrub off the make-up and change into a slinky black dress for her final appearance of the evening on stage in the background as Simon does an illusion with Onyx.

Pepper isn't needed for the Saturday matinee show as it is an abbreviated version of the weekday evening show. The Seven Sisters Illusion will be performed again Saturday night. Therefore, she remains behind at the compound with Sherry, Shelley and Shawn who take her furniture shopping at several stores. Pepper's style is Victorian cottage. The first thing she chooses is her bed, a queen-size white-painted iron bedstead. On either side of the bed she wants small tables with a drawer and shelves below for books. She likes the country white furniture finish. Sherry helps her select a double dresser, a tall chest of drawers and a book case. Pepper wants a white wicker rocking chair, a Victorian floor lamp with a damask off-white silk shade and beaded fringe and a wicker table for beside the rocker.

For her sitting area she chooses an antique-look settee, two armchairs in a floral chintz pattern that complement the maroon velvet-upholstered settee. She selects some tall potted artificial trees and another bookcase for this area of her suite. By lunchtime she has spent nearly all of the money that Simon has allotted her because she has also chosen two patterned area carpets, one for the sitting room, one for the bedroom. They have lunch at the Cavalier restaurant. Pepper gets a brief glimpse of Simon, out on the concourse, talking to a tall brunette in a skimpy outfit as they pass by a window on the way to the booth where they're being seated. She sees him place his hand on the girl's buttocks, catches the girl's wide smile. He is in profile but she doesn't see him smile before she can no longer see them.

Sitting beside Shawn, looking at the menu, the image of Simon with his hand on the girl's ass forms in her mind and she grows distracted and anxious. "What do you want to eat, Pepper?" Shawn asks her. She turns her head and realizes the server is waiting to take her order, that everyone else has already placed theirs. "Fish and chips," she says, naming the first thing she remembers reading on the luncheon menu.

"Tarter sauce okay with that?"

"Yes, fine. And a slice of lemon on the side."

The server walks away toward the kitchen to place the order. Sherry asks, "So, how did it feel performing last night? Were you terribly nervous?"

"I was at first but then I calmed down. In costume and with make-up on it's easy to become someone else."

"Clowns have known that for centuries," Shelley says.

"So have actresses," Shawn adds.

"And prostitutes."

All four of them look toward the voice and are surprised to find Simon standing there. He has just sort of materialized in the restaurant. "Aren't you supposed to be getting ready for the matinee performance?" Sherry asks.

"I am as ready as I'll ever be. I was passing by and saw the four of you come in here. How did you spend the morning?"

"We've been furniture and accessory shopping. Pepper should be in her own suite within ten to fifteen days. After lunch, we're going to Home Depot to pick out paint and window treatments."

"Have you blown your budget yet, Miss Rumford?" he asks.

"Yes, just about," she replies truthfully.

His dark eyes meet hers. "Are you satisfied with your purchases?"

"I am."

"If you could have one more thing for your suite, what would that be?"

She starts to look away but stops herself, returns her gaze to meet his again. "I'm afraid that would be something that we won't find at Home Depot, or in any other store," she answers.

"And why is that? What is it that you want, Pepper?"

"I want happiness. That's the one thing I would add to my suite to consider it complete."

He hesitates then says, "Well, good luck with that. I'm sure you, of all people, will find it in good time." He gives a slight bow. "Enjoy your lunch. It's my treat today." He turns and walks quickly away.

70

"If he's paying I should change my order and get a steak dinner," Shawn says.

"Is he always this generous?" Pepper asks.

"No. I mean, he's paid his previous assistants well enough, and given them an allowance to decorate and buy furniture to their liking, but he really has given you more than he's given anyone else. And he's never treated us to lunch out of the blue like this."

"I think he likes you, Pepper."

"I think he doesn't want to lose another assistant, is what I think. It must grow old having to train someone new so often."

"How often is so often?" Pepper asks. "How long does he keep an assistant?"

"He doesn't keep them is the whole problem with him. There was Diana, Lisa, Naomi, Vanity, Catherine, Marielle, Jana, Zoe and then Gillian."

"You forgot Yasmin."

"Oh, right. She lasted an entire two and a half weeks."

"So, I'm basically short term?"

"That's up to you, Pepper. He's only fired one girl, that Olivia who secretly made the sex tape and leaked it on the internet. He was furious about that and sent her packing."

"I still don't know why he got so ticked off. Everyone knows he's like a sex addict. He never hides that fact. He's pretty damn hot in that video."

"You watched it?" Sherry asks her sister.

"Of course. Haven't you?"

"Not all of it."

"Well, when we get home maybe you should. Be enlightened, girl! We work for a virtual god!"

"A lusty god," Shawn says. "Can we not discuss his physical attributes and his prowess in the bedroom? It's not a subject I feel comfortable with."

"Sometimes I wish you had been born a girl!" Shelley says teasingly. "You'd have been a lot more fun to hang out with."

Sherry looks across the table at Pepper who seems somewhat shell-shocked by what they've been talking about. "To put your mind at ease, they've all quit. He's never fired anyone. They just got fed up and left, walked out on him and never looked back."

"Because of his…um…strong physical needs?"

"Because he can be such a damn pain in the ass is more like it. He'll teach you a trick or an illusion, but he doesn't ever reveal everything to you. I've seen him do stuff that I have no idea how he does it and he won't tell. He likes fire, Pepper. Sebastian does all the water tricks and illusions. Simon does all the illusions using fire. One time, he performed this awesome stunt—he went out on stage in his formal magician's suit, started talking about fire and self-immolation and how gruesome burning ones' self to death is. Then, as he continued to talk about stuff like spontaneous combustion, he stripped off his clothes to the waist so that he was half naked on the stage. He told the audience that he was going to become a human torch, and before they could even conceptualize what he had said, he threw his arms out at his sides, threw his head back and gave an ungodly shout. And suddenly, he was engulfed in flames from the top of his head to his waist and down his arms. He was literally on fire. The damn sprinkler system went off. People got soaked. We were standing backstage and Sebastian was totally freaking out, but then he got really mad, utterly furious with Simon. Simon was out there sort of staggering around, batting at the flames as if he couldn't put them out. He looked like he was struggling. We all had our hearts in the back of our throats.

72

Sebastian grabbed a fire extinguisher and rushed out onto the stage and sprayed this white powdery stuff all over Simon. He looked like a damned ghost! And all he did once the flames were out was take a deep bow and shout, "Your mothers were right, don't play with fire! You only get burned!"

"They had a huge fight after the show. That's when Simon took the suite here. He lived here for almost a year. They didn't talk, except their usual banter during the show, for almost that long. We thought for sure they were going to break up the act."

"But they seem bound together by some sort of bond. They have these terrible fights and live apart awhile then suddenly Simon is back at the compound and everything is fine again."

"They're like an old married couple," Shelley says. "Only worse."

"Are they a couple?" Pepper asks.

"Are you asking if they're bi-sexual? Sebastian and Charlotte are a couple. Simon's got a whole string of girlfriends. I've never seen them do anything that would make me think they're partners in anything other than magic."

"They both like females. Definitely."

"Can we change the subject?" Shawn asks.

They discuss the best clubs in Vegas, the best casinos, restaurants, arcades, amusements, boutiques and salons. They discuss the best shows in Vegas and suggest Pepper try to catch Penn and Teller, Lance Burton and David Copperfield, if she has a chance, just so she can see other magicians in action.

Their food arrives and they dig in, hungry after all the shopping they've done. They've certainly given Pepper a lot to think about for the rest of the weekend.

On Monday morning, Pepper is in the gymnasium where Simon has asked to meet her to begin her training. He wanted her there at eight o'clock but when he doesn't show up she just begins doing some exercises because she really hasn't been in a gym in a while. By nine o'clock, she is warmed up and comfortable enough to practice one of her old floor routines seeing that there is a large section of floor area covered with mats.

She has just completed a series of handsprings and stuck her landing, with just a bit of wobble, when someone applauds. Spinning around, she finds Sebastian, not Simon, has come into the gym. "Very nicely done," he compliments her. "Simon told me that you have a gymnastics background. It's good to see that your skills aren't so rusty that you can't be back at the peak of your performance in no time." He meets her at the edge of the mat. "Simon asked me to come and begin your training as he is, unfortunately, detained in the city this morning meeting with the police." He sees a flicker of worry in her eyes. "I'm sure he'll be here later this morning. Now, he's mentioned that he wants to bring back the levitation act. You seem perfectly suited for that. It does require that you wear a back brace that helps support you from neck to lower back during the illusion. It's rather stiff and uncomfortable but we don't want anything to happen that would injure your spine." She nods that she understands. "How much do you weigh?" he asks.

"One hundred-seven pounds." She's actually lost six pounds recently, something her doctor would not be pleased about as she is underweight for her height.

"Good," Sebastian replies. "That should be easily manageable. Simon's last assistant was taller than you and twenty pounds heavier. She wasn't suitable at all for this particular il-

74

lusion. It requires someone who is your height or less and very slender."

"I'll try not to gain any weight."

"Oh, a couple of pounds won't matter. As long as you stay at one twenty or less it should be fine." He smiles at her. "Let me see some more of your routine and then we'll practice another illusion that will test how flexible you are."

"I do this better to music."

"We have a sound system in here. If you tell me what music you have performed your routine to I can have Shawn load it into the system for you, if you want to practice and stay limber."

"I'll write it down for him later."

She walks to one corner of the mat. Sebastian stays where he is and in a few moments Pepper is in motion—running, vaulting, doing handstands, back flips, cartwheels, forward rolls, diving rolls all combined with graceful dance steps to stitch the routine into a cohesive whole. Despite there being no give to the gym floor, as it's laid on concrete with just a thin cushioning between, not like the springy flooring she'd be used to, she manages to gain some height with her jumps that impresses him. Dressed in a black leotard, black leggings and barefoot, her fiery red hair in a tight braid, Sebastian understands why Simon is so irrevocably drawn to her. She's a lovely girl, athletic, radiant. Her figure is not what Simon has gone for in the past, but feminine enough to catch the eye. By the end of her routine, he's considering Simon's suggestion to befriend Pepper, and perhaps more.

He's about to take her hand to lead her to another area of the gym when Charlotte comes into the room. "There you are," she says, looking from him to Pepper.

"Simon's detained in the city. He asked me to get a start on Pepper's training."

"Why don't I help you?" she offers. She's dressed in black leggings and a black t-shirt that hugs her curves. Her blonde hair is pinned up. "You're going to need a hand with some of the things that you'll be teaching her."

"Of course. That's very kind of you to offer. We're going to show her the Pincushion Illusion. She's the perfect size for it, don't you think?"

"Yes, she is," Charlotte replies, looking Pepper up and down. "You have to be thin and flexible to avoid being stabbed."

"Let me go find the cabinet in the prop storage area. You can tell Pepper about the illusion. I should be back in fifteen minutes or less."

As soon as he's gone Charlotte says, "First of all, I just want to tell you that Sebastian and I have been in a relationship for six years. Everyone in this company understands that. You will not be performing much with him, unless the act involves all the female assistants being on stage as part of the illusion. You're Simon's assistant and I have to tell you this, as well, he is more difficult to work with than Sebastian is. Simon can be very demanding, very intense at times. Sebastian is more easy-going. Simon can anger quickly. When he gets angry it's best to keep a low profile until his anger burns itself out, which it usually does. I also have to tell you that while Sebastian's accident rate is extremely low, Simon's assistants have regularly sustained some injuries during routines. He can be impulsive and reckless at times." Pepper glances down at her hand and flexes it to assure herself that she is not permanently damaged by the knife through the hand a few days ago. She frowns slightly, still not exactly sure how, if the knife had actually penetrated her hand, she has just the slightest of scars in her palm but no scar on the back of her hand. The minor pain that she'd had is also gone now. Her hazel eyes rise and meet

Charlotte's eyes. For the space of a few heartbeats she sees the older girl wants to tell her something else but makes a decision not to. "Show me how far you can bend your torso to each side," Charlotte says.

When Sebastian returns with a small, square cabinet on a rolling stand, Pepper thinks it's going to be impossible to sit in that cabinet with her head sticking out of the top and her arms out of the sides while trying to avoid being skewered while seated cross-legged inside. "It's a deceitful little cabinet. The knives are a foot long. The cabinet walls are actually six inches thick on the sides and back and while the blades look long the handles are four inches so in reality only two inches of the blade is actually penetrating the interior of the box from the sides and back. You just keep yourself centered in the box and you'll be fine. The danger lies in the front of the box as its thinner. So you'll have to learn your safety zone inside the box. It's not all that difficult. We're going to practice so you get a good feel for it today."

"It's all about deceiving the eye of the viewer and presenting the trick in a manner that makes it appear to be dangerous for the girl inside the cabinet, but in reality, you'll be perfectly safe once properly trained."

"We haven't lost anyone to a stabbing death yet," Sebastian tells her as he lifts her up onto the platform. "During the show we roll out steps that you use to get onto the platform, or maybe Simon will simply lift you up and put you up here."

"Okay," she says.

"Now, just sit cross-legged in the middle of the box and get comfortable. I'll give you a few moments to make any adjustments you need to make."

Charlotte picks up a knife from the platform and stabs it into the box with an abrupt thrust. In the box, Pepper yelps in surprise but the blade does not quite reach her. "Was that absolutely necessary?" Sebastian snaps at Charlotte. "What if she hadn't been in a good position?"

"Then she'd have been stabbed, but not seriously. Just a superficial wound. She would have learned respect for the blades. And the magician," Charlotte replies.

"I'm all right," Pepper says. My arms go through the holes?"

"Yes. Put your arms through if you're comfortable with your location in the box." Sebastian gives Charlotte one last, long look, then closes and latches the cabinet doors, picks up the knives and slowly, methodically thrusts them into the cabinet.

"Ow!" Pepper cries as one blade jabs her in the knee.

"Sorry. Try to keep your knees low. Are you bleeding?"

"I think so."

"Copiously or lightly?"

"Lightly," she answers.

"Then we won't need to call the paramedics." He continues to insert the knives. Pepper is a little wild-eyed as he's moving faster now, but he doesn't stab her again. "Very good, Miss Rumford! Only one minor injury on your first attempt at this trick." He then shocks her by picking up a sword. "Now, the grand finale!" he says loudly and before she can react he thrusts the sword through the space between the two front doors of the cabinet. Her torso sits directly in the path of the sword.

"Stop!" she cries. He does not stop. "Stop!" she screams. And then, "*Stop!*"

"Sebastian! Stop!" Simon shouts as he comes rapidly into the room. "When your assistant sounds that frightened and frantic it means there's something terribly wrong! Those are not the cries of a young lady merely suffering an anxiety attack during a trick!"

Sebastian looks from Simon, whom he has not expected to see since he thought he was in the city, back to Pepper and he sees that her face is chalky white, her eyes dark with shock. "Damn it!" he shouts, looking down at the sword with horror. A little stream of blood is running from beneath the cabinet doors, cascading onto the floor.

Simon comes up to the cabinet. "Let go," he says tersely to Sebastian. As soon as Sebastian relinquishes his hold on the hilt, Simon wraps his hand around the grip. "Pepper, look at me. Look here!" She blinks, shifts her eyes to meet his. "You're fine. I'm going to pull the sword out slowly and then I'll let you out of the cabinet. Do not move when I open the doors, just sit tight. Charlotte and Sebastian have to remove the other knives before I can help you out. Just sit very still." She nods slightly. He gives her a quick smile to try to put her at ease, but he does not like the little beads of perspiration trickling from along her hairline high on her forehead. She is shocky. "Pepper, do you like to fly?"

"What?"

"Do you like to fly? Not in a plane. Imagine yourself flying like a bird. Imagine the lift of the air beneath your wings. Now, feel your body lifting off the ground, defying gravity. You're rising upward. How exhilarating it feels to fly! You are as light as a butterfly!" She is calmer as he has put her into a trance. "Just fly, Pepper and be at peace. I'll tell you when to return to earth." He shifts his gaze to Sebastian, giving him a dark, angry glare. "What the hell were you thinking?" he hisses. "Didn't you test the sword before just thrusting it through?"

"Everything looked to be in order when I brought it in here. It all should have been in perfect working order!" Sebastian looks nearly as shocked as Pepper had looked. "Have I killed her?"

"Not quite." Simon focuses on the sword. "I need this right now," he mutters. "I bake three showgirls and now my brand new assistant has a sword thrust nearly through her. If you've paralyzed her you're dead!" By his tone of voice Sebastian knows Simon will probably succeed in killing him he is that angry.

Sebastian glances at Charlotte who is standing off to one side. He can't tell if she is as horrified about the accident as he is, or if she looks disappointed that Simon suddenly appeared and intervened. But why would Charlotte want the girl dead? He hasn't touched her. He was just rehearsing her, although he'd had a few random thoughts about seducing her. However, he had pushed them aside, had done nothing to make Charlotte this obscenely jealous.

Simon concentrates for several long moments before he slowly eases the sword back through the doors. Pepper gasps slightly and a trickle of blood spills from the corners of her slightly open mouth. "Fly, little one. Keep flying. The sky is such a beautiful shade of blue. The sun is warm on your wings and face," he murmurs as he pulls the gory sword completely out and throws it aside. He grabs the handles of the doors, hesitates, head bowed, eyes closed for one long moment, then pulls the doors open. "Go to sleep!" he commands and Pepper's eyes close, her body falling toward him. He catches her, hauls her out of the cabinet, lifting her in his arms. "Charlotte, I need Sabrina. Tell her I'll be in my house."

"Simon...." Sebastian begins to say in a warning tone.

"I need to do what I can for her. And if you're half the angel you think you are, you'll come with me and do whatever you can for this girl!"

The two magicians get Pepper over to Simon's home. He directs Sebastian to go get a clean sheet from the linen closet.

Sebastian gets the sheet and covers the sturdy library table in Simon's study. Simon produces a pair of scissors and slices the front of Pepper's bloody leotard from collar to crotch. The torn place where the sword went through adheres to her skin which looks burnt as if she was struck with a hot iron. Simon had heated the sword to cauterize the wound as he removed the blade.

Sabrina rushes into the room and stops dead with a gasp of shock. "What the hells' happened to her?" she cries.

"Sebastian didn't test the sword blade to see if it would retract easily. He ran her nearly through."

"I'm going to need my kit."

"Call over to the mansion and have someone run it over, and I mean *run* in the literal sense," Simon says as he rolls up his shirt sleeves. He nods toward the phone on a nearby stand. "Charlotte, make yourself useful and bring me a basin of hot water, some clean towels, and my Glock."

"What do you need your gun for?" she asks.

"To shoot you with if you ever deliberately allow this girl to get hurt this seriously again." He raises his head, his dark eyes burning with fury. Charlotte gasps and takes an involuntary step backwards. "No, let me make that clearer for you. I will kill you if you ever hurt her again, deliberately or even accidentally. Do you hear me? Have I made myself crystal clear?"

"Simon," Sebastian says warningly.

"And you worry about me hurting her! I might be a demon and a bastard but, damn it, Sebastian, I would never hurt her physically like this! I mean her no harm!"

"Have you stopped to consider that this was purely an accident?"

"I reek of guilt!" Simon hisses in response. "But if you think that I can't smell it on other beings then you don't know me at all despite all the centuries we've been together!"

"Stop fighting!" Sabrina orders tersely. "Your arguing like this does nothing constructive for Pepper. Put it aside right now, hash it out later. I need to open up that wound and repair the damage from the inside out. Simon, I need you to hold this rod and cauterize the bleeders. Sebastian, you come and help with the sponges to keep my work area clear so I can see what the hell I'm doing." She works swiftly, starting an IV in Pepper's hand, washing the wound with antiseptic sponges. Simon flinches as she uses a scalpel to reopen the wound.

Sabrina works quickly and efficiently. "No spinal cord damage. You missed the heart. I've repaired the lung laceration. I'm leaving a drain in. I'll talk to Dr. Traynor, as she'll most likely develop pneumonia from the blood in her lung." She looks at Simon. "She's going to be in a world of hurt."

"I can hypnotize her so she doesn't feel it."

"She belongs in a hospital. She's a human being."

"I already have big enough problems to cope with. We can take care of her here and thereby avoid any further scandal and potential legal issues. I do not relish the idea of going to prison, even though there isn't a damn prison in this world that can hold me."

"Maybe you should do as I suggested and think before you act in the future."

"I had nothing to do with Pepper getting injured this morning! I wasn't even here!"

Sebastian knows this is true, but he has also just realized that Simon has some connection with this human girl already because he materialized in the gymnasium fast enough when she got hurt. Simon knew that something had happened to her. He hopes that Simon wasn't someplace where there were witnesses to his vanishing from the room or wherever he was at the time. "Did you leave witnesses behind?" he asks.

"Did I what?"

"Where were you just before you appeared in the gym immediately after she got hurt?"

"I was…" He pauses to think. "In a stairwell. Alone. I was leaving the attorney's office and took the stairs."

"Are you absolutely certain that you were alone?"

Simon suddenly looks angry. "Of course I was alone! I'm not exactly Mr. Popularity in certain circles at the moment!"

"As long as you weren't in some girl's bed!"

"What are you implying? That I don't give a damn about anything anymore? Well, you're wrong! I feel like I'm starting a new chapter in my life and it's because of her!" he says, pointing at Pepper. "I'm looking forward to working with her. She makes me *happy*! Do you know how long it's been since I've felt happiness? Too damn long! I don't want to screw this up! I need this!" He looks down at the girl lying so still on his library table, bows his head, and closes his eyes. "Do not take this away from me," he says quietly.

"You haven't touched her, have you?"

Simon shakes his head. "No."

Sebastian's heart aches for his longtime partner. "All right then. Charlotte and I will be extremely cautious with her in the future. This *was* an accident, Simon. Neither of us wanted her to get hurt, or die. The sword failed to retract like it should have. I'm sorry."

"Go away."

"Simon…"

"I said, *go away*!"

Simon hires a live-in nurse to take care of Pepper. He puts her in a room at his house, the nurse in the adjoining room. Food is brought over from the mansion. For nearly two weeks, Pepper requires oxygen and antibiotics as she battles pneumonia and a moderate infection. Dr. Traynor has provided morphine for the nurse to use in Pepper's IV for the pain. She sleeps a lot at first but as her breathing gets easier, the nurse cuts back on the morphine and allows her to be more awake.

At the start of the third week, Pepper is restless and tired of being in bed. The nurse gets her up, allows her to walk in the upstairs hallway, but tells her she is not to try to negotiate the stairs yet as she needs to regain more of her strength. Piper, Poppy, Cym and Caroline have all come over regularly to visit her, bringing her small gifts and telling her about the shows. Sabrina brings her treats. Jack, the raven, often perches on the headboard and seems to watch over her.

On a Wednesday morning, the door opens and Simon walks in. He has Onyx with him. "He's been anxious to properly meet you," he says. "He's been aware of your presence in the house for weeks but I didn't feel that you were strong enough to meet him until now." He motions for the big cat to leap onto the bed. Pepper's eyes widen but the panther does not step on her. It is very cautious as it checks her out.

"You haven't come to see me at all," she says.

"I've been busy."

"Training a new assistant?"

"No, I have a new assistant already. I've been busy reinventing the show every night to account for your absence." He walks to the side of the bed and strokes the panther's head. "The police have concluded that what happened at the hotel was a tragic accident, the result of a combination of foolish actions and basic disregard for the dangerousness of the situation on the part of the young ladies who were waiting for me."

"So you're not going to jail?"

"No, I'm not."

She smiles, obviously relieved to hear that. "Good. It'd be a real trick trying to do an act with you behind bars and me alone on stage." This makes a corner of his mouth quirk up in a half smile. "And I don't know how to work with Onyx or Jack yet."

"I'll teach you. Do you feel like getting up and taking a walk with Onyx and me?" He lifts her robe from the foot of the bed, gives the cat a signal to get off the bed. Pepper throws aside the covers, swings her legs over the side of the bed and sits up. She is very thin and frail, and even more pale than usual. He holds her robe open for her. She stands up, turns, holds her arms out backwards. He gets her arms through the sleeves, settles the robe on her shoulders. His knuckles brush her fiery curls and in response his heart aches for what he cannot have. "Would you like some fresh air today?"

"That sounds nice."

They go outside to the patio where they walk slowly around the pool. Pepper is barefoot. He is dressed entirely in black. Her gown and robe are snowy white. Onyx prowls about for a little bit then flops over in the shade beneath the overhang. Simon walks with Pepper one more time around the pool and then they sit down near Onyx. "Any pain?" he asks.

"Not too much. I'm good."

"Have you spoken to your parents recently?"

"I talked to my mom two nights ago."

"Are they aware that you were so seriously injured?"

"No. By the time I had strength enough to call them I was doing much better, so I didn't see any point in worrying them for no reason."

"If things had gone badly, I would have called them and then flown them here." She nods. "Has Sebastian said anything to you?"

"He came and apologized profusely at the end of week one. Charlotte came a few days after that. Mostly, the other girls have visited with me and kept me from going stir crazy."

He nods, signals Onyx to come to him. He is perched on the edge of a chair and the big cat stops and sits before him. He taps his own shoulders and Onyx rises up, placing his huge paws, one on each shoulder. Simon rubs the cat's face briskly, vigorously, just behind its glossy black whiskers. The big cat makes a throaty noise, indicating his pleasure. "The secret to living with and working with a big cat is to let it know that you are the alpha animal in the pack. Onyx thinks of himself as a part of the troupe. He sees me as the one in charge. I also hand out the rewards for good work, for being obedient. He will view you as one of his pack mates. Today, I am introducing the two of you now that he has accepted your presence here. You may pat him if you'd like. He loves to have his ears scratched, the back of his neck scratched, his chin rubbed, but be careful because he'll try to nip and you have enough puncture wounds as it is. You may look him in the eye but allow him to look away first. Never turn your back on him. Never let your guard down. Never trust him, not completely anyway. He is well-trained to do his tricks and illusions. We never vary his routines. He is a creature of habit. Make no sudden moves around him or loud noises. Do not fight with me in front of him."

"I don't want to fight with you," she says.

He sighs. "I'm afraid that's a given. I can be quite impossible on any given day as you've probably deduced by now. It's not show biz ego. That's what everyone blames it on. I'm just a naturally contrary person who doesn't like to be confined by the rules." He glances sideways at her. "There, now I have revealed the whole awful truth about myself."

"Hardly the whole truth," she replies wryly. "But, it's a good enough start. You don't want to frighten me off all at once. That would place you in the awkward position of having to find yet another new assistant and start the training process all over again."

"You are a perceptive young lady."

"No, not really. I didn't perceive the damn sword was jammed and I was about to be stabbed."

"Did you know it was a trick sword?"

"No. He'd only shown me the knives. I didn't even know about the sword." She leans over and digs her fingers in behind Onyx's left ear. The big cat rolls his head toward her and closes his eyes, content with all the attention he is garnering from the magician and the girl. "I'm so lucky you got home exactly when you did," she says, looking directly at Simon. His dark eyes flick to meet hers for one brief moment and she sees something in their depths, sees that he wants to say something as well but he looks back at the cat.

"Yes," he finally says when she doesn't say anything more. "You are lucky." He tells her to sit back slowly. She does and he pushes Onyx away. "Swim!" he commands. The panther turns and leaps into the pool. "This cat loves to swim," he says.

"Wow! I didn't think panthers could swim!" She slowly stands up and walks to the edge of the pool.

Simon watches her. The gown and robe are made of a thin cotton material. Her body and limbs are visible as shadows through the material with the sun shining through it. The sun hitting her hair makes it flame like fire. Again, he finds it difficult not to grab her, throw her down on the cement and have his way with her, but he digs deep and finds one more ounce of restraint and remains seated.

Sebastian comes out of the mansion, frowning. "Pepper, what are you doing out here! You'll burn to a crisp you're so fair skinned! Simon, have you no common sense?"

"She needs sunlight. She's been confined in the house for weeks. Even a flower will fold into itself without the touch of sunlight on its petals." Pepper turns from the pool and looks at him with an odd expression on her face that he finally recognizes, with a jolt, as admiration. "Onyx! Out!" The big cat snorts water from its nose and swims away from the stairs used to get out.

"He listens well," Sebastian comments wryly.

"He has a streak of independence. He's just going to take one last lap and then he'll climb out." Onyx does exactly that. Like a dog he comes loping over, skids to a halt on the tiles and shakes himself vigorously, startling Pepper who steps backwards and falls into the pool, arms pinwheeling.

Simon is up and at the side of the pool before Sebastian fully comprehends what's happened. "Good Lord!" he cries.

Pepper surfaces—smiling! "The water feels so nice!" she says, reaching to take Simon's hand. He expects to pull her closer and up, out of the pool. He does not expect her to tug his arm, especially not so hard. His dark eyes meet hers, and in their depths he sees a flash of mischief and playfulness. In a heartbeat he understands what she wants. He allows her to pull him into the pool. She laughs as he surfaces, and then shrieks as Onyx leaps back into the pool.

"Shh! No loud noises," Simon warns her.

"You're both crazy!" Sebastian says, shaking his head. "Just don't let her drown. She's still weak."

Pepper unties her robe and peels it off, balls it up and then throws it onto the cement pool surround. She swims a bit although she doesn't have anywhere near her former strength back yet, however she loves the buoyancy of the water, the coolness of it, the heat of the sun. Simon keeps himself between her and Onyx, allowing her time to enjoy the sun and water. He hasn't failed to notice that Sebastian has not moved, that he is watching her. Her thin gown is clinging to her, is virtually transparent. He, too, is mesmerized by the pale pinkness of her beneath the water. "You could be a gentleman and fetch a towel for her," Simon remarks.

"So could you."

"I have to control the cat."

"Order it out of the pool."

"Someone has to keep an eye on Pepper."

"And you think that should be you?" Simon glares at him but he finally walks to the pool house. He brings back a white, waffle-weave robe. "Pepper! Time to come out before you drown."

She obeys, swimming to the steps and carefully walking up them out of the water, gripping the railing. Simon thinks his heart is going to implode, he wants her so desperately. His skin crawls as he watches Sebastian help the girl on with the robe, as he turns her and hesitates, his eyes feasting on her before he pulls the robe closed and ties the belt. He smiles at her, reaches out and brushes a few stray red curls from her wet cheek. Simon wants to leap out of the pool and hurl Sebastian out into the desert, although he realizes that he is the one who suggested that Sebastian befriend Pepper and even take her as a lover to save her from himself.

Sebastian sends Pepper inside and she goes. They both watch her until she is indoors. Then Simon climbs out of the pool, orders the cat out. "Forget what I said. I won't touch her, but I want you to keep your distance from her, too."

"Make up your mind what it is you really want and then let me know," Sebastian replies as he turns and walks away.

Simon motions for the cat to follow him and they go back into the house. By the time he has Onyx fed and back in his enclosure, has stripped off his soaked clothing, showered and dressed in black jeans and a black t-shirt, he finds Pepper asleep in a dry nightgown, sprawled on top of her bed. He stands gazing down at her for a long time, drinking in every inch of her, soaking up her radiant essence, basking in her beautiful glow. Then, slowly, he shifts her so that he can get the sheet over her as she is lying in the draft from the air conditioning and becoming too much of a distraction for him. She murmurs in her sleep, her hand brushing his arm. His skin tingles at her touch as if sparks dance across his flesh.

Quickly, he turns and leaves the room.

While she has been laid up recovering from her injury and illness, Shawn has painted her room a soft, pale green. Sherry and Shelley have arranged her furniture which had been delivered. They have consulted with her on bathroom décor and accessories and added the finishing touches to the suite so that everything is ready for her the day after her swim with Onyx and Simon when she is allowed to move back into the mansion.

The very next day, Simon has her in the gym. She is thin and weak but gamely tries to do everything that he asks of her. He doesn't quite realize how weak she really is until she steps out of a cabinet and drops straight to the floor. He stands looking down at her for a long moment then crouches down, scoops her up in his arms. "Had enough for one day?" he asks her.

"Yes," she replies wearily.

"You need to work on your communication skills. If you had told me half an hour ago that you were this exhausted I would have let you go back to the house to rest."

"Sorry."

"Always one to push the envelope, aren't you?" She gives him a half grin. "Take a rest, have your lunch then meet me back here at two o'clock for a brief rehearsal of the Vanishing Girl Illusion. You'll be performing it tonight."

"I will?" Her eyes open wider.

"It's time for you to start being my assistant. Two acts with me tonight, Vanishing Girl and I will throw knives at you. The audience seems to like that one. You just have to hold yourself very still. We'll do it early on when you're steadier and more rested. We'll make you vanish later on." He carries her to the patio, sets her down. "Go on. Take a nap, eat. I'll see you at two."

During the following weeks, Pepper trains, pushing herself to get stronger. She loves being part of the show and the audience likes her. She's happy they've accepted her. The only thing that bothers her is the jealousy and sometimes hostility she senses when she's out in the hotel running errands and encounters a showgirl from one of the clubs. They all seem to know Simon and think that he's theirs. She doesn't quite understand their attitudes until it finally dawns on her that they think she's sleeping with him, too! When one girl more or less comes right out and makes that remark, she replies that she's just his assistant and he's never touched her. The girl laughs, not believing her. "You just wait," she tells her. "Your number will come up."

On a Saturday morning, she decides she really needs to buy some new clothes. Piper tells her to just go out to the garage and ask Andrew for the keys to one of the cars so she can go shopping. She's really not all that familiar with Vegas yet. In the carriage house, she meets a young man named Andrew who services all the vehicles and keeps track of the comings and goings. He works for Adair who manages the company's fleet of vehicles and is also Sebastian and Simon's chauffeur. "If you're going to live out here with us you're going to need to apply for a Nevada driver's license," he tells her as he looks at her Connecticut license. "I can set that up for you, if you'd like." She nods. "You're not very talkative."

"What do you want me to say?"

"Say that you're free tonight and you'd love to go to a club, dance with me and have dinner."

"I work every night."

"Then how about Saturday or Sunday? You're not in the matinee performances, are you?"

"No, I'm not."

"Do you like motorcycles?"

"I don't know. I've never been on one."

"Racing across the desert, the wind blowing through your pretty, red hair, a big powerful machine between your legs. It's…" He stops talking because Simon has come into the carriage house. "Think about it," he says in a lower voice.

Simon comes up to them. "Poppy told me that you're borrowing one of the cars to go shopping," he says to her. She nods. He pulls a roll of money from his pocket and holds it out to her. "This is compensation for the injury you received during training. I've asked Poppy to accompany you. She'll be along shortly. First, you don't know Vegas. Andrew can program destinations into the GPS and our home location, but you shouldn't be out driving around on your own until you're more familiar with the city. Secondly, Poppy knows what you're going to need. Besides ordinary, everyday clothing you'll need more formal attire for dinners out and various functions and events that we must attend. Sebastian and I take our seven ladies along to a number of these affairs. She has a list. Since you're going out, you might as well start working on the professional aspect of your wardrobe as well as your personal wardrobe." Pepper is just looking at him. "Do you have any questions?"

"Do I ever have any time off?"

Something flickers in the depths of his eyes. A muscle bunches and vibrates briefly along the ridge of his jaw as his dark eyes shift to Andrew then back to her. "Your free time is when you are not training or performing. Once you're familiar with the illusions, you will have more free time, although I'd ask that you maintain your gym schedule as your flexibility, strength and endurance are vital to the act and your own safety and wellbeing on stage. I am not going to ask you to perform in the matinees. I perform solo illusions and if I do need an assistant, Sabrina is always willing and able to assist me." He glances at Andrew who has been listening to this with interest. "Use your free time wisely, Miss Rumford." He turns and walks away.

Pepper unrolls the money he's given her and is astounded. He's given her nearly ten thousand dollars! Andrew gives a low whistle. "Guess he wants to see you all dolled up!" He smiles at her. "For me, when we go out on the bike and have a picnic in the desert, jeans, a t-shirt and boots will do. You need boots so you don't get bitten by a snake." Her eyebrows rise and he grins at her. "Don't worry. I carry a gun. If a rattler threatens you, I'll take care of it."

"Are you serious?"

"Yeah, I don't want Simon killing me for letting you get hurt! I know who pays my salary."

Poppy comes into the carriage house office. "Ready to go, Pep? I know a great boutique where they have some fabulous gowns. You're like a size zero, right? Kalia will love you—model skinny and easy to dress. Simon wants me to take you to Greta for a haircut, too, while we're out."

"A haircut?"

"Only a few inches."

"Well, okay." Her hair is rather long, nearly to her waist. It's the longest that she's ever grown it. Losing a few inches won't be so bad.

By the time the two young women return to the compound, the car is loaded with bags of clothing and garment bags containing stunning gowns, some beaded but the majority lovely, but understated, as Pepper is not a glitz-loving girl. Her hair has been cut to a few inches below her shoulders, Greta having cut thirteen inches off. Pepper's head feels lighter, but as Poppy and Greta have both pointed out, the new, shorter length can be easily styled for when she needs to look glamorous although another inch or two might need to come off to achieve some styles.

That night, when she gets to the theater, there is a message waiting for her in her shared dressing room. The note asks her to come directly to Simon's dressing room upon her arrival. She frowns, drops her bag and goes to see what he wants.

When he doesn't respond to a knock on the door twice, she turns the knob and pushes the door open, sticking her head into the room. He is sitting in the tall canvas chair idly shuffling a deck of playing cards. There are two men in shirt sleeves and slacks, with badges clipped to their belts, and shoulder holsters, standing in the room. Their suit coats are on the loveseat. "Come in, Miss Rumford," says one of the men. "I'm Detective Brownley and this is Detective Gates." They wait for Pepper to come in and close the door. Simon glances at her, looks away and then returns his gaze to her, having noticed the haircut. "Mr. Crowe tells us that you can vouch for his being at the compound in the desert this morning."

"Yes."

"Can you elaborate? Give us a time that you saw him?"

She looks at Simon for a moment, wondering what this is all about but returns her attention to the detective after a moment. "I was up early. I get up at five-thirty. When I looked out the window, I saw Simon out exercising Onyx, his panther. I got dressed and went to the gym for six. I was there for forty-five minutes and then went back to the house to shower and get dressed for breakfast. He came into the dining room for a cup of coffee then went back to his house. About seven-forty or so, I went to the carriage house to ask about borrowing one of the cars so I could come into the city to shop. I was talking to Andrew when Simon came in about eight o'clock and gave me some money for clothes and a haircut. Poppy and I left about eight-fifteen. I didn't see him again after eight o'clock because I wasn't there."

"You're sure you saw him at five-thirty when you got up?"

"Yes, I am. I always look out the window. I'm originally from New England where it's just part of your everyday routine to look out the window to see what the weather is like. I'm not used to living out here yet where it's pretty much hot and dry every day. I also like to look at the sky at that hour." She shrugs. "That's how I saw him. He's usually out about then letting Onyx have a run, when he's home."

"So you're saying he was home?"

"Yes, I'm saying that he was home this morning. I saw him. I talked to him. I think I'd know who I was seeing and talking to. I work with him."

"Do you live with him?"

"I live in the mansion with the other girls. Simon lives in his own house. So, sort of, but not in the way you're asking." Here Simon gives her one of his quick, wry smiles that she catches from the corner of her eye.

"Thank you, Miss Rumford. You may go get ready for the performance now."

"I need to ask Simon something first."

"Go right ahead."

Simon looks at her and she looks at him. "Without all the weight of it my hair is kind of crazy. Do you want me to tie it back for the knife throwing act?"

He shakes his head. "No. If you recall, the silhouette has curly hair. It has to be loose to match that."

"Oh, right."

"Go get changed now, Pepper. I'll see you in a little bit." She nods and leaves.

"Well, since the girl says that you were in her room at six o'clock this morning and forced yourself on her, and your assistant states that she saw you exercising the panther at five-thirty and you were having coffee an hour and a quarter later, I suppose it's safe to say that you were at home at the compound and not in the city at the time she tells us you were."

"I was at home, like I said."

"We can't close the investigation just yet, you understand."

"Yes, I understand," he says, sounding weary.

"We'll be in touch again after we speak to other potential witnesses." Simon nods. They grab their jackets and leave.

The cards that he has been toying with all the while they have been in his dressing room suddenly burst into flames. He lets them fall to the floor where they burn and leave scorch marks.

Later, Pepper hears Sebastian and Simon arguing. When she hears Sebastian say her name she listens more closely and hears him say, "You're a master manipulator, Simon. You could hypnotize her and make her think she saw you on the moon if it would serve your purpose! I didn't see you this morning."

"Were you looking for me?" Simon counters.

"You're way out of control!" Sebastian hisses angrily.

"You're wrong. I am holding myself in unnatural control," Simon replies coldly.

"Ever since you hired that girl, you have been losing it, my friend. If she makes you so miserable then fire her! Get rid of her! Or just go ahead and...."

But Pepper doesn't stay to listen to what Sebastian is going to say next. She walks quickly to where she is supposed to be waiting for the knife throwing act, but she is fighting an emotional disturbance within her caused by what she has just overheard the magicians arguing about. Can Simon hypnotize her and make her think that she saw him at the house this morning? When would he have done that? And wasn't Andrew there? Hadn't Andrew witnessed Simon handing her the money? He was there. He gave her money. She spent the money on clothes and accessories, well, nearly all the money. She still has nine hundred odd dollars left. But the thing that is really bothering her, gnawing at her is Sebastian coming right out and saying that Simon made a mistake hiring her, that somehow she is making him miserable. How is she disappointing him? The sword accident was not her fault. She'd pushed herself to recover from that injury. Her training had been delayed and he'd had to rework acts, use Sabrina in illusions that he had intended Pepper to be in, but she was working hard, doing the best she can. Maybe that explains why he really doesn't spend much time with her—who wants to be around someone who has not lived up to their expectations?

"Yo, Pepper! Get out there!" Cym says, giving her a push.

Pepper gasps. Simon has introduced her and is waiting for her on stage for the knife act. She tries to pull herself together as she walks out onto the stage. "Here she is, ladies and gentlemen," Simon says, looking directly at her. "The late Pepper Rumford!" She sort of sleepwalks into the act.

As Simon arranges her against the board, he says in a low voice, "Why so grim?"

"It's nothing," she replies.

He tilts her head up to match the outline. "Just hold still," he says.

He selects the audience member to test the knives, to confirm they are real. Then, he rapidly hurls six of them at her in quick succession. She's wondering why the audience member has been allowed to remain on stage. In a few more moments she discovers why when Simon produces a black silk handkerchief and asks the young man to blindfold him. The young man will be handing him the knives and Simon will be throwing them blindly at her.

Peppers legs turn to jelly. They have not practiced this. He has not even hinted that such a twist on the act is a possibility. How on earth can he know where she is? After having a knife embedded in her hand and a sword thrust through her mid-torso she is terrified that he will miss and quite possibly kill her, especially since he doesn't seem to be happy with her. He can always blame it on the trick going terribly wrong, or her moving, even if she is too petrified to move at all! She is scared speechless.

"Pepper! Will you recite the alphabet for me!" he calls, the first knife already in his hand. "Slowly and steadily!" Her mouth is so dry that she croaks when she tries to say the letter A. "A little louder, please."

"A," she manages to get out. He seems to be locating her position by the sound of her voice, as if he is a bat using sonar or a dolphin using echo location.

"Keep going," he urges.

"B...C...D..." He hurls the knife. There is a collective gasp from the audience as it thuds into the board just above her shoulder. "...E...F...G..." Every third letter, he hurls another knife. She thinks her legs will give out on her at any moment but she's too scared to stop because he could just hurl a knife at her if she tries to move away. "...N...O...P..." The blade comes dangerously close to her hip. "...Q...R...S..."

"Faster, Pepper!"

Her stomach clenches. She grits her teeth. "T...U...V...W...X...Y...Z." The last blades have come fast and furious. One has pinned some of her curls to the board.

Simon whips off the blindfold, as he turns to the audience. There is wild applause and cheers. "The not so late Pepper Rumford!" he says, coming to the board, wrenching the knife out that pins her hair so that she is free. "Take a bow, Pepper," he says, his voice low. "Do not vomit until you reach the wings."

She manages a smile for the audience but can taste vomit in the back of her throat. He lets her go and she walks rapidly off stage and does exactly what he expects she will do, she vomits violently. Everyone is busy getting ready for the next illusion which is one of Sebastian's.

Simon comes from the stage, side-steps the mess on the floor, and keeps walking, ignoring her. Pepper's knees are wobbly but she staggers around the mess and stumbles after him. He's just closing his dressing room door when she reaches it. Without hesitation, she shoves the door open hard, startling the half-naked girl winding herself around the magician like a snake. "Get out!" Pepper flares. "Get the hell out!"

Simon looks down at the girl and says, "You'd better do as she has so politely asked. But don't go far. This won't take long."

Before the girl is even completely out the door, Pepper has walked right up to him and slapped his face so hard her hand aches and burns. "If you think you made a mistake then just say so!" she shouts at him. "If I make you so unhappy you want me gone you don't have to scare the goddam life out of me like that! I get the message!" She spins around. "I quit!"

"For the record, Miss Rumford, I do not think I made a mistake. If you feel compelled to quit then at least be professional enough to finish the show tonight. Then you are free to go, if that is what you want to do."

"Sabrina can…"

"Sabrina cannot replace you!" he says vehemently. "She is a poor substitute at best."

"I heard what Sebastian said."

"Did you? Or did you overhear a small part of a conversation not meant for your ears? Did you misinterpret what you did overhear?"

"I don't think either of you wants me here," she says.

"I have a visitor, Pepper. We will continue this discussion later. I expect you to finish this show tonight. We can meet afterwards. Now, send Lorinda in and I will see you shortly on stage."

Pepper walks out the door and mutters, "He's all yours," to the topless girl.

"Of course he is. A child like you would never be able to handle him. You can barely manage a stage act with him."

Pepper keeps walking. She finally veers into a stairwell, hurls herself down on the concrete steps and bursts into tears. She's held them back for quite a while, but now there is no stopping them.

When she finally gets her tears under control, she realizes that she has no idea how long she's been sitting in the stairwell. She's supposed to be on stage again with Simon for another illusion and then again for the Seven Sisters Illusion a short time later. Leaping up, she runs to the door and turns the handle, but to her horror, the door won't open. "No," she says. "No! Come on! Not now! Open already!"

And then she hears a noise behind her that makes her blood run cold. It sounds like a low, deep laugh. An evil laugh. Next, she hears movement, as if something is coming down the stairs from above. She can't see what's coming because the stairs turn back and there are no open railings. There is also an odor in the air, like burnt matches, only ten times stronger. Her heart is suddenly hammering in the back of her throat, nearly choking her with terror. She is absolutely certain that Satan himself is coming to get her. She has no idea why that would be but the idea has formed in her head and she knows it is a certainty.

Turning back to the door, she tugs on the handle again, twists the knob, bangs on the door with her fists. The laugh comes again, louder, closer. Whatever is coming, it is close to turning the corner. It'll be right upon her in just a few moments. "Let me out!" she screams.

Suddenly, the door is shoved open, pushing her back against the wall. Something tall and black moves with lightning speed past her and she gasps. In a heartbeat, it is up the stairs and around the corner. There is a terrible growling and hissing, a low, snarling voice. Pepper is frozen in place.

A huge serpent comes slithering around the corner of the stairwell. It starts to slither down the stairs toward her. It has glowing amber eyes. It's is the size of a crocodile's. It can probably devour her quickly. She can't even scream. Her voice is locked in her larynx. Just when she thinks she's going to die, the black form leaps onto the serpent and she sees its fierce face for the first time—it's burning red eyes, pointed teeth as it grimaces, wrestling with the snake. It has talons. It grabs the serpent by its upper and lower jaws, opening the things mouth wider, exposing the long razor sharp fangs, the forked blood-red tongue flicking forward toward her. "Look at me!" the black creature commands in a rough voice. "Look…at…me!" She raises her eyes away from one horror to meet the red eyes of the other horror. The black creature makes several quick moves, grimacing but not breaking eye contact with her. The snake hisses, whipping itself side to side, nearly throwing the black creature off its back but then there is a sharp cracking sound as the black creature breaks the thing's jaws, then it lets go, and pounds a clenched fist into the serpent's skull, shattering it. It leaps up, flames rippling across its shoulders, down its arms. "Get out!" it orders her. "Go!"

She forces herself around the door, steps out into the corridor. Glancing back, she sees the black creature hurl a ball of fire down the serpent's throat. She staggers three steps further along the corridor before she crashes to the floor in a dead faint.

"You are a trial to me," Simon says quietly as soon as her eyes open. "Something not agree with you at dinner? Do you have the flu?"

"What?" Pepper rasps.

"You failed to show up for the next illusion. I had to improvise after sending whoever was free to search for you. Vincent found you passed out on a corridor floor way at the back of the theater. What were you doing back there?"

"I don't know," she replies. Why would she have been back there? But then memories begin surfacing. She'd confronted him in his dressing room. There had been a topless girl there. She'd quit. Her world had suddenly crashed and burned around her and she'd lost it. And then…! There had been a huge snake and a…a…something! A hellish looking beast with red eyes! But the black thing with red eyes had saved her from the snake! Hadn't it?

"Pepper," he says, shaking his head. "It's time to go home." He rises from his chair. "I'll see you at the house."

She watches him walk out of the dressing room, realizes that she is in his dressing room because his clothes are all over the place. "Come on, kiddo. I'll drive you home." She hasn't even been aware that Andrew is in the room, too. He's been leaning against the wall at the head of the loveseat where she couldn't see him. "Get up slowly. If you feel faint at all lie back down."

Piper comes in with Pepper's tote bag. "Here's her stuff. How is she?"

"A little woozy still but she'll be fine."

They get her out to the limo the girls travel in. Andrew is their driver tonight because Jake is sick. The other girls question Pepper, but she really doesn't know how to explain what happened to her. "I think it was just a shock, his throwing knives at me while blindfolded. It scared me half to death."

"Poor kid, he's never done that before. I have to confess, my heart was in my throat, and I wasn't the one he was throwing knives at!"

"Simon has no qualms about endangering his assistants, as you've just discovered firsthand."

"He probably has some secret room in his house that he practices this stuff in with mannequins. I mean, he can't just suddenly decide he's hurling knives at a real live girl while blindfolded without ever having practiced it! That would be crazy!"

"Crazy? It's insane!"

"Please! I don't want to talk about it anymore!"

At the mansion, Pepper goes up to her room, strips off her filthy clothes and takes a quick, nervous, shower, fearful that at any moment a monster will jump out at her. She dries herself, towel dries her hair, pulls on her nightgown then goes out into her bedroom and screams. She has not expected to find Simon sitting on the side of her bed.

"Girls scream all the time when they see me, but not in terror like that," he says mildly.

"You scared me."

He pats the bed. "Come over here, climb into bed. You've had a hell of a night." She walks to the bed, climbs in, pulls the covers up to her upper chest. He glances at her, cocks a black brow at her modesty. She is a charming young lady and it is taking monumental restraint to sit here on the side of her bed with nothing between him and her but a thin cotton nightgown and a bed sheet, and his own clothing, black jeans and a black t-shirt, his usual at-home casual attire. "Let's try to keep this little talk brief," he says. He holds his hand up to stop her from speaking. "It will be mostly one-sided. I want you to hear what I have to say, then I want you to think about it for a day or two before you make your final decision about whether or not you stay or go. Agreed?" She nods. "Sebastian thinks you are too young and naïve. I do not. Young, yes. But I don't think there is a girl alive in this world these days who can honestly be called naïve unless she has been raised in a damned convent with no outside contact whatsoever with anyone or anything. Children are exposed to the adult world and all its ugly realities from the moment they begin suckling at their mother's breast. There is no innocence in this world anymore. You, Pepper, are not innocent, but you are inexperienced. And that is what I believe is the crux of Sebastian's issue with you. I could have chosen anyone at all, but I chose you. I do not have any issues with you. I want you to stay. I can sway Sebastian's opinion of you. It will just take a bit more time." He looks away, his gaze traveling about her room. It is a very feminine room, yet he feels comfortable enough in it. It's the girl in the room who raises his discomfort level. He continues. "I believe Andrew has let you know that he is interested in getting to know you better. I encourage you to allow that, if you feel he is someone you might develop feelings for. Perhaps you need a first fling."

"I…"

"Let me finish. Sampling the variety available in the world allows one to discern ones' own likes and dislikes. Go and have a picnic in the desert with Andrew. If another young man shows interest and asks you out, go. Enjoy your life, Pepper. You're free to see whomever you choose." He clasps his hands loosely, elbows on his knees. "I want you to remain as my assistant. I apologize for not preparing you for the trick tonight. It was something that I have been practicing on my own for some time. I apologize profusely for springing it on you so abruptly. I am sincerely sorry that it upset you so much that you were ill. However, I do have to tell you that you were impressive. You did exactly what you were told to do and that was exactly what I needed in order to do the trick safely." He stands up. "You do not make me unhappy, Pepper. Quite the contrary. You make me very happy." He walks to the door of her room and opens it. "On that note, I bid you a good night, Miss Rumford."

"Pepper. Just Pepper." He nods once, turns away. "Simon, wait!" He hesitates in the doorway. "Don't turn the light off!"

"Are you afraid of the dark?" he asks.

"Yes, tonight I am."

He looks back over his shoulder at her. "There are no monsters under your bed or in your closet."

"Only in my head?"

"Only in your head. Goodnight, Pepper."

"Simon!" She scrambles out of bed and runs to the door. He turns and looks down into her upturned face. "About your… um…friend. I'm sorry I interrupted you."

"Well, you probably should knock before you fling doors open like that."

"I'm sorry. Really and truly."

"Apology accepted." He turns and walks down the hall-way.

Pepper leans out of her doorway and watches him. At the head of the stairs he pauses to look back, sees her watching him. For a long moment their eyes meet and hold then she ducks back into her room and closes the door. He remain where he is for a moment more then quickly descends the main staircase and returns to his own house, but the agony of desire consuming him soon sends him out into the desert where he burns it off running as far and as fast as he can.

The house is a mere glimmer on the horizon when Simon stops running. He is far enough away now to allow the fire to consume him. Flames leap and dance from his shoulders, down his arms to his hands. He hurls fireballs the size of cannon balls into the desert until, exhausted, he drops to his knees into the sand, slumping forward.

It is at that moment that the only other large creature in the desert drops gracefully down from its perch with a few quick flutters of its wings. "Feeling better now?" Sebastian asks.

"Another demon was after her tonight," Simon replies.

Sebastian looks away, then up toward the stars twinkling in the night sky above their heads. "Why do you think that was?"

"I don't know. I think…" He shakes his head. "I think it was because she was so emotionally volatile. It was feeding on that."

"What'd you do?"

"I killed it."

"Did she see you?"

"Yeah."

"And?"

"I can't make her entirely forget what she saw."

"Great."

"I told her to go out with Andrew. I more or less told her to go out and have sex with someone, anyone."

"Except you."

"Except me."

"You're an idiot," Sebastian concludes.

"So you tell me on a daily basis."

Sebastian sighs. "Did you rape that girl?" he asks.

"No," Simon replies.

"You have an amazing ability to teleport yourself. You could have done that and Pepper would have been none the wiser."

"I was outside exercising Onyx. I know what time she gets up. I enjoy looking at her as she studies the morning sky. She is a vision. Sometimes she sees me, but most of the time she doesn't even know I'm there feasting my eyes on her."

"So you had nothing to do with that girl that morning?"

"No. I was here. I'm here more than I've ever been before."

"Since you immolated those showgirls and burnt out your suite."

"Since Pepper moved in," Simon says.

"You like torturing yourself?"

"Not especially."

Sebastian is quiet, his wings gently moving back and forth. Finally, he says, "Why do you think this demon was so interested in her? There are a lot of emotionally volatile girls in the world. Why Pepper?"

"I don't know, Sebastian! There's just something about her. Can't you feel it? Can't you see it? She's…she's radiant!"

"Maybe she's not all human?" Sebastian suggests.

"She has human parents. I met them. They seemed ordinary enough."

"Yes, okay, but is she their natural daughter? Did you ascertain that fact? Is she a product of their union, his sperm penetrating her egg thereby creating the being we all know by the name of Pepper, or did they adopt her?" Simon seems to comprehend that this could be a possibility. The couple he met could have conceivably produced a red-haired offspring if he understood human genetics correctly. Then there is the fact that Pepper is an only child. Her parents either failed to create a second child or perhaps couldn't conceive again. Or, if they had adopted Pepper, had perhaps felt their family was complete.

"I'll have to delve more deeply into her early years," Simon says.

"What do you think she might be?"

"I thought she was human but now you've got me questioning that. I don't know what she is. All I know is that I have never been drawn to any creature as strongly as I am drawn to her. It's maddening!"

"Then maybe you need to let her go before she does drive you insane."

"No! I need to know why this is, what it means. I need to find out if she and I can be together the way I want for us to be. I do not want to destroy her. I just want to keep her with me forever."

"Well, you're certainly a demon who likes it both ways."

"I'm a demon who's been waiting a damn long time for a mate," Simon growls.

"I heard that you entertained another dancer between acts." Simon shrugs. "That's how gossip starts. The police are watching you, you know."

"I'm aware of that. I'm always their number one suspect whenever anything happens to any girl in this city. It's become a pain in the ass, if truth be told."

"Then try to control yourself a little better and stay out of trouble!"

"Easy for you to say!" Simon fires back hotly. "Trouble follows me around like a thirteen foot long tail."

Sebastian stands up as he has been crouching for some time. He stretches his wings. "I'm heading home." Simon shoots a sharp glance at him. "Not there," Sebastian says looking up at the stars. "I haven't redeemed myself yet, and may be permanently grounded for all I know. I meant home to the compound. Neve was anxious tonight."

"I'll be home in a bit."

He watches Sebastian run a few feet, wings flapping vigorously before he rises up into the air and flies toward the distant glimmering lights surrounding the compound. It is very still and quiet in the desert tonight. He taps into Pepper's mind and is surprised to find that she is dreaming of him. It catches him off guard to realize that this is somewhat of an erotic dream. They are kissing rather passionately under a star-strewn sky and he has his hands on her buttocks, pulling her close against himself. She has one hand on his shoulder, and while he can't see her other hand he can feel it, feel her touching him, stroking him.

With a roar of hunger, he pulls himself back from her dream, his entire body throbbing with want, with need. She will be the death of him—death by desire.

Pepper has now seen for herself that Simon likes to work with fire in his illusions while Sebastian prefers to work with water. Both magicians make her nervous when they are fooling around with their chosen elements, but on stage they are strictly professional and use caution, well, except for Simon having moments when he seems to throw all caution to the wind as he performs some wildly, dangerous stunt, but he never seems to get burned.

He is including her in more of his illusions by the end of three months and she is finally feeling as if she is earning her salary as his assistant. She's also found a friend in Andrew, although she is not in love with him. He has told her that he loves her but she has not been able to reply in kind. He wants intimacy with her but so far she's only allowed him to go so far and no further. He's beginning to comprehend that she just doesn't want to be with him that way, but he's not giving up on her.

They are lying on a blanket on the sand out in the desert, watching the stars late one Sunday night, or rather very early Monday morning. Pepper'd had a huge fight with Simon backstage after the Saturday evening performance because he had changed an act right in the middle of performing it, leaving her in the awkward position of having no idea what he was going to do next. He had caught her totally unprepared, had shocked her by placing her in a black sack, her hands tied behind her back, her ankles bound and her eyes blindfolded. The sack had been attached to a hook. She'd had a panic attack inside the sack that had only worsened when she'd realized that he'd set the rope that the sack was dangling from afire. The sack had been raised twenty feet or more above the stage and she had thought that she was going to die. She still didn't know how she had ended up at the rear of the auditorium, but that's where she had suddenly found herself. He had been standing on stage, the burnt sack still smoking on the stage at his feet where it had fallen. "Ladies and gentlemen, Pepper, the Phoenix who has risen from the ashes!" She had walked down the aisle and joined him on stage, feeling as if she were in a trance state. It wasn't until she was back on stage that she had noticed that she was no longer wearing her usual black leotard and black tights, that she was now dressed in a slinky red gown with red boa feather trim. There were red feathers tied in her hair as well! How this had all transpired, she had no clue, but it had made her furious with him, especially when he had not answered her myriad questions about how the illusion had been accomplished without her having even been aware of what was going on. He'd only looked at her and said, "I perform magic, if you recall."

She is thinking about that as she watches the stars and then Andrew is leaning over her, kissing her. "You were so beautiful in the red dress the other night. It hugged every curve of your body."

"I don't have any curves," she replies.

"Of course you do. You're not a plank. You have some curves here," he says, caressing her hip. "And here," he adds, moving his hand to her breast.

"Andrew…"

"My heart was in my throat during the entire illusion. He comes up with the scariest illusions. I could see you struggling to get loose in the sack, then all of a sudden the rope had burned through and the sack fell with a thud onto the stage. I thought he'd killed you, but then it sort of went flat and he was pointing toward the rear of the auditorium and there you were. You looked so gorgeous, Pepper. Like a fiery, red bird coming down that aisle."

This is the night Pepper loses her virginity to Andrew and discovers her own fiery passion. This is the night that heat lightning streaks across the sky and strikes the desert around them, frightening her badly, and Andrew as well. He's never seen a storm like this one. There is no wind, no rain, just one bolt of hot bright lightning after another streaking down all around them from the star spangled sky. "I need to get you back to the mansion. It's too damn dangerous out here!"

Somehow, they make it safely back to the mansion. Andrew kisses her quickly at the door then goes to put the motorcycle away. Pepper stands for a minute watching the lightning. It seems to have followed them from all the way out in the desert to the compound on the plateau. As she lowers her eyes, there is a bright flash of lightning and in that flash she sees a dark figure standing across the patio between Simon's house and the carriage house. Its fists are clenched and it seems to be staring at her. She loses sight of it and is startled when Simon suddenly appears right in front of her. But as she starts to ask him what on earth he thinks he's doing, a bolt of lightning strikes the patio right where he is standing, the force of it throwing her back against the glass door. She can feel the electricity prickling against her skin, feel the radiant, burning heat of it. She stumbles through the door into the house, terrified, screaming.

Caroline comes running downstairs first. "I think Simon was just struck by lightning!" Pepper cries. There's someone lying on the patio, smoke rising from the body.

"Oh, no!"

Sebastian comes running into the house through the conservatory. Pepper is sobbing hysterically. Caroline nods toward the still open door and he looks out, winces. "Stay inside," he says, going to the door, slipping outside.

He walks to the figure, crouches down, examines it then stands up. He seems to be searching the area before he notices the lightning still flashing in the sky, but not as close to the house as it was. It's moving back out over the desert. "Damn it all!" he says aloud then he hurries back inside. "There's nothing we can do. He's badly burned. He's gone. It wasn't Simon though, it was Andrew." He catches Pepper who suddenly collapses in Caroline's arms at that announcement, throwing Caroline off balance.

Sabrina stays with Pepper who is inconsolable. "It was just some sort of freaky lightning storm, Pepper. It was just one of those unpredictable things. Poor Andrew! But he died a hero. He got you home safely, right? You're not hurt, just burned a little." Pepper's skin is reddened as if she has been lying in the sun too long. It stings and burns but is not blistering up. "Look, I have some sedatives in my room. Do you need one?"

"No," Pepper says, shaking her head. She doesn't want to take anything like that. She thinks that maybe Simon has been drugging her so that she can't remember learning the new tricks, but she can't understand why he would want her to feel that kind of terror and confusion. She also can't figure out how he could be drugging her either. He's never given her food or beverages. She's never felt any needle pricks when she's near him.

"Pep, what were you and Andrew doing out in the desert at this time of the night anyway?" Sabrina asks, setting Pepper off again. "Oh. Sorry." She pulls Pepper into her arms and holds her. "I'm so sorry! He was such a nice guy!"

Her door is suddenly thrown open and both Sebastian and Charlotte come into the room. "The police are downstairs. They need to talk to you," Sebastian tells her. "Do you know where Simon is?"

"Simon? No. I thought I saw him on the patio but it was Andrew. It turns out it was Andrew!" Tears fill her hazel eyes again.

"He's not home," Charlotte tells her. "The bastard isn't even home! He's probably off having his way with...."

Pepper leaps up and quickly leaves the room, half running down the hallway then down the stairs to the main floor. There are three police officers standing in the hall below. They turn and stare at her. "That's some burn you've got. How close were you to the lightning strike?"

"Too close," she replies, brushing tears off her flaming cheeks, wincing. Her tears sting her skin.

"You were out in the desert with Mr. Tate?" one of them asks her.

"Yes. I was kind of wound up after Saturday night's performance. I was still upset, so he suggested we take a ride out into the desert and look at the stars. It always calms me down to star-gaze. We were lying on a blanket on the sand just looking at the stars." One officer looks skeptical. "Then we made love and all of a sudden this freaky lightning storm came out of nowhere. There were bolts of lightning hitting the sand all around us. We both got scared. We thought we were going to die. Somehow, he got us back here safely. I jumped off the bike and ran to the back door. I waited for him there. He was putting the bike away. I was just standing there near the door watching for him. There was still lightning all around and it scared me because the storm seemed to have followed us. I saw someone," she says.

"Who did you see?"

"It must have been Andrew. I think all the bright flashes did something to my depth perception because I thought he was further away than he was and then I blinked again and he was closer. And then the next moment he was struck by lightning and I was thrown back against the door. I don't know why, but I thought it was Simon. Because of all the bright flashes it was like strobe lighting outside. I thought the figure had come from across the patio where Simon's house is, not the carriage house. But that wasn't the case."

"Unfortunately no, that wasn't the case. Do you know where Mr. Crowe is?"

She shakes her head. "No. Maybe he stayed in Vegas?"

"Sebastian mentioned that you and Mr. Crowe had a rather vehement argument after the show the other night. What was the argument about?"

"The act we performed near the end of the show. He changed it on me. I was mad about that. If he's going to change an act, any aspect of it at all, then he should have the decency to discuss it with me before hand."

"Decency? That's not usually a word we hear associated with Simon Crowe."

Cym and Caroline come from the rear of the house. "Here, Pep, we made you some chamomile tea. It'll help calm you down."

Sebastian comes downstairs holding his cellphone. "Here. He's finally deigned to answer his phone." He hands his phone to the officer who appears to be in charge.

"Mr. Crowe, this is Lieutenant Hadley. Where are you, sir?" He listens, frowns. "But Mr. Cross has told us that you rode home in the limo with him." He listens again. "I see. Look, there's been a death at the compound. We'd like to come and speak to you. Yes, I know you weren't here but perhaps you have a young lady with you who can collaborate your alibi. I thought so. Please remain at that location. We'll be there in less than an hour." He disconnects the call. "He's holed up at the Jack Rabbit Club in one of the private member's only suites with some girl he met there at the bar. We're going to go talk to him now. Are you going to handle contacting Mr. Tate's immediate family?"

"Yes. His father lives in Silver City," Sebastian replies. "I don't know where his mother is. They divorced when Andrew was fourteen. He's never mentioned her."

"Sorry for your loss, Miss Rumford," he says to Pepper who is standing with her head bent, tears dripping from her cheeks to the tile floor. "Perhaps you'd best go up to your room, drink your tea and try to get some rest." Caroline and Cym steer Pepper to the stairs and get her to climb up them. "Poor kid, damned rough way for a romantic night to end."

There is a mountain of tension between Simon and Pepper in the following days. The Vegas show is winding down. The company will be packing up and moving to their winter quarters in the Berkshires soon. From what Pepper understands, there is a second compound there and the design is like an Adirondack hunting lodge—a central lodge, smaller lodges and log cabins, rustic outbuildings housing a gym and an indoor pool. Sebastian shares his large lodge with Charlotte. Simon has a smaller lodge somewhat separate from the other structures, located in a private wooded glen. Rumor is he prefers his privacy and, surprisingly, usually stays by himself with no female companionship. He only has Jack and Onyx for company there. Everyone else lives in the central lodge building. Pepper will have her own room there, if she decides to stay. The rooms are all furnished nearly identically-comfortable but nowhere near as elaborately as their Nevada compound rooms.

Pepper decides that she'd really like to go home for a few months, so, although she moves into the Lakemont compound, she is there only a few days before Adair helps her with her bags and drives her to Chandler, Connecticut about eighty miles away, delivering her to her childhood home—a two and a half story colonial on a tree-lined street that is classic Americana in Adair's mind.

When he gets back to the compound, he gasses the limo at the private pump on the grounds and then moves it into the garage. He gets out and is surprised to find Simon waiting for him. "Was the prodigal daughter welcomed home?" he asks.

Adair shrugs. "Nobody was there when we got there. I carried her bags in, took them up to her room. She said they hadn't touched anything during her absence and seemed relieved about that. I guess the folks were working. She said she'd call them to let them know that she'd made it home safely, and then probably start dinner." Adair's mouth twists wryly. "Nothing special about the place. Small town America. Comfortable. The old man hasn't spent the million you gave him fixing the place up any, that's for sure. Kind of outdated, old-fashioned, but neat and clean."

117

"Does it seem odd to you that a man who makes his living selling real estate lives in a house you describe as outdated, old-fashioned?" Simon asks.

Adair shrugs then nods. "Yeah, you'd think he'd have scooped up some bigger, fancier, nicer place at a foreclosure sale or something. Realtors usually live in nice houses in case they have clients over. Gotta keep up the image."

"What image do you feel the Rumford's project?"

He shrugs again. "Ordinary, middle class folk."

"Did she seem happy to be back home?" Simon asks.

Adair scuffs the toe of his boot on the dirt floor of the garage. "Hard to tell. She's been so stressed out the past few weeks. If you want the truth, I think she's just relieved to be the hell away from us."

"If you're going to tell the truth then tell the whole truth. She's relieved to be away from me," he says before turning and leaving the garage.

"Yeah, that about hits the nail on the head," Adair says quietly before he closes up the garage and heads to the building where he lives with the other drivers and the stage hands who don't go home for the two months they're here. He's been missing Andrew. Andrew loved to play poker. He used to win a lot of spare change off the guy but sometimes Andrew got lucky and won a hundred bucks off him, so it all sort of evened out in the end.

For three weeks things go pretty much the same as they always have when the company breaks between the hectic four months of touring and the six months stay in Vegas. Everyone un-winds and relaxes. They takes day trips, go skiing. Some come and go for a few days, staying elsewhere visiting family or friends, or just going off on their own. Simon pretty much remains alone in his private lodge. No one sees much of him at all. Only Sebastian has the nerve to go and visit him every few days, to more or less check on him.

On the Monday before Thanksgiving, Sebastian comes to the house with an incredulous look on his face. "Simon is going to the Rumford's house for Thanksgiving," he says as they all sit down to dinner. Charlotte drops her fork with a clatter on her plate, shocked. Simon Crowe has never celebrated any holiday. He never has once vowed that he never would. Holidays mean nothing to him. So why has he accepted an invitation to Thanksgiving dinner at his assistant's parent's house? It makes no sense.

"I think it's because there's just over a month of vacation time left and he has to start making things right between them if he wants her to stay with the company. They were not in a good place with one another when we left Vegas. She's had a few weeks more to work through her feelings about Andrew dying like that. That really hit her hard."

"Can you see Simon Crowe sitting down to dinner with these middle class people when he's used to lavish Vegas spreads, showgirls, dancing, drinking, doing whatever he damn well pleases? He's a different sort of animal than the Rumfords are used to entertaining, I'm sure."

"He'll be home early, you wait and see," Charlotte predicts. "They will bore him into a stupor!"

For the next two days, there is much speculation that Simon will cancel the trip to Lakemont, but he does not. At ten o'clock on Thanksgiving Day morning, they watch him from the main lodge windows. He comes down the path leading from his lodge dressed in a black suit with a black banded collar shirt with a knee length black winter coat over all. There has been a light snow overnight and it's frosty out. He glances toward the lodge, as if

119

aware of all the eyes watching him, primarily because he *is* aware of them watching. He has dark glasses on. His longish, black hair is pulled severely back into a ponytail. He looks grim-faced but determined. As he turns onto the path to the garage he offers them a rude gesture with his upraised middle finger.

"Have you ever even seen Simon eat turkey before? He likes red meat."

"He eats fish, sometimes."

"Have any of you ever seen him eat fowl?"

"Only foul things," replies Piper with a grin.

"Let's not go there!" Poppy cries, elbowing her.

"Okay, what time will he be back from this fiasco?"

"He'll get there about eleven fifteen, piss them all off by noon and be home by a quarter past one."

"Well, can't top that, unless he speeds and makes it home by one," Cym replies.

"Unless he drives off someplace, like to New York City to indulge his carnal appetite since his gustatory appetite will remain unrequited, then we won't see him until Christmas. Once he gets started, you know he hates to stop."

Simon parks in the road in front of the pale yellow house and checks his watch. It is eleven-thirty. He has been driving a-round town a bit, psyching himself up for this dinner and visit. Removing his sunglasses, he tosses them onto the dashboard of the black Toyota Highlander he's driving from the compound's garage. With a muttered curse, he throws open the door and steps out into the slushy street. They have a bit more snow here than they do at the lodge. He really does not like snow, but since they live in the hot desert six months out of the year he can't grumble too much about Sebastian's choice of the Berkshires for the two snowy, cold months they're here on the east coast.

The driveway has been shoveled at least, and the walkway, as well. He mounts the cement steps to the front porch, crosses it then hesitates. An uncharacteristic anxiety permeates his body and mind. He'd been surprised when Pepper had called his cellphone and quietly, very simply invited him to dinner on this day. He believes he knows why. Whatever it is she has to tell him, she needs the security and comfort of family around her while doing so. He's pretty certain that she's going to tell him that she's quitting and will be remaining here to sit behind the damned receptionist's desk at her father's real estate office, wasting her life, being an obedient daughter. His deeper fear is that she will tell him this, and also that she's pregnant by Andrew who had foolishly failed to use a condom in his haste to have sex with her. If she tells him this, he doubts he will be able to stop himself from snapping her neck. He cannot bear the thought of her having anyone's child but his own, and that prospect seems less and less likely with every passing day.

He presses the doorbell, hears its muffled chime inside the house. Steeling himself, he waits. It's Mrs. Rumford who answers the door, smiling. "Hello, stranger," she greets him, opening the storm door then stepping back so he can enter the foyer. "It's so good to see you again, Mr. Crowe."

"Likewise," he replies carefully through clenched teeth. She reeks of gardenia perfume, never a favorite of his. There are other smells in the house—turkey roasting, the fragrance of freshly baked pies, vegetables cooking, and the smell of burning wood and paper from the fireplace in the living room.

This is where they find Mr. Rumford, on one knee in front of the fireplace, attempting to get the fire started. "Damned flue isn't drawing," Mr. Rumford grumbles as he turns and looks at

Simon after pushing his reading glasses up the slope of his nose, making a face to try to hold them there. "Crowe! You know anything about fires?"

"A little," Simon replies, but neither Rumford notices the ironic tone of his voice. "Let me help you with that." He shrugs out of his coat, hands it to Mrs, Rumford who stands stroking the fabric appreciatively. It is a very expensive cashmere coat.

The older man, who is dressed in brown, wide-wale corduroys, a pale blue shirt with a red tie and a gray cardigan sweater stands up, brushing off the knees of his pants before giving up his place on the hearth to the tall, black-clad magician. "Be careful, son," he murmurs.

The flesh on the back of Simon's neck crawls at that word 'son'. He now doubts that he will ever sire one of his own. Briskly, he uses the poker to manipulate the kindling, using his demon skills to make the kindling catch. When the kindling is burning and there are some embers beneath the grate, he adds small logs, adjusts the flue then adds a couple of larger logs on top of the now burning smaller logs. Satisfied for the time being, he gracefully rises. "That, sir, is how to build a fire," he says. As he turns, he catches sight of Pepper in the archway across the room and he freezes. She is, if anything else, more beautiful than he remembers her being. Her red curls are pulled back into a ponytail. She is wearing a pumpkin-orange corduroy jumper over an autumn print turtleneck shirt. The jumper clashes horrendously with her red hair and makes her look like a kindergarten teacher, in his opinion, but he adores her just the same. She has on green tights and brown loafers. It is a truly hideous outfit but he's not about to tell her so. For that matter, her father's attire is atrocious as well, and if he remembers correctly her mother was wearing some sort of retro hostess gown, floor length in an awful avocado and gold paisley pattern. It's as if the Rumfords' closets hold nothing but 1970's clothing. "Pepper," he says.

"Hello, Simon. Did you have any trouble finding the house?"

"No. There's a GPS in the car."

"You're a little late. I was beginning to think you'd changed your mind."

"I lost track of time sightseeing here in your little town."

"There's not that much to see," she says with a shrug.

No, he thinks. The only thing worth seeing in this town is now standing before him. He starts to cross the room but she holds up her hand to stop him, tells him to have a seat and a chat with her Dad while she and her mother put dinner on the table. "I thought dinner was at one," he says.

"It's already quarter past," she says, pointing to the mantle clock.

For the first time in his life, Simon Crowe feels off balance. The mantle clock definitely reads a quarter past one. He pushes his coat sleeve up, looks at his watch and finds that his watch is in agreement with the mantle clock. He looks toward the archway, but Pepper is no longer there. With a slight sense of disorientation he walks to an armchair and drops down into it. "I must have spent more time driving around town than I thought."

"That can happen. Quaint New England villages have a way of drawing one in."

Mr. Rumford is holding a pipe that Simon does not remember seeing him with previously. Now, he notices the fragrance of pipe tobacco in the room. Turning his head, he glances at the fireplace and is jolted to see that the fire has burned down substantially. He literally jumps up out of his chair, looking around a bit wildly. "How can this be?" he murmurs, his senses tingling.

"Dinner!" Mrs. Rumford announces. "Oh, Mr. Crowe, would you put a few more logs on the fire, please, before you join us across the hall in the dining room? You have such a way with fire."

Simon stokes the fire, pokes at the embers, closes the fire screen across the mouth of the fireplace then walks across the foyer. The stairway rises steeply to his left to the second floor.

In the dining room, Mr. Rumford is already carving a golden brown and glistening roast turkey. "Light meat or dark?" he asks the magician.

"Dad, I told you, he doesn't eat fowl," Pepper says as she comes through a swinging door which must connect the dining room to the kitchen. "Here, Simon. I broiled you a piece of sword-fish." She sets the oval plate down at one of the two unoccupied places at the table. "Sit here."

"You didn't have to go through the bother of cooking something just for me."

"It was no trouble. I couldn't find a venison steak and all the prime rib was sold out, so I had to get the swordfish or you'd have been eating bacon." She drops down into the other unoc-cupied chair.

Simon sits down, still feeling odd. Mr. Rumford slices turkey for Mrs. Rumford, Pepper and himself then sits down, shaking out his linen dinner napkin, tucking it into the collar of his shirt. "I hope you're not offended if we bypass the blessing?" he says to the magician.

"Not at all."

"I didn't think you'd be, fella like you."

"Dad!" Pepper picks up a bowl of steamed vegetables, serves a spoonful to herself then passes the bowl to Simon. He spoons some vegetables onto his plate, and as he passes the bowl to Mrs. Rumford his eye is drawn to a piece of broccoli on his plate. Narrowing his eyes, he realizes that there is a small green caterpillar on the floret that has been cooked with the vegetables. He happens to find caterpillars a delicacy.

Pepper passes him sweet potatoes. He's not fond of them and foregoes that dish. He does take winter squash and some black olives. The Rumfords, excluding Pepper, have loaded their plates with an astonishing amount of food. Pepper has taken only one small spoonful of each item, the food on her plate meticulously separated. He now realizes that she has always eaten this way, no foods on her plate touching. Her eyes meet his then she looks down at her plate as if trying to decide what to start with.

Simon stabs the broccoli floret with the caterpillar and pops it into his mouth. He is still chewing it when he senses Pepper's eyes on him again. His dark eyes meet hers and the corners of her mouth curve up in a rather enigmatic smile before she eats a bite of turkey. "Delicious," he says, just to see what her response will be. He has an uneasy feeling that she is well aware of the caterpillar he has just consumed.

"I thought you'd like it," she replies.

"Pepper is an excellent cook, just like her mother," Mr. Rumford remarks before shoveling another huge bite into his mouth.

"I'm surprised you only had the one child," he says.

"I couldn't have children," Mrs. Rumford responds quietly. "Tom and I adopted Tessie. She was found in a cardboard box behind the fish market. There was a little, coal-black kitten curled up asleep in the box with her. The police tried for months to find her birth mother. Tom and I fostered her. Everyone in town knew how desperately we wanted a child of our own. When Tessie was declared an orphan, we, of course, put our names in as adoptive parents. Naturally, since she'd been living with us for some time by then, we were allowed to adopt her. No one else volunteered. She's been our pride and joy for twenty-three years."

"No one ever stepped forward to claim her?" Simon asks.

"No. Abandoning a child is a criminal act. Do you honestly think some troubled, desperate young woman would step forward and admit she'd abandoned her newly born baby like that?" She shakes her head. "We were so fortunate."

"What happened to the kitten?" Simon asks.

"Oh, we still have the cat. I believe it's sleeping upstairs on Pepper's bed. He missed her terribly while she was away. But she's home now and he's quite content."

"He must be quite elderly, for a cat," Simon says, looking at Pepper. He's wondering about the cat and also about the statement made that she is home now. Does Mrs. Rumford mean that Pepper has told them she is home for good?

"He's as old as me but you'd never know it. He's still quite frisky."

He glances across the table and again feels off balance as he finds Mr. Rumford's plate empty. The man is leaning back in his chair with a satisfied expression, his hands folded over his literally bulging belly. Mr. Rumford sighs contentedly. Simon looks down at his plate and finds that he has consumed over half of his own meal. He does not remember eating anything but the one bite of broccoli with the caterpillar.

Pepper picks up the vegetable dish. "Here," she says, digging through the remaining vegetables for another few broccoli florets. She places them on his plate then sets the bowl and spoon back down. He looks down, sees that each floret has a caterpillar. "You look like you're enjoying the broccoli the most, although you've done well with the fish."

"Yes." He eats the broccoli and caterpillars while quickly trying to regain his bearings in this strange house. If he were one to be susceptible to drugs he would swear he had been drugged somehow, but he knows he hasn't. His head is quite clear, yet something is going on here that he can't quite figure out. It's rather disturbing and maddening for a being like him to feel so off kilter.

Mrs. Rumford and Pepper clear the table then bring in a pumpkin pie, an apple pie and coffee. Simon accepts coffee. He drinks it black. He chooses pumpkin pie. While Pepper serves the pie, Mrs. Rumford serves the coffee. Conversation is a mix of topics—the magic show, Pepper's work, his work and real estate. Mr. Rumford asks if he's developing any new illusions.

"I have a few in the design stage," he replies.

"Simon, can I talk to you privately?" Pepper asks as she rises from her seat. "Upstairs?"

"Go ahead, dear. Dad and I can handle the clean-up," Mrs. Rumford says.

"I wish I had a magic wand. I could whisk all these dishes right into the dishwasher and be done with it!" chuckles Mr. Rumford as he hauls himself up out of his chair. "There's a football game on that I'm anxious to catch."

Simon follows Pepper out of the dining room, up the dark staircase to the second floor. He is now certain that she is going to tell him that she will not be back. He follows her into her bedroom at the rear of the house. Her room is not the one that would be over the kitchen, but the other back corner bedroom. There is indeed a sleek, black cat on her double bed. The cat raises its head and glowers at him through amber eyes. "Go," she says. The cat hesitates a moment then jumps off the bed and saunters out of the room. Pepper swings the door shut and leans against it.

"I know what you're going to say," he says, preempting her.

"Really? Are you a mentalist as well as a magician?" she counters.

"All magicians are mentalists in some respects. We need to know how to deceive and manipulate people in order for them to believe in our magical abilities."

"But not you. You're different." She comes toward him and he finds himself taking a step backwards. "You really *are* rather magical," she says.

"I suppose I am," he acknowledges without coming right out and admitting that he has abilities that human beings do not possess.

"When I tell you to close your eyes, I want you to close them. When I tell you to open your eyes, you may open them."

"All right. Are you going to perform a magic trick for me now?" he asks. He has no idea what she is going to do.

"I'll let you be the judge of that," she replies. "Close your eyes." He closes his eyes. "Open your eyes." It has only been a few seconds at most between commands, yet, when he opens his eyes, he sees, not Pepper, but some other being, slender and grace-ful, its body covered with a pelt of soft, short ginger-colored fur. Its eyes are almond-shaped and hazel, its nose somewhat flattened. It has very fine whiskers. The tips of its fingers have claws.

Simon recoils back against the footboard of the bed, eyes wide with surprise and shock. The creature's eyes have oval pupils but they gradually become rounded as it moves closer. "What are you?" he asks.

"A demon, Simon, like you," it replies in Pepper's voice, only there is a sight trilling purr to the voice.

"I don't understand."

"Magic is the perfect place to hide. You and Sebastian have incredible disguises but you're not happy, are you?"

"No. I am not," he acknowledges. He is still reeling from this unexpected transformation. Pepper? The sweet little girl from a rural town in the northwest corner of Connecticut, a demon? He cannot believe it. He cannot believe that she has fooled him, a master manipulator, for months. Has she known all along? If so, she is a brilliant actress and a great manipulator herself. He has never been aware of this side of her, although, when Sebastian had mentioned the possibility that she had been adopted the thought that she was not all that she appeared to be had flitted through his mind, but he had dismissed it! What a fool he's been! "What do you want?" he asks warily.

"I want you to show me your real self. I've seen you before and I find you quite alluring."

"Do you? We're entirely different species of demons." His hands are literally itching to stroke her glossy fur. If he transforms then she will be able to see how wildly aroused he is as he will have nothing with which to hide that fact. He is unused to feeling so vulnerable and exposed.

"Let me see you, Simon," she says.

"Pepper, I cannot control myself at times like this."

"I'm aware of that."

"Your parents are downstairs."

She gives him a coy smile. "My parents? What parents would they be?"

"The Rumfords."

She takes a step closer, her eyes locked to his. "Simon, you said you drove all around Lakemont prior to arriving here. Do you recall seeing a Rumford Realty office on Main Street?" she asks.

Now that she's made him think about it, he did not see any such place. He can remember just about every other building on the street, but there was no realty office. "No," he admits.

"Transform for me," she says in her now purry voice and he complies, unable to resist her any longer. She comes right up to him, pressing herself against his black, scaly body. He places his hands on her buttocks as he looks down into her eyes. And then he is kissing her and he feels her hand move between them to touch him, to stroke him and he remembers her dream that he had visited. This is so similar, except that they were in their human forms in her dream.

"Are you sure you want to do this like we are now?" he asks.

"Yes," she purrs.

He groans as he picks her up and carries her to her bed, throws her down on it then climbs onto the bed and moves over her. "You know what I want to do, don't you?"

"I know," she replies. "I just needed to be sure *you* were the one *I* wanted to mate with."

He joins himself to her and they lose themselves in love-making, in mating. Her claws dig into his scales, opening tiny wounds. His talons leaves scratches on her, and he bites her hard on the throat, making her throw her head back and howl, eyes closed. But then her eyes open wide and she is panting. He raises his head, looks at her, realizing that she is approaching her climax. This realization sends a flare of heat through his entire being and he quickens his movements, pushing her over the edge and then he follows her as he releases in her, connecting himself to her for all eternity with the siring of this offspring she will bear for him. "Show me your human form," he whispers hotly in her ear. Beneath him she transforms into the pretty redhead he adores. He remains in his demon form for a few more minutes, kissing her pale, warm flesh, savoring her. Then he transforms back into his human shape. Pepper grins, pulls his face to hers and kisses him passionately. "I take it that I have met with your approval?"

"You have," she answers.

"Just in case I have not yet impregnated you, we should do this again, don't you think?"

"Oh, I felt it. It happened," she replies as she runs her fingers through his black hair which has come loose. "But we can do it again."

"I'm not too intense a lover for you, am I? Too vigorous?"

She lowers her hand to his shoulder where there is a deep scratch. "No," she replies. "Simon Crowe, I think you have finally met your match."

"Do you?" She yelps as he plunges into her anew but then she throws her head back and laughs with delight at what he does to her, how he makes her feel. His heart feels unusually light. She is a radiant being, in almost complete contrast to his darkness. With her, he feels a deep satisfaction, not the sharp, biting torment of disappointment after sex that he's experienced with human females. "Why did you make love with Andrew?" he suddenly asks.

"He wanted it, and I was curious to see how you'd react."

"I did not react well at all."

"You had a monumental temper tantrum. You scared me." She pulls his mouth to hers and moans. "You scared me half to death!"

He kisses her hungrily, driving into her. "I could have killed you that night. I thought about it. I wanted to do it, but I couldn't. I saw you on the patio and you looked so afraid."

"I did see you then," she says. It *had* been Simon, not Andrew.

"Yes. I walked right up to you but backed away because I could not destroy you. I could not kill what I loved so deeply. I then exchanged places with poor Andrew and struck him dead so that you would know how displeased I was, how hurt I was by what I perceived as your betrayal of my affection for you."

"Yet you never showed me any sign of your affection."

"I did, Pepper. I accepted you, trained you, gave you everything you could want and need. I saved you from what would have been a fatal sword wound. I saved you from a serpent demon that would have devoured you if I had not come to your rescue."

"You showed me you weren't a demon to be messed a-round with. You showed me you are ruthless when you want to be. You showed me you have no problem killing if it suits your purposes. You made me nervous, Simon. You're so damn reck-less at times."

"I was bored. I was frustrated."

"Are you bored and frustrated now?" she asks, then gives a little shriek at his physical, rather than verbal, response.

"Stop talking now and kiss me," he says.

After, they lay tangled together on her bed, both of them breathing hard. It has grown dark in her room as twilight has arrived. "Do your parents exist?" he asks, his head beside hers on her pillow. He is toying with a red curl, winding it around one of his long, slender fingers.

"Yes."

"Then answer me this. What do they think we are doing up here in your room?"

"Having a conversation about my continued employment. I've been on the fence about whether or not to go back."

"Have you been?"

"Yes."

"Have you decided one way or the other?" She points toward a corner of her room. He lifts his head and peers into the gloom. Her bags are packed in front of her closet. He drops his head back onto the pillow. "Are you going back with me tonight?"

"Yes."

A ripple of pleasure inside him makes his abdominal muscles flex. Her hand is there and she turns her head toward his, kisses him. "They will be sorely disappointed," he predicts.

"Give Dad more money. That'll make him feel better."

Simon blows out his breath. "I've paid a small fortune for you as it is."

"Pay another small fortune and I will be yours forever. There will be no more payouts after this evening."

"Miss Rumford, you are as much a manipulator as I am. You are deceptive and cunning, clever and an astounding actress."

"Well, part of the time I was not acting. I really was scared and disturbed, having second thoughts about you. And sometimes, just desperate for you to throw me down wherever we were and make me yours."

"I wish I had known about that part."

"Oh, Simon, how could you not have known?"

He thinks about that and is surprised to realize that every glance he has ever exchanged with her has been meaningful, has sent a message. The only ones they have been fooling have been themselves in those moments. "What is your element?" he asks.

"Air," she replies. He grins. "If you want to know the absolute truth, I can do the levitation illusion a lot more easily if we skip the support and you just let me have control. You can give the illusion that you're levitating me and moving me around." She winks. "Our new levitation illusion will be jaw-dropping."

"How so?"

"You'll make me float right out over the heads of the audience members. You can levitate me right up to the catwalk and then command me to fly down into your arms. And I will. I will fly straight into your arms, Simon Crowe. I'll show Jack a thing or two about flying."

He laughs. "I'm sure you will. I'm going to hate to break it to him that I will enjoy catching you more than I enjoy his landing and perching on my arm."

She sits up. He pulls her back down and kisses her again. She pushes him back. "It's late. We need to get dressed, go downstairs and let my parents know that we've worked this all out between us."

"What have we worked out between us?" he asks as he gets up and begins sorting out their clothes. "By the way, your outfit leaves much to be desired."

"I could hardly wear an evening gown to Thanksgiving dinner at my parent's house in Lakemont," she replies, sitting down on the edge of the bed to put on her tights.

"Never dress like this at home for me, please."

"I won't." She tugs the tights up, grabs her turtleneck and pulls it on over her head. "How was I wearing my hair?" she asks.

"Ponytail," he replies, buttoning his cuffs.

After pulling on her jumper, she walks to her dresser, picks up her brush and brushes her hair, finds an elastic band and ties it back. He brings her the pumpkin-colored ribbon, ties it around her ponytail with a neat bow. She hands him her brush and he uses it on his hair, brushing it back severely. She finds his elastic band on the floor, hands it to him.

She opens her door. He grabs her suitcases and follows her diagonally across the hall to the staircase, down the stairs. He sets the suitcases down by the door. Her parents are in the living room, her father watching football, her mother crocheting. "You were upstairs for quite a while," Mrs. Rumford remarks, not looking up from her needlework. "It's getting dark."

"We had a lot of things to discuss and then some negotiating to do," Pepper replies.

"So, what have you decided?" Mr. Rumford asks, turning in his chair to look at them. He notices Simon has his arm around Pepper. "Ah, I see. Fame and fortune beckons you, Tessie, and you cannot resist."

"Sorry, Dad. Simon proposed and I couldn't say no." She feels Simon's startled reaction to the announcement that he is apparently engaged to her, but then she feels his hand slip around behind her and fondle her butt. "I'm going wherever he goes from now on."

"Well, we'll miss you," Mrs. Rumford says. "And I hope you're taking that damned cat with you. The fool thing did nothing but howl and mope around the house for months when you weren't here."

"Can I take my cat?" she asks Simon.

"I suppose so. Just keep it away from Onyx."

"Oh, I have a feeling they'll get along well enough, after a few days feeling one another out."

"Coffee before you kids go?" Mrs. Rumford asks.

"That would be nice, Mom. Let me help you. I think Simon has something to talk to Dad about." They go to the kitchen.

"So, you've finally realized what a treasure you have in my little girl, have you?" Mr. Rumford says.

"Yes, sir, I have indeed."

"Phyllis and I, we'll be lost without her."

135

"Perhaps I can compensate you for that sense of loss, although I'm sure we will find time to visit when our schedule allows."

"Compensation?" Mr. Rumford says with interest, drawn back to the magician from the television screen.

"Let me write you another check, if I may."

"Certainly! Don't let me stand in the way of a rich fella and his checkbook, son."

Simon reaches into his inside jacket pocket, pulls out his checkbook and writes out a check for two million dollars. He tears it out of the book, hands it to the man, replaces his checkbook into his pocket. He's quite certain that he and Pepper will easily make that money back once they work out a number of new routines in the show featuring her element.

Coffee is brought in and enjoyed. Simon carries Pepper's bags out to the Highlander. There is a light, frosty snow falling. She coaxes her cat, Jet, into its carrier, kisses and hugs her parents goodbye. Simon shakes hands with Mr. Rumford, kisses Mrs. Rumford's cheek much to her blushing delight, then he takes the cat carrier in one hand, Pepper's hand in the other and they leave the house.

"Will you miss all this?" he asks as he pulls away from the curb.

"No," she replies truthfully. "I've been waiting for you. I just wasn't sure where you'd be. I only knew that one day I would find you, that I would be somewhere other than here." She rolls her head against the headrest to look at him in the glow of the dashboard instruments. He is a devilishly handsome man, and a gorgeous beast. She feels her heartbeat quicken. "Am I how you imagined I'd be?"

"No, not at all," he admits. "I knew you'd be beautiful, but I thought for sure you'd be a showgirl on the strip. You're much more alluring then I thought you'd be. I am not displeased, only in that I did not recognize you for what you are immediately."

"But you must have, Simon, on some deeper subconscious level, and that was the whole problem. We were far too wary of one another at first."

"I suppose," he agrees. That is probably true. "And I suppose I will have to spend some more money and buy you a ring worthy of your finger."

"You've spent way too much money on me already."

"Allow me this one last indulgence—you choose your ring, what you like, and I will pay for it. Agreed?"

"Agreed," she replies. She is quiet for several long minutes as he drives then asks, "Simon, what about Sebastian?"

"What about him?"

"How is he going to take this? You and he have been together for a very long time."

"Our time as Sebastian Cross and Simon Crowe is rapidly coming to an end. If he chooses to, he can go with us and we will transform ourselves once again. I kind of like magic and illusion."

"You are a bit of a showoff."

He smiles. "I am at that." She closes her eyes and rests as he drives on toward the Berkshires and their future. They will have a child together. He thinks it would be nice to include the child in the act once it is old enough. Perhaps, if Sebastian chooses to go off on his own with Charlotte, he and Pepper can create a family act with their son.

There are a lot of avenues that can be explored, but for now, he feels more settled. He feels quite happy, in fact, which is something he has never actually been before. He likes the feeling and hopes it will last for a very long time. He hopes it will last for an eternity.

THE GIRL WITH THE IVY TATTOO

Tuesday, September 9th

Eveleen Glenrowan came hurriedly down the outside wooden stairs from the apartment above the livery garage and dashed across the rain swept pavement then up onto the small rear service porch of the huge yellow brick mansion now known simply as The Cedars. It was a funeral home and she had recently started working there as a receptionist/secretary. The Mitchells had been kind enough to offer her the four room apartment in the former carriage house as she had been living with her father, John "Jack" Glenrowan, a renowned tattoo artist, across town in the Dockside District and his girlfriend, Fidelity Finn, and working at Rampant Ink, the tattoo and body piercing parlor that Glenrowan co-owned with Max Leary, after a nasty break-up with her biker boyfriend, Richard "Rogue" Walker, until Fidelity had announced that three was a crowd and he'd kicked her out onto the street. Eveleen was twenty-three years old, Irish-American, and an uncommonly pretty girl with wavy light-red hair and unusual jade-green eyes. She was tall and willowy, slender to the point of being too slim. She was soft spoken and sweet. The only aspects of her appearance that the Mitchells had remarked upon when she had applied for the job were her multiple ear piercings, the tiny diamond stud nestled in a hollow of her nose on the left side and her tattoo. She had agreed to wear long-sleeved shirts with collars and long pants at work to cover the tattoo which was of an ivy vine. The vine began behind her left ear, trailed down the side of her neck to her shoulder then spiraled down her left arm ending with an ivy leaf on her wrist bone. The vine branched from her shoulder, across her clavicle then plunged down between her breasts, girdled her hips then, from her right hip, spiraled down her leg to end with an ivy leaf on her right ankle bone. It was beautifully rendered, exquisitely detailed. Her father had tattooed her when she was sixteen. It had caused quite a scandal at Somerset High School, that a father would tattoo his daughter in such a manner, but it had also sent a lot of business Rampant Ink's way.

This morning, Eveleen was dressed in a crisp, pale green blouse, a dark green vest with some matte-black embroidery on the front in an art deco-reminiscent pattern, slim black slacks and black ankle boots. Her hair was still damp from the shower, combed back from her face. She let herself into the rear service hall and then into the back hall. There was a large, old-fashioned kitchen to the right. She went in there to start the coffee maker. This was one of her jobs, to make the morning coffee. She also ran the dishwasher at the end of the day so all the mugs and spoons and whatever other dishes that had been used the previous day were clean.

The coffee was brewing, the aroma permeating the kitchen, as she started unloading the dishwasher. Andrew Veale, one of the two embalmers, came in the same way she had. He had two sky-blue boxes from Carmelita's Bakery, speckled dark blue in places from raindrops. He set the boxes on the table. "Good morning," he said. "Damn rotten day for a funeral."

"It's supposed to clear up," she replied.

He stood watching her work. She was an exquisite crea-ture, he thought. He and Adrian had talked about her off and on since she'd been hired. Adrian was the other embalmer, a funeral

140

director and usually drove the hearse. Andrew was thirty-two years old and married to Beth Parker-Veale. Beth was about three months pregnant with their second child. They had a little boy named Vincent Adam who was three-years old. They were hoping for a girl this time. Beth was due to have her ultrasound this afternoon. They might find out then if they were having another boy or a girl. He thought Eveleen was nice but he liked her Rampant Ink co-worker, Hollyce Santos, better. Hollyce was the product of a Puerto Rican mother and a Jamaican father. She was exotic, beautiful and sexy with her long, kinky, ebony hair, her coffee-colored skin tone and large hazel eyes. She could easily have been a model, she was so striking in appearance, so sensual a being. Hollyce had helped Eveleen move her scant belongings into the carriage house apartment. Fortunately, the place had been furnished or else Eveleen would have been sleeping on the floor. "Not soon enough," he said. "Have you seen Adrian yet?"

"No. I just got over here. He usually doesn't come downstairs until seven-thirty." Adrian Frey-Dayne lived on the third floor of the Second Empire style mansard-roofed mansion with the tower. Eveleen had always thought of the house as the super-sized Psycho house. It still seemed somewhat unreal to her that she was working there, living on the property. Her world had totally been turned upside down in the past month.

"You hear Maddie or Jim moving about?" Madeline and James Mitchell lived on the second floor of the mansion. She shook her head. He glanced around the kitchen then took a step closer to her. "Hey, I was wondering if your friend would, you know, like to go out for a drink some night?" Eveleen glanced at him and he could see in her eyes that she had been caught off guard by his question. "I've been kicking around the idea of

getting a body piercing, but I'm chicken. I thought talking it over
with a professional might convince me one way or the other."

"Why don't you just go to the shop and ask her?" she
answered. Then she shrugged. "Either way, she'd talk to you
about it."

The elevator was coming down from the third floor. There
was a door in the back hall that looked like an ordinary paneled
door that might open onto a closet, but behind the door was the
brass cage door of the small two person elevator that went to the
second and third floors. It was mostly used by Adrian who did not
like to use the main staircase or the former servant's back stairs
early in the morning for fear of disturbing the Mitchell's. The
elevator was fairly quiet but could be heard on the first floor and
third floor due to the mechanical apparatus that ran it.

Andrew busied himself opening the pastry boxes. Eveleen
set out three mugs on the counter and filled them with coffee. She
already knew how Andrew and Adrian took their coffee. Adrian
liked his the color of *café au lait* with one sugar. Andrew drank
his black with three sugars. She liked her coffee light with two
sugars. The coffees were ready on the counter when Adrian came
into the kitchen. This morning, he was wearing his new suit in a
color called Onyx. He had on a medium green shirt with a dark
green tie. He was a couple of inches taller than six feet, lean, and
handsome. He had coal black hair that curled over his collar, very
dark, black coffee-colored eyes, gorgeous sooty lashes. His skin
had a mild olive tone from a distant Greek relative, but he was
mostly Scotch-Welsh in ancestry. He liked to have his suits tai-
lored for a more fitted look.

He made Eveleen's heart beat more quickly. He seldom
spoke to her, showed no signs of interest in her and she rarely even
saw him, but he had an effect on her that made her feel as if she

was the most awkward and socially inept person in the world. She took her mug from the counter and spilled it, grabbed a paper towel and dropped it into Andrew's mug, compounding the mess as she plucked it out and reached for another one to clean up that mess as well. Her cheeks were flaming. She could feel the heat radiating from them. Neither man said anything. She threw the wet paper towels out, took her mug and quickly left the kitchen.

She heard the Mitchell's come downstairs at seven-forty. At seven-five, Adrian came into the small room, the former morning room, where her desk was located. He set a plate with a spiced apple muffin down on the corner of her desk. She looked up at him but he was reading what she had been writing on a legal pad, a slight frown on his face. She was horrified that he was reading her notes and tried to cover them with an invoice. "No, let me finish," he said.

"I didn't mean for you to read this," she said, her voice barely audible. His dark eyes flicked up to meet hers for a mere moment and she shrank back in her chair, her heart pounding.

"You have some valid points, although I don't agree with everything you've written." He turned and started for the door. "Miss Glenrowan, I'd like to talk to you later. Would you come downstairs to my office at three o'clock?"

"Your office in the basement?"

"It's the only office that I have. Yes, that one." He was out in the hallway already when he called back, "Would you please unlock the front door."

Usually the front door was unlocked at eight. She quickly went and unlocked the inner vestibule door, then the massive front door with the ornate brass knob. She had just returned to her desk when the phone rang. It was rather early in the day for a call, but not unusual, as people died at all hours of the day and night. She answered, "Good morning, you've reached The Cedars. May I help you?"

"Sparks? It's Max. Look, Fidelity just called me. The cops were at the apartment bright and early this morning asking for you. Something to do with your dad, apparently. She told them where you live and work now. Don't be surprised..." He was still talking but she had heard the front door open and looked up. There was a police officer standing in her doorway now. Slowly, she replaced the receiver in the cradle, cutting off Max, who was still talking.

"May I help you?" she asked, her mouth feeling frozen, as if her jaw did not want to work.

Madeline had come from the rear of the mansion. "Good morning, Officer. What can we do for you?" she asked.

He'd turned at the sound of her voice and spoke to her. "I'm looking for Evelyn Glenrowan."

"What has she done?" Madeline snapped, making Eveleen, who could hear her perfectly well, cringe.

"She's not done anything that I'm aware of. I need to speak to her, about her father, John Glenrowan."

"The tattoo artist? What's about him? Has he gone and gotten himself arrested?"

"No, ma'am, it's not that." Something in his tone tempered Madeline's attitude immediately and sent a cold shower of sparks across Eveleen's skin. He turned back to her. "Miss Glenrowan?" She managed a nod. "I'm sorry to have to tell you this but there was an accident early this morning. A motorcyclist was struck at the intersection of Pierce and Ferry Streets. We have reason to believe, from identification found at the scene, that your father was the motorcyclist." The girl was white-faced and he hated to have to continue but he plunged on. "I'm, sorry, but he was killed. As next of kin I need you to...hey!"

Madeline pushed past him into the room at the sound of Eveleen hitting the floor. "Andrew! Adrian!" she cried.

They had been in the reposing room across the broad reception hall making sure that everything was in order for the viewing of Frances Harper and came running. Andrew didn't seem to know what to do. Adrian pushed past him, knelt down as he plucked the handkerchief from his coat pocket, then pressed it against the gash on Eveleen's temple where her head had struck the corner of the desk. "What happened?" he demanded. "How did she fall?"

"I was telling her that her father had died last night. She just passed out and fell out of her chair. I didn't know she was going to faint!" the officer replied. He was younger than Adrian, who was almost thirty.

"Madeline, get a glass of water. Andrew, help me move her to the couch."

The three men got Eveleen onto the couch, Adrian lifting her shoulders, the officer steadying her head and keeping the handkerchief pressed against her wound and Andrew lifting her lower body. She was starting to come around when Madeline returned with the glass of cold water.

Eveleen opened her eyes and saw four concerned faces peering down at her. "I'm sorry," she murmured, not exactly sure what had happened.

"You fainted," Madeline said. "This young officer was telling you about your father's accident."

Eveleen started, trying to sit up, but Adrian pressed her shoulders back down. "Don't try to sit up too quickly. You've cracked your head against your desk." She raised her hand but he had his hand on the handkerchief against her injury. Her hand touched his and she quickly pulled it away with a gasp.

"I'll drive Eveleen to Wheaton Medical Center to identify the body, but I think she may require a few sutures prior to being able to do that. Let me get Gillian. She can clean up the mess. Then I need to speak to Fred and Brian. Adrian, you can handle this funeral without Jim, can't you?"

"Yes, of course."

"He'll have to stay here until Eveleen and I return."

Eveleen did not speak during the drive to Wheaton. She sat with a clean cloth against her temple, silent and stunned. Madeline stayed with her in the emergency room. "She's just received a bad shock." Eveleen glanced at the woman as if she did not know who she was. Madeline had never exactly been friendly with her. It had been James and Adrian who had actually made the final decision to hire her. Madeline had never liked the idea and never been anything but cool or downright cold toward her.

With three sutures in her temple and a large Band-Aid covering the injury, she took the elevator to the basement with Madeline and the young officer who had waited in the corridor for them. The hallway to the morgue was painted institutional green with only a black stripe painted on it indicating that they were following the correct corridor. Turning a corner, they reached a set of double doors, steel, painted dark green. A small white plaque with black lettering, reading "MORGUE", was attached to the wall beside the doors. Eveleen seemed to freeze up as the officer pushed the right hand door open. "Go on," urged Madeline, giving her a nudge.

The officer led them to a small room with a couch. There was a window, like a picture window, opposite the couch. The curtains were on the opposite side of the glass, controlled from the room beyond. "Pete has the body on a gurney behind the curtains. When you're ready, tap on the glass and he'll open the curtain. Only the head will be exposed. He's been cleaned up, will look like he's just sleeping. If the man is your father you can nod. If he is not your father you can shake your head. You can turn away at any time." Eveleen nodded. "All right? Whenever you're ready."

Eveleen bowed her head. She was shaking. Madeline put her arm around the girl's shoulders and gave her a light squeeze. "I know this is not easy. Are you ready?" Eveleen nodded. Madeline rapped sharply on the window. The curtains slid smoothly apart to reveal a man lying on a gurney beneath a clean white sheet. His head and neck were exposed. His dark hair was longish, combed back from his face. It was still damp from being washed. There was abraded skin on his right cheek, jaw and temple, a bloodless gash where his helmet had dug into his left temple. There was no visible blood at all.

Eveleen slowly raised her head. A low, keening sound rose up in her throat and she cried, "Dad!" before moving forward to press her hand against the glass as if she could touch him through the barrier.

"He's your father?" Madeline asked. The man had been quite handsome. It was a shame he had met such a gruesome end.

"Yes!" Eveleen cried.

Madeline nodded and the morgue attendant closed the drapes. The young officer, afraid Eveleen would pass out again, grabbed her and steered her to the couch, making her sit down. She was still keening. Madeline looked at her then said, "She's probably going to be sick. Help me get her to the ladies room." They got the girl onto her feet, steered her across the corridor into the ladies room. The officer seemed nervous about being in there. "There's no one else here," Madeline snapped. Eveleen bent over the sink and vomited the coffee that she had drunk. And then she started sobbing.

Madeline let her cry until the worst of the sobs were past, then she turned on the taps. "Wash your face, rinse your mouth. There's paperwork you need to sign so they can release the body. I'll call Jim. He'll send Adrian over to pick up your father as soon as he returns from the Harper funeral. We'll handle your father's funeral."

"I don't have the money for it!" Eveleen cried.

"Don't worry about that now."

The paperwork was signed. Madeline told Pete that Adrian would be picking up the body that afternoon. She and the officer got Eveleen out to the black Lexus. "I'm really sorry about your dad," he said. Eveleen nodded, murmured a quiet thanks. He shut the door.

Madeline got behind the wheel of the Lexus and headed back to Juniper Avenue. "The death certificate will be ready when Adrian picks him up. Is there anyone we should call for you? Your mother, perhaps? Another relative? A friend?"

"My mother is dead. My relatives live in Ireland. I need to call Max. He'd called me to tell me what had happened but I hung up on him."

At The Cedars, Madeline sat her in the kitchen, made her a cup of tea and some buttered toast. She left the girl alone, went to talk to her husband. When she returned, she found Eveleen at the table, her head down on her folded arms. She was weeping quietly. Gillian was sitting across from her sipping coffee. "I've called Rampant Ink. Mr. Leary is on his way over," Madeline said.

"I'll sit with her," Gillian said. Madeline seemed relieved and left. "She's not exactly a warm, nurturing person," Gillian said softly.

Eveleen finally got herself under control, went and used the lav in the hallway, washing her face again. She grimaced at her reflection. Her pale skin was mottled with pinks and reds. Her green eyes were preternaturally vivid, as her eyes were reddened and raw-rimmed from crying. "Ugh!" she said, wrenching open the door, returning to the kitchen. She made a fresh cup of tea, thanked Gillian for being so kind and then went to her office, sat behind her desk hunched forward staring down into her cup.

Max Leary, a great grizzly bear of a man with his shaggy salt and pepper hair and full matching beard, came into the room. "Eveleen, hey, about your old man, baby, I'm so sorry!" She raised her head and looked at him. He was in his usual faded and frayed jeans, tie-dyed tank top and boots. He had thrown a short-sleeved denim shirt on over the tank top. "What a freakin' shame!"

"Uncle Max, I can't believe he's dead!"

"Yeah, I heard a Hummer mowed him down. He was road pizza." Eveleen's eyes widened then filled with tears. "Hey, sorry! I know it's hard on you. So, what's the deal? Is he being waked and buried from this joint? How you ever goin' to afford that?"

"I don't know," she replied.

"You get a company discount or something?" She shook her head, shrugged. "Okay, look, a coupla bars have put out pickle jars for donations. We'll have to wait and see what the Pirates can cough up by way of a donation. I got a coupla thou in the bank."

"This is my problem, Uncle Max," she said.

"He was my business partner, sweetie." She looked sad and resigned. "You want to go talk to your employers now, make some arrangements?" She nodded.

They went down the hall, found Madeline and James who led them to the consultation room. "I want it simple," Eveleen said. "He wasn't an extravagant man."

"Of course." Madeline looked at her husband then asked, "Did he belong to a church?"

"He occasionally went to St. John's. Father Martin knows him."

Madeline managed to hide her surprise. "I'll see if he's available for the funeral service here and at the church." Eveleen nodded. "What hours would you like for the wake?"

"Just one evening, seven to nine?"

"With a brief service here before the funeral the following day?"

"Yes."

"Adrian will take care of finding a grave site for him in St. John's Cemetery."

They selected a basic casket, the wording for the memorial cards and the pictures on the reverse side—ocean views as Jack had loved the sea. Max took Eveleen out to lunch at Maxine's Café near Rampant Ink. He brought her back at one o'clock.

Adrian was in the hallway as she came through the front door, having been left off there by Max. "Your father is downstairs," he said. She looked at him a moment, then biting her lip, looked away. "I'm going over to St. John's to see about a grave site. Would you like to go with me?"

"I have some work to do," she said, her voice barely audible.

"It's nothing that can't wait for an hour or so." He thought she'd shake her head, go to her office, but she took a deep breath and nodded.

He used his black Toyota Highlander for errands like this. The cemetery was managed by the church. The office was in the parish house across from the church. Adrian asked to see a cemetery layout and where plots were available. The secretary unrolled a map of the whole cemetery. Available plots were marked with blue pencil. There were different price ranges.

Adrian watched Eveleen look over the map. He saw how her eyes kept returning to the knoll overlooking the bay, how she forced herself to look at the least expensive plots at the rear of the cemetery. She was gnawing her lip raw with anxiety. Finally, he made the decision for her. "Section K, plot 103." She gasped as she raised her head, her green eyes meeting his. "He loved the sea. He should be buried there."

"But I..."

"Section K, plot 103," he repeated to the secretary who nodded and pulled out the contract for that plot from a filing cabinet. Adrian took out his checkbook and wrote a check for the full amount. Eveleen had left the room. He found her standing in the hallway when he came out with the paperwork in his jacket pocket. "Next, we need to arrange for the vault and marker."

"It's way too much money," she said as they left the parish house. "How will I ever be able to pay you back?"

"Don't worry about that right now," he replied.

They went to Bayside Monuments. She selected a small granite marker that would have his name, birth date and date of death on it. Adrian wrote another check for, what to her, was another small fortune. Back in the SUV, he asked about clothing for the burial. She looked at him almost wildly then said, "His clothes are at his apartment. His girlfriend is there."

"You're his daughter. You're handling the funeral arrangements. We can't bury him naked."

He drove her to the apartment which was on the second floor over Sharkey's Bar and Grill, two blocks down the road from Rampant Ink. Eveleen was nervous. Adrian knocked on the door.

The door was opened by a bleached-blonde, young woman with the largest breasts he'd had ever seen, obviously implants. They were like barely restrained watermelons in a clingy yellow cotton tank top. She had on spandex, leopard print pants and was barefoot. "Whatta ya want, Gorgeous?" she asked, eyeing Adrian as if he was a tasty morsel she wanted to devour. Her eyes flicked to Eveleen with obvious disdain and annoyance.

"Eveleen is here to pick out burial clothes for her father."

"Well, ya can't take his leathers. I promised them to Rogue, who by the way, has a helluva piece in his pants, girlie! Yer outta yer mind, blowin' him off like you done!" She stepped back. "Go on and have a look. I don't know what the hell he's got worth sendin' him off to eternity in." She grabbed Adrian's arm as he started to move past her. "She can handle it. You stay out here and have a nice little chat with me, why doncha? You wanna beer?"

Eveleen went to the bedroom, pausing to glance back at Adrian who did not look comfortable at all with her father's amply endowed girlfriend. Quickly, she made her way across the trashed bedroom, ignoring the unmade, stained bed. The room smelled strongly, of sweat, sex and stale perfume. Eveleen fought the urge to gag as she tugged open the closet door and dug past Fidelity's array of flimsy attire in search of something fairly decent for her father to wear. She pulled out a soft denim shirt, a pair of faded jeans with ragged cuffs, a navy blue t-shirt from a dresser drawer, a pair of briefs that were fairly decent, dark socks and his cowboy boots. She carried these things out into the other room, where Fidelity was telling Adrian all about her implants, encouraging him to feel her breasts to see if he could tell they weren't real. He had declined to touch her so far and she was getting mad at him. "I've got what I want him dressed in," Eveleen said.

Fidelity jumped up and snatched the cowboy boots out of her hand. "Oh, no you don't, missy! These are expensive boots! You ain't buryin' his damn cowboy boots when I can pawn 'em and get some good money for 'em! He was behind on the rent and I don't want my ass out on the streets because he went and got hisself smeared all over the road!"

Eveleen abruptly shoved the clothes she was holding into Adrian's arms and then slapped Fidelity's face so hard the woman's head snapped around. "He is being buried in his boots!" she said angrily. "You need money, you know how to earn it yourself!" She snatched her father's boots back and then pushed past Adrian. Fidelity was cursing her, cursing them both as they went back downstairs.

Eveleen was stonily silent as he headed back toward the other side of town. Finally, he said, "I have no doubt she'll have the rent money before your father's buried."

"Oh, no doubt about that! None whatsoever."

"Was there anything else of your father's that you wanted before she pawns it all?"

Eveleen shook her head. "No. My dad's tattooing equipment is at Rampant Ink. Max won't let anyone steal that and pawn it. He can keep it to compensate him for what he's going to lose in revenue by not having my dad there. The only thing I really want is my Dad's ring. Do we have his effects at The Cedars?"

"They're downstairs in my office," he replied. "That's where they're usually kept until we turn them over to the next of kin."

"It's a silver ring—a Claddagh ring."

"The heart in the hands." She nodded. "You can have his things when we get back."

At the Cedars, she followed him down the cement stairs to the basement entrance. There was a wide ramp as well leading to this door, for wheeling caskets up and down because there was no freight elevator in the house. Andrew was not around. Gillian had gone for the day, as well. Adrian switched on the lights in his office and Eveleen followed him in.

He took some papers from his coat pocket and laid them on his desk. Eveleen looked around the room because she had never been downstairs before. It was a fairly large office. He had a nice mahogany desk and leather chair, a leather side chair, a leather couch against the far wall. There was a row of brass hooks on the wall, several four drawer wooden filing cabinets that appeared to be antiques. He had a brass lamp with a blue glass shade on one corner of his desk, his flat screen monitor on the other corner. There was a water cooler beside the couch. The painting on the wall over the couch was a Pre-Raphaelite repro of Ophelia floating dead in a stream. She was looking at it when he turned from the filing cabinet with a plastic bag in his hands. "Eveleen?" She turned and looked at him. He stood looking at her. She was beautiful in the same ethereal way as the Pre-Raphaelite models had been beautiful. She had their coloring—the red hair, the green eyes, the pale and delicate skin, faintly luminescent. He had noticed it before, but now he noticed it again, with John Everett Millais' *Ophelia* behind her. That he wanted her so badly surprised him. He had been attracted to her, yes, but now he could barely restrain himself from walking around his desk, pulling her into his arms and kissing her, touching her. He was reacting to her. "Your father's things," he said, laying the bag on the desk.

She looked from him to the bag and back. "I want to see him," she said.

"What?"

"I want to see my father. I want to kiss him goodbye before you change him into a cold, rigid parody of his real self."

"That's not possible."

154

"At the hospital he was behind glass. They wouldn't let me touch him."

"He's biohazardous waste..." he said and when she gasped, shocked, he paused. "I mean, a biohazard. He hasn't been treated yet."

"He's flesh and blood is what he is," she said. "And I want to see him. I want to touch his cheek and kiss him goodbye."

"Eve..."

"Adrian, when a loved one dies in the hospital, or a nursing home, they let all sorts of relatives traipse in and kiss the person goodbye, touch their hands, their faces! No one worries about germs! I'm here because my father chose her above me. We had an argument. I want to tell him that I'm sorry. I want to tell him goodbye. I want to kiss his undamaged cheek! Why can't I do that? Is it really such an unreasonable request? Or do I have to live with the fact that he's twelve feet down the damn corridor in an icebox, dead as a doornail and I can't even look at him! He's *my father*! He's the man who kissed my scraped knees and elbows, who tucked me in at night and kissed my cheek when I was a little girl. He's the man I loved all my life! He's never going to touch me, kiss me, hold me or tell me that he loves me ever again! Please! Let me say goodbye to him, Adrian. Please, before he's full of chemicals and Gillian paints his face like a mannequin's!"

He was silent for a long moment then he said, "You'll have to wear gloves and a mask. He'll be cold and he will not smell good." She nodded that she understood. "Give me a minute." He took off his jacket, hanging it on a brass hook then rolled up his shirt sleeves and left the office. Eveleen loved the olive color of his skin.

He returned a few minutes later, handing her a pair of pink gloves and a blue mask. He told her she could have thirty seconds and no longer. She was not to touch the sheet or move it in any way. She nodded again. He let her into the refrigeration room then stood in the tiled hallway hoping that no one would come downstairs. He heard some small wounded sound from Eveleen and felt a flash of anger. Had she moved the sheet, seen the tremendous damage his body had taken, trapped under his bike, under the Hummer as he was dragged down the street a hundred or so yards before tumbling free and being run over by the rear wheel of the vehicle?

She came out of the room. "Wait for me in my office," he said, going in to slide the body back into the unit and close the door. He discarded the used mask and gloves, discarded his gloves. She had not touched the sheet as it was just as he had left it. As he slipped out into the hall, he heard the door at the top of the stairs open, heard Madeline call his name. Quickly, he went to his office. Eveleen was sitting in the side chair, her head bent. He filled a paper cup at the cooler and handed it to her.

She was sipping water as Madeline came into the office. She stopped dead when she saw Eveleen there. "What is she doing down here? She is not authorized to be downstairs!"

"We just returned from picking up the burial clothes for her father. I retrieved his effects for her and when she saw them she felt faint. I've given her some water."

"You should have brought her upstairs, not down here."

"This is my office. If I need to meet with her, she can come down here and meet with me. She works here."

"But she's also a client of ours now and her father's body just happens to be down here! How do you think she feels about that?"

"Please don't argue," Eveleen said as she stood up, setting the cup on the desk. "Thank you for taking me to pick out a plot for my Dad, and to get his clothes. If it's all right with you, Madeline, I'd like to go to my apartment now."

"Yes, of course. It's been quiet upstairs. Go and lie down. It's been a difficult day for you." Eveleen picked up the plastic bag lying on the blotter and excused herself. She let herself out through the basement door. "Granted, the girl lost her father, but really, Adrian! Let's not try to break all the rules in one day!" She turned and walked out into the corridor. "Oh! I came down to tell you that Andrew and Beth are having another boy. He called with the ultrasound results while you were out."

"I forgot today was the day."

"Too bad it's not a girl, but, boys aren't so bad, at least not until they're grown." She left the office, went back upstairs.

Adrian dropped down into his chair with a deep sigh. He thought about Jack Glenrowan and the blonde woman. She was not someone that he would ever be interested in, but evidently Eveleen's father had been crazy enough about her to toss his own daughter out onto the street. Eveleen still worked at Rampant Ink on Saturdays and two nights a week, Tuesdays and Thursdays. It was Tuesday. He wondered if she would be going to work tonight. He had caught glimpses of her leaving for work at the tattoo and body piercing parlor. She usually wore tank tops, black jeans that rode low on her narrow hips and ankle boots. She kept her hair combed and controlled at The Cedars. When she worked at Rampant Ink, she let the natural curl rule, just scrunching her hair and letting it air dry. She wore make-up that gave her an edgy look, a studded leather wristband and other jewelry. He liked her like that too, wild, provocative, edgy, yet, when he had talked to her one evening as she was leaving and he'd just finished putting the hearse away, she had been the same sweet person she was when dressed nicely for work at The Cedars. He never heard her curse foully or speak disrespectfully.

He went upstairs. Madeline and Jim had closed up as there was nothing scheduled that night until a seven o'clock grief counseling session in a reception room. They would be upstairs relaxing, getting ready for dinner. He should be thinking about dinner himself. Instead, he walked through the first floor and let himself outdoors. He had no reason to be outside, but he went to his SUV and opened the door, pretending to be looking for something.

Eveleen came out of her apartment, clattering down the stairs in her short black boots. "You lose something?" she called to him as she stood beside her tan Toyota Corolla.

"One of the papers from the monument company," he replied.

"Do you want me to help you look for it before I go?"

"No, thanks. Maybe I just missed it and it's downstairs. I don't know. I'm not that worried about it yet."

She threw her black leather bag into her car, and then came around it, walking over to where he was standing. "I wanted to thank you for letting me say goodbye to my dad. I know you can get into a lot of trouble for that so I'll never tell anyone what you did for me." Her green eyes met his.

"They can't fire me," he said. "I own fifty-one percent of The Cedars." She looked surprised at that information. She'd been under the impression that the Mitchells owned the place and he worked for them. "Long story, keep it under your hat." She nodded. "Look, I still want to talk to you, but it can wait until after your father's funeral."

"Okay." She hoped he wasn't angry about what she had been writing on her legal pad, seeing as he was the majority owner of the funeral home. "I have to go. I probably shouldn't work tonight, but if I stay home I'll just keep crying, so I might as well work and keep busy." She took a step closer, boosted herself up onto her toes and kissed his cheek. "Thank you so much, for everything."

He nodded. He wanted to grab her and crush her to him, kiss her, take her upstairs and make love to her, but he didn't move. "See you in the morning," he said.

"Goodnight, Adrian."

He watched her walk to her car. He liked her sweet little ass, her long legs. He liked everything about her. She smelled like honeysuckle and a hint of orange. She'd most likely eaten an orange for dinner.

Wednesday, September 10th

In the morning, Adrian came downstairs early. Eveleen was making the coffee. He took down three mugs. She glanced around then took a card from her pocket and slipped it into his coat pocket. He was wearing his Onyx suit again with a deep, sapphire-blue shirt, black, amethyst and dark-blue striped tie. His black curls were still damp from the shower. Before he could ask her about the card in his pocket, she grabbed her mug and left the kitchen.

He slipped his hand into his pocket, took out the card and examined it. It was a Rampant Ink business card. Flipping it over, he saw that she had written on the backside in her bold, direct style, 'Good for 1 FREE ear piercing—diamond stud.' He smiled, shook his head then slid the card back into his pocket.

Madeline came downstairs early, fuming. "I cannot believe he's drunk at seven-thirty in the morning!" she said, outrage and frustration in her tone. "And what was that inappropriately dressed little trollop doing kissing you last evening out in the parking lot?" she demanded of Adrian who was sitting at the table reading the morning newspaper while he drank his coffee.

"Did I miss something? What little trollop would that be?"

"Our little resident red-haired tramp!" she flared as if he had rocks in his head.

"Do you mean Eveleen?"

"You know that's who I mean! Don't act stupid! Why was she kissing you last night?"

"She was just thanking me for helping her get through a bad day, make some tough decisions, help her get clothes for her father from the whore he had living with him, who obviously doesn't give a damn about his daughter. She was grateful and gave me a kiss on the cheek. There's nothing wrong with that." He went back to reading the paper thinking that Madeline would be thoroughly shocked if she knew the thoughts that were going through his mind in regards to Eveleen. He'd broken up with Virginia over a month ago, but he had considered calling her, maybe going over and persuading her to have sex so he could relieve the sexual tension he felt thinking about Eveleen. He'd managed to talk himself out of that foolishness. He really didn't want to renew that relationship for any reason.

"She looked like a trashy little tramp and I am appalled when she leaves this property looking like that, and returns late at night looking like she's just left the biker bars!"

"Eveleen is not a tramp. She dresses appropriately for her job at the tattoo parlor, like she dresses appropriately for her job here. Just leave her alone."

"Adrian, you're letting your standards slip! Even two months ago, you never would have considered hiring a girl like that! Now look at you, you're sitting there defending her!"

"I am sitting here telling you that there is nothing wrong with her work here. And it's none of our business if she goes to her part time job looking like whatever the hell she wants to look like! That's her business, not ours!" He stood up. "If you'll excuse me, I'd like to meet with her this morning. I might as well go and get that done now before anyone shows up and finds the whole place in a surly mood." He left the kitchen, walking down the hallway, past the display room where an assortment of caskets and accessories were displayed, the reception room where guests of the bereaved could have coffee, tea, water, and sometimes, small pastries or cookies if the bereaved wanted snacks made available. He passed the consultation room, Madeline's office, Jim's office, the door beneath the stairs leading down to his realm below. Eveleen's office was almost directly across from that door-way. Her door was open and he wondered how much of what Madeline had been shouting about in the kitchen she had heard in the otherwise quiet house.

She was filling out a form and did not look up as he entered. "Is now a bad time to talk?" he asked.

"Yes," she replied.

In her one word response, he had his answer. She had heard everything. He was annoyed with Madeline. "I embalmed your father last night. I'll be downstairs embalming Miss Sawyer this morning. We have the afternoon two to four o'clock wake for Mr. Tucker. Would you mind very much if we discussed your ideas over lunch rather than next week?"

"I have no appetite."

"Then how about tonight, after the seven to nine calling hours for Mr. Tucker?"

"It would probably be a waste of your time and mine as I'm not going to be staying here much longer."

"Eveleen, don't make any hasty decisions, especially right now when your emotions are already in turmoil."

"She hasn't wanted me here since I was hired. She obviously thinks you made a grave error in judgment. I'm not stupid. You made a mistake. I'll go."

"I did *not* make a mistake when we hired you," he said. "And I will see you at nine-thirty tonight in my office. No argument." He walked out of her office, crossing the hall and opening the door to the basement. He passed through it, closing it firmly behind him. Now he was angry. He would not allow Madeline to drive Eveleen out of The Cedars!

The day was raw, a cold rain falling, a stiff wind coming in off the bay. Summer was definitely over. It was only the second week of September, but already the beach weather was over. The trees were beginning to be transformed, subtle color flaring here and there in the leaves. Adrian ate lunch upstairs in his apartment, sharing some leftover chicken with Reynolds, his tabby cat. The cat had been a stray that had begun hanging out in the Serenity Garden beside the carriage house. It had liked to sun itself on the pavement, had rubbed itself against his legs when he was out washing the livery vehicles. He'd let it in last winter during a blizzard and the cat had made itself quite at home and had never asked to go outside again. It was comfortable in its new environment.

He caught glimpses of Eveleen during the afternoon wake, busy in her office making phone calls, typing on her computer. He left her alone. She worked eight to five with an hour off for lunch, so was gone during the evening wake hours. It was a little after nine-thirty by the time all the callers and the bereaved had departed for the night. The funeral service was at nine o'clock tomorrow with a ten o'clock church service followed by burial. It was still raining hard. Adrian locked the front door, went through the first floor turning out lights and securing the house for the night. He glanced out the rear door window and saw that there were lights on in the apartment above the garage. He was late for his meeting with Eveleen. Rapidly, he walked back through the darkened house, and let himself downstairs. Walking quickly along the corridor, he went to his office. It was empty, dark. He was tired, and his anger and frustration had been growing all day. Flicking on the light, he walked around his desk and reached for the phone. He would call her and tell her to get over here immediately! As he began punching in her cellphone number, he noticed the envelope propped against the base of the lamp. He set the phone down, grabbed the envelope, tore it open and removed the sheet of paper from inside. He scanned it quickly, then read it again more slowly. A muscle in his jaw twitched. It was a letter of resignation! "No, damn it! I will not accept this!"

He got up and left his office. Letting himself out through the basement door, he strode across the parking lot, taking the outside wooden stairs two at a time up to the apartment door. He pounded on the door with his fist, in which he clutched her letter. As it was still raining hard, he was getting wet, growing cold. "Eveleen! Open the damn door!" he shouted.

She finally opened the door. She had been in the shower. Her hair was wet, a towel draped around her shoulders. She had another towel wrapped around her torso. "What is the matter with you, banging on my door and shouting like this? It's late and I want to go to bed." He pushed past her into the living room of the apartment. It was sparsely furnished. There were very few personal effects in the room. She swung the door shut, lifted a corner of the towel that draped her shoulder to dry her ear, the side of her neck.

Adrian shook the letter at her. "I will not accept this!" She shrugged a slender shoulder. The towel slid off her shoulders. She still had it gripped in her right hand. "You can't just quit!"

"I already have since you're holdin' the letter!" she fired back. "You've clearly read it! What more do you want me to say?"

"I want you to be rational about this, is what I want you to do!" He could not stop himself from looking at her tattoo. He could see where it came from around the backside of her ear, down the side of her neck, how it ran across her shoulder and spiraled down her left arm, ran across her left clavicle then plunged down between her breasts from the hollow at the base of her throat. His eyes traveled to her thigh where the ivy spiraled down her right leg and ended at her ankle bone. "You can't let Madeline's attitude…"

"That's the problem, I can't take her attitude anymore! Who does she think I am? It's obvious *what* she thinks I am and she's wrong! She's dead wrong! My father raised me better than that! Maybe he liked girls like that, but he would have killed me if I'd ever behaved that way! Just because I have a tattoo and I worked with my dad in his and Uncle Max's shop doesn't mean anything more than the fact that I wanted to spend time with him, learn his trade and help him out. I wasn't sleepin' with his customers! I've only ever had two boyfriends in my entire life! Danny moved to California and I broke up with Rogue because he was treatin' me so bad! I'm *not* a tramp!" Tears shimmered in her eyes. "I just don't fit in here," she said.

He tore up her letter. "I'm not accepting this resignation. You need to bury your father first and foremost. Tomorrow is his wake, Friday his funeral. Take the weekend and think things through. Don't make any decisions until you've taken time to thoroughly think about your future."

"My future!" She stormed off through the apartment. "I most likely won't have one if Rogue gets a hold of me!" He followed her, found her in the bathroom. She'd dropped the towels, her back to him. She grabbed a thin, cotton, calf-length gown and pulled it on over her head. His eyes were on the ivy girdling her narrow hips, ivy leaves tattooed on the enticing swell of her buttocks on either side of her lower back. The vine was truly exquisite. She turned around, saw him in the doorway and glowered at him. "You can go now! I've nothin' more to say to you that you'd care to hear!" She moved to brush past him but he grabbed her by the wrist, spun her around and pushed her up against the hallway wall. She went rigid in his grasp, throwing her free arm up to protect her face—the reaction of a girl who expected a physical blow to follow such a violent action. He grabbed that wrist as well and pinned both her arms over her head. She was breathing hard and looked frightened.

"This is primarily my business. I choose the people I want to work for me, and I want you here. You're exceptionally kind and compassionate with the bereaved when they come in. Madeline can be a little abrupt at times. Jim is drinking far more than he should and I don't need him offending people. I need you here. I can't be both upstairs and downstairs. If Madeline and I can't get Jim to agree to rehab for his drinking problem, to get counseling for his gambling addiction, then I'm going to have to hire an embalmer and another driver and take over his job upstairs. I don't want to have to do that just yet! There's a lot going on around here that you may not be aware of. I have a problem with Andrew, too. He seems to have developed this fascination with your friend Hollyce. He's a married man! His wife is expecting their second child in six months! He's on the verge of destroying his marriage and his life!"

"Are you blamin' me for what she's done?" she demanded hotly, her fear having dissolved once she'd realized he was not going to hit her.

"No, of course not! I'm just letting you know why I'm so damned pissed off right now. I can't deal with you quitting like this when I already have a lot of other things on my plate to worry about!"

Her eyes met his. He was angry. "Will you please let go of my wrists. You're hurting me." He released her immediately. "Thank you." She laid her right hand flat against his chest. His shirt was damp from the rain that he had run through. His black curls were dripping onto his shoulders. She could hear the rain coming down in torrents outside. "Adrian, would you like a cup of coffee before you go back to the house?"

He wanted more than a cup of coffee. He wanted her, naked beneath him on her bed. "I can't stay here," he muttered, pushing away from the wall, walking back to the living room. He was humiliated by his physical reaction to being so close to her. She had to have been aware of his hardness pressing into her belly. "Just promise me that you'll be at work tomorrow morning as usual," he said, his back to her as he stood near the door.

"All right, I'll be there, but I can't promise you that I'll be there much longer."

"We'll talk about this again on Monday." He wrenched open the door, letting himself out. Eveleen walked to the door, locked it then switched off the interior light, watching him hurry across the pavement to the rear door of the mansion in the slanting, driving rain. He turned and looked back at the apartment. She let the lace curtain fall back across the window, backed away, shaken by the realization that he wanted her. She hadn't been wrong about that, had she? She'd thought he was going to kiss her in the hallway when he'd had her pinned against the wall, and she realized now that she would not have pushed him away. She would have grabbed the front of his shirt and pulled him even closer. She would have kissed him the way that she had dreamed about kissing him since she'd started working here. "Oh, this is so wrong with my dad lying across the way," she muttered as she went to her bedroom and threw herself into bed, pulling the covers up because now she felt cold with the heat of his body no longer radiating against hers. She switched off the bedside lamp and lay in the dark listening to the rain, a few hot tears seeping from the corners of her eyes. "I don't know what to do, Dad. I can't afford this funeral for you. I'm goin' to owe The Cedars a fortune. I already owe Adrian for your nice bay view plot and your marker. I'll be payin' this off for half my remainin' lifetime!" She sat up, twisted around, punching her pillows. "Damn it! I can't quit this job! I need the money!" She fell back onto her pillows with a sob. "Madeline hates me! She doesn't even know me! How can she be so mean and cruel when I've never done anythin' to deserve that kind of attitude from her?" It was a long time before she finally fell asleep.

On the third floor of the mansion, Adrian stood looking out of his bedroom window toward the carriage house, at the dark apartment. He had come so close to kissing her, to telling her how much he wanted her! But that was not the way to handle this crisis. He didn't want her to feel obligated to stay because of his feelings for her. She probably didn't even care about him. He'd frightened her, grabbing her like he had, spinning her around and pinning her against the wall like that. That former boyfriend of hers, he must have beaten her, treated her badly because there had been genuine fear in her reaction, not anger. "I handled that all wrong," he said aloud. Reynolds meowed and wound between his ankles. He sighed, scooped up the cat and lay down in his chilly bed. Reynolds licked his bristly jaw then settled down against the pillow beside him. Adrian pulled the covers up, but he could not sleep. All the more professional ways he could have handled this situation with Eveleen were running through his head. She was grieving. She was upset with Madeline. She was probably over-whelmed by the expense of the funeral, but he would pay for the whole thing if he had to. He knew she had nothing. Tomorrow, he'd have to treat her with kid gloves. Her father was being waked in the evening. She shouldn't even be working. Most businesses offered bereavement leave. He should have asked her if she wanted to take a few days off. "I just don't think sometimes!" he said, frustrated and upset with himself. It was a long time before sleep finally claimed him.

Thursday, September 11th

At seven-thirty, Adrian made the coffee since Eveleen had not shown up yet. Andrew had arrived at twenty past seven looking as if he'd just rolled out of bed. Adrian wondered whose bed he'd been in, but held his tongue. Andrew's personal life was none of his business. Madeline came down at quarter of eight, frowning. "Where's Eveleen?"

"She probably had a bad night. Maybe she forgot to set her alarm clock? Her father's being waked this evening. We should have given her today and tomorrow off."

Madeline waved her hand, brushing aside that suggestion. "If she'd wanted the time off she would have asked." She prepared her coffee. "Looks like I'll have to open the door this morning," she remarked, sounding put out about it as she walked out into the hallway. The rear door opened and Eveleen came in. It was still raining. She had trouble closing her umbrella. "Well, look who the cat dragged in!"

"I'm sorry! I forgot to set my alarm last night!" She came hurrying down the hallway, glancing into the kitchen. "Thanks for makin' the coffee. I'll open." Her Irish was still very noticeable this morning, making Adrian wonder if she was still angry and upset.

He prepared her coffee and brought it to her office. She had unlocked the front doors and was booting up her computer. "You know, you can take today and tomorrow off for bereavement leave."

She shook her head. "I'd rather be here because this is where my dad is," she replied. She noticed he had two mugs. He set one on her blotter. "Thanks."

Madeline stuck her head in. "Eveleen, we have the Tucker funeral this morning. Would you make an urn of coffee?"

Eveleen took a sip of her own coffee then got up and came around her desk. Adrian was still standing there looking at her. "I'd be drivin' myself mad if I wasn't here stayin' busy."

"You still sound so Irish," he commented.

"Oh, sorry, I hadn't noticed." He walked with her as he was heading back to the kitchen. Gillian had arrived as he'd left the kitchen to bring Eveleen her coffee. She had brought in donuts from Smithies Donut Shop.

"Donuts in the kitchen if you want one," he said as she went into the reception room to grab the kettle they used to fill the urn as it was too heavy for her to lug from the kitchen full of water.

He hated rainy funeral days. After finishing his coffee, he and Andrew went out to move the cars into position. Buck and Fred were just arriving. "You guys are late!" Adrian remarked.

"Yeah, big accident on the main road, we had to detour!" Fred replied.

"We stopped and handed out business cards, tucked a few in the pockets of the deceased for good measure," Buck said, earning him a black look from Adrian, a chuckle from Andrew. "Jeez! Just kidding! Cars were burning. We couldn't even get close!"

"Great." Adrian did not like working with burn victims.

Madeline had welcomed the family and some relatives by the time they came back inside, hanging their black knee-length rain coats on hooks in the back hall. Adrian heard Eveleen talking to someone and glanced into her office as he passed. It was Max Leary. He seemed to be arguing with her, trying to keep his voice down. Adrian reached in, drew her door shut and continued to the foyer where Madeline stood stony-faced. "The riff raff snuck in with the mourners. He caused quite a ripple among them in his fine attire," she murmured.

"Look," Adrian said, "lighten up on her. She dresses appropriately, she does her job well. Just leave her alone and let her be."

"What are you talking about?" she demanded, causing a few heads to turn.

"She heard you making derogatory comments about her yesterday and left me a letter of resignation on my desk last night."

"Oh, happy day!" The look he gave her made her gasp. "Oh, Adrian, don't tell me you have a soft spot for that little hussy! She's been around the block more than a few times, and besides, she's much too young for you! You can't associate with someone like her, a man in your position in the community! What would people say? Why, we'd lose business faster than you could blink an eye! People would lose all respect for The Cedars!"

"And that wouldn't happen with your husband lurching a-round in a drunken stupor, slurring his words on the phone, reeking of alcohol in the consultation room?" His counter jab had struck true. Her face blanched, then color flared high across her cheek-bones and her eyes glittered. "Leave her alone!" he said firmly. "She's not a disgrace to The Cedars, but your husband is rapidly becoming one."

"I won't stand here and take this from you!" she huffed.

"Well, you'd better, because if you storm off and leave me standing here alone I'll suspend you for three days."

"You don't have the authority to do that!" she snapped.

"Unfortunately for you, I *do* have the authority," he replied.

"This is James' and my business!"

"Not anymore. I've been the majority shareholder for the past three months. You and I own this business."

"What do you mean? How can that be?" she cried.

"Ask your husband, but not right now. You stay put." He walked to the door of the reposing room and glanced in. Every-thing appeared to be under control. A few more mourners arrived and he greeted them as Madeline stood glaring at him. He walked back over to where she was standing at the foot of the grand staircase. "Why don't you go upstairs for a while? I'll ring the buzzer when we're ready to load the casket. Eveleen can help me down here."

"Don't be ridiculous! She's a receptionist, not a funeral director!"

"Well, she's a lot more pleasant to look at than you are at the moment."

"I do not like you speaking to me this way! What has gotten into you?"

"Dissension in the ranks pisses me off!" he hissed. "If you can't say anything nice about her, then keep your damn mouth shut! I shouldn't have to tell you this!"

Max came out of Eveleen's office scowling. He grunted as he passed by them then let himself out, closing the door rather firmly behind him. "Well, he's not a happy camper," Madeline commented.

Adrian went to Eveleen's doorway. "Everything all right?" She had been sitting with her elbows on her desk, head in her hands, but looked up at the sound of his voice.

"No," she replied, sounding distressed.

"What's wrong?"

"Rogue is back in Somerset. He's already heard about my dad. He was at the shop asking for me. Max didn't tell him I was working here. He'll find out though. There are a lot of loose lips in this town. I'm sorry, Adrian."

"Will he come roaring over here on his chopper and assault you, make a scene? Or will he try to start something with you to-night at the wake?"

"I don't know." She sounded distraught, miserable.

"I have a few contacts in the police department. We had some trouble with Big Bear Brown's wake and funeral last year. Let me give them a heads up that there may be trouble tonight."

"Adrian, come in for a minute and close the door." He glanced down the hall at Madeline who was watching him through narrowed eyes. He signaled that he would be just a minute, then stepped into the office and closed the door. "I need to tell you that Dad was a member of the Pirates Club. They're rivals with the Snakes and Adders, bad blood between the two clubs. Max just told me that Dad and Fat Joe had a heated argument and exchanged a few blows the night Dad died. The police are looking into things to see if anyone connected to the Snakes and Adders has a red Hummer, or knows someone who does. They may have been lying in wait for Dad when he left the bar and headed home." He was looking at her, his expression neutral. She looked away. "Yeah, I know. My life is chaos on all levels."

"Not all," he replied. Her eyes came back to meet his. "I'll request a subtle police presence tonight. We'll have an officer in the kitchen in case trouble arrives in the form of one former boy-friend with a short-term memory problem. You're no longer his."

"No, I'm not," she confirmed. "But you're right. He still thinks I am."

"You'll be all right."

"I should have had him waked and buried elsewhere."

"We survived Big Bear's wake and funeral. We'll get through this one for Jack Glenrowan."

It was almost one o'clock when they returned from the Tucker funeral. Buck, Fred and Andrew had gotten take-out. Adrian had decided that he was eating in his apartment. He hung his raincoat up, smoothed back his black hair then walked down the hallway. Madeline was eating a sandwich at her desk, reading a magazine. She just glanced at him as he walked by. He stopped in Eveleen's office. She was staring out the window at the side yard. "Have you eaten?" he asked. She shook her head. "I make a mean grilled cheese and tomato sandwich, if you'd like to come upstairs." She did not reply. "You need to eat something."

"I can make some soup later."

"How about some tomato soup and a tuna sandwich?" he suggested.

She sighed. "You won't take no for an answer, will you?" She spun around in her chair and he saw that she had been crying. "All right, maybe it'll take my mind off things."

"Reynolds will distract you."

"You have a cook?"

"No, I have a cat."

They walked back down the hallway. Madeline did not even look their way, but he didn't fail to notice the set of her jaw. They took the elevator up to the third floor. Although he'd been right in her face last night, he was nervous being alone in the small elevator with her as it slowly made its way to the third floor. They exited into a hallway in his apartment. "Bedrooms and bathrooms are back that way, living room, dining room, kitchen and study are this way." He led her toward the front of the apartment, showing her the layout. It was very spacious, definitely masculine décor with black leather furniture, rich dark woods, a big screen TV in the living room, a bar. The kitchen had stainless steel appliances with cherry cabinets, a black and white tile floor, black granite countertops. "You like the color black," she observed.

"I guess so. I tend to wear black a lot." She gave him a sideways glance and smiled. "You never see a funeral director in a bright blue suit with a bubblegum pink shirt and a shiny purple tie."

"No, you never do." Reynolds had woken up and come trotting down the hallway into the kitchen. He skidded to a stop when he saw Eveleen.

"Hey, there! You must be Reynolds." She crouched down, holding out her hand toward the cat. He looked up at Adrian, then sauntered to Eveleen and rubbed his cheek against her fingertips. She scratched under his chin, behind and in front of his ears. He began to purr. "How'd you come up with a name like that for a cat?" she asked.

"He likes to play with small balls of crumpled up Reynolds aluminum wrap," he replied as he went to the pantry behind where the elevator was on the other side in the hall. He came back out with a can of tomato soup and a can of tuna fish. "Which would you like to prepare?"

"I'll make the sandwiches. Do you have celery?"

"Look in the crisper in the fridge. It should still be good. I had a salad this past weekend."

While she got out the celery, he opened and drained the tuna fish, Reynolds weaving around his ankle. "Stop it," she scolded him. "You're getting fur all over his pant legs!"

"I have a lint roller. No pet owner should be without a half dozen of them scattered around their home and office." He handed her the glass cutting board and a knife.

"You're pretty trusting, inviting a girl you hardly know up to your apartment and handing her a big knife," she commented as she snapped off two stalks of celery and then rinsed them under the faucet. His kitchen had all the modern amenities. She liked it. There was plenty of room for two people to do prep work and cook, unlike her former tiny studio apartment where she'd had a two burner hot plate, a small microwave oven, a toaster oven, a tiny single basin sink and a mini fridge. This was luxurious in comparison! "Bowl?"

He indicated a cabinet and she took down a terra cotta-colored bowl to mix the tuna, celery and mayonnaise in. She found the mayo in the fridge on her own. Adrian was stirring the soup. "Bread is in the second drawer over there. Whole wheat or multi-grain."

"Do you have a preference?"

"No, whatever."

"Whole wheat it is then." She pulled open cabinets until she found two luncheon size ceramic plates and two matching ceramic bowls. Opening drawers, she found his stash of flatware and set two places at the granite-topped counter using placemats that were neatly stacked at one end and grabbing paper napkins from a basket as well. "What would you like to drink?" she asked.

"Milk." She grinned. "What?"

"Nothin'! I like milk, too. You just don't see too many men macho enough to drink milk in front of a girl." She had seen glasses in one of the cabinets and got out two, poured the milk, then made the sandwiches. He filled the bowls with soup. "Here you go," she said, bending to place a small saucer with a table-spoon of plain tuna on it on the floor for Reynolds. "Enough to satisfy your love of fish, but not enough to give you mercury poisoning."

Adrian liked that she cared enough not to poison his cat. They sat down on tall stools at the counter. She'd cut the sand-wiches on the diagonal. His mind flashed back to his grandmother cutting his sandwiches that way when he'd been with her during the summer. He'd had one or two weeks with her before she sent him off to camp for six weeks, then he was packed up and sent back to school. Eveleen was still looking around, taking in everything. He realized that she was trying to get a feel for the kind of man he was. "You don't find this creepy at all?" he asked.

"Creepy? Have you got skeletons in the closets you haven't shown me yet?" she asked, her amazing green eyes meeting his.

"No, just a lot of dark-colored suits."

"No hooded grim reaper robe? No big, bloodstained scythe leanin' in the corner?"

"Uh, no, nothing like that." He set his spoon down. "But that reminds me. I want to show you something." He shrugged out of his jacket, draping it over the next stool, then loosened and removed his tie. Next, he began unbuttoning his shirt. Her spoon had frozen halfway to her mouth. "Just the shirt and t-shirt are coming off. Nothing else, I promise. I can't show you unless I half undress."

"Uh, okay." She ate the spoonful of soup as he pulled his arms out of his shirt sleeves. Her eyes went to his right arm and he saw them widen. She set her spoon down. He tugged his t-shirt out of his waistband, then off over his head. "Oh, my God!" she cried. He had a grim reaper tattoo! It started high on his right shoulder, the reaper's blade curving back behind his shoulder. It was full figure and ended just above his elbow. It was well-done. It was lyrical. It was exquisitely rendered. She'd instantly recognized the artwork as her father's and tears filled her eyes. "When did he do this?" she asked, barely able to speak. She hesitated then touched the tattoo, stroking his arm as if she could draw her father's essence from his handiwork on Adrian's upper right arm.

"I was twenty-two, had just graduated from college. A bunch of us went out drinking. We all decided to get tattoos to celebrate. Having studied to be a mortician and funeral director, I decided I wanted a grim reaper. We ended up at Rampant Ink because we were told the best tattoo artist in the area worked there, a guy named Jack. I thought he'd start it that night but he'd shaken his head, told me to sober up first then come back if I still wanted a reaper. Meanwhile, he'd sketch a few designs for me to look at, if I came back. I sobered up and went back a week later. He had three designs for me to consider. The first one was just the hooded skull head and draped shoulders with the blade behind, showing at both sides. The second sketch was half figure, holding a scythe in one hand, an hourglass in the other. The third drawing was this one. It was simpler than this. After I chose it he nodded, started working on it, and added embellishments. He designed the reaper as poised to swing the blade. He added the hourglass on the chain around the waist. He added the little red-haired angel peeking out from inside the robe." Eveleen gasped. She hadn't noticed that, but now that he had pointed it out she saw it, and was stunned to see the angel looked like she had looked when she was a child. Tears started rolling down her cheeks. "Did he put you on my arm?" he asked quietly. She looked at him and nodded. "She has her little, pale hand on his sandaled, bony foot as if she wants to stop him from taking that step forward and harvesting another soul." She slid off the stool and began pacing the kitchen.

"How old are you?" she asked.

"I'll be thirty next month."

"So, it was like eight years ago that he did this?"

"Yes."

"That was the year before he gave me the ivy tattoo." She brushed at tears on her face. "Oh, my God. I can't believe you of all people have one of my Dad's tattoos! You seem so…so conservative!"

"You've only seen me at work. I'm just more mature than I was at twenty-two. I don't think I'd run out and get another tattoo any time soon." She wiped tears off her face with a napkin.

178

"But I might consider a diamond ear stud." Her eyes met his. "But only if someone I trust does the piercing."

"Do you trust me?" she asked.

"I believe I trust you enough to jab a hole through my ear lobe with a sharp implement."

She came back around to stand just behind him on the right side. He sat still, let her trace the design with her fingertip. When, upon closer scrutiny, she discovered that the small angel was wrapped in ivy she gasped again. Had he already been planning her tattoo a year in advance? Had he worked it into this man's design as a trial, to test his ability to draw and color ivy in ink? Without thinking she leaned forward and pressed her lips against the reaper's bony face. "Oh, Dad! I love you and I miss you so much!" she whispered. She raised her head and stepped back. "Thank you for showing this to me," she said.

"Sit down now and finish your lunch." He got up, grabbed his t-shirt, turning it right side out. He noticed that she was watching him as he redressed. "Why'd he wrap you in ivy?" he asked.

She chewed and swallowed the bite of sandwich she had in her mouth. "Ivy is eternal. You can cut it back, cut it down and it regenerates. It binds. It's for binding, bonding. It's for fidelity." He made a face. "No, not that horrible woman!"

"I know what you meant, but it reminded me of her." He tucked his shirt in. She noticed he wore tartan boxers. She liked that he did. She thought boxers were far sexier than the terrible, supposedly sexy, crotch slings Rogue wore to impress the ladies. They had never impressed her.

She finished her soup, then rinsed the dishes at the sink and loaded them into the dishwasher. She would kill for a dishwasher! They were so convenient, although sometimes washing dishes could be fun, if you had someone you liked helping. "You have a lot of books in your study," she said as they headed back to the elevator.

"I like to read."

"So do I. What sort of books do you like?"

"Mystery, historical books, books about antiques and architecture. I also read some contemporary fiction, classics." She nodded. "What about you?"

"I like mysteries and historical fiction. I like books about odd historical subjects, too, like the molasses flood in Boston, and the leather man in Connecticut."

"I heard about the leather man when I was at school in Fairfield, Connecticut—a tramp dressed all in handmade, heavy leather clothing who made this huge circuit year after year through New York state and Connecticut. He was so predictable you could practically set you watch by his appearances."

"Yes! You do know about him then!" She was surprised and pleased.

"You have a book about him?" She nodded. "Can I borrow it?"

"Yes, of course." They exited into the rear hall. "Thank you for lunch, Adrian. That was nice of you to distract me like this."

"No problem. I have work to do downstairs. I'll see you later for your father's wake. We'll be bringing him up in a few hours." She nodded. "I'll let you know."

"Oh, I'm sure I'll hear you truckin' him past my door." They would be bringing him through the side entrance then down the hall to the front left reposing room.

Max, Stitch, Trace, Hollyce and Pitch, all from Rampant Ink, came to collect Eveleen at four-thirty. "We brought pizza and beer," Stitch said. "Jack wouldn't want us eating a fancy sit down dinner before his wake."

They went across to the apartment. Madeline came out of her office, a look of disdain on her face. Andrew and Adrian were setting out the guest book and memorial cards. On an easel, just inside to the right of the vestibule door, was a display of some of Jack's best tattoo work. Evidently, he had taken color photographs of almost all of his best work. Adrian couldn't remember if Jack had photographed his arm or not. If he'd been honest with Eveleen, he'd have confessed that he'd been pretty drunk for every tattoo session. It'd helped ease the pain, and by the time Jack was done for the evening Adrian had been stabbed and inked sober enough to drive himself safely home to his apartment. He'd been working as an embalmer for Forest & Lake Funeral Home back then. He'd joined The Cedars when he was twenty-five. Neither Madeline nor James knew about his tattoo. He wore t-shirts that came to his elbows in the summer. He always wore long-sleeved shirts for work, no matter how hot it was. Sometimes, if it was scorching hot out, he substituted a tank top jersey for the t shirt. If he was bare-chested in his apartment and heard someone at the door or the elevator coming up he put on a long-sleeved natural cotton shirt that he kept lying around for that purpose. "Well, that tells you what kind of a night we're in for," she said acidly.

"There won't be any trouble," Adrian said. "Officer Taylor will be in the kitchen and there'll be an unmarked car cruising nearby."

"Boozed up bikers and drugged-out, tattooed idiots! This is outrageous!" She marched upstairs to prepare hers and Jim's dinner.

Adrian and Andrew went to the kitchen. Buck was getting Chinese take-out. They got out paper plates and plastic utensils, paper napkins. Buck arrived and they filled their plates at the counter, sat down and dug in. Andrew had a six pack in his car that he brought in. Adrian had one, Buck and Andrew each had two then split the last one. Fred didn't drink, he just had a Coke. Adrian didn't approve of drinking on the job, but it was going to be an interesting night, to say the least.

Eveleen came back at six-thirty with her co-workers. She had changed into a t-shirt style black dress, black tights, black ankle boots. All the black made her naturally pale skin look ghostly white. The tattoo on her left arm was visible, the ivy vine circling it to her wrist. She had her father's Claddagh ring around her neck on a silver chain, a black leather, silver-studded wrist band around her right wrist. Stitch, Trace and Pitch all had a combination of leather and denim on. Hollyce had selected a curve-hugging black leather mini dress, thigh high black stockings, stiletto-heeled black boots that reached her knees. She had her hair loose and wild, wore a black leather, silver-studded dog collar, silver bangles and silver dangling earrings. Adrian saw both Buck and Fred swallow hard when they saw Hollyce. Andrew grinned, his eyes aglow. Adrian ground his teeth and kept his mouth shut.

"You ready for this?" he asked Eveleen, who was standing in the doorway of the reposing room looking toward her father in his casket. Gillian had performed a miracle on his face, hands, and his upper body, stuffing him with cotton batting. Adrian had stitched him back together afterwards. He and Gillian had dressed Glenrowan then Gillian had applied the make-up, arranged the hair. He looked peaceful, no trace of the trauma he had suffered visible to the casual viewer. The lower half of the man was a nightmare of shattered bone and torn flesh. Adrian had done his best to preserve him. The room was cooler than normal and he saw Eveleen shiver and rub her arms. "Sorry it has to be so damn cold in there."

"I understand. It's just for a couple of hours." She turned her head and looked at him. "Gilly did a great job. He looks better than he did in real life." She gave him a rueful smile. "He always looked a little bit scruffy."

"Hard to give a corpse that five o'clock shadow look."

She touched his arm. "Thank you, Adrian, for all you've done for my Dad and me."

Motorcycles roared into the yard. "Here we go," he said. She nodded and went to stand with her friends near the casket to greet the callers. Adrian thought she looked pretty tonight, her hair loose and scrunched into somewhat wild curls, a bit of black mascara brushed onto her copper lashes, a little smoky eye liner and shadow. She had not colored her lips. They were her usual pale coral color. She looked young among her co-workers and he realized that she was young. He was seven years older than her. What had he been thinking? She needed someone closer to her own age, not him. He turned away, walking across the hall to greet the rowdy bunch of bikers who had just come through the front door.

"Swank place you got here, man!"

"I think it's creepy! Is Norman Bates' mother upstairs or tied up in the basement with the rest of the stiffs?" asked a girl with scarlet hair and purple eyes that had to be tinted contact lenses. She was wearing a skin tight, black leather top and bottom, the top leaving not much to the imagination. If she sat down, well, Adrian hoped she had something on underneath that skirt or else there would be an orgy going on in the reposing room in no time.

"Holy shit," Buck muttered. "I feel like I'm standing in the middle of the making of a porno movie! Man! This is awesome!"

"Wipe your chin and be quiet," Adrian hissed as more of the same came through the doors, flooding into the hall, pushing their way into the reposing room. It was getting loud.

Madeline came halfway down the stairs, scowling. "Is that cop here?" she hissed.

"Yes, he's in the kitchen eating leftover Chinese food."

"They're parking their damned bikes all over the lawn!"

"It's only for two hours."

"I'm going upstairs to see if Jim has any whisky left. I need a stiff drink!" She turned and went back up the stairs.

Fred made a soft buck-buck sound to indicate he thought she was a big chicken. Adrian gave him a half smirk to say he agreed. Andrew was standing in the doorway of the reposing room talking to Hollyce. He led her down the hallway, toward the bathroom. Adrian frowned. She ought to be able to find the bathroom on her own. There were signs and arrows.

The front door banged open and another raucous contingent spilled in. This lot reeked of alcohol and pot, and included a clearly drunk, or high, Fidelity in a black dress that looked painted onto her body it was so tight. She was weeping and wailing like a grieving soap opera widow, her mascara running down her cheeks in rivulets as her entourage led her into the reposing room. It was getting even louder and rowdier now. Adrian adjusted his tie. He could not imagine that Eveleen was thrilled about the show Fidelity was putting on. He was surprised that she hadn't thrown herself across the casket yet. He wanted to go in there and haul her out, throw her out the door on her ass, but he continued to stand stoically near the door knowing it was not his place to interfere. Buck and Fred, he noticed, had moved further down the hall.

At seven-fifty, the front door was thrown open and three young men in black leather entered. The one in the middle had long, dirty-blonde hair, a soul patch on his chin. He was handsome, had a certain dangerous glamor about him. Adrian knew instantly that this young man was Rogue, Eveleen's former boyfriend, the one who was not so willing to acknowledge that their relationship was over. "Where's my goddam little redheaded bitch!" he said loudly. "Eveleen!" He glanced at Adrian and sneered, "Nice suit, Mr. Spiffy." Adrian managed to keep a neutral facial expression, although he was already seething inside.

"You look almost as stiff as the stiffs," one of Rogue's companions said, flipping Adrian's tie outside his coat as he passed by him. Adrian calmly tucked his tie back inside his coat.

Rogue strode into the reposing room, rudely shoving people aside. He called to Eveleen again, using an even more foul word in reference to her. His companions followed and within moments all hell broke loose in the room with people yelling and shouting. Adrian heard Eveleen cry out, Max's gruff voice cursing and shouting. Furniture began falling as the sound of a scuffle broke out. "Damn it!" Adrian said. He looked down the hallway and saw no one. Buck and Fred had vanished. "Hey!" he shouted, hoping to get the officer's attention. Surely he had to have heard that something was going on that needed police intervention.

As Adrian started toward the viewing room, Rogue came out, dragging Eveleen, in a headlock, beside him. "She don't want to be with her dead daddy no more tonight. She wants a real live man with a real live..." Adrian had taken in the whole scene in a glance. Eveleen was practically blue, he had her in such a tight headlock. Her eyes were dark from lack of oxygen. Without pausing to think about it, he threw a solid right that connected with Rogue's nose with a sickening crack. A gusher of blood shot out of the man's broken nose. He immediately dropped Eveleen, who fell on the floor, gasping for breath. Max, Stitch and Trace came shoving through the throng of onlookers. Trace grabbed Eveleen up off the floor and practically threw her into Adrian's arms.

"Get her the hell out of here!" he shouted before turning to defend himself against one of Rogue's friends.

Adrian scooped Eveleen up, throwing her over his shoulder. Quickly, he strode down the hallway. Officer Taylor was just coming from the kitchen. "A little late, aren't you?" Adrian snapped.

"I called for back-up. Do you think I'm crazy? One cop against hundreds of drunk or high bikers? They'd kill me in a heartbeat!"

There was shouting and screaming from up front. "I'm taking her upstairs where she'll be safe."

He noticed Andrew peeking out from around the display room door. He didn't stop to be outraged that Andrew had taken Hollyce in there. He wrenched open the door to the elevator, shoved the brass gate open, got in, slammed the door shut, turned the deadbolt so no one could summon the elevator and follow, crashed the gate shut and hit the button for the third floor. Behind his back Eveleen was gasping, retching and then vomiting down his back.

Upstairs, he carried her to his bedroom, not bothering to switch on the lights. He veered into the bathroom, flicking on that light and setting her down. Because he was a man and lived alone, the toilet seat was up. She fell onto her knees and vomited the rest of her dinner into the bowl. Reynolds came into the room and stopped, looking from her to Adrian. "Can you breathe?" he asked her. She nodded. She was still having trouble but her color was improving. She was white again, with high color in her cheeks. "I have to go back downstairs," he said, stripping off his coat that was covered down the back with partially digested pizza. He kicked off his black shoes, unbuttoned his shirt, pulled off his cufflinks and threw them onto the counter alongside the sink. Eveleen scuttled backwards, after flushing the toilet, to sit against the wall. She was watching him warily, her eyes teary. He removed his shirt, his t-shirt, then unfastened his pants and pulled them off as the back of the legs had been spattered with vomit. He was only in Black Watch tartan boxers and black socks when he went into his darkened bedroom. A dim light came on. From where she was sitting, she saw him pull on a black t-shirt, black jeans and black biker boots. In a matter of moments, he had transformed himself into one of the bikers downstairs, his black curls tousled. He came to the bathroom doorway. "You stay put. Do *not* leave this apartment. Do you hear me?" She nodded. "Answer me!"

"I won't go anywhere," she said, her voice raspy.

"Good girl. I'll be back. I've got a mess to clean up downstairs."

"Adrian!" she cried.

"What?"

"Am I bleedin'?"

"No, that's Rogue's blood in your hair. I smashed his damn nose!"

"Can I wash my hair?"

"Do whatever you want. Just don't leave, and don't let anyone in!" He vanished. The black t-shirt was snug on him and the sleeves rode high enough to reveal his tattoo, a good portion of it. She'd glimpsed the little red-haired angel with her hand on the sandaled foot of the reaper.

She glanced at Reynolds. The cat had sat down in front of the sink near Adrian's discarded clothes. "I'm a mess," she muttered, getting herself up onto her feet. She tugged her stained dress off over her head, kicked off her boots, peeled off her tights, panties and unfastened her bra. She stepped into the shower stall, closed the door, turned on the water. At first the water was cold and she stood with her back to the spray, hugging herself, but when it got warmer she turned and tilted her face up into the water, letting it wash over her. Then she shampooed her hair with his shampoo. This was the source of his evergreen scent, his shampoo and soap. She liked it, scrubbed herself thoroughly, as if Rogue had left a stain on her skin from head to toe. When her fingers began to pucker, she turned off the water, grabbed a fluffy gray towel and dried herself.

She put her panties and bra back on, then grabbed his discarded eggplant-purple shirt and pulled it on, buttoning it. The tails, front and back, covered her thighs about halfway to her knees. She balled her dress up and threw it in the sink. Her leather wrist band was on the counter with his cufflinks. She threw his t-shirt into the hamper, grabbed his suit coat and used a damp wash cloth to wipe her vomit off of it. She did the same with his pants then went out into his bedroom, to the closet to find some hangers. He owned a lot of suits, she saw. He had expensive clothes. No wonder he always looked so good! She hung the sponged suit in the bathroom from a towel bar, then rinsed out her dress in the sink and threw it over the shower stall. His suit would have to go to the cleaners first thing tomorrow morning.

She left the bathroom, following Reynolds to the kitchen. Rummaging around, she found a box of tea bags, put the stainless kettle on to boil. She found a can of cat food, dumped it onto a plastic plate for the cat because it seemed hungry. She gave Reynolds fresh water, then made her cup of tea and sat at the counter sipping it. Her stomach rumbled. She had lost her dinner and now felt queasy. She got up and made herself some wheat toast, buttered them and ate them.

After washing the few dishes she'd used she went out into the living room, curled up on the black leather couch, pulling a midnight blue, burgundy and gold throw over herself. Reynolds came and snuggled against her. Warm, safe and cozy, she closed her eyes wearily and drifted off to sleep.

Adrian rubbed his jaw. He had been struck a couple of times but there'd been no serious damage done. He might have a bruise along the ridge of his jaw in the morning though, and grimaced at that thought. Rogue had managed to get away but the police were looking for him for assault and battery charges and causing a near riot. When cruisers had begun to arrive, a lot of people had fled, jumping onto their bikes and roaring away in all directions. He could just imagine what the lawn looked like. Stitch had been slashed by a knife. He'd been taken by ambulance to Wheaton Medical Center. Trace had taken a beating but refused medical treatment beyond ice packs. Even Max had some bruises and scratches on him. Pitch had made it through unscathed as he had stayed behind to guard Glenrowan's body so no one tampered with or desecrated the corpse.

Officer Taylor was gathering statements from those sitting around the kitchen table. Madeline had come downstairs outraged, very vocal, but she had grudgingly brewed fresh coffee. She had not failed to notice how Adrian was dressed, had not failed to see his tattoo. She had looked shocked, but now she just looked angry about the whole terrible business. "I knew that girl would bring trouble upon us," she said, earning a dark scowl from Adrian.

Adrian had noticed that Andrew and Hollyce had simply vanished. He'd wanted to send Hollyce upstairs to stay with Eve-

leen. Glancing at the clock, he frowned. He wondered what Eveleen was doing. It was after ten o'clock already. He'd left her a-
lone far too long. He finished writing his statement, signed it,
dated it and slid it across the table to Officer Taylor. "If you don't
mind, I'm going to run up and check on Eveleen."

"I'll need her statement," Officer Taylor said. He slid a
form across to Adrian. "Have her write it up when she's able and
I'll swing by to pick it up. The funeral is at nine here, ten at the
church?"

"Yeah."

"If she feels up to it, have her write it first thing in the
morning. You sure she doesn't need medical attention?"

"She was all right when I came downstairs. Talking. Her
breathing was a little wheezy but she was okay." He took the
paper. Buck, Fred, you two straighten up the chairs and lock
everything up tightly. I'll be down early to make sure things are in
order for the funeral. Keep the air on high in the reposing room or
he's going to go bad."

He left the kitchen, took the back stairs up to the third floor
since the hall access door to the elevator was still dead-bolted from
inside. He came into his apartment through a door in the second
bedroom that looked like a closet. He looked in his bedroom and
bathroom, saw his suit hanging up, her dress over the shower stall
door. Her boots were under the bench with his black shoes. He
found her in the living room because Reynolds had meowed softly.
He had stayed on the couch with her, guarding her. "Hey, fella,"
Adrian said, scratching the cats ears. "Good boy. Keeping an eye
on her are you?" He crouched down, ran his hand over her hair.
Her hair was soft. She smelled of evergreens and he realized that
she'd washed her hair. He leaned closer and sniffed. Her skin
smelled of evergreen, too. He remembered seeing the towel

hanging over the shower stall also. She had taken a shower. "Eveleen," he said, caressing her cheek. Her skin felt soft, delicately warm. "Evie." Her eyes opened and she looked at him.

"Hi," she murmured.

"Hi. Sorry to wake you. Are you comfortable enough? You can sleep in the guest room tonight if you want. I don't want you alone over in the apartment. Rogue got away. There's going to be an officer patrolling the yard all night, but I'd still prefer that you stay in the main house where you're more protected."

"Okay."

"I'm going to grab a shower then hit the hay. There's a paper on the kitchen counter. The police need you to write your statement about what happened tonight, how he grabbed you and nearly choked you. You were turning blue." He couldn't stop himself from leaning forward and pressing his lips to her forehead. "Try to get some sleep."

"I was asleep. Reynolds is like a heating pad." She pulled her left arm out from under the throw and touched his stubbled jaw. Her eyes met his. "You're like a dark version of Superman."

"I'm hardly super. Adequate man, that's more like me."

"I think you're super."

"I do my best." He tousled her curls then stood up. "I need a shower."

He'd hoped to find her in his bed when he came out, but she was not. With a sigh, he shut off the light and got into bed, pulling the covers up. Reynolds would probably sleep in the living room with her. He'd have the bed to himself tonight, and that made him feel lonely.

He wasn't asleep yet when he heard her light footsteps in the hall. "Adrian?" she whispered.

"What's the matter?"

"I don't know what's wrong with me. I can't stop shivering."

"It's probably just a stress reaction."

"Can I come in?"

"Yeah, come and lie down with me for a while." She came into the room, climbed into his bed. He could feel her shivering. "Come here, curl up beside me." She shifted closer, snuggling up against him. He put his arm around her. "It's okay. No one's going to hurt you anymore."

"I was so scared he was going to beat the crap out of me. I thought he was going to kill me. He was high on something. He'd probably been smoking crack or meth." He curled himself around her, holding her close. The tremors were deep inside of her. "He used to beat me so bad," she whispered.

"He's never going to lay another finger on you," he promised her. She raised her head to look at him in the starlight and moonlight coming through the window. The rain had passed and the night had become clear.

"You have such dark eyes," she said softly. She touched his face, tracing the line of his nose, the curve of his cheek, the angle of his jaw. Her fingertip brushed across his lower lip. His lips parted. She laid her finger in the middle of his lower lip and he touched the tip of it with the tip of his tongue. Her eyes widened and then she smiled. "Can I kiss you?" she whispered.

"Do you want to?"

"I want to."

"Be my guest."

"I can't kiss you unless you kiss me back."

"Oh, I will," he quietly assured her.

"You're my employer," she whispered. "I shouldn't be in your bed wanting to kiss you like this."

"No, probably not but, here you are. It has not been a typical night at The Cedars by any means." She boosted herself up a bit and caught his mouth with hers, kissing him softly. He pulled her even closer. She unfolded her long limbs, stretching out. He straightened his legs out also and then she nudged his legs apart to slide one of her legs between his. "Evie..." he murmured as her hip brushed against him. She didn't say anything, just kissed him a little differently, the tip of her tongue pressing against his lower lip, then slipping between his lips to lightly duel with his. He groaned, pulling her under him, moving over her. "As your employer, I should not be doing this either."

"Should I file a sexual harassment grievance with you?" she asked.

"Only if you think I'm harassing you."

"Oh, Adrian..." she said, as he unbuttoned his shirt that she was still wearing, slid his hand inside, unhooking her bra. She pushed her breast against his palm. "You're not harassing me."

"Can I make love to you?" he asked.

"If you don't, I'll be so disappointed."

"I feel like I might be taking advantage of you."

"No, you're not. I want you." She kissed his face all over. "Adrian, I want you so bad right now I will cry if you stop what you're doing!"

"Don't cry," he whispered in her ear as he tugged her panties down. She raised her hips to make it easier for him to get them off of her. He wrestled the shirt and bra off her. "I want to follow your ivy tattoo," he said.

"It starts behind my left ear."

"I know," he whispered, his breath warm in her ear. She had stopped shivering, but now he felt her tremble. "I know." He turned her head to the right, bending her left ear gently forward so he could press his lips to the leaf that was behind her ear. "Evie, how many men wear your image on their bodies? On how many men did your father tattoo you wrapped in ivy?" he asked, his mouth moving down the side of her neck, following the vine to her shoulder.

"I don't remember ever seeing him put my image on anybody," she replied. "I was in high school when he tattooed you. I was a sophomore. He started the vine that spring when I turned sixteen." He kissed her down the length of her arm then followed the vine back up to her shoulder, across her collarbone to the hollow at the base of her throat. "No one really noticed my tattoo at first. I had long hair. They could really only see it on my arm. He worked on it all summer. He did all the ivy on my torso. It took a long time. In my junior year, they noticed it in gym class, in the locker room and the girls began to talk. They thought it was scandalous, that there was something going on between me and my Dad. The school sent the police to the apartment and to the shop to question him. A counselor and the principal questioned me at school. He'd done nothin' inappropriate. I was always covered." She gasped as he reached the leaves tattooed on her breasts, just the inside areas near her sternum. "He finished with my leg that spring. Everyone at school had begun to treat me differently, like I was tainted somehow. It hurt. My Dad had given me a gift and I loved it, but everyone else saw it as some sort of perverted, terrible thing that he'd done to me." She laid her hand on his head, lacing her fingers through his loose curls as he kissed the leaves on her hips. "Danny was nice but his parents didn't think very highly of me. I met him at the end of junior year. He worked at the ship-yard. I hardly saw him all summer. We dated at the beginning of senior year then his father was transferred and he was gone." He was working his way down her leg now. "Dad started training me

194

when I was seventeen. I really didn't want to do tattoos though. I worked in the shop, behind the counter as the cashier. I ordered the supplies, kept the shelves stocked, ran errands. After he hired Hollyce, she trained me to do piercings. Sometimes I helped Dad ink in designs just to keep my skills up to snuff." He was coming back up the vine now, having reached her ankle. "Adrian, you're the only man who has ever followed the vine like this. Rogue couldn't have cared less about my tattoo. Dad had done a lot of work on him. People have to always look at his tattoos." She gasped as he urged her thighs apart and kissed her there. "Oh, my God," she whispered.

"Has anyone ever made love to you?" he asked.

"Not like this." She thought about it as his lips moved back up the ivy vine. "No," she concluded. "No, never."

"He just took what he wanted from you and you thought that was love, didn't you?"

"Yes," she replied, her voice barely audible.

"Did he ever give you any pleasure?" She turned her head away, closed her eyes that were suddenly full of hot tears. She bit her lip. He kissed the vine and ivy leaves on her neck. "He didn't, did he?"

"No."

"Do you want me to give you what he denied you?" He was back near her ear again. "Do you want me to show you how it's supposed to be when two people make love together?" He turned her face toward his. "Do you trust me?"

She opened her eyes, looking into his. "Yes."

He dried her tears with kisses. "Then let me love you."

"Okay."

"You don't have to be afraid of me. I'll never hurt you."

"I know you won't. You've always been so good to me."

He took his time, ignoring the fact that it was late and they both had to be awake early for her father's funeral. She had come to his bed willingly and he was not going to lose this opportunity to show her how much he cared about her, how he felt about her. He whispered suggestions in her ear, ways that she could position herself and move with him, against him to heighten her own pleasure, and his. She really was quite naïve about sex. He hated Rogue all the more for being so cruel to her, for not giving her anything in return for all he'd taken from her. He knew when she was close. "That's it," he urged her. "This is how love is supposed to be."

"Oh, my God!" she cried, her fingertips digging into his shoulders

"Fly to the moon and stars, Evie. I'll be right behind you," he said quietly. He kissed her to stifle her cries, not wanting anything they did together to be overheard in any way by Madeline and Jim on the floor below. She was quivering beneath him. He moved quickly, buried himself in her warm body and released. It was as if the gates of Heaven had been thrown open and all of its beauty lay spread before his eyes. He felt as if shafts of sunlight had pierced him through, lighting him from within. All the darkness of his life was dispelled in the glory of his union with Eveleen.

"Adrian," she said, stroking his curls as his head was down, his face buried against her neck where he could feel her pulse throbbing. "Are you all right?"

"Never been better," he replied, his voice muffled.

"Me too," she said. "Never been better."

He raised his head as he slid away from her, but he pulled her along with him, gathering her in his arms. "Can you sleep now?" he asked.

"I'll sleep like a baby."

He twisted toward the bedside table, turned on his alarm clock. "My alarm goes off at five-thirty. I know it's early but I always start my day then. You'll have to go down the fire escape and back to your apartment to get ready for your father's funeral."

"I'm so sorry about your suit."

"I have others."

She giggled. "Lots of them," she said.

He laughed quietly. "That I do. Goodnight, Evie."

"Goodnight."

Friday, September 12th

Although she wanted him to make love to her again when the alarm went off, he didn't. He switched off the alarm, threw the covers aside, then turned and kissed her cheek. "Time to rise and shine."

"What time do the Mitchells get up?" she asked as she scrambled out of bed, began searching for her bra and panties. He was sitting on the side of the bed, having pulled on his plaid boxers, watching her.

"Six or six-thirty. I'm not exactly sure."

"They won't see me sneaking down the fire escape will they?"

"No." He stood up, grabbed his deep purple shirt off the floor and went to her, putting it on her, slowly buttoning it, bending to kiss a few of the leaves on her upper chest as he did so. "You're so beautiful," he said.

"I don't think so."

A wry smile tucked itself into the corner of his mouth. "You'd better go while you can." He walked with her to the door to the fire escape. She slipped out and went down the iron stairs quickly and quietly. It wasn't until she was across the pavement and up the wooden stairs that she realized she didn't have her key. Adrian had been watching her and he realized her problem, motioned for her to wait. He didn't know where she'd left her keys, probably in her office downstairs. He grabbed his key ring off the dresser, found the master key to the carriage house and worked it off. She had come back to the foot of the iron stairs. He stepped outside, leaned over the railing and dropped the key into her cupped hands. She mouthed, 'Thank you,' smiled then ran back across the cold blacktop and up the stairs, letting herself into the apartment.

At seven-thirty, he went downstairs via the elevator. Buck and Fred were there, sitting at the kitchen table. "Sorry we bailed on you last night," Fred said, not making eye contact with Adrian.

"Well, as far as I know, no one got killed," Adrian replied as he got out a coffee filter and measured out the coffee into the basket. He shoved it into place, filled the plastic pitcher that was marked so the carafe wouldn't overflow. He added the water and the machine started the brewing cycle. Almost instantly the kitchen began to fill with the aroma of coffee.

"That bastard nearly choked Eveleen," Buck said. "I can't believe you busted his damn nose like that! Jeez, Adrian, you're a marked man today. Rogue and his buddies will be gunning for you."

"I suppose so," Adrian replied. He didn't relish that idea, but he wasn't going to let it ruin his day. He'd had Eveleen in his bed last night. He'd made love to her. Nothing was going to ruin his day.

Andrew arrived with Hollyce in tow. She was in a clingy black mini dress that displayed all her assets to their best advantage. They had brought a bagful of various breakfast burritos and a box with a dozen assorted muffins. At seven-forty, Madeline and James came into the kitchen. "The kitchen is just for Cedars staff," she said when she spotted Hollyce.

Hollyce shrugged and stood up. "I'll go wait with Jack then."

"We don't open until eight."

"But I'm already here, already inside. He's certainly not going to mind if I'm a little early." She sauntered down the hall on her four-inch heels. Madeline shot Andrew a withering look. He slunk out of the kitchen, heading toward the front of the house. "Adrian, you have got to talk to him before he ruins his marriage completely." She helped herself to coffee. Jim had grabbed his coffee and a burrito and unobtrusively retreated to his office. "Where's Eveleen? Is she still upstairs?" she asked, shooting him a piercing glance, sure that she would make him react.

"As far as I know, she's over in the apartment."

"Oh, I didn't hear her leave last night. She was upstairs in your apartment, wasn't she?"

"I took her up there to keep her safe. She fell asleep while I was dealing with the bullshit down here. I woke her when I went upstairs, after the house was straightened up and secured. She went home after." He was not going to say any more about it. It was none of Madeline's business.

"Do we have the police coming to maintain order this morning?"

"Yes. As far as I know, Rogue is still out there."

"You should have just let him take his property and leave last night. Instead, you had to agitate him and now he'll be out for revenge."

Adrian shrugged. "If he wants more damage, so be it."

"You cannot fight the bereaved and their friends."

"If he behaves and leaves her the hell alone he'll be fine. I won't touch him."

She had a sour expression on her face as she said, "You defend that girl as if she means something to you."

"She's one of our employees. If someone grabbed you and put you in a chokehold like that, I assure you, I would have broken their nose to get you free, too. No one should be treated like that."

"But I understand she has a history of men abusing her. Maybe she likes that sort of thing. Some girls do."

"I don't think she looked as if she was enjoying that." He took his coffee and left the kitchen, not wanting to discuss the matter with her anymore. He made his way to Jim's office, knocked and then went in and sat down. "Have you thought about rehab?" he asked.

"You're asking me *now*? It's not even eight o'clock in the morning yet."

"I just want you to know that I will suspend you if I ever see you downstairs drunk again. I expect you to come down sober, be neatly dressed and groomed and capable of doing your job. If you can't do that, then I don't want you here."

"Who died and left you boss?"

"No one yet, but you're well along that path. I don't want you to go any further. Turn it around, Jim. Maddie and I can't make that decision for you. It has to come from your own resolve to get your life back on track. I can help you with the gambling debts. I've told you before, when you sold me your fifty-one percent of the Cedars, that I would buy the house and property, buy the business from you for more than enough to settle your debts. You and Maddie can remain here. Once all this stress is off her shoulders I'm sure she'll turn herself around, too. She's become a freakin' bitch lately." He stood up. "I have a personal interest in Eveleen Glenrowan," he said. "I think she's an excellent receptionist and secretary. She has some ideas that I want to look at, and explore further with her, that may help us out."

"You said personal interest," he pointed out.

"I'm attracted to her. I'm considering asking her out."

Jim looked at him for a long moment then sat back in his chair, folded his hands across his belly and grinned. "She's a pretty girl. Damn, she has long legs! Beautiful eyes." He sighed. "What the hell, Adrian, you want it, go for it. Maddie was a looker back in the day."

"She's still a lovely woman," Adrian said. "I have to speak to Andrew now."

"Ah, yes, I saw him walk by with that body piercer girl."

Adrian went to the reposing room where Jack Glenrowan was. It was unoccupied. He walked in after turning the lights on low. Making his way to the open casket, he looked at the man lying there. He wished now that he'd asked Glenrowan more questions when he was being tattooed, wished he hadn't been so drunk and stupid that he had never even noticed the little red-haired girl for almost a year after the fact. She was more toward the backside of his arm, difficult for him to see without a mirror. "You gave her to me way back then. I'll protect her, Jack. I don't know if you knew the truth of things when you did it, but as much as you've bound her in ivy, you've bound her to me by means of this tattoo. I'll do whatever I have to do to keep her safe."

"You talkin' to a dead man, honey?" Hollyce asked as she came into the room.

"I talk to the deceased occasionally," he replied.

"Well, at least they don't talk back to you, right?" She came up to him. "Look, Andrew says you're pissed he and I are having a little fun together. I just want you to know, it'll be over soon. He's really not my type. He's so vanilla."

"He's married with a little boy and another on the way." She rolled her eyes. "His wife is upset."

"She'll get over it, and he'll be a much better husband for his little foray onto the wild side. He'll get over me. He loves her. I'm just gasoline on his fire, baby. I'll burn off quick enough." She looked at Jack. "God, he was great in bed. Eveleen doesn't know the half of what he was really like. She worshipped him, saw only the good in him. The rest of us knew otherwise. Guess when he tossed her out of the apartment in favor of Fidelity she had a wake-up call!" She turned and looked directly at Adrian. "How the hell did she end up here of all places?"

"She answered an ad in the online classifieds," he replied.

"And she was the best choice of all the people who re-sponded to the ad?"

"Yes." He did not reveal that there had only been three respondents. One had been sixty-one years old and a heavy smoker. The second had been eighteen-years old, addicted to her cellphone, texting throughout the interview and unable to spell cedar correctly. Eveleen had been the gem, outshining the other two by far.

Madeline huffed as she passed the reposing room. "Why isn't the door unlocked yet! This place is going to hell in a hand basket!"

"Excuse me," Adrian said, leaving Hollyce with her thoughts. As he came out into the hall, he saw Eveleen going into her office. Madeline had unlocked the door then stomped upstairs. He walked to Eveleen's office and leaned against the door frame. She was searching through her desk, frowning. "What's wrong?"

She looked up at him. Her hair was still damp from the shower. She had on a dark green dress with a tiny floral print. "My keys are missing. I thought I'd left them down here last night."

"I don't remember anyone going into your office, but when the fight broke out, I admit I wasn't looking. Then I was upstairs for a few minutes with you before coming back down. You didn't have them upstairs?"

"No." She straightened up. "But my shoes are upstairs in your bathroom under the bench. Can I go up and get them?"

"Use the elevator. The doors are locked today, main door and rear door."

"I'll be back down in a few."

"Eveleen, can you do me a favor while you're up there? Can you feed Reynolds? I think I forgot to do that this morning."

She nodded. He watched her walk barefoot up the hall and smiled, enjoying the subtle sway of her now very familiar hips.

Father Martin arrived at eight-thirty, going directly to the kitchen where he knew he could get hot coffee and something to eat before the service. Max Leary and the three younger men from Rampant Ink arrived a few minutes later. Eveleen had come back down and gone to be with her father. Adrian had already looked in on her twice as he paced the front hall near the vestibule door, somewhat tense, not knowing for sure what trouble lay in store for them this morning.

There were about fifty people who attended the service, among them, Fidelity in a low cut, black dress that drew every male eye in the room. Adrian didn't know what in the world was restraining her breasts, keeping them from falling out. "Duck tape," Andrew whispered, catching Adrian looking and frowning. Adrian looked at him. "Naw, just kidding, but ladies do have this adhesive stuff they use to prevent wardrobe malfunctions, as if us guys care about them falling out of their clothes like that."

"Damn stuff must be as strong as Super Glue to keep those things from falling out."

"It's pretty good stuff. You remember Beth's low cut wedding gown? She used that stuff to keep from popping out. It took a lot of effort to clean that crap off her boobs afterwards though."

At nine-thirty, people began moving out to their vehicles that now were adorned with purple "Funeral" flags courtesy of Buck and Fred. All the vehicles had been parked in the order in which they would be following the funeral procession. Andrew was driving the lead car, a black Cadillac that would carry Jim and Father Martin to the church and cemetery. Next, Buck would drive the flower car. Adrian would follow in the hearse. The limousine, driven by Fred, would carry Eveleen, Fidelity, Max, Hollyce, and Stitch. Trace and Pitch would follow the limo in a black pick-up truck belonging to Trace. Mourners had been lined up behind the black pick-up. As the mourners went out to get into their vehicles or onto their motorcycles, Buck and Fred were out there telling them which vehicle to follow in the procession, to keep their headlights and hazard lights on for the drive to St. John's. They could park wherever they liked once they got to the church, except in the curved driveway in front as the funeral livery vehicles would be parked there and couldn't be blocked in.

"You ready to say goodbye, lass?" Max asked Eveleen, as he slipped an arm around her.

"Is anyone ever ready to say goodbye to their Dad?" she replied. "Or to anyone for that matter?" She let him lead her to the casket. "I'm going to miss you but I think you left me a sign. I got your message last night. I'll be okay. Thanks, Dad. I love you, and goodbye." She bent forward, lightly kissing her father's cold, stiff cheek.

"Ready?" Adrian asked. He and Andrew were waiting to close and secure the casket and then wheel it out to the hearse. She nodded.

"I'll take her out to the limo," Max said.

It took almost fifteen minutes to get the casket out the side entrance and around to the rear of the hearse. They loaded it in then Andrew moved to get behind the wheel of the Caddy while Adrian slipped behind the wheel of the hearse. He put on his dark-lensed sunglasses since the sun had decided to shine on Jack Glenrowan today. As he reached over to adjust the air conditioner, he caught movement in the passenger side mirror that startled him. Eveleen pulled open the passenger door and got in, closing the door. "You can't do this," he said.

"I'm ridin' with my father," she said, her tone brooking no argument from him.

He stared out the windshield. It was against the rules, yet, she was an employee and there really wasn't anything that said a second employee couldn't ride shotgun in the hearse. But, she was also the bereaved, the daughter of the deceased. She really should not be sitting there beside him, however, he couldn't deny that she had spunk, and he liked that she was there. "Madeline will hear all about this from Jim and Andrew," he said. "And I'm sure Buck saw you also."

"He's my father. This is his last road trip. I'm goin' to the church with him. I'll behave and ride in the limo on the way back." The mourners could walk from the church to the cemetery if they wanted to, but Adrian guessed all the bikers would want to roar through the narrow lanes and line up alongside the road to see Glenrowan off. They would drive the family, priest, casket and flowers over as the knoll where his grave was waiting was all the way across the cemetery. "I don't mean to get you into trouble."

"I'm not worried about it."

"I didn't think you would be. What are you going to do? Write yourself up? Give yourself a few days off without pay?"

"I could use a few days off," he said. "Maybe I'll suspend myself for three days, go up to Maine and walk the beach, relax a little." He turned his head and looked at her. "I haven't taken a vacation in almost four years."

"Why not?"

"There's been no place I've wanted to go." He shifted the car into gear as the lead cars began to move forward slowly. "You get a five-day vacation your first year with The Cedars."

"I've really only worked here for like six weeks," she pointed out.

"Why don't we find someplace nice to go near the end of May, before the tourist season really starts?"

"Where would you like to go?"

"It doesn't matter as long as you're with me." She flushed then smiled. "Miss Glenrowan, you shouldn't be smiling like that. This is a funeral, after all."

"You really want to take a vacation with me?"

"Yes, I do."

"Wow."

"Last night, I hope you know it wasn't just a one-time thing." She looked nervous. "I think we need to get to know one another a little better, go on a few dates, eat some popcorn while watching a movie after work some nights, take walks on the beach to look at the stars. I'm interested in a future with you."

"I'd like that, Adrian," she said, her heart beating faster.

"I didn't bore you, did I?"

"Oh, no! Not at all! I found your company very stimulatin'." He saw the dimples she was trying to restrain, wanted to lean over and kiss her, but they were crawling along the road now, more motorcycles and other vehicles joining the procession. "Looks like there'll be a crowd," he commented.

Eveleen was suddenly gnawing her lush lower lip, looking worried. "There'll be trouble if Rogue shows up," she predicted, her voice low.

"Don't worry about it."

"He's got it in for you now."

"It'll be all right," he replied.

"I don't want you to get hurt."

"I'll be fine."

They arrived at the church with a huge funeral procession behind them, hundreds of leather and denim clad, tattooed bikers. They milled about outside as the casket was unloaded and some of the flower arrangements were brought in. Eveleen stood looking at all the mourners. Adrian could tell that she was searching among them for Rogue. He wished he could reassure her that nothing was going to happen to her, or to him.

He and Andrew, once the casket was inside, the chosen burly pall bearers had escorted it down the aisle on the church truck and the casket had been draped in the Catholic manner, stood out on the sidewalk. "I'm going home to Beth tonight," Andrew suddenly said.

Adrian turned his head away to look at Buck who had a toothache. He was prodding his tooth with his finger. "Make a damned dentist appointment!" he called over to him. Buck nodded, pulled out his cellphone and made a call. The tooth had been bothering him all week. "He's calling his girlfriend to ask her to make him an appointment. I can almost guarantee it."

"He's such a baby."

"Good, I'm glad you're going home. That'll get Beth off my ass. She thinks it's my fault that you haven't been going home nights, that I have you out carousing every night."

"She thinks of you as a womanizing, confirmed bachelor."

"She really doesn't know me all that well, does she?"

"Are you seeing anyone?" Andrew asked. "Or have you given up because chicks just don't dig a mortician who lives in a funeral home?"

"I'm seeing someone," he replied.

"Oh, yeah? Who? Does sour puss Maddie have a hot, horny, kid sister I'm unaware of?"

"No, I'm seeing Eveleen."

"Are you shittin' me? You're hittin' her?"

"Andrew," he said, a hint of warning in his voice.

"Is she as hot as Hollyce in the sack?"

"No, she's sweet and passionate. She's nothing like her love 'em and leave 'em friend."

"So you've jumped in the sack with her already?"

"Look, we're just establishing a relationship. I'm not discussing it with you. All you need to know is she's my girl-friend."

"Well, okay. Have at her. She's pretty enough, although she's plainer than Hollyce, and she's too damned skinny for my taste."

"That doesn't matter. I like her just the way she is."

"Well, good for you. Hope it works out, although Maddie'll flip out when she finds out you're sleeping with the hired help. She's already going to be all over your case for letting Eveleen ride in the hearse today."

"I'll explain that to her, make her understand."

"Good luck with that."

Jim signaled to them, a short time later, from the church door. Adrian opened the back door of the hearse. He and Andrew went inside to supervise the proper removal of the casket from the church.

Rogue showed up for the graveside service, roaring into the cemetery on his custom chopper moments after the service had begun, disrupting Father Martin. Adrian, who was standing at the head of the grave with the priest, Jim, Andrew, Buck and Fred, saw Eveleen tense as her former boyfriend sauntered over, a swagger in his step as he elbowed his way through the crowd. His eyes were blackened and bloodshot, his nose swollen and misshapen. Max glared at him. Stitch and Trace looked ready to pounce on him. Rogue slipped an arm around Eveleen pulling her to his side. She turned her head away, would not look at him. Adrian could see that she was terrified he would do something to her, or him.

As the priest launched into his ashes to ashes, dust to dust reading, Rogue grabbed Eveleen, pulling her closer and shouted, "Just throw the damn bastard in the ground and cover him up with dirt already! I'm taking my girl home now! Enough is enough of this shit!"

Eveleen twisted herself around, looking toward where Adrian was standing, and gasped. She did not see him, but she saw something that sent a shockwave through her, enough of a jolt that Rogue noticed and hesitated, looking back to see what had happened. Her eyes were riveted on something. He looked toward where she was focused and saw only the priest and the funeral home men in their somber black suits. He thought she was looking at one of them in particular, and he knew which one it was, that black-haired son of a bitch who'd broken his nose last night! He snarled at Adrian.

However, what she was actually looking at was a tall figure in a black, hooded robe surrounded by swirling, deep gray fog or smoke. The figure had a gruesome, grinning skull face, very dark eyes. His eyes burned with rage. He stepped forward and she saw that he held a huge curved blade, a scythe. She thought for sure that Death had come to claim her. Her heart was hammering. "Don't take me!" she cried. "Please! Don't take me!" Everyone around her assumed that she meant she didn't want Rogue to take her away, but no one dared move to help her.

"I'm not here for you," the grim reaper replied. His voice was at her ear, soft, quiet—familiar. Her breath caught at the back of her throat. It was Adrian's voice! She blinked but the image did not alter. "Eveleen, get down!" he ordered. She obeyed instantly, knowing what was coming, wrenching herself sideways away from Rogue, letting herself fall. Her falling down like that pulled Rogue off balance, as he was still gripping her arm. She heard him grunt, and then he was on the grass beside her, his body wracked with spasms as if he was having a seizure. People began screaming and shouting.

Max grabbed her, lifting her up and hauling her away from Rogue, who was writhing on the ground, his eyes rolled up into his head. "Damn fool probably overdosed," he growled.

Eveleen raised her head, looking for Adrian, finding him standing to the left of Father Martin. He looked somewhat grim-faced but she thought it was just concern for her safety. She looked away, searching for the figure she had seen, but he was gone. "Has anyone called an ambulance?" she asked.

An hour and a half later, Adrian walked into her office at The Cedars. He came up to her desk and laid her key ring on the blotter. She looked up at him. He could see all the questions in her eyes. "Will you have dinner with me tonight?" he asked. She hesitated. "Please."

"Can I think about it for a bit?"

"Yes, of course. Take as much time as you need. I'll be downstairs. I have a lot of paperwork to catch up on." He turned and walked across the hall then through the door with the frosted glass window to the basement.

Eveleen sat looking at her keys. Where had he found them? Had Rogue had them? Had one of his cronies snuck into her office and stolen them for him. Had he planned on breaking into the apartment at some point and raping her? Beating her? She shuddered. She didn't know what had happened at the cemetery this morning. For over an hour now she had been debating with herself whether or not what she had seen and heard had merely been a figment of her imagination, caused by stress, fatigue and fear. There was the fact that Adrian had a grim reaper tattoo she had seen for the first time last night. That could have planted the idea in her head. That the reaper would speak in Adrian's voice also made sense to her, since he was Adrian's tattoo come to life. Adrian had said he would keep her safe, that he would protect her.

"I am so confused!" she cried, putting her head down on her folded arms on her blotter. Her mind was in a whirl.

She didn't see him again all afternoon. At close to five o'clock, she locked her office door. She was not going to leave it open anymore even though, from the state Rogue had been in, she guessed he would no longer be a threat to her, but he had friends. There was no one around on the first floor. She went to lock the front door for the dinner hour. There were no wakes scheduled for tonight, but there were bodies in the basement that needed to be embalmed and Madeline would be holding a grief counseling session this evening. She assumed Adrian was still in the basement, unless he had left through the basement entrance then come back in through the back door and gone upstairs. But why would he be avoiding her?

Crossing the hall, she put her hand on the embossed brass doorknob. She was not supposed to go downstairs, but she wanted to see Adrian and talk to him. He was waiting for her answer about dinner and it was close to dinner time. She hoped he hadn't changed his mind while waiting for several hours for her to make up her mind. Taking a breath, she turned the knob and opened the door, slipping past it, pulling it closed behind her and then slowly making her way down the staircase that came to a landing halfway down before turning back on itself the rest of the way so she came out in the tiled corridor, facing the back entrance. As she stepped off the last stair, a dark figure came out of the room where the bodies were stored. She caught her breath sharply. It heard her and turned its head to look at her. For a long moment they stood silently looking at one another. Her heart was pounding again and her knees felt weak. She hadn't been hallucinating! She had seen the grim reaper at the cemetery and here it was again, coming out of the refrigeration room. It turned its head away and started down

212

the corridor away from her. "Adri....," she began to say, but her voice seemed stuck in her throat. It did not stop. "Adrian, wait!" It went into the office. She hurried down the hall, terrified, but also desperate to know the truth. "Adrian!" She turned into his office and stopped. He was standing near the desk looking the same as he usually looked to her. "Oh."

"What is it Eveleen?" he asked.

"I thought..." He did not say anything. She looked into his dark eyes. The reaper had the same beautiful, black coffee-colored eyes. "I know who you are," she said.

"Do you?"

"This is the perfect place for you to work."

"I've always thought so," he replied. "Have you thought about dinner?" he asked.

"Yes, I'll have dinner with you." He nodded. "Adrian, we need to talk about this."

"Yes, I suppose we do. It's curious how your father gave you to me, isn't it?" She nodded. "Do you think he knew?"

"A lot of the Irish have the sight," she replied.

"You must have it, too. You saw me."

"Twice."

He adjusted his tie, checked his cuff links, smoothed the front of his coat. "Are you afraid of me?" he asked.

"No, I'm not afraid of you," she replied. Why would she be afraid of him? He'd told her that he'd never hurt her. She believed him. She trusted him.

"I tend to frighten women away."

She didn't say anything for a few moments but then she said, "Well, if I'm ever in the shower and you come up behind me lookin' like that and run a bony finger down my spine, I can't promise you that I won't scream." She lessened the distance between them. "Can I ask you something?"

"Certainly."

"I'm just curious. What did you do to Rogue?"

"Well," he began, then hesitated, debating with himself whether to continue or not. His eyes met hers again and he went on. "I intended to merely paralyze him from the neck down. But you pulled him off balance and the blade did some damage to his brain instead. It caused him to have a grand mal seizure. He'll have to be medicated and restrained frequently so he doesn't harm himself thrashing around like that."

"Oh."

"I could always go and take him, if you think that's cruel, his having to live that way."

"He won't bother me ever again, will he?"

"His brain got a bit stirred up, like oatmeal. He probably doesn't even remember you. He's not going to be walking, or driving ever again. He lacks coordination and cognition." He shrugged, a rueful look on his face. "I messed up."

"He was going to rape me, beat me and then probably kill me, wasn't he?'

"That appeared to have been his game plan. I believe he also planned on shooting me, and if that failed, knifing me. I'm not fond of being shot or stabbed."

She stepped closer. "So how's this going to work?" she asked.

"The same way it has worked for the past six weeks, only, I might suggest that you move in upstairs with me in the near future. We'll work here, continue to reside here, live our lives here, take vacations to the beach or in the mountains or wherever you might like to go. It will be life as usual."

"Except for one thing that is very unusual."

"Well, there's that, yes, but it doesn't have to interfere with anything. I am who I am."

"Did you go to school for that?"

"To be a mortician? A funeral director? An embalmer? Yes, of course."

"No, the other job you do."

"Oh, no, that just came naturally."

She laughed. "Oh, Adrian, you're so funny!" She slipped her arms up around his neck. "Can you...I don't know what you call it...um...transform yourself at will? Or are you only like that around dead bodies?" She yelped as he transformed in her embrace. "Oh, my God!"

"Does that answer your question?"

"Wait! Stop! Stay like this a minute!" She moved his hood aside, slipping her hands inside to touch his skull, caressing his bony feathers. "You've got gorgeous teeth!"

"Thanks."

"And your eyes, they're so dark there're bottomless."

"If you say so."

"What do you have under your robe?" she asked.

"Miss Glenrowan, you certainly are a curious girl," he murmured, sounding amused. "Bones."

"That was probably a stupid question, but how would I know?"

"There are no stupid questions. This is all new to you. Can I answer any more questions for you?"

"What exactly do you do? Do you kill people?"

"I do *not* kill people. Maniacs with assault rifles, machetes and other assorted deadly weapons kill people. Natural disasters kill people. Illness, disease and advanced age kill people. Lightning strikes and accidents kill people. I harvest souls from dead bodies and send them on their way into the afterlife."

"But…"

"I know there's a whole grim reaper culture out there. Look me up on Wikipedia and you can read for days. However, I'm really not that complicated."

"But you would have killed Rogue, wouldn't you have?"

"I'm rather protective of what is mine," he replied.

"Can you be Adrian again? You don't have lips when you're like this." He transformed and was Adrian again. She pulled his face to hers and kissed him. "I'm hungry," she said.

"What would you like?" he asked.

"You!"

"I meant to eat."

"That's what I meant." She felt him react to that. "Oh, you probably meant for dinner, right? Can we go to that little Italian restaurant three blocks south of here? Luigi's, is it?"

"Yes, all right."

"I'm dying for spaghetti and meatballs."

"You don't look like you're dying to me. I ought to know."

She smiled. "That's very good news, that I'm not dying. After dinner, can we bring home the rest of the wine and go upstairs and finish it and then…"

"We'll throw Reynolds off the bed and…"

"Make love all night long," she concluded.

"Sounds like an excellent plan to me." He kissed her. She melted against him. "Do you know how much I love you?"

"You turned a man's brain into mush for me. That tells me right there how much you love me."

"No one is ever going to hurt you again. I promise you that."

"I believe you." Her stomach growled. He smiled. "I'm starving to death."

"You may be starving, but death is not in your immediate future, I assure you."

"Sorry, stuff like that just slips out."

He laughed. "I can see you're going to be the death of me."

"I am not!" she cried, following him out of the office. "Unless you mean that I'm going to love you to death!"

"Just try, Evie, just try to do that and see what it gets you."

"Ecstasy? Rapture?" she hazarded.

"Maybe a little of each," he replied as he locked the basement door. They climbed the stairs. His black Highlander was in the lot. "Maybe a whole lot more."

She climbed into the passenger seat. He hesitated, turning to look up at the house. High up on the third floor, Reynolds was sitting in the bedroom window watching him. "I'm not sharing my bed with you tonight, my friend. You can have the couch or the bed in the guest room." He got behind the wheel, looking at Eveleen. She was looking at him. She was so pretty. Her pale skin was luminous in the low light. "You look like an angel," he said.

"Who knows? It's been a strange and interesting day. Maybe I am, Adrian, maybe I am."

"Your father seemed to think so."

"Daddies dote on their little girls."

"But the majority of them don't tattoo their little girls onto strange men's arms, who turn out to be more than they appear to be, and then surprisingly enough, fall in love with the real girl when she answers a help wanted ad years later."

"You needed my help," she said.

"I did and I still do," he acknowledged. She had given him that help and more. She was not afraid of him. She liked his third floor home in the funeral home. He had begun to think that there was no female companion, no female lover in the world who could understand him and live with him, who would want him and stay with him to ease the loneliness of his existence. But, then, Eveleen had shown up in his life. He had carried her around on his arm for eight years without realizing what a gift Jack Glenrowan was going to give him when he threw her out of his apartment. The wheels had been set in motion then. Adrian was happy with how it had all worked out. From the look on the face of the girl with the light, coppery-red hair and the incredible ivy tattoo sitting beside him, she was happy about the way things had turned out, too.

Death didn't always have to mean the end, he realized. Sometimes it also meant a new beginning.

THUNDERHEADS

Autumn

A series of thunderstorms is passing through the area today. It had been raining now for over an hour, great flashes of bright, blue-white light illuminating the yard, followed closely by deep, reverberating rumbles of rolling thunder sounding like a freight train colliding with a rock slide in a gully. I have been busy doing nothing in particular, mostly avoiding my mother, my aunts, my father, my uncles, and my siblings. In a sprawling, Gothic Revival mansion with thirty-nine rooms, you would think it would not be so difficult to isolate ones' self, but I have been dodging their shadows and footsteps for hours now. I have grown weary of the diversion and despondent over this game of hide and seek. I do not wish to be sought. I wish to be left alone to my own devices, my own dreams and designs.

Finally, as a last resort, I slip into the upstairs billiards room and walk straight toward the fireplace to the left upon entering. At the last possible moment I veer to the right of the massive structure, my eye already on the secret knot that when pressed will reveal a narrow doorway disguised as a mahogany panel like every other panel in the room. Glancing over my shoulder I slip through the fifteen-inch wide opening then pull the panel closed again from inside the wall. I ignore the soft sweep of cobwebs across my cheek as I bend and feel blindly for the flashlight that I secreted here months ago. My fingers brush the cool aluminum cylinder. I press the rubber button and bright LED light floods the small space I stand in. This house is riddled with secret passages and staircases. I have only recently begun to explore these marvels after accidentally discovering this secret panel one spring afternoon when cleaning the woodwork after being ordered to do so by my father. Frustrated and annoyed, I had scrubbed the paneling with a vengeance. The applied pressure of the rag I was using had been enough to trigger the release mechanism—a soft click and this wonder had been revealed.

The passage was exceedingly narrow. I was glad I was small and thin in size and stature. I had braided my hair today to avoid catching it on random nails, pulling it out in little clumps like I have done in the past. This passage led away from the fireplace and then, at the juncture with the Vermillion Guest Room, it branched continuing on in the same direction, but there was also a narrow stairway leading up to the third floor. The house was three stories high with an assortment of attics above in the peaks and gables.

I chose the stairway and climbed upward, stepping carefully because the wood, though thickly furred with dust, creaked and groaned with dryness and age. I did not want anyone wondering where these stray sounds originated. My Aunt Beatrice, Mother's older sister, and her husband, my Uncle Reggie, have a suite of rooms on the third floor. Uncle Reggie had lost his fortune due to an addiction to horses, those of the racing variety. They had lost their house, their vacation home in the Bahamas, their fleet of vintage automobiles. Aunt Beatrice has one solitary diamond ring on a thin gold chain that she wears around her neck all the time. She never takes it off. It is the only piece of jewelry that she has left from her fabulous jewel collection. Their tumble from the heights of prestige and wealth had been at nosebleed speed. They had landed awkwardly, senseless, in shock and horror in my parent's formal parlor, literally begging for a roof over their heads and food to put in their hungry mouths. What could my parents do? They relegated them to the third floor with Mom's spinster sister, my Aunt Louise, who was three years younger than my mother, but so unconventional that no man had ever managed to get a grasp on her personality and discover the charm in her addle-brained sweetness. Aunt Louise has a tower room. I've always thought of her as our Rapunzel because she has very long, blonde hair turning silvery-gray and white in random streaks. Her hair is *extremely* long. Washing it is practically an all-day project, but one of her quirks is that no one can cut her hair. I am the only one allowed to trim the ragged, split ends once every two or three months, but I have to use a certain pair of silver-handled scissors. I have to collect the clipped hair and place it in a hair retainer made of celluloid, manufactured to look like ivory. When the hair re-tainer is full it is added to the shelves where other hair retainers sit, all containing the snipped ends of Aunt Louise's pride and glory. She only leaves her room to join the family for breakfast. She never dresses for this meal as it is too early in the day. She comes downstairs in her nightgown, robe and slippers. My siblings and I sometimes called her The In-Valid Louise. We are careful not to let anyone overhear us, but I think our overworked housekeeper, Thayer, has heard us once or twice as we whispered together in the hallways or shadowy corners of vast rooms.

I reached the top of the little staircase and found I could go in either direction. I chose south, past Aunt Beatrice and Uncle Reggie's suite. The curious fact that there were little knot holes that could be removed at various places left me feeling slightly disturbed. Who, in previous generations, had prowled these nar-row paths and stairways to spy on whom exactly? I had scoured the walls in my own bedroom and bathroom, searching for secret panels and suspicious knotholes. I had found a panel but could not figure out how to open it from my side. I'd left exploring that wing of the house for another time, when my family went out and I would not be attracting undue attention if I happened to make any noise at all within the walls.

I suddenly came upon another very narrow staircase leading upward to one of the attics. Who in the world would want to bother prowling the perimeter of an attic? And why? To spy on dressmakers dummies? Dusty old hump-backed trunks with rusted padlocks? Dust-furred boxes of old, glass Christmas tree ornaments stashed on shelves for safekeeping and forgotten through the years as the resiliency of plastic replaced the delicate beauty of these fragile relics of the past?

I debated only a moment before squeezing up the narrow staircase, feeling a vague sense of claustrophobia in the tight space. But, being curious and adventurous by nature, I followed my instinct and reached a panel at the very top that, when pushed in a certain place, made a soft click and swung outward into the attic. I heard what sounded like a sharp intake of breath that gave me pause, thinking I had startled one of my brothers or sisters up to some nefarious deed in the dim room. There was a window, tall and narrow with a gothic arch at the top at each end of the room, draped in cobwebs and smeary with the grime of ages, which dimmed the gray and gloomy light of early afternoon. Up here, the sound of rain drumming on the slate roof tiles was loud, like hundreds of thousands of fingers tapping restlessly above my head. A thin, sharp whistle sounded high in the eaves from some defect in the wall or an unseen vent partially clogged with debris of some sort, perhaps hornet nests or dead bat wings. A rumble of thunder shook the floor beneath my feet.

I crept cautiously through the small door, shining my light around the perimeter of the room. It was surprisingly neat and clean, well ordered. It's pristine nature sent a shiver rolling down the length of my spine, a cold steel ball of trepidation lodging at my vestigial tailbone. There was a massive Victorian-era bed set up at the far end that was blocking the majority of the west window that faced the rear of the property. The bed was unmade, as if someone had just slipped from between the covers to go fetch a glass of warm milk from the kitchen. Against the wall, where the door I had just come through was located, there was a tall, Victorian wardrobe blocking my view of the near back corner of the room to the right of the bed. In the other direction, there was a crimson-colored velvet settee and some rather uncomfortable looking chairs set up with a mahogany table at the center. An antique, Persian carpet, threadbare and dusty, defined the sitting area. I noticed some tapers, candleholders and a matchbox on an end table. There was a bookcase crammed full of books to my left on the other side of the little door.

I took a quiet step forward into this strange attic room, my head turning left and right, taking it all in. There were dark oil paintings hung on the rough batten board walls. There were heavy, crimson drapes framing the front window. High above the Gothic arch at the top of the Victorian headboard there was a thick, black fabric roll that could be lowered to cover that bit of window. "How strange," I murmured. It was another moment before my mind registered the fact that my eyes had naturally fallen upon a figure crouching in the corner to the right of the bed. I thought, at first, that it was a dummy of some sort left over from a long ago Halloween tableau, but my flashlight struck it in the eyes and the eyes squeezed shut and a hand came up to shield the closed eyes from the too-bright LED light. I lowered the light, my heart skipping several beats in shock. "Who are you?" I cried. I didn't think anyone had been relegated to the attic! My parents were prone to stashing desolate relatives in any location, evidently. How was it that this one had escaped my notice?

"You should go away and pretend you never saw me," he replied, for it was a young man somewhere around my own age, which was nearly eighteen. "If you know what's good for you."

"Apples and fiber are good for me. I'm not very fond of either though. What are you doing hiding up here?"

"I'm not hiding," he said, although it sure looked as though he had been hiding from me since he was still crouched in the dim corner. I really couldn't see him that well.

"Then come over here and let me see you."

"You need to leave."

"Are you supposed to be up here?" He did not reply. "How did you get in?" He seemed to have nothing further to say to me, but I was curious about him now that I had discovered him. "You might as well stand up and come over here and talk to me because I'm not going to be thrown out of my own attic. You have some explaining to do." His dark eyes had opened and he'd been watching me, but now they narrowed. I wasn't exactly afraid of him. He hadn't rushed me and attacked me, beaten me senseless for invading what was obviously his space. If the shoe had been on the other foot and he'd come creeping into my room unexpectedly, I might have gotten hysterical and outraged to a degree that would have been discomforting to anyone within a twenty yards or so distance. Finally, the rebel in me surfaced, the conspirator and negotiator took control. "I don't particularly care that you live up here. You can stay for as long as you like. But this is my home and I do have an inalienable right to know who is residing under this roof. I am a great believer in privacy, so your secrets, whatever they may be, shall remain perfectly unspoken, uncommunicated to anyone else in this house. I solemnly promise you that." He gave a short snort of skepticism. "Come over here. I don't bite and I won't clock you with the flashlight or anything. I'm avoiding my brothers and sisters today because they are *the plague* and will be the death of me if I let them near." I walked to the crimson settee where I perched on the edge of one cushion. "Come talk to me for a minute and then I'll go away and no one will be the wiser for my having been here at all."

"You have a weird way of talking," he said as he slowly stood up to his full height which was perhaps an inch or two shy of six feet. I was exactly five feet short.

"I read a lot. I do not care to watch television. It's insulting and noisy and…well, I do like the BBC broadcasts. I indulge in them occasionally." He was coming closer, warily watching me as if I was a cat and he was a mouse, that he expected me to pounce on him when he was close enough and bite his head off. "Do you have a name?" I asked.

"Of course I do, but I'm not telling you what it is."

"Are we in school together?"

"No."

"Oh." I clicked off the flashlight. The room grew very dim and dark. "Can we light a candle? I like candlelight, don't you?"

"No, let's just sit in the gray light and get this inquisition over with."

I nodded. "You do know some big multi-syllable words yourself. I'm impressed."

"You're annoying me," he said. He hadn't sat down yet, even though he'd given me the impression that he was coming to this end of the room to join me for that purpose. "You're Jessie," he said. My expression made one corner of his mouth turn up in a sly grin. "You're not the only one who creeps around inside the walls of this house. You'd be surprised what a person can discover just listening from behind a wall. You're not the youngest, but you are the oddball and your brothers and sisters harass you when your parents aren't within earshot. You have a crazy aunt who lives in a third floor tower room. She sits in her rocking chair and makes up weird little rhymes all day. She likes to embroider, but she only embroiders black moons and silver stars on white handkerchiefs. There are literally a thousand of them all over her room. I don't know which one of you is weirder, you or her!"

"Why are you living in our attic and prowling around inside the walls of our house listening to us and evidently spying on us, as well? Are you on some sort of secret mission? Did the mayor hire you to do surveillance on my family? Do you work undercover for the police? Are we under investigation?"

"You have a very vivid imagination," he said. "No to all of that farfetched nonsense."

"Then what are you doing here? Surely, you weren't built into the house back at the turn of the twentieth century?"

"Do I look that old to you?"

"Where do you go to the bathroom?" I asked, looking a-round. There were no bathrooms in the attics as far as I knew.

"Do you really want to know?" he countered.

I guessed not. "Where do you wash your clothes? Take a shower?"

"In your pool house, if you must know. There're a washer and dryer there, and a shower," he replied. "And a bathroom," he added.

I hadn't thought of that because the pool had cracked long ago, when there had been a small earthquake, and was now a third full of stagnant murky water. No one swam anymore. No one used the pool house. It was hidden behind a tall hedgerow, invisible from the main house. A body could live there without our being aware of it, as evidently had happened already. "What do you eat?"

"The same things you eat, only I eat my meals in the form of leftovers."

That explained Cook's peeved attitude. I thought she had bunions or hemorrhoids, or something, and that was what was making her so irritable. She was miffed about food going missing from the fridge and pantry. "There's always plenty. She cooks for an army. My mother, sisters and Aunt Louise are always dieting. Aunt Beatrice threw in the towel on having a nice figure when they moved in with us."

"You're not going to tell anyone that I'm living in your attic, are you?" he asked, a hint of a threat or a warning in his tone.

"No, of course not. What do I care? The place is crawling with castaways, what's one more?"

"Do you have a spare key you can loan me? I'm getting tired of crawling in through the cellar window."

"You want a key?"

"Yeah, to the back door."

I shrugged. "I'll try to find one for you then." He nodded, walked to the front window and stood looking out at the rain. "You aren't planning on murdering us, one by one in our beds, are you?"

"No. I've never killed anyone," he said, leaning his forehead against the cold glass. "I'm not going to hurt anyone if I don't have to. I just need a roof over my head, a place to stay for a while. This house is so huge I thought, maybe, I could just sneak in and find a place to escape from the world where no one will bother me." He glanced back at me and I got the message. I was bothering him. I'd disturbed his solitude.

I stood up. "Sorry to intrude upon your space. I was just exploring the interior of the house. I saw the stairs and came up. I didn't know you were up here."

"Can I trust you?" he asked.

"Yes." I wasn't going to elaborate. I had told him I could keep a secret. I could. I shouldn't have to reiterate that. "Where did you get all these books?" I asked.

"From the library. From boxes in some of the other attics. From your room." I caught my breath. "I risked it when the house was empty about five weeks ago. You always have your nose in a book. I figured you might have something worthwhile to read. You do. I haven't had a chance to bring the books back yet."

"You can keep them up here for now." I walked to the little door. "Does my room have a secret door then?"

He turned his head to look back at me over his shoulder, and again the corner of his mouth curved up in that sly smirk of a smile. "Maybe," he replied. The way he said it sent a shivery sensation down my spine, but this wasn't like the cold finger of death tracing my spine. This sensation hit the base of my spine then unexpectedly burst like a firework in my pelvis and I gasped. Heat rose in my cheeks like an after effect. I hadn't blushed in ages!

"I have to go," I murmured.

"Maybe, one night, I'll sneak down and visit you," he said, his voice low.

I slipped through the small doorway back into the narrow stairway feeling strangely jittery with a blend of nervousness and excitement. I had found a strange young man living in our attic! I was not going to betray his presence in our house. I was not going to tell my father, who would be prowling the attics with an elephant gun in search of this interloper in our midst in a heartbeat if he learned of his inhabiting our little garret. "Is this how you get in and out?" I asked from inside the wall.

"Yeah," he replied, his voice closer. I looked back and saw he had come to the doorway and was looking at me. "I certainly don't go waltzing down the stairs to the third floor hall and make my way through the house to get in and out. Have fun exploring these secret routes, Jessie, but don't bother me again."

"I won't," I said. At least, I had no intention of doing so, not then anyway.

"Hey," he called as I started back down the steep stairs. I hesitated. "Leave the key for me in your room, on the mantle next to the raven statue."

"I will."

"Don't wait up for me," he said and then the panel clicked shut. I was alone inside the walls, carefully making my way back down to the third floor, my thoughts in a whirl from my conversation with our mysterious attic inhabitant.

Dinner was a painful affair held every night at seven o'clock sharp. We had to be the only family in existence who were still required to dress for dinner, like we were somebodies instead of some bodies. I had chosen an Edwardian-era ball gown, rescued from a trunk a number of years ago. I was quite fond of the sapphire-blue color, the empire waist, the puffed sleeves, the sumptuous materials used to concoct this high-end garment circa 1912. I felt like a first class passenger going to dine in the elegant dining room of the fated Titanic. Well, *fated* more or less described how I felt about dining with my siblings and parents and assorted relatives, except for Aunt Louise, of course, who never came down to dinner.

Tonight, I had chosen to wear my red hair pinned up. I was not very good at doing an up-do on myself so it was a bit lopsided and already stray coils of hair were escaping the pins designed to hold hair in place, except on my head. I had to have the slipperiest hair of any living human being on this planet. My cheeks still bore traces of hectic color. I had been thinking about our mystery resident as I'd dressed, all the while very self-consciously aware that he could be watching my every move. I would have to go over every inch of wall area in my room. That he had gotten books from my bookcases meant that he had to have a means of entering my room because I locked my door whenever I left my room. I did not trust my brothers or my sisters. They were mean creatures, spiteful, nasty and vicious. For some reason, my red hair provoked them, as if I were a matador's red cape and they were enraged bulls with a loathing for the dreaded target.

My mother was already at the table, as were Aunt Beatrice and Uncle Reggie. My mother and Aunt Beatrice were talking in hushed voices at the far end of the table. Uncle Reggie was helping himself to the liquor laid out on the sideboard, bourbon, whisky, gin—he could easily be annihilated before the rest of the family trickled in for the evening repast. I chose to avoid walking down the length of the table adjacent to the sideboard because Uncle Reggie was a butt pincher. I did not fancy having my butt pinched as if it were a ripe tomato.

"Jessamyn, that is an interesting gown you're wearing tonight," Uncle Reggie commented, his myopic, predatory eyes gleaming behind the narrow lenses of his glasses.

My mother glanced at me and scowled slightly before returning her attention to her sister, with whom she had a particularly close relationship. I could not boast of any such closeness with any of my three sisters. We did not wear one another's clothing. We did not share shampoos, cosmetics or perfumes. We either avoided one another as much as possible, or squared off for minor skirmishes that occasionally flared into major battles with damages being incurred to community property and our persons.

I sat down in my seat, tilting my face up to study the still life displayed in a huge gilt frame above the sideboard. It had hung there for generations. The painting was both lush and disturbing. It depicted numerous varieties of fruits, severed by a knife, their pulpy or pitted centers spilling out, mingled juices staining the tablecloth, dripping over the edge. The knife had a large and rather deadly looking blade with a slight curve to it, the blade set into a bone handle. I frowned, began to look away, however, from the corner of my eye I saw a slight movement to the left of the frame and realized that it was not a dark knothole, but a dark eye staring back at me.

I suppose some young ladies would find being ogled from a knothole in the paneling quite disturbing. I found it merely surprising and uncomfortable. I picked up my napkin and used it to polish an imaginary smear from my sharp, silver-handled steak knife. Then, in a fluid and graceful series of actions, I rose from my seat and hurled my knife at the knothole. Well, not directly at it since I didn't intend to take his eye out, but it struck the wall true about a half inch from the hole, quivering slightly with the force of the throw.

"What the deuce!" cried Uncle Reggie who had been refilling his scotch at the sideboard. The knothole had transformed into a knothole once again; it was no longer an eye.

"Spider," I said. "Missed it, I guess." I shrugged.

"What the devil do you think you're doing throwing knives in the house!" cried mother, aghast.

"I told you, didn't I? That one's loaded with repressed violence," Andrew said. I didn't exactly know when he had entered the room, but there he was. He was my nineteen-year old brother, the one who strongly resembled our father with his brown hair and blue eyes. "Really, Mother, she should be confined!"

"There'll be no more knife throwing in this house, do you hear me, Jessamyn?" Mother said.

She didn't even wait for my response but turned back to Aunt Beatrice, her mothering duties finished for the evening. As I went around the table to retrieve my knife, I heard her murmuring that I was hardly college material, that they would be saddled with my upkeep for the remainder of their days since no man would look twice at such a volatile creature as me. I wiggled the knife loose from the wall, rubbing my finger down the new wound in the paneling. No, it was not the first time a knife had been thrown at the walls in this house, nor would it be the last. If truth be told, we were all ticking pressure cookers and occasionally we needed to let off a bit of steam in a quick burst of mischief or mayhem before settling down to a simmer again. "Don't stare at me," I said aloud to the knot hole.

"Nobody's staring at you," Glenn, my fifteen-year old brother, muttered as he brushed past me to take his place at the table. He had mother's ash-blonde hair, green eyes. Tonight, he was dressed like an orchestra conductor in a cutaway coat, white shirt, white bow tie, white vest with exquisite, little, jeweled buttons and black trousers with satin stripes down the outer seams. He was wearing sneakers, lime green with electric blue insets and neon orange laces.

I returned to my seat as Caroline, my eldest sister at twenty-two, breezed into the room like a princess. Laura, a year younger than Caroline followed in her wake. Both of them wore cocktail dresses circa the fifties with chunky rhinestone jewelry. Caroline's strawberry-blonde hair was in a sleek chignon, while brunette Laura always wore her hair in a page boy because she didn't like to fuss with it and the look suited her. They took their seats at the table. Uncle Reggie resumed his seat.

My father strode into the room, his eyes moving from person to person, counting heads and finding the table lacking by several. Thirteen-year old Ruth and eleven-year old Jonathan came noisily into the room arguing over a hand-held video game. My father snatched the game from Jonathan's hand and tucked it into his inside jacket pocket, shooting them both a look that quieted them instantly. They slunk into their seats like scolded puppies, even though no word of reprimand had been spoken. "Where's Baxter?" father asked, shifting his gaze to Uncle Reggie.

"Damned if I know," Uncle Reggie replied with a shrug as he lifted his glass and took a healthy swallow of amber liquid.

"He was showering when I was getting dressed. I could hear his wretched baritone from across the hall," Andrew replied.

"Then we shall wait another minute or two for him."

"Ah, jeez!" Jonathan cried.

"You may leave the table," Father said. There was nothing in his tone of voice, no threat, no condemnation, no anger, but Jonathan, looking both incredulous and rueful, rose from his chair and left the room, trained to obedience since birth.

"Must you be so harsh with the children?" Mother queried. It was her standard patter after father's show of supreme authority. She really didn't care, if truth be told.

"The mouth on that boy will be the death of him one day, mark my words," Father replied.

We all sat silently around the table, trying with all our might to become invisible, to not make a twitch or suffer an involuntary tic that might draw the laser beam of Father's eye upon us. I could feel a sheen of perspiration coating every bare inch of my skin as I suddenly worried that the exposed cleavage above the bodice of my gown might draw harsh criticism and banishment to my room with an empty stomach. I really didn't have much of a figure, but this gown was snug and pushed what I did have together in a manner that men might find of interest. I held my breath until I began to feel lightheaded with anxiety and lack of oxygen. Just when I thought I would slip unconscious beneath the table, Uncle Baxter strolled into the dining room and took his place, to my father's immense satisfaction.

"Charlotte! You may serve!" Father called. Immediately she came through the swinging door between dining room and butler's pantry with a huge tureen of soup. Curls of steam rose from the tureen. "Pea soup! Marvelous!" exclaimed father as he began ladling thick, yellow-green semi-liquid, with floating bits of grayish-pink ham, into bowls, passing them to left and right until we each had a bowl of soup, with varying amounts in them, as his ladling was inconsistent, before us. I felt blessed to have a bowl with a mere half ladle of soup lurking at the bottom. Pea soup, at least Charlotte's version of it, was more like pea paste with tidbits of porcine gristle scattered throughout. I figured I could choke down this much without gagging on it.

I actually pitied poor Ruth who had gotten a bowl with two ladles worth in it. She looked as if she was going to be ill as she lifted her soup spoon. The spoon hesitated above the murky pond scum-colored contents of the bowl. Her eyes darted left and right as if beseeching someone, anyone, to help her avoid her terrible fate. I saw her realize that no help would be forthcoming. Trouper that she was, she stiffened her back, squared her shoulders and began eating. Before long, her face was the same color as the pea soup and I thought for sure, would have put money on it, that she was going to spew across the pristine damask tablecloth. I was a lousy gambler and was grateful that I hadn't placed a wager on her ability to control her gag reflex.

The meal ground on, salad, fruit, potato, entrée—tonight veal cutlets, not a favorite of mine by far, white asparagus (nothing like eating severely chlorophyll-anemic green vegetables), cheese, bread and then, thank God, Charlotte's amazing turtle cake. I confess, I have a passion for caramel. It wasn't a secret by any stretch of the imagination and, as a result of that general knowledge, the slice my father cut for me was razor thin. My eyes met his as I took my plate. In their depths, I saw the silent challenge in his gaze. He *wanted* me to protest, to make a remark that would get me exiled to my room. That was the cruelty of Randolph Edwin Pemberton. I had been the victim of his peculiar depravity plenty of times growing up. But, as with anything, when you have a lot of exposure to something over time you build up an immunity to it. I merely gave him a Mona Lisa smile and ate my practically see-through slice of cake without uttering a word. Of course, the razor blade has two edges, and one never knows how deep the cut will be on the back swing. "Jessamyn, you do not have the breasts to do justice to that gown. Do not trouble yourself to wear anything that revealing again, as quite frankly, there is nothing to see on that scrawny frame of yours that would appeal to anyone with an appreciation of the female form."

The sting of the bee can be fatal to someone with an allergy to bee venom. I could feel my throat closing up, not due to anaphylactic shock, but to the sudden rush of tears, so many I could not swallow them all without drowning myself. What saved me was my father rising abruptly from the table and stalking out of the dining room, our signal that the meal was over. Chairs were slid back and the room emptied like a theater where the word *Fire!* had just been shouted from the balcony.

I was in my nightgown, sitting on the window seat, staring out at the back lawn. There were no lights on in the room. It was after midnight, still raining with an occasional distant flash of lightning and low rumble of thunder. I could not sleep. I suffered from insomnia. Not every night, just when I was wounded. Sometimes it was hard to staunch the flow of blood from the internal injuries inflicted by my father's sharp tongue.

One moment I was alone, and the next, I sensed a presence in my room. I did not, however, feel threatened. If the Angel of Death had come for me, so be it. If a bogeyman had come up from the dank cellars to try to frighten me to death, then he was in for a hard nights' labor. If my grandfather's ghost had decided to haunt me, instead of Laura or Caroline, who was I to complain? Ghosts will do whatever they please.

I heard a slight metallic sound and realized that it came from the area of the fireplace. Attic man had come for the key I had laid on the mantle hours ago. I did not move. All my dark thoughts scattered, leaving me suddenly with the sensation of empty-headedness. I bent my head, resting my forehead against the cool glass and closed my eyes. I willed myself to be invisible, but the cloak of misery mantling me seemed to be a beacon for I sensed that he had moved, was standing just behind me now. "For you," he said. I felt him set something down beside my hip on the cushioned seat.

And then he was gone. He moved so silently it was eerie. I just sensed that he was gone. There one moment, gone the next. I waited a few moments then shifted my eyes to glance down at the seat. Raising my head, I took a closer look. He had brought me a very generous slice of turtle cake on a paper napkin. Tears threatened again, but these did not feel as if they were about to strangle me. I smiled. Had he watched the whole grim proceeding in the dining room? "Thank you," I said aloud.

I ate my cake, jaws aching as I savored every bite of it. Then, I soaked the paper napkin in the sink until it was a soggy, sodden, limp vestige of itself before flushing the final bit of evidence away. I climbed into my four poster bed, pulled the covers up and stared at the crocheted canopy above me. A piece of cake in return for a key that gave him easy access to our house. I think he had gotten the better deal in that trade, but I was grateful just the same for his kind gesture, bringing me the cake that my father had deprived me of, assuaging a wound. Stranger in our attic, you have moved up one notch in my opinion and I shall not betray you. I will keep your presence in our home a secret. Whoever he was, he understood what I was.

I suddenly sat up with a gasp. What about poor Jonathan, sent to his room without his dinner? Here I was well fed, indulging in a big slice of purloined cake while my, admittedly annoying, littlest brother, lay in his bed with an empty belly gnawing on his ribs. I wished I was as adept at moving through the mysterious inner workings of the house so that I could slip down to the kitchen to raid the pantry and refrigerator in order to bring my brother something to soothe his rumbling tummy.

I lay back down with a new resolve to do further, more extensive explorations within the interior walls of the house. I would map out the secret passages and stairways. I would be the explorer who conquered the unknown—only those passages were not entirely unknown. The young man with the ebony hair and dark eyes, the one dressed all in black like a shadow man, knew these routes intimately. How long had he actually been living in the attic that he was thus so familiar with the passages? How long had he been studying the dysfunctional aspects of my home life?

And why exactly was he in our house anyway? That was the big money question. Yet, I knew I would never ask. That was his business, not mine.

It was late October before I saw our secret attic dweller again. I was glad when I ran into him in a passage, even though encountering him at a turn startled me badly. "I need to talk to you," I whispered urgently. He nodded, pointing upward, indicating we should meet in his attic garret. I shook my head. I had a mountain of homework and would be confined to my room all night.

He reconsidered, leaned close and whispered in my ear, "Then I will come to you, but it won't be until late." I nodded. He glanced at the notebook in my hand, saw that I was mapping the secret routes behind the interior walls. He gave me a smirk and a speculative look then squeezed past me, muttering, "Later," as he did. I did not look behind me to watch him go. My heart was beating too fast and so hard that I felt dizzy. I leaned against the rough wall, ignoring the cobwebs and dust kitties.

When I could trust my knees not to give way, I continued in the direction that I had been going. The beam of my flashlight soon caught something unexpected on the bare wood floor. I stood looking down at the hundred dollar bill for several long moments before bending to pick it up. It was crisp and of the most recent U.S. Treasury design. How in the world had it come to be lying on the floor in a secret passage? Yet another mystery!

I concluded my explorations for the day as it was nearly time to dress for dinner. I peered through a knothole in the Lilac guest room before slipping through the secret panel. This room was directly across the hall from my own bedroom. Quickly, I darted through the door, pulling it closed behind me then turned to cross the hall to my own room. I actually gave a chirp of shock when I found Andrew standing there. "You scared me!" I said.

"What have you been up to?" he asked. "God, you're filthy! What in the world were you doing in there?"

My brain whirled then clinked as a plausible excuse fell into the slot connected to my mouth. "I was on my way to change for dinner when I heard a noise in the Lilac Room. I thought it might be a rat. Charlotte's been complaining on a daily basis that food has been disappearing. I went in, closed the door so it couldn't escape into the hall, and I searched everywhere for the little devil. Yes, I did crawl under the bed. It's filthy!"

"Did you find any rat?" he asked, his tone telling me that he wasn't buying my tale.

"No, of course not. And I don't have time to haul all the furniture away from the walls to look for a hole he might get into and out of the room through. I'll have to do that tomorrow."

"Maybe we should both look," he said. "We should do it right now." He grabbed my wrist, twisting it a bit as he flung the door of the Lilac Room open and shoved me back inside, following right behind me. His blue eyes searched the room as if he expected to find someone or something in the room. Swinging the door shut, he pushed me toward the bed. "Let's find that rat," he said, his voice cold.

"It could come in through the closet," I said.

He gave the closed closet door a glance then shook his head. "I doubt it." He got down on his hands and knees and looked under the bed. He looked for what I felt was a long time before he slowly stood up. Abruptly, he grabbed me, lifting me right up off my feet and hurled me onto the bed. He pounced on the bed, straddling me before I could even react to his having thrown me like a sack of potatoes. He grabbed my wrists, taking them in one hand and pinning them over my head.

"Let go of me and get off of me!" I cried.

"You didn't crawl under the bed," he sneered. "At least not this one. Now, tell me how you got so damned filthy!" He drew his free hand back and, when I didn't answer quickly enough, he slapped my face so hard I saw bright flashes of light and tasted blood. "What are you up to, Jessamyn?" he demanded. "There's something going on around here. Father's on edge. He's angry as all hell. Things have been disappearing from all around the house. What do you know about that? Tell me!"

"I don't know anything!" I shouted, blood spraying from between my lips.

"Tell me!" he shouted right in my face, his spittle flecking my skin. When I didn't say anything more, he hit me again fore-hand and backhand until my ears roared, my eyes blurred with tears, and my lip split.

"Stop it, Andrew! Stop!" I cried.

"You are a sick girl," he said, his voice so like father's it nearly stopped my heart. He slid backwards off the bed, hauling me up, my wrists still trapped in his vise-like grasp. "You need to be taught a lesson, is what you need! Father has never been hard enough on you!" He threw me across the room. I crashed against the dresser, the wind chuffing out of me. I crumpled to the floor. He strode angrily across the room, kicking me in the ribs, then the hip. I covered my head and took that blow just above the elbow of my left arm. "You need to be punished!" I heard him rip the leather belt from around his belt loops. He struck me with it a dozen times before the door suddenly burst open and my little sister Ruth stuck her head into the room. "Get out of here!" Andrew barked at her.

"It's time for dinner," she said, her voice hushed and urgent. "We have to go downstairs now!"

"Get out!" I heard the soft click of the door. Andrew struck me three more times, his breath coming in snorts like an angry bull's. "I'll tell them you're indisposed and won't be down for dinner. You're staying up here. You'd better not show your ugly face downstairs tonight or, I swear to God, Jessamyn, I will snap your neck like a dry twig and that'll be the end of you!" He strode to the door, letting himself out.

I lay on the floor for I don't know how long before I finally found the strength to get onto my hands and knees and then haul myself to my feet. I staggered across the hall to my room and locked the door, wedging a chair under the door knob. I then stumbled to the bathroom where I peeled off my bloody, filthy clothes and climbed into the deep claw foot tub, pulling the shower curtain closed. The water was icy cold at first. I sat on the edge of the tub shivering until it was the right temperature, or rather, the temperature I could bear on my battered flesh. My knees wobbled. I had to kneel in the tub to finish washing myself so as not to fall and further hurt myself. With effort, I shut off the taps, but I did not have the strength to climb out of the tub.

It was there that he found me, lying in a cold, pink puddle at the bottom of the tub, curled into a fetal position. "Jesus," he said softly.

He lifted me out of the tub, sat me on the closed toilet lid then draped a towel around my bruised shoulders. He used another towel to rub my hair dry, the part that had been in the puddle. He left that towel draped over my head and face. I wondered why, until he switched on the bathroom light and I groaned, squeezing my eyes shut. My face hurt. My eyes hurt. My mouth hurt. My body hurt as well as ached. I heard him open the medicine cabinet. "What are you doing?"

"I'm looking for something to treat your injuries with."

"Look in the narrow cabinet over there." I lifted one hand to point to the cabinet behind the door.

"What the hell happened to you?" he asked, his voice quiet but angry.

"Nothing," I lied, keeping my voice soft and flat, devoid of emotion. If I let the emotion surface, it would not be pretty. I would crack like a fragile porcelain vase. I would shatter.

He rummaged around in the cabinet then came back and crouched down in front of me. Pushing the towel back off my head, he looked at my face. I carefully avoided making eye contact with him. "Was this your father's doing?" he asked as he tilted my chin up. I averted my eyes. "Keep your head up." He soaked a cotton ball with water and hydrogen peroxide that he'd mixed in an emesis basin then daubed the cut on my right cheek with the cotton, making me wince. "Hold still."

"That hurts," I said blandly.

He blew air out through his nose. "You're not so tough," he said. "Go ahead and cry. I've seen girls cry before."

"I'm sure you have." I winced again as he treated the cut on my jaw. "Charlotte's been complaining about the food going missing."

"Yeah, I figured she would eventually." He threw that cotton ball away, soaked another and blotted the blood from my shoulder wound. I risked a glance and saw that my skin was the color of a plum. He pulled the towel away, exposing me completely, his dark eyes taking in every deep bruise. "Girl, your family is beyond sick." Rising gracefully to his full height, he went to the door and grabbed my nightgown from the hook where it hung. "Can you raise your arms?" I shook my head. My shoulders felt as if they had been wrenched from their sockets. He unbuttoned the bodice completely to the waist. "Then we'll do it this way." He crouched down again and dressed me from my ankles up, helping me stand so that I could get my arms into the long sleeves. He leaned close to me, my breasts brushing his chest as he lifted the top of the nightgown from behind and settled it on my shoulders. His hands moved to my waist and slowly, carefully, he buttoned each pearl button except for the top one. His knuckles lightly stroked my jaw. "Now, let's get you into bed." Catching me off guard, he lifted me up in his arms, carrying me to my bed. He set me down on the edge of it so he could pull the covers down then got me settled in bed. "I should let you sleep," he said.

"Don't go!" I whispered when I felt him shift as though to rise. He was sitting on the side of the bed.

He was silent for some time before he lay down beside me. "I can stay for a little while," he said. "I don't like leaving you a-lone when you're hurt this bad." He shifted onto his side so that he could see me. "Who did this to you?"

"Andrew."

"Bastard!" He got up, went and shut the bathroom light off, then came back to the bed. I heard him remove his shoes. "Move over." I could barely move. He flung the covers aside, shifted me to make room so that he could lie down beside me, then he pulled the covers over us. I was icy cold, shivering. He curled himself around me, his arm across my waist. "Why'd he do it?"

"Because I lied."

"Lied about what?"

"What I had been doing in the Lilac room. I told him I thought there was a rat to explain why I was so filthy from exploring the secret passages."

"Stay the hell out of the walls from now on," he said. "You don't need to be in there. And I don't need you to be caught in there." He realized he'd spoken harshly to me. "I'm sorry," he said more calmly. "If anyone catches you sneaking around in the passages then that puts my being in the attic in jeopardy." His breath was warm against my aching shoulder, his arm around me surprisingly comforting. I don't think anyone had been this close to me in a non-aggressive manner since I was a child. "Jessie," he said, "there are secrets here even you aren't aware of."

"Are there other people living in the attics?"

"No. Just me."

"What do you mean then?"

"One day I'll tell you, but for now, I can't say anything."

"Why are you here?" I asked.

"I heard rumors." He stopped himself and was quiet for a few minutes. Then he said, "Your family is incredibly rich."

"I know."

"Not all their money was legally obtained."

"What do you mean?"

"There have been certain activities, since before this house was even constructed, that have added wealth to your family's coffers. The sins of the Pembertons are unusually extensive." His lips were at my ear. "You are an innocent," he whispered. "Stay that way. Finish school. That's all you need to do."

"My mother won't let me go to college."

He was silent again. And then, gently, he turned my head slightly toward him and he pressed his lips against the corner of

244

my mouth very lightly. "Go to sleep," he said softly. "You're starting to distract me."

"What's your name?" I asked. He'd been living in the attic for at least two months, maybe longer.

"Look, you have to promise me that you'll never throw another knife at me," he whispered.

"I won't. I promise."

"When you do stuff like that it draws attention to things I don't want certain people aware of. Understand?"

"Yes. I'm sorry."

"No more knives."

"No."

His breath was like warm butterflies wings, soft and fluttery against my cheek. "My name is Pen."

"Like quill pen? Ink pen? Fountain pen? Ballpoint pen?"

"Shh! Yes, like all of those." He moved his hand again, lightly caressing my breasts before circling my waist again. "And for what it's worth, you were beautiful in that blue gown that night. You have perfect breasts, although at the moment they're somewhat bruised." I found the will to turn in his embrace. His face was close to mine. "Your ability to keep secrets is going to be severely tested in the next few months," he warned.

"I'm not very good at lying. I'll work on that. I am, however, an expert at keeping secrets."

"The fact that I'm still here attests to that trait in you." And then he kissed me. My lips hurt, but my aching heart and soul rejoiced in the thrill and awakening I experienced from my first real kiss. "I should not be doing this," he murmured, but he kissed me again. "Now we're both in danger of discovery."

"I won't let them discover you. I will protect you to my dying breath and keep your secrets safely locked within my very soul."

"Good girl. Now close your eyes and try to get some sleep."

"Will you stay with me?"

"Until close to dawn, then I really have to go."

I slept after a while. It was a comfort to have him with me, even though I knew it was very odd to have a near stranger in my bed, one I did not know anything about, other than the fact that he was living in our attic and he knew some of my family's darkest secrets, whatever they may be. I, curiously enough, felt safe with him, unlike how I felt with my own brothers and sisters. Andrew had never hurt me this badly before. I had been afraid of him to-night, afraid of his shocking violence and cruelty. That he had grown up to be so much like father disappointed me quite deeply. Were none of us capable of rising above the darkness that flowed through our veins like shadows, nurturing us on malevolence and moral corruption? I had never thought of myself that way, but was I really any different from my siblings? My parents? My ances-tors? That it troubled me so much must mean that on some level, at least, I was concerned and aware that this was all very wrong.

It was not quite dawn when I felt Pen slip from my bed. He tucked the covers close around me to preserve the residual warmth from his body being close to mine all night. I struggled to disen-tangle myself from the shreds of a chaotic dream. "Pen," I mur-mured, his name stumbling over the swelling of my lip. "I found a hundred dollar bill on the floor."

"Where was that?" he asked from across the room.

"In the passage, not far from where we met yesterday."

"Where is it now?" His voice was suddenly terse and I was afraid that he was now angry with me.

"The front pocket of my jeans," I whispered.

"You can't be found with that. It would be too dangerous for you. I'll take it for safe keeping." He wasn't mad at me, only worried for me.

"Where did it come from?"

"You don't need to know." I heard him go into the bathroom where my clothes were lying in a bloody heap on the floor. "Be careful, Jessie," he said when he came back into the room. "Just go on with your life as usual."

"I will."

"I hope you do, for both our sakes." And then he was gone.

Nothing was said about my injuries, not even at school, although there, I did receive some frank and curious stares. Still, no one said a word to me about my appearance. My teachers studiously avoided looking at me. If they did not see me, then they did not have to concern themselves with issues like abuse in all its myriad varieties. They made it their job not to notice that I had been beaten again, even though this time it was more severe.

And thus October passed. I healed physically. I made a more conscious effort to avoid my eldest brother. I stayed out of the walls and passages. I concentrated on my class work, my homework, and spent long hours alone in my room reading books, some of which disappeared from my bookcases, but I knew where to find them if I wanted to read them again. It didn't trouble me. I left messages on the fireplace mantle if I heard anything that I thought Pen should be made aware of, like the night when Charlotte set an elaborate trap to catch the food thief. Thank God, he found the note and avoided the trap—a series of empty aluminum pails and random handheld bells, gathered from around the house, strung on wire that crisscrossed the pantry and kitchen at ankle and shoulder height, guaranteed to make enough noise to wake the dead if disturbed. I'd managed to conceal some of my own dinner in a napkin, leaving the bundle on the mantle with the note. The soiled napkin was left in my bathroom sink where I found it the next morning. I had stashed it in the laundry basket in the utility room before leaving for school.

I didn't see Pen again until one night in late November when snow was being predicted for the following day. I was asleep when he slipped into my bed. He was cold, having traversed the chilly passages to reach my room. I startled awake at the touch of his cold hand on my hip. "Shh!" he hissed. "It's only me."

"You've got the hands of a corpse!"

"Sorry, damned cold tonight." I shifted, turning toward him. I could not see anything but darkness, but I could feel him. "I need to talk to you."

"About what?"

"I'm leaving for a while. It's going to snow soon. I can't be leaving tracks to and from the pool house and all around the yard and up to the back door." He pulled me close. "It's too dangerous to stay during the winter. And it's too cold in the attic now."

"Where are you going?"

"I have a place to go."

"Will you ever come back?"

"In the spring, when the snow is gone, I'll probably come back." And then he groaned and pulled my face to his and kissed me. "I have to come back," he murmured. His mouth caught mine again as his cold hand found my breast and fondled it, sending a river of heat flowing throughout my body. I moaned into his mouth, my lips parting as I gasped. "Damn it, Jessie," he said. "Some days I wish you had never discovered me. Yet other days, I don't know how I can live without you."

"What do you mean?"

"You are the monkey wrench in the plan." He kissed me again. "I want to sleep with you every night. I dream about you. I think about you more often then I should. This was not supposed to happen."

I wasn't so ignorant that I didn't know what he was talking about. It was such a rush to realize that Pen liked me, wanted to be with me. I'd always thought of myself as some sort of human malignancy, a carrier of some virulent plague everyone was careful to avoid. That this man wanted me, had these kind of feelings for me was a revelation. That my own dormant sexuality had been stirred, awakened made me tremble in his arms. There was a void inside of me that ached. I knew he was the one person who could remedy that ache. His caresses and kisses were like a salve on all the physical and emotional wounds I suffered on a daily basis. It would take even more to satisfy the hungry ache inside of me, but he would not go that far with me. Later, I would be grateful for his restraint as it would have been disastrous for both of us if he had not maintained such rigid control of his wants and needs.

Before dawn he woke me with a gentle shake. "I have to go." He kissed my cheek.

"Pen..."

"Don't say my name aloud again until I come back."

"Will you come back?"

He pulled me against his body. "I am a moth drawn to the flame of your beauty. I am a ship lost at sea reveling in the beacon of light you cast across the dark waters, summoning me to your shore. How can I stay away from you now?" He kissed me, leaving me breathless, panting for air, my heart pounding. "See you in the spring when the snow has thawed."

And with that, he walked out of my life. I forced myself to shut the doors in my heart against him lest he creep back inside and ignite the fire I kept banked there for him. That would be the death of us, the ultimate betrayal of his trust in me to keep his secrets. I shut Pen, the black knight, in a room in my mind, and only when I was alone in my locked room, did I dare open the door and visit with him in memories.

Winter

With fall had come further fractures in the façade of my family. My father, never a kind man, nor a man of any particular warmth or compassion, became a ferocious beast prone to nerve-wracking verbal abuse and increased physical violence. With winter now upon us, it was like living with a caged and irrational wild beast that no man or woman could tame or control. While the rest of the world was enjoying their religious and secular holidays, he laid siege to the entire house, ranting and raving about how people had been stealing from him, stealing him blind and he was not going to tolerate it any longer! He fired Thayer, the housekeeper, threatening her with prosecution for theft. I watched the befuddled and traumatized woman trudge to her Volkswagen Jetta, echoes of her shocked cries of, "Why, I never, sir! I never done such a thing!" echoing in my ears. She was so upset she nearly backed into a birch tree, but corrected her trajectory of exit at the last possible moment, merely sideswiping it, leaving a fresh wound in the fragile papery bark. And then, he released Charlotte from the bonds of servitude in the kitchen, accusing her of taking all the missing food and eating some of it herself as she had put on considerable weight since the date of her first hiring. Charlotte had backlashed at him, rearing up like a confronted grizzly bear, shouting vile names and accusations in his face. He'd slapped her down, reduced her to acrimonious tears and mutterings—and then, she too was gone from our lives. I was convinced, that with one well-spoken word, my father had the capability of slaying another, of taking a human life and so utterly destroying it that the will to live would evaporate like a puddle on a hot sidewalk during a scorching August afternoon.

I sat reflecting upon all of this turmoil in the house in my window seat, occasionally tracing the words *HELP ME* in the fog of my exhalations upon the glass. I wept bitter tears for the loss of Charlotte and Thayer. Since childhood, they had been the rocks to which I had tethered the raft upon which my very existence floated in this treacherous, churning black sea in which I lived. There were no alliances in my home any longer. We were each separate combatants struggling for survival. There were no lifelines to be thrown from one hand to another, no hope of aid or assistance as we struggled into adulthood trailing the wreckage of our childhood, the flotsam and jetsam of our adolescences behind us sorry, tattered things that they were still clinging to us— our battle flags mutely displaying our multitude of defeats.

Father hired a woman named Henshaw to take control of the kitchen and pantry with an iron fist. Her inventories were epic and meticulous with nary a crumb remaining unaccounted for at the conclusion of each day. She was a middle-aged woman with a face seemingly carved by a few deft strokes of a hatchet, all sharp angles and ridges with the small, beady, dark eyes of a weasel. She was thin as a rail, and looked as if she had never eaten a decent meal in her lifetime. Her legs were the size of my arms, yet she hauled large pots and kettles around as if she were made of steel. We learned, quickly enough, not to make eye contact with her lest she accuse us of eating more than our allotment—our allotment being the amount of food father served us every evening, his portions according to his whims, as usual. Andrew looked well-nourished as did Caroline, who would be leaving home shortly after her upcoming marriage to the son of one of Father's business associates, a fellow with prematurely graying hair named George Nevers, who seemed to me to be too smarmy and self-assured. He called my father Randolph as if they were golf partners and lifelong friends. Father didn't seem to mind. George was the only person I ever saw my father become anywhere near jovial with. They knew things, shared intimate knowledge and made cryptic remarks to one another that brought tight smiles to their hard faces. Laura was also dating an associate of father's, but I could tell she was not all that fond of the young man, one Jason Langley. I often passed her room, these long winter nights, hearing her bitter weeping, and occasionally her outright sobbing. She was losing weight much like I was. We were becoming mere wraiths haunting the house, sticking close to the shadows, our eyes downcast, our lips compressed lest any word escape them that might condemn us or cause father's head to turn our way. We avoided the focus of his attention like circus hands trained to stay just beyond the sphere of the spotlight, only rushing in to perform our duties when the light was shone upon another ring.

Glenn became rather hefty. With the added weight came added surliness. Little Jonathan was wasting away, sent more often than not from the table for no apparent transgression other than his mere presence among us. His eyes were sunken, darkly ringed like a raccoon's, his cheeks hollowed. Ruth, at thirteen, was just blossoming into a beauty. Father took to doting on her.

She took to looking like a frightened doe as he led her from the dining room after dinner nearly every evening to have "a little chat" in his study. Often, Uncle Baxter went with them. I recollected Caroline, and then Laura, being treated the same way, but never had father doted on me. He had told me often enough that he did not like redheads, that he thought girls with red hair were far inferior to blondes and brunettes and had unmanageable temperaments. He said he couldn't be bothered bringing my tempestuous nature under control. I was too much trouble, in his opinion. He and mother seemed anxious for me to finish high school. Since I had already been told that there would be no college for me, I assumed they intended to throw me out onto the street to fend for myself, therefore, that knowledge began to eat away at me from the inside, upsetting my stomach and throwing me headlong into melancholy moods.

Father next hired a married couple, Julius and Nancy Blackstead, to manage the housekeeping. He set their parameters, told them what rooms they could oversee the care of and what rooms they could not even set foot into. It seldom surprised me, as March came along, when Nancy Blackstead would suddenly throw open the door of my room without as much as a quiet tap or a by your leave to announce her intention to enter. She laid siege to my room with carpet sweeper, mop and bucket, dust rags and cleansers for the bathroom while I struggled to concentrate on researching a paper on the history of the Pemberton Asylum, established by my great-great grandfather in the mid-eighteen hundreds. My great-great grandmother had been an inmate of the asylum within two years of its grand opening. I was startled to discover, among family papers, that she had been a redhead. I carefully avoided mentioning that fact in my paper lest my father deign to read what

I was writing about the subject and discover the presumed madness of a prior redhead in the family tree.

It was during my research at the town library, scanning through documents related to the asylum that the headline *Renowned Philanthropist Deemed Insane- Pentheus Beresford Committed! Pen's Friends Rally to Right a Grievous Wrong!* The name 'Pen' leapt from the page causing me to sit back in my seat with an audible gasp. My heart began beating rapidly and my mouth went dry. Could my Pen be related to this man named Pentheus Beresford? Whole avenues of exploration began opening in my brain and I shuddered. Had my great-great grandfather ruined his great-great grandfather? I had recognized the name Beresford since I was presently sitting in the Beresford Library.

Leaving my seat, like a mesmerized person under the control of a hypnotist, I climbed the dank stone stairs from the basement archives to the main level of the library, making my way through the stacks to the reading room. Above the fireplace in this room, there hung a dark portrait of Pentheus Beresford, the library's founder and benefactor. I stood before the fireplace, in which a low fire crackled for the enjoyment of the patrons who had brought books and periodicals here to read while ensconced in comfortable wingchairs and club chairs scattered about the room, and looked up into the dark eyes of Pentheus. He, like so many people whose portraits had been commissioned at that time, had a severe scowl upon his countenance, but in the depths of his dark eyes shone a warmth and vitality that bespoke a generous and glowing heart. At the corner of his mouth was a familiar subtle curve that made my breath catch. Hadn't I seen that sly quirk at the corner of Pen's mouth? I saw traces of my Pen, as well, in the line of the nose, the curve of the cheek, the angle of the jaw.

Shaken, yet stimulated by their comparison, I sought out the shelf on the second floor of the library containing all the yearbooks of our town high school and those of surrounding communities. I knew Pen was older than I was. He had been finished with high school before I had even started. I searched through the yearbooks for the years when I was in middle school, and found the name Pen Beresford listed for the year before I started high school in the town of Granger Falls where my great-great grandfather's asylum had been constructed on the cliff overlooking the falls. There was no photograph of Pen among the senior class individual pictures, but I found a photo of the Granger Falls baseball team in which P. Beresford was pictured with his teammates. His hair had been long and unruly, past his shoulders, then, but his face, though tiny, was the same. I sat down and looked at every page in that year book, finding only one other photograph in which he appeared, in that of the Science and Mathematics Club. In this picture of only nine students, he was grinning, as were they all, as if someone had told a joke or informed them that they had all won the lottery just before the picture was snapped. He was gorgeous! That he had his arm familiarly around the shoulders of a girl named Faith Marston, a beautiful girl with light-colored hair, caused a painful sensation similar to a knife being plunged into the center of my chest. Had they been a couple? Were they still together five years later? If so, how could she have tolerated all the time he had lived in our attic without him at her side? A million questions flooded my head, pummeling me, wounding me. I had begun to think of him as mine, but now I realized that he was mine only in the sense that I had discovered him living in our attic and prowling the secret passages in our home. He was mine in the sense that a butterfly landing on my hair and resting there for several long minutes while gently flapping its wings was mine. He was mine in the way a breathtaking sunset was mine—only in those few moments before the rotation of the earth causes it to slip from my view. Hot tears of disappointment stung my eyes as I snapped the cover of the book closed, rose and hastily jammed it back into the stack.

I went back to the basement, printed off the article as I gathered my research materials together, shut down the computer, snatched the printed article from the tray, cramming it into my notebook. Putting on my coat, I grabbed my canvas bag, heaving it over my shoulder and fled the library, striding quickly through the crunchy remnants of an icy rain, heading home.

I was thoroughly chilled by the time I reached the house, yet, I stood in the driveway looking at the tall peaks, the long glittering gothic-arched windows, the stonework, the massive front doors, the wrought iron lightning rods on the roof, the stoic chimneys, a couple of them grudgingly chuffing out dismal gray smoke. The designer of this house had taken inspiration, I realized, from the great Gothic buildings comprising the Pemberton Asylum. I essentially resided in a downscaled version of it.

The middle weeks of March were spent researching Pemberton Asylum more deeply. The Historical Society, I discovered, had cartons of old documents and records rescued from the asylum just after it had burnt down in 1974. The inmates at that time had been few as there had come into existence new programs allowing the mentally ill to live within the community in group home settings with supervision. Some were even allowed to live in apartments with case managers and caregivers checking on them daily. The perception and treatment of mental illness had changed vastly since the days when husbands could commit wives merely on the basis of the wife rejecting his advances, or disagreeing on how the furniture should be arranged in a certain room.

I read chilling reports of neglect and abuse labeled "treatment attempted and failed." It shocked me how human beings had been subjected to such tortures in the name of medicine, that my family history was full of sadists and cruel men professing to be experts in the field of psychiatry and psychology, pioneers in the treatment of mental illness. Part of our vast fortune had been made at the cost of terrible human suffering. It sickened me and filled me with a deep shame that this was where I had come from, the dark roots of the family tree sending their poison upward through each generation.

I embarked upon a snubbing of my family, appearing only at dinner as required, properly dressed, but abstaining from any conversation, though conversation in my family was seldom attempted as it only led to dissonance and verbal volleys of a vindictive nature. At first, no one noticed my stony silence, my lack of eye contact. But as the end of winter came, my father did take notice. At dinner one night, he threw his soup spoon down the length of the table, striking me across the cheek, leaving a smear of tomato basil soup. I turned my head away from him instead of toward him. "I have had quite enough of you!" he shouted. "Go to your room! I will deal with you later! Leave this table! Now!"

I rose as gracefully as possible from my chair and walked quickly from the dining room, sweeping past him disdainfully. I was driving nails into my own coffin at this point but I didn't care. I went up to my room, threw myself into the chair at my desk and applied pen to paper, documenting every real and perceived form of abuse ever suffered at my father's hands. My hand grew cramped, my shoulders began to ache and still I wrote, spilling everything that I had locked down deep inside of myself onto the pages, shocked and shaken by the memories I'd unleashed.

At ten o'clock, my father came into my room, the reek of alcohol and tobacco wafting from him. His blue eyes glittered with rage as he came at me. I jumped up and away from my desk chair, but the gown I'd worn at dinner caused me to stumble. "Don't you dare touch me!" I cried, but he already had a hold of my arm, was half dragging me to the center of the floor where he pushed me down onto my knees and then struck me a blow that nearly sent me into oblivion. My ears were still ringing when he began to rain blows from his belt upon me. I took the first few then scrambled to get away. His belt buckle tore skin, gouging me, making me bleed. My arms ran red with streams of blood.

"I clearly see that I have made a grave error allowing you to behave as you have this winter. I should have disciplined you like this long ago, but, I confess to you now, I hesitated due to my less than fatherly feelings toward you!" I barely registered what he was saying as my arms were up protecting my head from damage. "You are a siren, Jessamyn, and as such, you are a dangerous creature! You lure men with that red whore's hair of yours! You drive them to thoughts of lust and depravity! I should have locked you away long ago!" He hit me until I was no longer struggling, no longer able to try to escape him, and then he sat on the floor, tears streaming down his face and cradled me in his arms. "Forgive me, Jessamyn, forgive me, but I am a weak man!" he cried as he rocked with me on the blood smeared floor. "I do this for your own sake! Do you hear me? For your own sake!" From his coat pocket, he produced an old-fashioned, bone-handled straight razor, the handle of which was finely carved with a hunting scene of a hound pursuing a fox. I thought he meant to slash my throat, but instead he grabbed a handful of my hair and began hacking at it with the sharp razor. He threw handfuls of my shorn hair around the room, grabbed another clump and swept the razor across again. I was afraid to move, afraid that if I so much as uttered a sound of protest or distress that he would tilt my head back and cut my throat as easily as he was cutting off my hair. When he was finished, he dumped me off his lap and unsteadily got to his feet. "That your mother and I have tolerated such a defective being astounds and alarms me," he said as he went to the door. "You are preternaturally brilliant, as your school records indicate, however, there is something deeply and fundamentally wrong with you. I should have begun addressing that flaw in your character, your very psyche when you were yet a child. Consider this the first of many treatments I will administer to you in the pursuit of perfecting you." He left the room, closing the door firmly behind him.

I lay on the bloody floor in my tattered gown, surrounded by clumps and strands of my long hair, my head practically shorn, the rim of my right ear bleeding from a deep cut, the lobe of the other ear slashed nearly clean off. I was in shock, not feeling the pain yet.

Late that night, I was treated in the kitchen by Henshaw, who completed slicing off my ear lobe as Julius Blackstead and his wife Nancy held me down in a chair, a kitchen towel stuffed into my mouth to stifle my screams. Henshaw then cauterized the bleeding wound with the heated edge of the knife she had used to complete the amputation. I clenched my teeth against the searing pain then meekly subjected myself to having my head shaved by Mr. Blackstead since my father had left my hair beyond being able to be styled in any manner. At close to one o'clock, I was sent up to my room. Mrs. Blackstead came up a short time later to sweep up the hair and scrub the bloodstains from the floor while I sat watching her wretchedly from the edge of the bed. My bare feet were cold. I was still in the ruined, bloodied gown, looking, perhaps, like a Cinderella who had been sucked into the engine of a jet and spit back out again.

"Get to bed now," she said gruffly as she trundled her mop, pail and the carpet sweeper from the room, closing the door behind her.

I continued to sit on the edge of the bed for some time, my ears throbbing, my body wracked with terrible trembling and pain. Finally, I walked across the room and locked the door then I stripped off the gown, stuffing it into the wastebasket before stepping into the little dressing room where I surveyed all the damage at once in front of the full length mirror. I had clotted-over gouges, raised welts, angry bruises and bloodstains from my head to my knees. Miraculously from the knees down I was unscathed, small compensation that it was. I walked to the bathroom and washed at the sink. If I took a shower at this point, all the wounds would open and weep and I did not have the energy or strength or presence of mind to deal with it at this time. I washed the streaks and smears of blood off my bruised skin, carefully blotting the wounds and patting them dry. When I was finished, had put on my nightgown, there was a sudden roiling in my stomach and I vomited. The adrenalin had dissipated from my bloodstream and the pain was now a roaring beast with a hundred snarling heads demanding to be assuaged. I retched, my stomach empty. Rinsing my mouth, I tried to swallow pain relievers but I gagged on them and spit them out. For a long moment, I stared into my own eyes in the mirror and did not recognize the young woman staring back at me in stunned disbelief and horror with her shorn head, torn cheek, damaged ear lobes and mottled bruises. She was an alien being. Only the green of her irises was familiar, wrenching. I had to lower my gaze from hers, humiliated by how I had failed her a hundred, a thousand times in the course of my lifetime. "I am nothing," I murmured as I switched off the light and headed to my bed.

I missed two days of school. When I returned on the third day, I was there no more than ten minutes before I was summoned to the principal's office. "Please sit down, Jessamyn. I had a call from your father yesterday. He explained how you'd been in a terrible accident. I want to assure you that the school staff here is very supportive and understanding. The nurse is available should you need anything during the school day. Your teachers have been advised."

"I'm all right," I murmured, although I was not. I had not eaten anything but two bowls of a rather vile beef broth in three days. I felt leaden-limbed with weakness. My mind had lost the ability to focus clearly. My thoughts skittered like wild animals on ice. My entire body felt stiff with the physical insults of the beating my father had given me. "I'll do my best as always."

"You are an exceptional student. I wish there were more like you." He gazed at me for several long moments as if there was much, much more that he wanted to say. Finally, he pushed himself up out of his chair and came around the desk. "There are only a few more months until graduation, young lady. The last time I looked, you were top of your class. I'm very proud of you."

"Thank you," I murmured as he opened the door and I passed through into the outer office. Mrs. Dearborn, his secretary, could barely hide her shock at my appearance. Every step I took was like another step forward into a long tunnel that kept telescoping further ahead of me, leaving me despairing of ever seeing the doorway at its end.

That was how the next week passed, too. And then it was the vernal equinox.

Spring

Spring came rumbling in with great flashes of lightning and a cold driving rain mixed with sleet. I sat at my desk before the window, revising my report on the Pemberton Asylum, adding and deleting, changing, amending, and strengthening the terminology to get it just right. My ten-to-fifteen page mandatory report had swollen to forty-nine pages of prose and downloaded vintage photographs of the asylum, my great-great grandfather and some of the interior chambers of the asylum from the archives at the historical society. My paper had turned into a scathing analysis of the behavior of the supposedly intelligent and sane medical professionals toward the allegedly mentally infirm and troubled inmates confined within the walls of that institute of horror. I tried to excise my own personal opinions from the report, but the tone of the entire paper remained one of disgust, revulsion and outrage. There was nothing I could do about it now. I printed it, punched the pages and inserted them into a half-inch black binder. The title of the paper was *"An Examination of the Pemberton Asylum for the Insane and Infirm of Mind and How the Abuse of Power and Authority Destroyed the Lives of Many in This Community and Surrounding Communities in the One Hundred Twenty-Five Years of Its Existence."*

I shoved the binder into my backpack, switched out the light and sat in the dark on the window seat watching the great blue-white flashes of lightning strobe in the sky, followed by deep reverberating rumbles of thunder that shook the window panes. The rain slashed hard against the glass, streaking it with nature's harshest tears. I felt tired, lethargic. I still had not been allowed back in the dining room. My meals were delivered to my room by

Henshaw after the family had eaten. Occasionally, I bought lunch at school, usually a peanut butter sandwich and a carton of milk. I was the thinnest I had ever been and my clothes hung off me as if I were a scarecrow. There were still thick scabs on my damaged ears and on the deepest of the wounds my father had inflicted on me. The bruises were green and yellow with some traces of purple and lavender-blue.

I lifted my finger to write 'Help' in the fog on the glass, but a hand came from behind me to grasp my wrist and prevent me from writing my usual plea. To my credit, I did not even flinch. "You're still wet," I said. "Did you just come in? Isn't Henshaw still in the kitchen?" She had just come up a half hour or so ago to remove my tray.

"I came in through the cellar and up through the walls," he replied. The sound of his voice was like balm in my ears. "Turn around. I want to see you."

"No. You don't."

"Do you think I haven't heard all about what that bastard did to you?" I opened my mouth, but he jerked my hand down rather roughly. "There was no accident," he said, anger searing his words. "Let me see what he did to you."

"Close the drapes and turn on the light then. You might as well get the whole picture if you're so intent upon knowing the full extent of the damage."

He drew the drapes at all three windows then flicked on the overhead light. He came back and knelt before me, his dark eyes taking in the shorn hair, now slightly grown out, the damaged ears, the thinness of my face, the scars on my cheek and jaw. He tilted my head back and saw my clavicles sticking out. "Oh, Jessie," he murmured. "My God, Jess." And then he was standing up, pulling me into his arms, holding me tightly, his face against my head. It

263

was awhile before I found the strength to raise my arms and wrap them around him. He felt solid and real, warm despite the dampness of his dark clothing. "If I'd been here I would have killed him," he said, his voice low. I nodded. "Are you hungry?"

"I don't feel hunger anymore," I whispered.

"You need to eat. Come on. I'll share my sub with you." He let go of me and I nearly toppled over. Steering me to my bed, he sat me down, lifted my legs up onto the bed then propped me up with pillows. Retrieving a long, slender, brown bag from the dressing room, he sat on the bed and pulled out an eighteen-inch long grinder. The smell of warm tuna fish salad and cheese almost made me sick, but he urged me to take a bite. When the flavors filled my mouth, I moaned. Saliva began pooling in my cheeks. "Eat slowly," he counseled.

We sat on the bed eating in silence. He seemed ravenous. I managed half of what he had given me, which was actually about a third of the entire grinder, more than my stomach had held in quite a while. I felt bloated, stuffed. He gave me sips of Coke and I suddenly belched loud and long. He looked at me and, there it was, that sly grin, the light of amusement dancing in his eyes. For the first time in many long, dark months, I felt a flare of heat behind my breastbone. I laughed, revealing my chipped front tooth, the edge of the belt buckle having damaged that as well. "That wasn't very ladylike," I said. "Sorry."

"I don't mind," he replied. "It's the carbon dioxide in the soda talking."

I sighed, fell back against the pillows, my hands over my stomach. "Where have you been?" I asked.

"Home." He did not elaborate.

"And now you're back?"

"Now I'm back," he confirmed.

264

"For how long?"

"As long as it takes," he answered, getting up, crumpling the paper bag and tossing it into the fireplace where there was a low fire burning. "I've heard you've been spending long hours at the library. What have you been doing?"

"Writing a report for school."

"What's the subject?" His tone was casual, but something about his posture betrayed that it was not mere curiosity making him ask.

"The Pemberton Asylum, and how people were incarcerated against their wills and subjected to a mindboggling number of tortures, all in the name of *modern* medicine." His spine stiffened briefly before I visibly saw him will himself to relax.

He nodded. "I've heard about that place. I've actually been up to the ruins and hiked around there. The place burnt down, but some of the walls are still standing. It was constructed of stone. You can see the great gothic stone arches of the main corridor. They're like strange dominoes poised to be toppled one day." He turned back to me, "Why'd you choose that subject?"

"We were assigned to write about something local and historical. Being as I *am* a Pemberton, I chose the asylum as my topic."

"You're about as much a Pemberton as I am," he said.

"What do you mean by that?" I retorted.

"Never mind. It's not important right now. What is important," he said, as he came back to the bed and stood looking down at me, "is that you get your strength and health back. I'll bring you food, better stuff than subs and pizza. I didn't realize things had gotten as bad as this for you. We'll get you built back up."

"Can you get me a prosthetic earlobe?"

He shook his head. "Sorry, but no, I can't do that. You'll just have to let your hair grow out to cover it. I won't be buying you earrings in the future, that's for damn sure." He gave me that quirky smile again as he reached over and ruffled the very short red hair on the crown of my head. "Who gave you the prison haircut?"

"Henshaw."

"Ah, Iris Henshaw, the former women's correctional facility cook."

I cocked an eyebrow at him. "Do you know everybody and everything that goes on around here?"

"I've been making a close study of your family, as you might have concluded by now. Why else do you think I'm here? Or do you think I'm merely here to seduce you?" Again there was that bright, dancing light in the depths of his dark eyes.

"Well, a girl can hope, can't she?" I replied as casually as I could.

He sat on the edge of the bed and pulled me into his arms, holding me close. He kissed my temple, my scarred cheek, the ridge of my jaw, the tip of my nose and then his mouth found my lips, somewhat chapped as they were from dehydration, and he kissed me. "Of course you can hope," he murmured against my lips. "Hope allows you to persevere when the path ahead seems darkest and baited with bear traps and trip wires." He kissed me more possessively. "Hope makes the heart light and protects it from utter despondency."

"Are you a philosopher? A sage? A wise man?"

"No, none of those things. I'm an avenger." He sat back, looking away, aware that he may have revealed too much, regretting that he had let those words slip across his lips.

"I won't tell a soul, Pen. You have my promise. I never break a promise."

"That's all well and good," he answered as he stood up and began pacing the room. Just when he was about to say something more there was a rap on my door and Caroline ordered me to unlock the door and let her in. He glanced at me then slipped into the dressing room, closing the door, but not completely. I got up and went to the door, unlocking it, letting my eldest sister in. "I thought I heard voices," she said, suspicion in her eyes.

"I was talking to myself."

"Really, whatever for?"

"No one else talks to me these days. It gets somewhat lonely and my ears sometimes ache for the sound of a voice."

She rolled her eyes and in doing so noticed the bottle of Coke on the bedside table. "Where did *that* come from?" she demanded.

I turned and looked toward where she was pointing and saw immediately what she meant. My heart lurched, but the lie came surprisingly quickly to my lips. "I bought it at school today, found it in my backpack when I was packing my things for tomorrow."

She looked toward my backpack sitting on the floor beside my desk then her eyes searched every corner of the room. She strode to the bathroom, flipping on the light and walking in. I heard the shower curtain rings rattle around on the stainless steel halo over the tub. Of course there was no one there. My heart was hammering though as she came out, again searching the room with her eyes. Then she abruptly pulled open the door of the dressing room and walked into that area slapping at my clothes as if they hid a body behind them. I fervently prayed they did not hide anybody. Whatever route Pen used to gain access to my room was obviously hidden in my dressing room for he was not there. He had vanished as quietly as a phantom. The only sign that he had been with me was the nearly empty Coke bottle. I picked it up and drained it as she came back into my room. "Father wants to read your report before you turn it in tomorrow. Give it to me."

"I need it for tomorrow. I can print him a copy in the morning if he wants it that badly. I want to go to bed."

"He wants to read what you've written now."

"It's late."

"Give it to me!" she flared.

"Fine!" I went to my back pack, grabbed the binder from inside and threw it at her. She caught it awkwardly, glaring at me and then left, slamming the door shut behind her.

I booted up the computer, my heart racing. I downloaded a copy of the report to a flash drive that the Student Council had gifted to every honors student last month. My father didn't know I had this. Just as my paper finished downloading the network crashed. I hid the flash drive in my dressing room, just to keep it safe in case he stormed upstairs, broke down the door and conducted a full scale search of my room for a second copy. He would not find one.

He did come upstairs, banging on the door and shouting at me to let him in. I did so and he proceeded to do exactly as I had predicted. He had the original with him, and he tore the pages from the binder, practically foaming at the mouth with fury as he flung the pages onto the fire, accusing me of blasphemy against my family, of being a traitorous, ignorant little bitch who knew *nothing*! He prodded the fire with the poker then turned toward me. I thought he was going to kill me. I did not flinch. I stood my ground, glaring at him, my jaw tight, my fists clenched so hard my knuckles showed white through my delicate skin. We stood facing one another for what seemed like a very long time before he hurled the poker at me. It struck me across the shoulder, the side of my neck and jaw. It hurt, but it didn't kill me. It fell with a clang to the wood floor and I kicked it aside, my eyes narrowed dangerously, pinning him in place. In the space of a heartbeat, I saw a flash of shock in his eyes, shock that I would not cower before him. No one had stood up to him since he'd been a child. He recovered, strode to my laptop, grabbed it and then carried it out of the room with him. He, too, slammed the door, harder than Caroline had. It was as loud as a gunshot echoing throughout the house. I walked to the door, turned the lock, retrieved the poker and set it back in its place, after stirring the ashes of my report on the grate.

Finally, I went to bed, exhausted, as I tried to figure out how long it would take me to boot up a computer at the library in the school and what it would cost to print a copy there so that I could submit my paper on time. I was, however, too tired to think. I fell asleep.

The following morning, I had to submit to Mr. Blackstead searching of my backpack and person for any sign that I had a duplicate copy of the report on me. I, of course, did not. I did have the flash drive hidden under the insole in my sneaker. On the bus, I retrieved it and tucked it into my jeans pocket. When I got to school and opened my locker, a black binder tumbled out at my feet. I frowned, stooped down and picked it up. Opening the cover, I found it was a copy of my report. Pen, I realized, must have watched me hide the flash drive in my dressing room, then retrieved it, taken it someplace, printed out a copy of the report, put it in an identical binder, then broken into the high school, into my locker and stashed it there for me to find. How he had managed to do all that was beyond my being able to comprehend. I was grateful just the same for his supreme efforts. I turned in my report promptly at nine o'clock.

Three things happened during the first week of April. My brother Jonathan slipped into a coma and was hospitalized. My sister Caroline married George Nevers. The stress and strain of the wedding and reception caused Ruth to crack. She had begun acting strangely at the reception, dancing wildly and then shouting angrily at the musicians, sulking, and then laughing merrily as if her outbursts had never happened. By the time we'd returned home, she was so out of control that my father had summoned an ambulance. He came home in the wee hours of the morning alone. I saw him from my bedroom window as he parked the car and walked to the door. I heard nothing more that week, still confined to my room, except to go to school.

When I went down for breakfast late the following week, for I was once again being allowed downstairs, only now, I had to eat in the kitchen, Henshaw informed me that Ruth had been committed to the psychiatric unit at Crowley Memorial Hospital for a long term stay. I absorbed this knowledge with a passive expression, although it truly rocked me to my very core. "Is there any word about Jonathan?" I asked.

"The lad's severely anorexic, emaciated. They've placed a G-tube and are feeding him that way, after he repeatedly yanked out the naso-gastric feeding tube." She spoke about these things as if they were ordinary, everyday occurrences, but to me they were signs that the fractures in my family had become fissures. Soon they'd be fjords and that would be the end of us.

"I want to see him," I said, as I stood up. She gave me a look that set me back on my heels. Really! Who did she think she was!

I did an unprecedented thing—I went in search of my mother, finding her in the morning room reading a sailing magazine that belonged to Uncle Baxter. She looked up, clearly startled by my appearance in a room that she considered her own private area, off limits to everyone else, including her sisters Beatrice and Louise. "I'm concerned about Jonathan," I said without preamble. "And Ruth."

"Are you really? Now that's something I never expected to hear from your mouth." She turned her attention back to the page she had been reading. I walked further into the room, catching a glimpse of the page. It was a full-page photograph of a sailboat plying through rough lake waters. The photograph seemed to fascinate her. There was no written text on the page.

I frowned. "I want to visit Jonathan."

"I'm afraid that's impossible. You failed your driver's exam."

"I did not," I said calmly, even though I knew it was pointless to argue with her. My father had taken me for my exam. I had performed well on the written exam and I knew I'd done very well on the road test, yet my father had steered me out of the registry telling me that I had failed miserably and there would be no license for me. He had done the same with Caroline and with Laura. Only Andrew had his license, and a car of his own, courtesy of father's magnanimous nature, and I say that with tongue firmly planted in cheek. Father did favor Andrew, though. I wondered if Glenn would be allowed a license. He would celebrate his sixteenth birthday soon, but he didn't seem to have the same character as Father and Andrew, although he had mean down pat.

And while on the subject of birthdays, my eighteenth would be in three days' time, but I expected nothing to mark the occasion. I'd had a birthday cake one year, had an allergic reation to the strawberries, got very sick and had never had another cake since. No one even bothered wishing me a happy birthday anymore. I knew it was my birthday only because I marked the calendar every year so that I'd remember at least. "Then, will Father keep us apprised of his condition, and Ruth's?"

"Why would he do that?" She shooed me away as if I were a bothersome droning fly that had blundered into the room. "Go to school."

Dismissed, as it was clear that she was through with me, I left the house, walking to the bus stop. I was feeling out of sorts about my younger siblings. None of us got along, that was true, but even in dysfunctional families, like mine, there was some sort of emotional stake in one another's lives. Jonathan had been looking sickly for months, and Ruth had been acting strangely since the night Father and Uncle Baxter had first left the dining room with her, which had become a tri-weekly event. I had the feeling that wheels had been set in motion and were now grinding toward their inevitable destinations.

"Jessamyn, may I see you after class?" Mr. Jenson inquired. He was my history teacher, the one I had written my research paper for. I nodded. He was probably going to chastise me for writing such a lengthy report. I suppose teachers didn't like to be handed things like that. After all, they had twenty-five to thirty reports to read and grade. He'd probably found mine tedious and inappropriate.

I couldn't focus on the lesson, yet my pen wrote constantly throughout the class period. When the bell rang I snapped out of my reverie and stared down at the page I had been writing on. I had written a series of phrases- *I am nothing. It has started. Jonathan will die. Ruth will not come home. A man lives in our attic. Aunt Louise is unstable. Train wreck. Aunt Beatrice grows fatter every day. Uncle Baxter is a molester. I do not belong here nor there. Father is a cruel man. He has a heart like a cold black stone. I think I am in love. Thunderheads are forming.* I gasped, heavily scratched over the line about Pen living in our attic, shocked that I had written those words when I had diligently kept his secrets for months. Quickly, I closed my notebook and stood up.

"Jessamyn, please have a seat here in the front row for a moment. I will write you a late pass to your next class." Mr. Jenson stood up, went to the door and closed it. He returned to his desk, sat down, picked up his pen and tapped the cover of the black binder lying on his blotter, my report. He was looking off into space above my head. I thought he would just stare at the ceiling, or back wall, forever, or at least until the final bell rang. I squirmed a bit in my seat, shuffling my feet. His eyes came down and found mine, held my gaze a long moment before lowering to the binder. "I've read your report. Twice, in fact."

"Was it that poorly written?" I queried quietly. "I apologize for its length. I know it's three times the length you asked for."

"Where exactly did you get all the material for this paper?"

"I documented my references and sources on the last three pages."

"Yes, I saw that, yet when I went to the Historical Society and asked for the cartons salvaged from the old asylum, I was told there were no cartons. When I went to the library, I found just two of the documents you cited, and one old newspaper on microfiche detailing the fire that destroyed the asylum in the 70's." His eyes finally met mine and he must have seen the disbelief in my eyes, the stunned look of a young woman who had just been dealt an unexpected and near fatal blow.

"My father demanded a copy of my report the night before I turned it in. He was less than pleased."

"Yes, he called me and advised me that your paper was full of conjecture and invention. He said you would not be turning in that report. Yet, you did. I have it right here." He sighed. "It is a very well written report, very intriguing in content, but, because I cannot find the sources or the references you cite throughout its pages, I cannot give you the grade I feel your effort deserves. I'm sorry, but, I have to give you a failing grade."

I stood up, willing myself to remain calm although it felt as if a tornado was spiraling inside of me, high velocity winds tearing me apart. I took the binder from his desk and dropped it into the wastebasket. "My father burned the original copy of this report. He is a wealthy man with a towering temper. He was not happy with me. How hard do you think it would be for a man of his stature in this community, with his means, his influence, to make things disappear? I researched this paper for the full two months you gave us to write it. I did not make up one fact. I held documents in my hands, read them on microfiche and on the computer. That he went so far as to expunge these things just goes to prove what the gist of this report states—the Pembertons, singularly and as a whole, are manipulative, cold, cruel, ruthless and quite possibly not mentally sound themselves. I'm sorry I can't produce my research materials. Since you can't find them, I can only conclude that my father had them purchased or removed from circulation, or he has simply had them destroyed. I'm sorry this has to ruin my perfect academic record here in this school but there's nothing I can do about it now. It's too late." I walked to the door and laid my hand on the doorknob. I did not look back when I said, "I am, every day of my life, deeply ashamed to bear the name Pemberton." With that said, I opened the door and walked out as the bell rang.

"Jessamyn, I can write you a late pass!" he called after me.

I would rather be thrown out of school than accept a late pass from a teacher who did not believe me, who thought me a liar, a fabricator of fiction!

Three days later, he again asked me to remain after class. I was reluctant to do so. My respect for him as an educator and a human being had been shaken. Still, I had been trained to obedience so I remained in my seat, fourth row back on the far side of the room. This time he did not summon me to the front of the room. He rose, went to the door, shut it and then came up the far aisle, stopping and turning toward the window. "I have a fax machine in my home," he said. "Two nights ago, I arrived home to find, quite literally, hundreds of pages of paper strewn across my den floor. The machine was still spewing pages and would do so for another half hour. Unfortunately, the ink cartridge had run dry, but many of the pages on the floor were quite legible. I was angry at first, thinking someone had pranked me by fax blasting my machine. Then, I began gathering the documents. When I saw what they were, I admit, I sat on the floor and spent several hours sorting them, forgetting my dinner in the process. I did not dine until well past ten o'clock that night. I have been reading the pages that did print out. I have to ask you this, did you find these documents in your home? Did you fax them to me?"

"No. I didn't even know you had a fax machine. And I don't know where the documents are. I assumed my father had burned them like he'd burnt my original report."

"Is the report on your computer at home?"

"No. My father cut off my network connection then he took my laptop. He probably destroyed it. I have a new laptop now and there's nothing on it at the moment. But I do have a flash drive with the report on it. I managed to make a copy before he severed my network connection and took my laptop away."

"Then who sent me the documents? Where were they found?"

I had an inkling who had sent them. He'd probably found the documents stashed either in the attic or the basement, or some unused room in the house. He'd probably watched my father carry them into the house then spied on him via the secret passages and their peep holes. But, how could I explain about Pen Beresford living a clandestine life in the attic and walls of my home without betraying him? Without sounding absolutely out of my mind, for that matter? I couldn't. "I don't know," I replied.

He turned and his eyes met mine. I saw him look at the scar on my cheek, the scar on the ridge of my jaw, my still short, choppy hair, my damaged ears. He had seen the bruises with his own eyes. I couldn't conceal them all with clothing. "Are you in some sort of trouble?" he asked.

"Trouble?"

"Do you have a boyfriend who's abusing you?"

I shook my head. "No."

"Do you want to speak to an advisor? Principal Schuman?"

"No. I'm okay." He did not look convinced. "Really."

"I have reconsidered your grade in light of this mysterious bombardment by fax of proof that you did do the research, that these documents had existed at the time you were working on your paper. I salvaged the report from the trashcan. I will not return it. I would like to hold onto it, if I may."

"I can't bring it into my home anyway, so go ahead, keep it," I said as I stood up.

"Jessamyn, if there's anything I can do...."

"There isn't," I said, cutting him off. "I graduate in one month and one week. I have plans to move far away as soon as I can after graduation. Thank you for your concern though, and your belief in me again. I appreciate it." I slung my backpack over my shoulder and left his classroom.

The very next day he did not report for school. I heard that the office had tried contacting him a number of times, then sent the police to his home for a well-being check. He was found dead at the bottom of his cellar stairs. The police felt that he had slipped and fallen on his way to the basement to do his laundry the previous night, as the basket, clothing and linens were found strewn at the bottom of the steps. They labeled his death accidental.

I knew otherwise.

That night, Pen came to me well after midnight. I cried my heart out for Mr. Jenson who had been a good soul. "I probably shouldn't have done it," Pen said. "Hindsight is always twenty-twenty, as they say."

"You found the documents?"

"Yeah, in the attic of the other wing. I was damned lucky he didn't choose my secret lair. He might have discovered me, or wondered at the arrangement of the furniture, at the very least. I've since made it look less like a living space and more like a jumbled storage space. I was too cocky. I've got to be more cautious now. He's riled up, like an agitated rattlesnake, striking out. I want you to be very careful. Don't do or say anything to anger him further. Promise me you won't."

"All right. I don't intend to anyway. I'm sick to death of my family, if truth be told. I just want to graduate and then get the hell out of here as fast as I can."

"Where are you going to go?" he asked. My tears had subsided. I'd washed my face, blown my nose and come back to bed. He'd lain down beside me, his head beside mine on the pillow.

"I don't know yet. I'm not even exactly sure how much money I have."

"Don't worry about that. I think you'll be pleasantly surprised."

"What do you mean by that?"

"Nothing. Forget I said it. Where do you want to go?" he asked.

"I'm not sure."

"I've always wanted to see the western states," he said.

"Okay, how about Montana."

"Lots of open space there."

"Wyoming? Colorado? Washington state?"

"Not Alaska?"

"Hawaii, maybe. I hear it's beautiful."

"You're a redhead. I'm afraid you'd burn like dry timber on the beach there with all that sunshine."

"Well, what's the darkest, gloomiest state there is then? I'd probably feel right at home there."

"I think it's this one that we're living in right now." I blew out my breath in frustration. "Think global," he advised. And then, he kissed me, starting with my cheek before moving to my mouth. "I never wished you a happy birthday. Belated birthday wishes."

"Oh, well, my birthday is never celebrated anyway."

"No?" I shook my head. "You're eighteen now. If you had a birthday cake with eighteen candles burning brightly on top of it, what would you wish for before blowing them out?"

"I don't know."

"You must want something?" he urged.

I paused, my heart pounding and then took another leap. "Okay, I want you."

That gave him pause, but then he laughed softly. "You already *have* me. What else do you want?"

"No, I mean, I *want* you." He caught the emphasis this time.

"Oh, now I understand. Well, I'm not prepared for *that* tonight. Kisses and caresses will have to suffice." He kissed me again. "No giggling, no shrieking, no nothing, except maybe some very quiet moaning, understand?"

"I do. Perfectly."

"God forbid any member of your family overhear you enjoying something, experiencing pleasure and happiness."

"No, those things are forbidden here. Totally taboo."

"I am totally taboo," he said, his voice a low growl as he unbuttoned the bodice of my nightgown. I shivered with anticipation and excitement. "Don't make me gag you."

"No, I won't. I will be as silent as the night." I inhaled sharply as he spread the top of my gown open, bent his head and kissed my breast, his mouth warm and moist, his breath hot through his nose as he took my breast in his mouth, teasing me in a delicious and amazing manner. I found myself gripping his dark hair, rather harder than I'd intended. When he murmured a protest, I loosened my grip and he went back to giving me a prequel to my real birthday gift. If this was just the prequel, I suspected the gift itself would be mind-blowing—and exactly what I wanted.

He raised his head way to soon and looked at me for a long time. I started to get nervous about his close scrutiny of my face in the moonlight. "This wasn't supposed to happen," he muttered.

"What wasn't?" I asked, my voice quavering a bit. He was so strange sometimes.

"My having these kind of feelings for you," he replied. He sat up. "Close your gown, it's too distracting."

"Pen, what's the matter?" I asked as I refastened my bodice with trembling fingers. He stood and began pacing the room, clearly agitated. I thought maybe he was overly aroused, and angry now about something to do with me. Maybe he'd realized he really didn't want me after all. That was the story of my life. Nobody wanted me. I was a Pemberton, from a mega-wealthy family. I wasn't drop dead gorgeous like Caroline, but I was pretty enough in my own right, at least I had been before that last nightmarish beating. Yet, boys continually shunned me, gave me looks as if I bore a scarlet 'A' upon my chest, the 'A' standing for abnormal, in my instance. I was as familiar with rejection as I was with dejection. "Never mind," I said, my voice low as I turned onto my side, my back to him.

He continued to pace for quite some time, then suddenly he was on the bed. He pulled my shoulder back until I was lying flat on my back and his face was close to mine. There was a look on his face that frightened me with its fierceness. "I've told you before, you've thrown a monkey wrench into my plans. I thought you were like the rest of the Pembertons, but you're not. I also told you I'm here as an avenger. I am, and you can't stop me, Jessie. I have to tell you what I'm doing here and I have to trust you to keep it just between us. Can you keep a terrible secret?"

"I keep all sorts of terrible secrets every day. I won't tell anyone anything. I've kept your presence in this house a secret since the day I happened across you in the attic, haven't I? I haven't told a soul about you."

"No, you haven't, and I appreciate that, but the truth may turn you against me."

"Tell me the truth, Pen. Let me decide if it will or not."
He dropped down beside me, his head on the pillow with mine
again. We both lay gazing up at the crocheted canopy above us, as
if we were outdoors looking up at the stars in the heavens. "No, let
me ask you something first. Are you Pen Beresford?"

"Yes."

"And my great-great grandfather ruined your great-great
grandfather."

"That was a long time ago," he replied, "but, yes, he did."

"That's about all I know about your family. I discovered
that while researching my paper."

"Yeah, I realized that when I read it. That's why I helped
you."

"You worked incredibly fast."

"Like you, I have insomnia quite often."

"You broke into the high school. How did you not get
caught? And how did you find my locker? How did you crack the
combination lock?"

He sighed. "Jess, you have your locker number and combination number in your memo book in your backpack. That was
pretty easy to find. I didn't break into the high school. I was there
at the crack of dawn and followed a custodian in. He was talking
on his cellphone. He never even noticed me. There's no great
mystery to what I do."

"Okay, then what about the research materials and your
faxing everything to Mr. Jenson's home fax. How did you get his
number?"

"From the internet. I Googled his phone number and found
his fax number. I went to my father's office and faxed everything
from there."

"Where's your father's office? What does he do?"

"You don't need to know that."

"So, how did you even know that my father had the materials I'd used?"

He raised his hands, running his fingers through his longish dark hair. "Jess, I know a lot of people. I figured there'd be trouble when he read your report. I asked the librarian, Kathy Leblanc, to call me if your father sent someone to make those files disappear. She did. I also talked to Pauline Johnston at the Historical Society. He didn't pay her off. Instead, he had the cartons stolen while she was locked in the bathroom."

"Do you hate my father?"

"Of course I do," he answered honestly enough. "The bastard has destroyed so many lives in this town and surrounding towns. Your family has been ruining lives, and actually killing innocent human beings, a lot of them women and children, if you really look closely at the asylum records. If you dig even deeper you'll find the staff raped women inmates, and they killed babies, hurling them off the cliff. Sometimes, they performed abortions, trying 'new and innovative' techniques. They ended up killing a lot of young women experimenting on them like that. Jess, it's really too horrible to even think about. And it's been ongoing since before that asylum was ever constructed. Your family is freakin' evil through and through."

"Well, hang onto your hat, but that's really not news to me."

"No, I suppose not. You must know, or at the very least suspect, what the man you know as your Uncle Baxter did to Ruth, with your father's consent." He didn't have to spell it out. He didn't have to speak it aloud. I knew. "He lets that bastard live in this house! He could have done the same thing to you when you were younger!" He turned his head and looked at my profile. "He didn't, did he?"

"No. He told me redheads are freaks of nature like hunch-backs and babies born with cleft palates. He found me disgusting, lucky me." So, if I had known what he was since I was a girl, why had I not done anything to protect my little sister? Primarily, be-cause my father had trained us all to turn a blind eye to what oc-curred in this house, to never question him about anything, to obey adults, to nurture animosity toward one another not kinship. Our mother was a mother only because she had born a number of ba-bies. Beyond passing a newborn like a kidney stone every year or so, until father lost interest in her, she'd had no interest in moth-ering anything. She had been aloof and distant all of my life.

"I'm going to kill your family," he said. I'd figured as much, but hearing the words coming so abruptly and coldly from his lips caused me to catch my breath. "If you try to stop me, I'll have to kill you too."

"Pen," I said, "there have been days when being murdered in my bed would have been considered a blessing." I turned onto my side, raising myself up onto my elbow, looking down at his face. I had thrown him into shadow, but there was some light re-flecting in his eyes. I saw his eyes meet mine, felt him looking at me. "Do you need my help?"

He pulled me down, kissing me as if he meant to devour me. "I don't need your help. I've got it under control. I just need you to suffer through another month or so of this shit before I set off the grand finale and set you free. I want you to graduate head of your class. You do know that there has never been a Pemberton at the top of any class, don't you?"

"No. No one's ever mentioned that. It doesn't sound like anything they'd brag about."

"It's not. You," he said, kissing me passionately again, "are an anomaly."

"Well, doesn't that make me feel special."

"You *are* special." He caressed my face. "Will you come visit me in prison?" he asked.

"Sure. I'll bake you cakes with files in them. I'll smuggle in whatever you desire—clean socks, jack knives, a bottle of whisky, a 60-inch flat screen TV, a Ferrari." He finally laughed. "I don't want you to go to prison," I said.

"It could happen. If I mess up, it *will* happen."

"I'll be the pen pal who sends you a thousand dollars in every letter. You'll have lots of friends in prison."

"Huh! I don't need those kind of friends!" He kissed me one more time then sat up. "I've got to get out of here. I'm not going to risk knocking you up."

"That's chivalrous of you."

"Maybe, in a few years, I'll reconsider that." He walked across the room. "Get some sleep."

The next month of my life was grueling. Father harbored immense animosity toward me. He wore me down psychological-ly. He beat me whenever the mood struck him. I landed in the emergency room a week and a half before graduation, when I passed out at school from a combination of abuse and malnutrition. The police came and grilled me about my boyfriend, because my father had told them that I was in an abusive relationship with a young man who regularly beat me and starved me. He'd told them I was living with this young man and was seldom home. Not sur-prisingly, my mother backed his outrageous story. But, I was eighteen and an adult. I was top in my class at school. Mr. Schuman was questioned and he stated that he'd seen bruises and wounds on me in the past and felt it was abuse in the home. He had told the police that he had never seen me with any of the boys in the school, that I was a loner and not one to socialize with my peers.

I refused to say who had beaten me so badly. I refused to explain how I had gotten so malnourished. I spent three days in the hospital being given fluids and liquid meals, working up to soft foods. On the fourth day, I agreed to go home with my parents. What else could I do? I had nowhere else to go since I didn't have an abusive boyfriend living in a trailer park or seedy apartment in his parent's basement or above a friend's garage. I went home and was locked in my room. There was no school since I would be graduating in one week. It was Senior Week, but I was too weak and hurt to participate. I would be lucky if I could walk on my own power to the podium to accept my diploma.

During that one nightmarish week, Ruth hung herself in the psychiatric ward. The brakes on Uncle Baxter's car failed and he was critically injured when he struck a dump truck broadside. Aunt Louise suddenly decided that she was a bird and leapt from her tower room window, breaking her neck. The fissures had broken wide open, creating the predicted fjords. Father roamed the halls ranting and raving, cursing and shaking his fist at the heavens. Laura loudly bemoaned the fact that these tragedies were going to ruin her wedding plans! Andrew advised Father that he planned to move out, that he was intending to explore all his options, as if he really had any other options. Caroline moved back home with her husband since their new home was not ready yet— the project plagued with delays and other on-site problems. They were tired of extended travel. Uncle Reggie suffered a massive coronary and toppled face first into his eggs Benedict the morning of my graduation. He died en route to the hospital. Aunt Beatrice did not go with him as she was too overcome by emotion and, if I was not mistaken, that emotion was elation rather than grief. To cap off that horrible week, Jonathan suddenly passed away in the rehabilitation facility where he had been transferred not too long ago. His heart had simply stopped beating.

I called a taxi to drive me to my graduation. No one in my family wanted to go. No one cared. There was too much happening at once, too many funeral plans to be arranged. My success as a high school student was unworthy of their attention. It really did not bother me all that much that none of my remaining family members wanted to watch me graduate. If truth be told, I didn't want them there anyway. They meant nothing to me, if I must be blunt about it.

I made it up on stage to the podium and received a hearty handshake from Mr. Schuman, who beamed at me and told me he was extremely proud of me. He wished me good luck in all my future endeavors. I smiled for my graduation picture, accepting my diploma, shaking hands with Mayor Branford. It all passed in a blur as I was exhausted, not having gotten much sleep due to everything that had been going on. I had a headache from the bright sunlight.

It caught me off guard when Pen suddenly appeared before me after the ceremony. "You don't look so good," he said. "Come on. I have my truck just over there." He led me to a black Dodge Ram pick-up, helped me climb up into the passenger seat. "Sorry I haven't been around much lately," he said when we were in the truck and he was inching out into traffic. "I've been busy."

"I've mostly been sleeping."

"Jesus, you look like crap. I'm sorry, Jess. I should have been paying more attention to you."

"It's all right. I haven't been such good company anyway."

"Want something to eat?" I leaned my head back against the headrest. "Good food, I promise."

"Okay, sure." We were passing the park. It was full of fire trucks and police cars—the annual Fire and Police Picnic. There was a carnival-like atmosphere there. "The whole town could burn down and be looted by vandals and thieves and they wouldn't care today," I commented and he laughed. "Isn't it strange, though, that they've scheduled their picnic for the same day as graduation?"

"Must have been some sort of scheduling screw up," he said, and the subject was dropped.

He took me to what I assumed was his home, well, not his place exactly, his mother's house. When he led me into the living room, he hadn't even introduced me yet before his mother was up and out of her chair, having thrown her book aside when she'd laid eyes on me. "You must be Jessie! Pen's told me so much about you! My goodness! You look as wilted as a daisy in a drought! Let me get you something cold to drink! Pen said he would be bringing you home for dinner. Dinner will be ready in half an hour."

I sat in the living room, sipping iced tea, nibbling cheese and crackers. She admired my diploma and, I swear to God, there was pride shining in her eyes as Pen told her of my academic achievements. I had never had any adult show pride in anything I'd done before in my life. It felt surreal to be sitting in Pen's mother's living room being oohed and aahed over. Finally, Pen cleared his throat. "You're making Jess uncomfortable," he said.

"I'm just so happy to finally meet her!" She glanced at the mantle clock. "I'll go put dinner on the table. We'll eat in the dining room."

"No, please. I prefer to eat in the kitchen, if that's possible," I protested.

"But it's your graduation day! It should be celebrated! It should be special! It's a tradition in our family."

"Well, okay then," I agreed, willing to concede.

"Dinner will be on the table in ten minutes," she said as she excused herself and left the room.

Pen shook his head. He was sitting across from me in an easy chair, that sly twist tucked into the corner of his mouth. "She's the boss," he said.

"She's very nice. I like her, but I'm sort of embarrassed, being the center of attention like this."

"You're the graduate girl. It's your day. We should celebrate it in style."

"Did you plan this?"

"I just mentioned it to her and, well, here we are."

"You've talked to her about me?"

"Of course. And she doesn't hold it against you that you're a Pemberton, by the way."

"I guess that's a good thing."

"A damned good thing. Pemberton's ruined her family, too, back in the day."

"Oh."

"Nothing personal. It wasn't your doing. We can overlook the fact that you're a part of that family."

"You haven't told her?" came his mother's voice from the dining room beyond the living room where she was bringing food to the already set table.

"Not yet."

"Well, when do you plan on telling her?"

"Maybe after dinner," he replied, sounding exasperated. "It's my gift to her. I'll give it to her when I feel the moment is right!"

"You're just like your father!"

"Thanks for the compliment!" He rolled his dark eyes, shook his head.

"What are you guys talking about?" I asked.

"Dinner's ready! Come and eat! You look famished—about to faint from hunger!"

Pen led me to the dining room. I almost did faint. She had made a pork roast, roasted red potatoes, made homemade applesauce, honey-glazed baby carrots, spinach salad. And it all smelled so delicious! "You get to sit at the head of the table today," he said, holding the chair out for me.

I sat down, feeling strange to be sitting where normally my father would sit to preside over the table, like the lord of the manor. Pen sat to my right, his mother to my left. They encouraged me to eat. For one crazy, fleeting moment, I experienced sheer panic. They were being too nice. They were making me eat, encouraging me, urging me. My family had ruined their families. I thought, in one flash of complete and utter paranoia, that they intended to poison me on my graduation day.

When Pen saw my fork freeze, my eyes widen, he snapped his fingers in front of my face. "Earth to Jessie! What's going on? We've lost the signal!" I looked at him, confused. He grabbed my wrist, brought my fork to his mouth and ate the bite of pork I had cut for myself. "As your official Graduation Day taste tester, I proclaim this meal fantastic and offer high praise to the cook for her supreme efforts. I also offer high praise to the Graduate for being such an amazing brainiac! That high school will never be the same without you roaming the halls and earning As left and right."

"Oh, hush up, Pen and eat your dinner. Go ahead, Jessie, dear. You, too. Dig in."

I ate. The food was mouthwateringly good. It was so good it made me realize that the meals Charlotte and Henshaw had cooked for my family were rather inferior. "I want to learn how to cook like you do," I said, just blurting it out.

"Thank you, honey, that is the best compliment I've ever received." She beamed at me, clearly happy that I liked her cooking. "I'd be happy to teach you how to cook. Pen, if you haven't noticed, can eat like a horse and never gain an ounce! I envy that boy!"

I was stuffed before too long, not having eaten much for a week. Pen helped clear the table and then they brought in a layer cake in my high school colors—red and white. I had to force down cake and ice cream, but it was awesome because we never had ice cream at home. Mother had never allowed it.

Afterwards, in the living room, Pen sat beside me on the couch and handed me an envelope. "Open it. It's your graduation present."

"What is it?"

"Something I found in the attic of your house."

I opened the envelope, pulling out the papers that were inside. There was a newspaper article about a baby disappearing from the nursery of the hospital. The newspaper was dated one day after the date of my birth. There was a color photograph of a teary-eyed young woman, the mother of the stolen baby. My heart ached for her. What a terrible thing to have happened to a new mother! The next article related how my father had given the young woman fifty-thousand dollars one month later when the kidnapping remained unsolved. Five months after that magnanimous gesture on his part, a mentally ill man had confessed to kidnapping the baby and throwing it in the river. The voices in his head had told him to do it, he'd said. The body of the infant was never found. "That's a truly tragic story, but why do you want me to have this?"

"Look at the picture of the mother," he said. I looked, and after a few moments it struck me like a bucket of ice water over the head. The young woman had red hair the same color as mine, green eyes like mine. She strongly resembled me! "That's your real mother," he said. "The woman you know as your mother had a stillborn baby the same day that this woman delivered a little red-haired girl. Money exchanged hands even before your father publicly bestowed fifty grand on her. She made a lot more than just fifty thousand selling you to him."

"Oh, my God!"

"That's why you don't look like any of your brothers and sisters. That's why you don't even look like your parents. They aren't blood relatives at all. They raised you to believe that you're a Pemberton, but you're no more a Pemberton than I am!"

"I don't believe this! Where did you find this stuff?"

"You're not the only one who can do research, Jess. I didn't have a clue when I first saw you, but after being in the house and observing your family for a few months, seeing how they behaved, and seeing how you behaved, I noticed differences, glaring differences. I found your real birth certificate in a file box in the attic. Your mother named you Paige Erin Kilpatrick."

"This is so strange," I murmured. My head was reeling. "I don't feel good."

"You'd better lie down." They helped me lie down, made me comfortable. "I'm afraid all of this has been too much for her," she said, looking worriedly toward Pen.

"Can you take care of her for a little while? I have an errand to run. I'll be back in about an hour or so."

"Pen," I said, not wanting him to go—not wanting him to do what he was going to do.

"I have to go, Jess. You just lie here and rest. I'll be back before dark, before you know it." He squatted down beside the couch and stroked my hair, my cheek. "It'll be fine. You'll be well taken care of."

"You'll be back, won't you?" I asked worriedly.

"Yes, of course I will." He kissed me. "I'm going to marry you one day. I can't do that if I don't come back for you, can I?"

I managed a weak smile. "No, I suppose not."

"Then wait right here for me." He stood up. "Promise me you'll wait here."

"I will. I'll be right here. I promise." He gave me that sly grin, and then he left.

I closed my eyes. Incredibly, I fell asleep. I was dreaming that I was an inmate in the old asylum, locked in a room, dreading the sound of every approaching footstep, knowing that someone was coming to abuse or torture me. And then, there was an earthquake. The earthquake was so real that it startled me awake. The house seemed to be trembling, glass knickknacks clinking across the room. I struggled to sit up. A woman was coming into the room, and at first I didn't recognize her. Pen's mother had brunette hair, but this woman had ginger hair, yet her face was the same. "It's all right, Jessie," she said. "There's been a massive explosion somewhere in town." I gasped.

"Where's Pen?"

"He'll be back in a little bit." She came and sat beside me on the couch. "It'll be over soon, sweetheart." She saw me looking at her. Calmly, she returned my gaze. Her features looked familiar, not as Pen's mother, but as someone else entirely. My eyes drifted to the envelope on the coffee table. I reached for it, but she stopped me. "I'm your gift," she said. "I'm what he wanted to give you today." I thought my heart would break. "I'm your real mother, Jessie."

"How did he find you?" I asked, tears welling in my eyes. "How on earth did he find you?"

"He found the articles. I'd moved away for a while after you were born, but this is my home town. This is where I wanted to live. I came back, married to a very nice man. I'd had you when I was seventeen and unwed. When your father offered me a lot of money for you, I thought I was doing the right thing by you. I thought, because he was a rich man, he would take real good care of you. I thought he and his wife would love you and cherish you, and be proud of you. When Bob and I moved here about nine years ago, I kind of looked for you, just to see how well you'd turned out, how you'd grown. I saw you around town occasionally. You were always alone. You looked sad."

"Why didn't you say something to me?" I asked.

"I'd promised your father that I would never mention you, never try to see you, and never do anything to indicate that you had once been my baby girl. He bought not only you, he bought my silence. There was a threat of a lawsuit if I ever said one word about you. I was just a scared teenager then. I thought I would go to jail for selling my baby. I let him tell his lies, and I cried real tears. I cried so many tears, through so many years, regretting what I did."

"Intimidation and fear, the tricks of my father's lifelong trade in misery." I brushed tears from my cheeks. "How did you meet Pen?"

"He found me last fall. He said he'd met you. He wanted to know if I wanted to meet you. Of course I did. I've thought about you every day since I gave birth to you. I regretted selling you so quickly. I spent the money foolishly. I was young and stupid and I wasted it. I should have put it in the bank, but I spent it all. I wanted to have fun. I'm thirty-five years old now. I'm not old by any means. When Pen said he had some plans and maybe he could reunite us, what could I do? What could I say? I worried about your father taking some sort of revenge on me, but Pen assured me that would never happen. It's only been gradually that he's been more open about his plans."

"His plans don't shock you?"

She looked at me for a long moment, looked away briefly then returned her eyes to meet my still teary gaze. "No, not really. I mean, look at all the lives the Pembertons have ruined, destroyed, and devastated through the years. I bet you can't walk down the streets of this town without rubbing elbows with someone your father, your grandfather, your great-grandfather, your brother even, hasn't hurt financially, psychologically, emotionally or even physically. My God, Jessie, look at what he's done to his own children! You do know only Andrew and Caroline are his natural children, don't you? Laura, Glenn, you, Jonathan and Ruth—he bought you all. God only knows for what reason, what purpose. I mean, Valentina has no real love of children. Has she ever cuddled you? Comforted you? Done anything in any way nurturing?" I shook my head. "He bought children so he could experiment with them. Not with Andrew, his heir. Maybe not with Caroline, as she is his own flesh and blood. But the rest of you…" She raised her hand to lightly touch the scar on my cheek, trailed her fingers to the scar on my jaw. "It's a miracle that you're still alive, is what it is." Her own eyes filled with tears. "Little Jonathan wasting away like he did; young, beautiful, little Ruth hanging herself after being so violently abused. Laura is desperate to marry and leave the house. Glenn, I hear, has an eating disorder, is as fat as a water buffalo." I nodded. "We can't save them. It's too late to save them. But we can save you, Jessie. You have a home here with me. You have Pen who loves you very much. You've been in freefall for years and we are your safety net."

"Pen's going to be arrested," I predicted.

She shook her head. "Chief Weller? His mother was committed in the early seventies. She died in the asylum. When his father tried to sue the asylum and your father, he was found dead in his garage, an apparent suicide by asphyxiation. The coroner, Doctor Yates? He discovered signs that Jim's father had been suffocated prior to being placed in his car in the garage with the hose running into it and the engine running. It wasn't carbon monoxide that killed him. When Dr. Yates tried to start an inquest it was quickly squelched. Judge Lincoln refused to pursue the case. He ordered the prosecutor to drop the case, said the evidence was tainted. Those of us who've suffered outnumber those in town that your father paid off with huge amounts of cash." She dried her eyes, shook her head then smiled. "Today, Pen Beresford is giving a lot of people in this town and the surrounding communities a huge gift in honor of your graduation. I have received the gift of my daughter. Everyone else receives the satisfaction of knowing that the Pembertons have gotten exactly what has been due them for a very long time—eternal damnation in Hell." She stood up, walking to the front window. "He should be back soon," she said.

"What am I supposed to do now?" I asked.

"Pen will take you out, and at some point during the night you will be informed that your home has been destroyed by some sort of an explosion. The house has imploded, gone up like a fireball. It will be ruled a natural gas explosion. There will be no other survivors, only you because it was your graduation day and you were out celebrating receiving your diploma with your boy-friend."

"Is he my real boyfriend, or is he just pretending?" I asked, the lines between reality and deception so blurred at the moment that I honestly didn't know.

She turned back. "At first, he was going to kill all of you to exact revenge upon the Pembertons for killing his great-great grandfather, for ruining his family so they lost their fortune. He had a hard life, but he's made something of himself since high school. He's a whiz with explosives. He earns his living as a demolition expert. He's been working locally at the quarry, doing blasting while he's been setting the wheels in motion. He origin-ally wanted to blow up the Pembertons on Halloween, but then he met you, and you utterly charmed him. You set him to thinking he might be killing an innocent young woman, one who was as much a victim as the members of his family were. He started prowling about the attics, listening at ducts and vents, observing your family from behind the walls, and what he saw deeply disturbed him. And in the process, he fell in love with you and wanted to keep you safe. He decided to wait until today, when you'd be out of the house. He was fairly certain that no one else in your family would bother attending your graduation. None of them care a fig about you. It had to be today." I nodded. "Jessie, this is bigger than you and I, bigger than Pen and his family. This is a community that is purging itself of evil."

I stood up and began pacing, worried because it was getting late and Pen had not yet returned. My mother, Emily Chase, not Mrs. Beresford as I had assumed when Pen had brought me here, began preparing supper for her husband and herself. They did not have any children. It was just after six o'clock when the black Dodge Ram pulled up to the curb and Pen climbed out.

I opened the front door as he came up the walk. He hesitated, his dark eyes meeting mine, trying to read me. "Where've you been?" I asked. "It's my graduation day. I thought you were taking me out tonight."

"I got detained. Sorry." He gave me that slow grin that set my heart beating rapidly. "Come here." I flew down the front steps, ran down the walk and leapt into his arms. He caught me, lifting me up, kissing my neck, my shoulder. "I have one small favor to ask of you," he said.

"What's that?"

"Try to muster a tear or two for the loss of your family in such a tragic manner when the police come to inform you of the explosion tonight."

"Are they looking for me now?"

"They don't know for sure whether or not you were in the house yet. It'll be an hour or so before Chief Weller remembers that you graduated today, that you're probably out partying with your boyfriend and our friends."

"I don't have any friends."

"We're meeting them in Granger Falls. They're my friends, and now they're your friends, too."

My mother came to the door. "It went all right?"

"Like a charm," he replied. "I'm stealing Jess now. We're going to Pirate's Pizza over in the Falls."

"Chief Weller knows that I have a room to put her up in?"

"Yeah, you're first on the list of townspeople the Red Cross will call to find a place for Jess to stay."

"Thank you, Pen. Thank you for Jessie, and for all you've done."

"I think we've all gotten what we wanted from this."

"I'll see you late tonight, dear," she said. I could not yet think of her as my Mom although in my heart I knew she was already more of a mother to me than Valentina Pemberton had ever been.

We went to Granger Falls where Pen had grown up. Pirate's Pizza was an amazing place, the interior designed to look exactly like what a pirate ship would have looked like, down in the hold. There were nets hung from the ceiling, old trunks and chests filled with fabulous fake doubloons and paste jewels, strings of glass pearls. The tables were scarred wood and there were benches and stools. The servers wore ragged cut off pants, striped jerseys and head scarves. The bartender wore an eye patch. There was a fake skeleton in manacles chained to a back wall with a tricorn hat, with a big snowy white plume, askew on his head. Someone had stuck a cigar between his teeth at some time in the past and the owner had left it there. It gave him a roguish appearance. There were pitchers of beer and a party size pizza on the table. I was too young to drink so I had Coke, but Pen had given me a few sips of his beer. I really didn't like it. He'd ordered a bottle of red wine and poured me a glass of it. I liked that better, but only had the one glass when everyone at the table toasted my graduation. They all acted as if they had known me for some time. I liked them. They were friendly and fun to be with. They made me laugh. This was what had been missing from my life—friends, fun, laughter, companionship and love. A girl named Mariah, who was sitting beside me, lived on a farm where they raised horses. She offered to teach me how to ride. I thought I'd like that.

At quarter past ten, a tall, good-looking police officer entered the restaurant. He paused, glancing around, spotted us and came over. "I hate to interrupt, but I believe there might be a Miss Jessamyn Pemberton at this table?" His eyes fell on me. He had dark eyes and he seemed familiar. "May I speak to you, Miss, over there where it's not so noisy?"

"What's this about?" Mariah asked. "Jessie hasn't done anything wrong. She graduated from high school today. This is my wine glass. I'm twenty-one. I'm legal."

"I'm not here to arrest her for having a glass of wine to celebrate her graduation."

I stood up and made my way around the table. Pen had also stood up, and he walked with me as we followed the policeman to the far corner of the room away from the loud music. The officer turned and said, "I have some bad news, I'm afraid." I just looked at him. "There's been a terrible accident at your home. They think it was a natural gas explosion. I'm afraid your home has been totally destroyed. I'm sorry to have to tell you, but, we do not believe there were any survivors."

I stared into his eyes for a long moment, and then let my eyes drop. My gaze fell on his name tag. *Chief Beresford.* Pen's father was the Chief of police in Granger Falls! That staggered me. My head whirled. "I've got you, Jess," Pen said, his arms coming around me from behind.

"Let's get her outside into the fresh air." They led me outside. "I'm sorry we have to meet under these circumstances," Chief Beresford said. "Pen's told me he'd met a great girl, he just hasn't gotten around to bringing her home to meet the folks yet."

"He didn't tell me you were the chief of police." He hadn't told me anything at all about his family.

"No, Pen plays his cards pretty close to the vest. I've been in touch with Chief Weller. Pen, can you take her back to town, meet the Chief at his office? He has a Red Cross worker there who'll assist Jessamyn to find lodging and clothing, whatever she needs. I know it's a terrible loss, but you're going to be well taken care of, young lady. You'll be amazed at how a community can pull together to help in a crisis like this." He looked at his son standing behind me. I was shaking now, the reality of my situation hitting me harder than I thought it would. Everything I had known since I was a child had been a lie, a fabrication, a parody of real family life. It staggered me that I was suddenly free of that life, that I had a mother who cared about me and wanted me in her life, a boyfriend who loved me even though he had loathed the Pembertons. I was overwhelmed by the fact that he had recognized in me a difference from the rest of my so-called family, that he had cared enough to spare me their fate. My life was going to be so different now. It was going to be a huge adjustment. I realized that. I was intelligent enough to know there would be residual effects from my abusive upbringing.

Pen pulled me closer, rested his head against mine. "You're going to be okay, Jess," he murmured.

"When things settle down some, son, you bring this girl around for dinner with me and your stepmom. We'd like to get to know her better."

"Yeah, I will," Pen replied.

"You'd best get her over to Chief Weller's office now."

We went back in to say goodbye and apologize for having to leave. Pen told them what had happened and they all looked shocked and concerned. "Do you have a cellphone?" Mariah asked. I shook my head. "Pen! Get this girl a cell so we can call or text one another! I want to keep in touch with her! When you get her a phone put my number in it right away!"

"Mine too!" called Cathy from the far end of the table.

"Mine too, Pen!" chimed in Dorie.

"All right! All right! Sheesh! Girls! Come on Jess. Catch you guys later."

On the drive back to Pemberton, I questioned Pen about his family. He told me that his mother had been an avid bike rider. One afternoon, she'd been pedaling her usual fifteen mile loop around Granger Falls when she had been struck by a limousine and killed. The limo driver had stated that Mrs. Beresford had swerved out into the path of the limo to avoid a rough spot on the side of the road without looking and he had been unable to avoid striking her. The death was ruled accidental. Pen's father had been a routine patrol officer at the time, Pen, a little boy of four years of age. His father had always felt that the Pemberton's limo driver's story was too pat. He'd scoured the scene and he'd never found any rough spot that his wife may have been trying to avoid. Yet, he couldn't accuse the chauffer of lying. He'd known, without a shadow of a doubt, that Randolph Pemberton had paid off the investigator, his supervisor, the prosecutor and the judge. He'd made the vehicular homicide case disappear. Pen's father had vowed to have his revenge one day. He had married Virginia Hayes when Pen was five and she was the only mother Pen really remembered. Chief Weller had been Pen's father's best friend on the force at the time of Rose Beresford's death. He was like an uncle to Pen.

In every life there are invisible connections, a veritable dot-to-dot web of lives intertwining and spreading outward from a core. The web I had called home had been torn asunder, yet I'd landed on another part of the web, a part that I had not even known existed. My salvation had been my boredom and desire to escape from my family. I had found secret passages that had led me to the young man who had taken on the responsibility of avenging a multitude of wrongs. As socially inept as I was, Pen had found me intriguing, fascinating, and worthy of being allowed to live. He had orchestrated a graceful fall for me from one part of the web to another, reconnecting me to my real mother and her husband, who did not feel threatened by his wife's eighteen-year old daughter being housed in their home in the days following the explosion. He was a very nice, warm and generous man who welcomed me into his home and gave me all the time I needed to reestablish a bond with my birth mother.

I met Pen's stepmother. I liked her. I liked everybody's mother I met in the months following my graduation and my release from the nightmarish ordeal of the first eighteen years of my life. Like a flower long denied sunlight, fertile soil and tender care, I bloomed amid my new friends and new family.

When Pen suggested that I buy a car so I could come and visit him, we went to the bank where I'd presented my brand new driver's license and a replacement copy of my birth certificate as proof that I was Jessamyn Pemberton, since my bank book had been destroyed, along with everything else I'd owned, in the explosion. I'd been astounded when I'd been handed a balance sheet telling me how much money I had in my account. I had seven hundred eleven thousand dollars in the bank. I'd nearly fainted. Pen had to put his arm around me. I paid cash for my SUV. Life was good.

Autumn

It has been exactly six months from the day I turned nineteen. Fall has arrived in a burst of stiff breezes and turning leaves. The Pemberton estate has been winding its way through the court system for over a year now. My father had left a will, but I was not mentioned in it. All petitioners who'd filed claims against the vast estate were being paid first. The state will take its share. The remainder will pass to me, thanks to my lawyer, Steven Thayer. I have been recognized by the court, the state and the United States Government as the sole surviving heir of the Pemberton estate. It will still be awhile before I see any of the money. But it really doesn't matter.

I'm going to marry Pen Beresford tomorrow. He had proposed on my nineteenth birthday. My mother has sewn my gown and made my veil. She's also designed and sewn her mother-of-the bride's dress and Pen's stepmom's mother-of-the-groom dress. Mariah will be my matron of honor as she had married her boyfriend Kenny at Christmas. Dorie, Cathy and a new friend named Diana will be my maids of honor. I am both nervous and excited.

A flash of lightning in the sky catches my eye. A rumble of thunder soon follows. Fat raindrops begin tapping against the glass. "Do you remember the day we first met?" Pen asks as he comes up behind me. I nod. I will never forget finding him in the attic garret. That was the day my life had begun to change. "A lot of people don't like thunderstorms, but I find them rather exciting, rather romantic, don't you?"

"Only when you're with me, otherwise, they make me a little nervous."

"You shouldn't be afraid, Jessie. You rode out a violent storm for eighteen years. What's a little thunder-storm in comparison to that?"

"I guess I shouldn't let it bother me, especially since I'm marrying a man who likes to play with things that go boom." I turn in his arms, look into his eyes. "I love you, Pen. Thank you for all that you've done for me. You saved my life."

"Yours and a thousand others."

"You're like a super hero." He shrugs. "My Mom's been crying all day."

"It's hard for mother's to see their little girls grow up and get married, more so when they missed the seeing them grow up part."

I nod. "Pen?'

"What?"

"When I get my inheritance, I want to be like your great-great grandfather. I want to use the money to help Pemberton, Granger Falls and the little villages and towns around us. My family owes them for what they did to all those people for all those years. I want to do good things. I can't erase the past, but I can help make a better future."

"I think that's a wonderful idea."

"We'll keep enough for us, enough so we can live off the interest and never touch the rest, unless there's a dire emergency or we have to put five or six kids through college or something like that."

"You want kids?"

"Do you?" I ask.

"I suppose we could have one or two. But we should wait a few years. We need some time for us first."

"Even though I grew up a Pemberton, that I'm not a Pemberton by blood, I still feel tainted by association. Any child of ours might be considered a Pemberton as well as a Beresford. I want our kids to be the generation that starts healing the old wounds."

"You're very altruistic for having been raised in an atmosphere of avarice, vice, greed, deceit, betrayals, cruelty, lies..." He suddenly kisses me. "But then again, as you've pointed out, you were a Pemberton in name only. Our kids are going to be lucky to have you for a mother."

"As long as you don't bring your work home with you and blow us all up." He laughs. "I mean it."

"I only play with explosives at work." A bright flash of lightning behind me makes me jump. "Boom!" he says softly. Then he kisses me again. I don't even hear the clap of thunder that follows that big flash. Love is pretty amazing—it can make you deaf to the things that remind you of your past, that set your nerves on edge and cause bad memories to surface. Pen is good about distracting me, by giving me all the love I need.

There will still be days when the reverberations of the traumas I've suffered will echo through me, but I'll have my mother and stepfather, my husband and his family and all our friends to distract me, to remind me that the past should remain where it has been left, in a pile of smoking rubble. I live in the here and now. I live for the future. I live with a lighter heart and a happier soul.

As far as thunderheads go, when I see them forming, I turn to Pen. He has a certain way about him that distracts me, comforts me. When the storm passes, but the rain still falls, if it's warm enough, Pen and I go outside on the back deck and we dance in the rain until we're soaking wet and laughing. If the sun happens to break through the low gray clouds we look for the rainbow. Whoever finds it first gets to choose where we will go for dinner that night. We are establishing traditions of our own. We have involved our parents in our lives. We have mapped out the funding of a huge variety of improvements and programs in our town and its surrounding communities—including a beautiful, family-oriented park on the cliff where the old asylum used to be.

The Pembertons will be paying for their sins through the generosity of my checkbook. And I think, at last, there will be peace in the little traumatized slice of the world in which we live. We're all, finally, beginning to heal.

About the Author

Susan Buffum works as a medical secretary. She has written for many years as a hobby, sharing her stories with family and friends. She lives in western Massachusetts with her husband, John, and her daughter, Kelly, who also writes. They have two literary cats, Revere and Riley-Beans.

Susan welcomes your comments and feedback. She can be contacted at sebuffum415@gmail.com

Made in the USA
Charleston, SC
17 March 2016